# Better than chocolate-covered marshmallows . . .

"Ellen, tell us who you've been having m—  I can cross him off my potential b

Sarah and Penny started ε

Grace smiled. "You didn't ɪent slide, did you? I love chocola much as the next girl, but better than sɛ ɪnk so."

Of the four of them, Ellen was the most secretive about her love life, but she now looked resigned to the fact that she was going to have to talk.

"You remember I told you about the IT guy who was revamping all the computers on campus? I went out with him a few times."

"Ellen, I'm shocked!" Sarah said. "A *few* times? And you gave it up that easily? What happened to your ten-date rule?"

"The ten-date rule is only good if you actually go out ten times. I haven't had more than four consecutive dates with the same guy in almost three years."

"That's because you're not giving it up fast enough," Penny said.

"Was it that bad?" Sarah asked.

Ellen reached for another marshmallow. "He was all right. But he certainly wasn't—"

"Heathcliff!" the three of them shouted.

"Honestly, Ellen," Grace said, "if you're going to have a crush on a fantasy hero, why him?"

"I have to agree with Grace," said Sarah. "What's the fascination? Because I don't get it. He's, like . . . sadistic."

"I know Heathcliff isn't perfect," Ellen said. "But nobody is, not *even* Mr. Darcy, which Grace would know all about since she has her own live version of him."

# the boyfriend of the month club

## Maria Geraci

BERKLEY BOOKS, NEW YORK

THE BERKLEY PUBLISHING GROUP
Published by the Penguin Group
Penguin Group (USA) Inc.
375 Hudson Street, New York, New York 10014, USA
Penguin Group (Canada), 90 Eglinton Avenue East, Suite 700, Toronto, Ontario M4P 2Y3, Canada
(a division of Pearson Penguin Canada Inc.)
Penguin Books Ltd., 80 Strand, London WC2R 0RL, England
Penguin Group Ireland, 25 St. Stephen's Green, Dublin 2, Ireland (a division of Penguin Books Ltd.)
Penguin Group (Australia), 250 Camberwell Road, Camberwell, Victoria 3124, Australia
(a division of Pearson Australia Group Pty. Ltd.)
Penguin Books India Pvt. Ltd., 11 Community Centre, Panchsheel Park, New Delhi—110 017, India
Penguin Group (NZ), 67 Apollo Drive, Rosedale, North Shore, 0632, New Zealand
(a division of Pearson New Zealand Ltd.)
Penguin Books (South Africa) (Pty.) Ltd., 24 Sturdee Avenue, Rosebank, Johannesburg 2196,
South Africa

Penguin Books Ltd., Registered Offices: 80 Strand, London WC2R 0RL, England

This is a work of fiction. Names, characters, places, and incidents either are the product of the author's imagination or are used fictitiously, and any resemblance to actual persons, living or dead, business establishments, events or locales is entirely coincidental. The publisher does not have any control over and does not assume any responsibility for author or third-party websites or their content.

PRINTING HISTORY
Berkly trade paperback edition / December 2010

Library of Congress Cataloging-in-Publication Data

Geraci, Maria.
  The Boyfriend of the Month Club / Maria Geraci. — 1st ed.
    p. cm.
  ISBN 978-0-425-23650-5
  1. Single women—Fiction. 2. Female friendship—Fiction. 3. Dating (Social customs)—Fiction.
4. Daytona Beach (Fla.)—Fiction. I. Title.
  PS3607.E7256B69 2010
  813'.6—dc22                                                   2010013512

PRINTED IN THE UNITED STATES OF AMERICA

10  9  8  7  6  5  4  3  2  1

*For my sister Carmen.*
*Thank you for being the Lettuce.*

# ACKNOWLEDGMENTS

There are so many people I need to thank for this one. There's my parents, Carmen and Fernando Palacios, whose love and support I can always count on. My sister Carmen, who's not just a fantastic sister, but a wonderful friend as well. My husband, Mike, whose patience knows no bounds. And of course my kids, Stephanie, Kevin and Megan. I hope you know how much I appreciate the sacrifices you all make when I'm writing on a deadline and don't have the time or energy to do the things I want and should do.

Thank you, Deidre Knight, for always believing in me. You're a super agent and super friend!

I'd like to also especially thank my wonderful editor, Wendy McCurdy, her editorial assistant, Katherine Pelz, and my publicist, Erin Galloway, as well as the fantastic folks in the art department at Berkley. Thanks for the awesome cover!

Thank you to all the wonderful friends who inspire me to keep writing. To my early readers, Lissa McConnell and Lisa Wallace. The Tallahassee Bunco Broads, and Pari and the rest of the nurses in labor and delivery at Tallahassee Memorial Hospital, who cheer me on and keep me motivated. A special wink to Amy Ruscher for coming up with the Céline Dion bit. Much better than Barry Manilow! And last but not least, to Melissa Francis, my critique partner extraordinaire, who listens to every plot point and twist, countless times over and over until I get it just right. Where would I be without you?

# The Ghost of Boyfriends Past

Grace O'Bryan didn't believe in ghosts. She also didn't believe in witches, vampires, love at first sight, that there was anything real about reality TV, or the ridiculous claim that you could lose ten pounds on the three-day cabbage soup diet (she'd tried it twice). If you couldn't see it, feel it, touch it, or taste it, then in all likelihood it didn't exist. Which made for some very practical thinking on Grace's part. Except for the one ripple in the otherwise smooth seas of her personal logic. Like her *abuela* Graciela—the Cuban grandmother Grace was named after—what she *did* believe in was curses.

How else could you explain tonight?

She had waited a whopping two months for Brandon Farrell to ask her out, only to wake up this morning on her period. Not that that in itself was a problem. She wasn't a have-sex-on-the-first-date kind of girl. Nor did she suffer from bad cramps. But she'd also woken up five pounds heavier than she'd been last night (maybe she should have given the cabbage soup diet one more try). So instead of the outfit she'd planned on wearing, she'd ended up borrowing her best friend Sarah's little black dress. Sarah had excellent taste in clothes—the dress was a winning combination of elegant yet discreetly sexy. Sarah was also a size larger than Grace, and the dress had fit perfectly. At least it had fit perfectly back at Grace's town house. It wasn't until Grace had folded herself into her tiny red VW Bug that she'd noticed the dress was a tad too short.

And now, thanks to some heavier than average Saturday evening Daytona Beach traffic, she was late for her date. She tugged on the hem of Sarah's dress and opened the door to the city's newest, most exclusive restaurant, Chez Louis, only to find herself nose to aquiline nose with Felix Barberi.

Grace sucked in a breath. It was a Dickensian nightmare. Too bad the man standing in front of her was one hundred percent real. Grace might not subscribe to love at first sight, but substitute lust for love, and in Felix's case she'd been a firm believer.

At first, Felix had been incredibly charming, despite his annoying habit of wanting to make out to Céline Dion's number one hit "My Heart Will Go On." But Felix worked in the restaurant business and the brutal hours had strained their relationship and tarnished his charm. The ultimate strain had come when Grace had returned early from a business trip to surprise Felix on Valentine's Day. She'd gone to his apartment with a bottle of red wine and a pepperoni and anchovy pizza, only to catch Felix going at it with a dancer from the Topless-a-Go-Go.

Grace didn't know which was worse: the fact that Felix had cheated, or that the someone he had cheated with had a rack that must have cost six months' worth of lap dances. The incident had confirmed, however, that the St. Valentine's Day Curse was alive and well.

The St. Valentine's Day Curse was a long-standing joke among Grace and her friends. Its roots went all the way back to third grade at St. Bernadette's Catholic School when Grace's first boyfriend, Richard Kasamati, broke up with her on the playground on Valentine's Day. The uncanny thing was that over the years, no matter how serious a relationship she seemed to be in, Grace always ended up alone on that day. If Grace began dating a guy in March, the relationship might last a whopping eleven months, and yet she would still find herself flying solo by the first week in February.

But joke or not, finding Felix in flagrante delicto with his topless dancer had been no laughing matter. Grace had driven back to her town house, packed up what few things Felix kept there (including his Céline Dion greatest hits CD), and unceremoniously dumped them on his doorstep.

That was nine months ago and she hadn't seen Felix since. Although she had to admit the sight of Felix in a tux still made her mouth water. It was Grace's one fatal flaw. She was hopelessly attracted to hopelessly attractive men.

Felix cleared his throat and straightened to his full height, and since Grace was wearing four-inch heels, it put them at the exact same level. Felix wasn't short, but neither was Grace.

"Grace, you look . . ." He paused, taking in the dress, the hair, the makeup. "You look fantastic!"

Felix's eyes didn't say fantastic. Felix's eyes said *hot*.

Grace felt a moment's vindication, but then her instinct for survival shifted into overdrive. Felix didn't hand out compliments without an ulterior motive.

She caught a glimpse of herself in the Versailles rip-off gilt-framed mirror behind the reservation desk. Grace had never thought of herself as beautiful. Her older brother, Charlie, had hogged all the beautiful genes. A better word to describe her was *interesting*. She'd inherited her mother's big brown eyes (a plus) and her father's Irish complexion (a negative—there wasn't enough sunscreen in the world to keep her from freckling). Her shoulder-length dark hair, usually an asset, wasn't cooperating tonight. Her upsweep with the sideswept bangs was supposed to be going for Julianna Margulies in *The Good Wife*. But the humidity outside made her look more like Julianna Margulies in *ER*. She had to admit, though, Sarah was right. Too short or not, the dress did look good on her. Maybe Felix's compliment was genuine.

"Thanks," Grace said. "You don't look too shabby yourself."

It suddenly occurred to Grace that she'd never worn anything like Sarah's little black dress when she was dating Felix. She'd always been more of a jeans and sneakers kind of girl. Maybe if she'd dressed sexier, Felix wouldn't have been tempted to cheat.

*Wrong.*

It shouldn't have mattered if she wore granny panties or tiny silk thongs. Cheating was about the cheater, not the person who had been cheated on. How many times had she consoled Sarah with that same platitude?

"So, how long have you been working here?" she asked Felix.

*Was she really making small talk with Felix Barberi?*

"I was hired to open the restaurant. I'm the general manager." He gave her a funny look.

"Congratulations, Felix. That's great." She meant it too. Why should she be a shit just because Felix was one?

"There was a big article in the paper when the restaurant opened last month. Lots of corporate types from all over Florida gunning for the job. My picture was on the front page of the local section. You sure you didn't see it?"

Grace shook her head. What was she supposed to say to that? Polite small talk was one thing. It meant she was an adult and that she'd moved on. But she wasn't about to throw her arms around Felix and give him a congratulatory hug.

"How's your job going?" he asked. "Still working at that tourist shop?"

"Florida Charlie's is a family business. Of course I still work there."

"I saw a billboard the other day on I-95 claiming you now have the world's largest alligator tooth on display."

The alligator tooth display had been her father's idea. Grace had found it tacky but she wasn't about to divulge that to Felix. "It's pretty cool, actually. You should come by and see it sometime." *Who knows, maybe it belongs to a relative of yours.*

Felix came in close. So close she could smell the starch radiating from his crisp white shirt and the expensive Acqua Di Gio cologne he always wore. A vision of writhing naked body parts (his and hers) made Grace's pulse race. Then she remembered more writhing naked body parts (his and *not* hers) and her pulse raced again—this time in anger. She hated to admit it, but a part of her was still reeling from Felix's infidelity. She thought she'd moved on, but seeing him again was like pulling the Band-Aid off an old cut only to find that you'd accidentally ripped the scab off too.

"Grace," he said in a low, intimate voice. "It's me, remember? You don't have to put on an act. I know how much you hate working for your father." He placed his hand on her bare elbow. "Baby, you're better than that. You have to break free. Be all you can be."

Career advice from Felix Barberi? This was too much. She'd like to break free all right. Free enough to clobber him over the head.

*Patience,* Grace thought, trying to squelch *Mal Genio*— which more or less meant "Bad-Tempered One" in Spanish. Her brother had christened her with the nickname at age five when Grace had kicked him in the shin after he'd told her there was no Santa Claus. The temperamental alter ego had proven convenient over the years. Whenever Grace did something she didn't want to own up to, she'd say, "*Mal Genio* did it!" It didn't get her out of any punishments, but psychologically it made her feel better to know she had an inner demon that she couldn't completely control.

She regretted that she'd confided her job woes to Felix, but she couldn't let Felix mess with her head. Not before her big date with Brandon. She stepped back to reclaim some of her personal space.

"Felix, I never said I hated working for my father."

The heavy scent of butter and garlic and freshly baked bread floated through the air. It smelled even better than Felix and his Acqua Di Gio. Grace felt herself sway. Five-pound weight gain or not, she should have eaten today.

"I wish I'd known you were stopping by," Felix continued. "I'm filling in for Pierre, the maître d', so I really can't take a break right now. But maybe in another thirty minutes?"

Stopping by? Did Felix think she'd come here to see *him*?

"I'm meeting a date," Grace said. "Maybe you've heard of him? Brandon Farrell? He's been named Daytona Beach's most eligible bachelor two years in a row by *Central Florida Magazine*. He's my new boyfriend."

Felix raised a brow.

Okay, so maybe that was a little over the top. Since this was their first date, technically Brandon wasn't her boyfriend. Not yet anyway. But the petty side of her liked rubbing it in Felix's face. *See? I've moved on. With a mature man who knows what he wants!*

"Of course I know Brandon Farrell. He's a regular customer," Felix said. "He also happens to not be here tonight."

Brandon was running late too? "That's Saturday night traffic for you," she said, laughing nervously. "Can you just go ahead and seat me? I'll wait for him at the table."

"Sorry but we're completely booked and there's no reservation." Although there was no one around to hear them, he lowered his voice. "When Farrell wants a table he calls ahead and we always accommodate him, regardless of how busy we are. I've been manning the phones all night and I can guarantee you he hasn't called." He gave her the same consoling look he'd given her earlier when he'd brought up the alligator tooth display.

"There . . . There must be some sort of mixup."

"Grace, you don't have to make up a story to come see me. The truth is I've been thinking about you too."

"Felix, I really *do* have a date with Brandon Farrell."

"Then why don't you call and find out what's holding him up?" Felix challenged. "Like I said before, Farrell's an excellent customer. If he tells me to seat you, there won't be a problem."

Only there *was* a problem because Grace didn't have Brandon's phone number. She'd been so giddy when he'd asked her out last Thursday night after Zumba class that she hadn't thought to get it. Come to think of it, he didn't have her number either, but there was no way she'd tell that to Felix. She tugged on the dress again and tried not to fall off the unfamiliar four-inch heels. Working in sneakers all day put a girl at a distinct disadvantage in the heel department.

"Um, funny thing, Felix. I don't know Brandon's number by heart. It's programmed in my cell but I accidentally left it at home." Not the truth, but not exactly a lie either. In her haste to get out the door, she really had forgotten her cell phone.

The house phone rang. Felix put a finger in the air to signal he wasn't done with their conversation. "Chez Louis." Was it Grace's imagination, or did Felix suddenly have a French accent? "Yes, of course," Felix said into the receiver. He glanced at her, his hazel eyes wide with amazement. "She's right here."

"Is it Brandon?"

Felix nodded and handed her the phone.

Grace squelched the urge to say "I told you so."

"Grace, listen, I'm sorry, but I'm not going to be able to make it," Brandon said. "I had a rugby game scheduled for four. I thought we'd be done by six but the game went into overtime and we just finished. I didn't realize until now that I don't have your number."

Grace didn't know which was worse. Her disappointment

over the broken date or the embarrassment of being stood up with Felix as a witness.

"It's okay," she said, trying to sound mature about the whole thing. "Maybe we can do it some other time."

"*Damn*, you're being too nice about this."

Grace wasn't about to argue with that.

"I really want to see you tonight. The thing is . . . I'm heading over to this bar across from the field. I scored the winning try and the guys want to buy me drinks. I wish like hell I could get out of it, but they won't take no for an answer. I know it's not Chez Louis, but . . . maybe you could meet me there instead?"

Grace knew the bar he was talking about. She'd never been inside the Wobbly Duck but she'd driven by a few times. From the outside it looked like it was falling apart. Probably not the best venue for her shrinking black dress and her four-inch heels. But the alternative was to go back to her place and spend the night alone, *or worse*, go back to the store for her book club meeting and have to face Sarah and Penny and Ellen and tell them she'd been stood up. On the other hand, if she went to the bar, she could show Brandon what a terrific sport she could be. Fifty years from now, at their golden wedding anniversary celebration, it would be one of those cute "first date" stories to tell their party guests during the toast.

"I know the place," Grace said. "Sure, I'll meet you there for a drink."

"Really?" he said with such boyish enthusiasm that Grace couldn't help but be convinced she was doing the right thing. The Wobbly Duck might not be Chez Louis, but she was still technically going out on a date with Brandon.

They said their good-byes and she handed the phone back to Felix.

Grace put on a fake smile. "Silly me! I got everything totally confused. We're meeting somewhere different."

"Grace, I know the . . . incident last February must have been a blow to your ego, but you shouldn't let it drag down your self-esteem. I couldn't live with myself if I thought I'd done that to you."

Grace felt her face go hot. Of all the conceited . . .

"Good news, Felix. You can go on breathing, because my self-esteem is just fine, thank you. Now, where's your bathroom?" She needed to check out the hem situation. And touch up her lipstick. And empty her bladder. She certainly didn't want to do any of that in the bathroom at the Wobbly Duck. She wasn't even sure the place had running water.

He sighed and pointed down a hallway to her left. "Remember, Grace. I'm here whenever you need me."

"Thanks. I'll keep that in mind."

Just a quick touch-up and she'd be on her way to meet Brandon. After tonight the Felixes of the world would be behind her forever.

She took the first empty stall and pulled the tiny shrink-wrapped tampon from her black clutch purse. Trying to balance herself midair (Abuela had always warned her against the evils of actually letting any part of her anatomy touch a toilet seat she hadn't personally cleaned herself), she tried to work the shrink wrap off the tampon by wiggling it between her fingers, but the outer wrap didn't budge. Grace blew out a frustrated breath and tried again, this time working the plastic more vigorously. Nothing happened.

Obviously, she was dealing with a defective product.

She fished around the bottom of her clutch to produce a lipstick, her driver's license, a credit card, dental floss, car keys, and two pieces of unwrapped bubble gum. *Ew, gross.* She tossed the bubble gum and upended her purse, but no more tampons. She had no choice. She'd have to open this one.

She tried to use the edge of her car key to rip into the plastic but that only ended with her jabbing herself in the palm of her hand. She could always use her nails, of course, but she'd gotten a manicure for tonight's date and she didn't want to chip her color. Bringing the end of the tampon up to her mouth she gnawed on the plastic with her teeth. After a minute of struggling, the plastic finally gave way.

*Thank God!*

Still, someone in the feminine hygiene department of Procter & Gamble was going to be the recipient of a very serious e-mail come Monday morning.

She finished up in the stall and washed her hands. *Huh.* Something felt weird. It wasn't her contact lenses, was it? She blinked. No, they felt fine. She rubbed her tongue against the edge of her bottom teeth. There was something stuck in there. It was probably a little piece of the plastic shrink wrap that had dislodged itself while she'd done her beaver imitation. Good thing she always carried dental floss in her purse.

She checked herself out in front of the full-length mirror. It was just as she suspected. The dress *was* too short. It had looked fine back at her town house with Sarah urging her on, but she could see now that she was showing too much leg. At least too much leg for Grace O'Bryan. Despite being a jeans and sneakers kind of girl, she did occasionally dress sexy. But this was *too* sexy, and she wasn't the kind of girl who could pull off "too sexy" without worrying that she looked ridiculous while doing it.

She grabbed hold of the dress by the back of the neck and twisted around to read the label. There was a giant P next to the size. *Of course.* Sarah was barely five foot two. The dress was a petite! No wonder the cut felt strange. Kind of the like the plastic stuck between her teeth. There was nothing she could do now about the dress, but she could do something about the plastic. She gave a great big smile to expose her teeth and leaned her face into the mirror to get a better view.

What she saw made her freeze. There was no plastic stuck between her teeth to get rid of. What felt so weird was that a tiny piece of one of her bottom teeth was missing.

Grace snapped her eyes shut. This wasn't happening. Maybe the lack of food today had made her delirious. Yes, that was it. She'd open her eyes and find the whole thing had been a mirage. She was like those people who wandered through the desert, dehydrated, and thought they saw a swimming pool—only instead of seeing something good, she'd conjured up something bad.

She took a deep breath and slowly opened her eyes.

It wasn't a mirage, because there it was, staring right back at her. Her previously even row of straight white teeth was no more. Somehow, she'd chipped off part of her tooth while unwrapping a tampon.

Who did that happen to?

People who were cursed.

That's who.

# Beware of Bars Named After Drunken Birds

The parking lot of the Wobbly Duck was nothing more than a muddy field. By the time Grace trekked her way to the front door, her shiny black patent heels were filthy. She tried to get as much mud off them as she could before entering the bar. The mingled sounds of laughter, football on TV, and singing blasted her ears.

> *We sailed the good ship Venus,*
> *You really should have seen us!*
> *The maidenhead was a whore in bed*
> *And the mast was an upright penis!*
> *Olee Olee Anna! Olee Olee Anna!*

Good grief. Were they singing what she *thought* they were singing? The stench of spilled beer and sweaty male made her nose crinkle, and the floor was so sticky she had to work to lift her foot up. It wasn't like she hadn't been in a grungy bar a time or two, but this place was gross. Plus, she was definitely overdressed. Or underdressed, depending on how you looked at it.

Maybe she should leave. Coming here now seemed like a bad idea. But she couldn't just not show up. Not after Brandon had sounded so pumped to see her.

She tried to make him out among the crowd. Despite the fact that she appeared to be the only woman in the bar, no one paid her any attention. *So much for the allure of a shrinking black dress and four-inch heels.* Still, she should be grateful. This wasn't the kind of bar she wanted to draw notice in. She tried to flag the bartender down, but he was busy listening to two guys in the middle of an animated play-by-play.

A male voice from somewhere behind her interrupted her futile attempts to get the bartender's attention. "What's a nice pair of legs like yours doing in a place like this?"

Apparently, she'd thought too soon. The magic powers of a little black dress were alive and well. She braced herself and did an about-face to find the man behind the voice.

Tall, broad shoulders, blue eyes. *Nice.* But she couldn't let him get away with that butchered cliché.

"I have to admit, that's original. Most guys notice my ass first."

He grinned, revealing an identical set of dimples. "Don't know how I could have missed that. Turn around and let me start over."

Before Grace could respond, the table in the center of the room broke out in song again.

> *The cook his name was Freeman*
> *He was a dirty demon*
> *He fed the crew on menstrual stew*
> *And hymens fried in semen!*
> *Olee Olee Anna! Olee Olee Anna!*

Grace rolled her eyes.

"The verses only get worse," said Dimples. A tiny trickle of blood oozed from his chin. Grace resisted the impulse to grab a napkin off the counter and apply pressure to the cut.

"I'm actually looking forward to them."

Dimples laughed. "I like you." He glanced toward the table where the singing had originated. "Are you sure you're in the right place? I mean . . . do you know what kind of bar this is?"

"An Irish pub?"

"That's currently full of horny, drunk rugby players. And then there's you. Wearing *that* dress." The way he said the last part made her feel naked. Grace didn't know whether to be flattered or annoyed. She thought of Felix's reaction to the dress. Were all men really this . . . simple?

"So which are you?" Grace asked. "Horny or drunk?"

"I'm not drunk. At least not yet."

"Hey, Rosie!" someone shouted in their direction. "Hurry the fuck up and bring us our beer!"

Dimples motioned to the bartender. "Sean, I need a couple of pitchers, fast."

Sean the bartender smiled at Grace, revealing several missing teeth. Grace pursed her lips together. She was visiting the dentist first thing Monday morning. "Well, well," Sean purred in an Irish brogue. "What can I get for *you*, love?"

"Eyes back in their sockets, Sean," said Dimples. "I saw her first."

"Rosie!" came another anonymous shout. "What the fuck! Where's our beer?"

"Get your own beer. I'm busy!" yelled Rosie aka Dimples. "Sorry about that," he said to Grace. "This place is filled with animals."

"So I see."

"Look," he said, glancing down at his muddy shirt and shorts. "I know I'm a mess, but there's a bar a mile down the road that won't kick me out for showing up like this. The drinks are watered down but the atmosphere is a lot nicer."

Was this guy seriously trying to pick her up?

"How do you know I'm not some crazy serial killer?"

He looked amused by the turnaround. "I can think of a few worse ways to die."

"I didn't say I was going to have my way with you first."

"Hey, life's a crapshoot, right?"

"Sorry, but I'm looking for someone."

He splayed his arms out to his sides and grinned. "I'm right here in front of you, sweetheart!"

Grace couldn't help but grin back. She also couldn't help but notice the way the skin around his eyes crinkled when he smiled, and what perfectly beautiful teeth he had. Dimples was more than just nice. He was downright gorgeous. Like a slightly older version of those brooding college-aged Abercrombie and Fitch models. He made even Felix look plain. The comparison to Felix made her lose her smile.

"Do women really fall for that semi-charming baloney you're trying to peddle? Or am I just that gullible looking?"

"I'll have you know it's taken me years to perfect that sandwich meat."

"I didn't come in here to hook up with some horny rugby player. When I said I was looking for someone, I meant someone in particular."

Dimples clutched his hand to his chest like he'd been wounded. "It's the story of my life. I meet the girl of my dreams and she's meeting someone else."

In another lifetime, Grace might have fallen for Dimples' phony charm. But her stint with Felix had taught her a thing or two. "Maybe you can help me find him," she said.

"I'm a nice guy, but I'm not that nice."

"I mean, maybe you know him. Brandon Farrell?"

He hesitated, then pointed to the large table in the middle of the room. "Try over there." It was the table where the singing was taking place.

*Chin up, Grace.* She hadn't fought her way through the parking lot mud to be intimidated by a raunchy song. "Thanks."

"Yeah, well . . . good luck with that." Dimples collected his pitchers of beer and made off for the other side of the room.

To get to her destination Grace had to slide between the closely packed tables. No one bothered to scoot his chair to make room for her, so it was either tits one way or ass the other, but at least she was getting some interested looks now. Of course the interested looks were more like leers. By the time she got to Brandon's table, her face was on fire.

"You made it!" Brandon said. He shoved the guy next to him out of his chair and offered it up to Grace. "So what'll you have? We have beer. And we have more beer!"

The guys at the table laughed.

This was her opportunity to show Brandon what a great sport she could be. "In that case, I'll take a beer."

He slid his mug her way.

She'd meant in her own glass. Oh well. She took a long drag of the warm beer. She'd prefer something colder but Grace wasn't about to make the jungle trek back across to Sean the bartender, and she didn't want to bother Brandon with such a silly request. She took a few seconds to study him. His dark hair was adorably mussed and there was a tiny smear of dirt on his right cheek. Up until ten minutes ago, she would have said he was the best-looking guy she'd ever met. She glanced over to the table where Rosie Dimples had deposited his two pitchers of beer. Someone sitting next to him said something that made him smile. Rosie Dimples was even prettier than Felix and Brandon put together. And he knew it too.

A guy wearing a backward baseball cap punched Brandon in the arm. "Hey, asshole. Aren't you going to introduce her?"

This produced a few snorts among his buddies.

"Sure. Everyone, this is . . . Grace."

For one horrible moment, she was certain Brandon had forgotten her name.

"Grace O'Bryan," she clarified to no one in particular.

"This is the gang," Brandon said, waving his hand around the table by way of introduction.

Something momentous happened on the TV screen that made the room explode in shouts. Guys began jumping up and giving each other high fives. The Tampa Bay Bucs had scored a touchdown. Brandon grabbed her and gave her a hug, beer mug still in hand. Grace felt something wet slide down her back. *Ugh!* She'd gotten beer on Sarah's dress. Or rather, Brandon had gotten beer on Sarah's dress.

She glanced around and noticed once again that she was the only female in the bar. Grace pulled down the hem of her dress in an unconscious gesture. With all the pulling and stretching and now the beer stain that was probably setting itself into the fabric, she might as well buy Sarah a brand-new dress. This one was never going to be the same again.

Dimples met her gaze from across the room. He wasn't smiling.

Baseball Cap caught the exchange. "You know that loser over there?" he said, motioning to Rosie Dimples. She wondered briefly what Dimples, or Rosie, or whatever his real name was (because it simply *couldn't* be Rosie) would think of her nickname for him. She ignored Baseball Cap's loser slur. It was probably just pumped-up macho rugby talk.

"I've never met him before but he was nice enough to point Brandon out for me."

"Hey, Farrell, I think you should kick Rosenblum's ass for talking to your woman!" Baseball Cap said.

"He's already kicked Rosenblum's ass!" said another one of the guys with a laugh.

"That was on the rugby field. I mean for real," Baseball Cap said.

Grace waited for Brandon to say something civilized to counter the Neanderthal sitting across from her. But he didn't.

*Well, that was disappointing.*

"So, Grace," Baseball Cap continued, oblivious to her disgust. "How do you know our boy Brandon here?"

"We met in Zumba class," Grace said.

Brandon began to cough violently. Grace slapped him on the back between his shoulder blades. "Are you okay?"

"What the hell is Zumba?" Baseball Cap asked.

"Did your beer go down the wrong way?" Grace asked Brandon.

Brandon tried to speak but nothing came out.

"Don't worry," Grace said in the calmest voice she could muster. "I've taken CPR. Do you need me to do the Heimlich?"

Brandon, whose face had gone the color of an eggplant, frantically shook his head.

Doing the Heimlich maneuver in Sarah's too-short little black dress would probably prove indelicate but Grace might not have a choice. No one else at the table seemed the least bit concerned that Brandon could very well be choking to death. What was wrong with these hooligans?

"Just make the international choking sign," Grace said, bringing her hands to her throat to demonstrate.

Brandon's arms flailed at his sides, but he made no motion to do the choking sign that would give her permission to do the Heimlich.

*For the love of God.* Was he too proud to ask for help?

"I'm . . . I'm o-kay!" Brandon wheezed pathetically.

Grace tried to remember what she'd learned in her CPR class. If Brandon was talking, then he couldn't be choking. She let herself relax a little and slid the beer into his hand. "Here, take a sip of this."

Brandon downed half the glass.

Satisfied that he was all right, Grace turned her attention to Baseball Cap. "Zumba is aerobics done to salsa music. It's a lot of fun. You should try it sometime."

Baseball Cap snorted. "Brandon, my man, when did you grow a pussy?"

"What she *meant* to say was that we met at the gym. Right?" Brandon croaked, his expression part pleading, part embarrassed.

"Um, yeah, we met at the gym."

Okay, so Brandon didn't want to admit he did Zumba. Grace could sort of understand that. Especially in this testosterone-overloaded crowd. "Dancing is an excellent way to keep in shape," she informed the guys at the table. "There are football players who take ballet, you know."

"Yeah, well, the last time I looked, I had a dick," Baseball Cap shot back. "I thought you did too, Farrell."

Brandon didn't say anything. Maybe his throat was still too raw from his near-death choking experience. If Brandon couldn't stick up for himself, then Grace would just have to do it for him. "That kind of macho posturing usually indicates a big problem," she said to Baseball Cap. "Or maybe in your case, it's a small one."

The guys at the table began to howl.

Baseball Cap gave a short laugh like he thought her joke was funny, but Grace could tell by the look in his eyes that he was seething. "Farrell, you didn't tell us you were fucking Dr. Phil." He turned his creepy smile on her. "So, honey, what do you do for a living?"

*Honey?*

"Are you *kidding* me?" Grace asked Brandon. "This guy is actually your friend?" Raw throat or not, how could he let Baseball Cap get away with this kind of talk?

"Grace, he's drunk. Ignore him. Doug's a good guy," Brandon said, shifting uncomfortably in his seat.

*Good guy, my ass,* Grace thought. From the way Brandon's words slurred together, it appeared Doug wasn't the only one who'd had too much to drink. Well, Rosie Dimples had warned her. The place was full of drunk, horny rugby players. And Brandon was no exception.

A huge wave of disappointment (and lack of food) sent her head spinning. This was so *not* how she had imagined this evening. Five more minutes. That's how long she was giving this date. Five more minutes, then she'd find an excuse to get out of here. Maybe Brandon would come to his senses and leave with her.

"So let me guess," baseball-cap-wearing Doug said, like he just hadn't heard the exchange between her and Brandon. He gave Grace a slow perusal that made her feel dirty. "Judging by that dress you have on, I'd say you're a hostess at that new restaurant Farrell likes to go to. The one he keeps a standing reservation at . . . What's it called?"

"I don't work at Chez Louis," Grace said.

"So where do you work, babe?" Doug asked.

*Babe?*

Somewhere inside her, Grace could hear *Mal Genio* begin to chuckle. Grace's fingers began to twitch. "I manage a tourist shop."

Brandon seemed to come alive. "Oh, yeah, which one?" he asked.

It occurred to her that Brandon didn't know much about her. He'd been a dedicated member of the Thursday-night Zumba class for the past two months at Grace's gym, the Total Package. He was one of only three guys taking the class, the other two being a couple. Brandon wasn't very coordinated, but he tried, and Darlene, the instructor, loved him. Brandon and Grace had gone out for coffee last week after class. They'd chatted about which circuit machines were good for which muscle group, and

Brandon told her all about his job as vice president of his family's bank, but they hadn't talked much about Grace.

"You've probably never been there," Grace said, taking another sip of their shared beer. She glanced at the TV screen. Now would be a good time for the Bucs to do something good again. Or even something bad. Anything to divert the table's attention from the current topic.

"Try me," Brandon said.

Grace steeled herself for the inevitable jokes. "I work at Florida Charlie's."

Doug's eyes widened. "*The* Florida Charlie's? The shop with the stuffed alligator in front? The one off the interstate where all the employees dress in costume?"

"I thought that place closed down," someone said.

"We stopped wearing costumes a few years ago," Grace said.

Doug laughed like he'd just won the lottery. "Hey, Farrell! Remember those commercials Florida Charlie used to do when we were kids? The ones where he wore the giant orange-head costume and ran around the parking lot yelling 'Ex-squeeze me'?"

Grace stiffened. The commercials featuring her father wearing the orange-head costume had been the scourge of her elementary school years. A vision of Richard Kasamati running around the playground doing an unflattering imitation of her father in the orange-head getup flashed through Grace's head. "*Your dad is weird and so are you!*" Richard had chanted. *Mal Genio* had taken care of the situation. She'd punched Richard in the stomach and made him cry. It had earned Grace a trip to Sister Perpetua's office, better known to the students at St. Bernadette's as the chamber of horrors, but it had been worth it.

Brandon grinned. "I remember those orange-head commercials. But I thought they were kind of—"

"So you work for Florida Charlie," Doug said. "It'd be worth the humiliation just to spend ten minutes talking to that guy. I saw him interviewed once on TV. He's like something off another planet. Is the crazy Cuban lady still around? Isn't she the one who makes the alligator his costumes?"

*Uh-oh. Mal Genio* was fully awake now and begging to be let out to play. The hell with the five minutes. Grace was out of here.

"For your information, *babe*," she said to Doug, "Florida Charlie is my father. And that crazy Cuban lady is my grandmother. Besides being an excellent seamstress, she also dabbles in *brujería*. That's witchcraft, *honey*, in case you flunked high school Spanish. So you better watch out, or I'll find a live chicken she can sacrifice to make a potion that shrinks your pecker even smaller than it already is." Grace stood and looped her purse over her shoulder.

Doug's eyes gleamed in satisfaction. "You've dated some crazy chicks in your time, Farrell, but I think this one's my favorite!"

Brandon grabbed her by the wrist. "Hey, I told you, he doesn't mean anything by it. Give me ten minutes—"

"I'm *gone* in the next five seconds. You can either come with me or not. At this point, I'd actually prefer you didn't."

"You're joking, right?" Brandon looked confused. "No one's ever walked out on me before."

"Then consider me your first."

"Tracy, I think you need to calm down."

Grace froze. "What did you call me?"

Brandon frowned. "I meant to say . . . Grace."

"But you didn't."

"Isn't that what your friend with the blond hair calls you in class?" Brandon asked in the tone of someone who was being wronged. "I have no idea how you'd get the nickname Tracy from Grace, but hey—"

Despite the horribleness of it all, Grace started to laugh. It was a high-pitched, scary sounding laugh. *Mal Genio* wasn't going to be stopped. Not tonight anyway.

"What's so funny?" Brandon demanded.

"That's *Gracie*, you idiot. My friend Sarah calls me Gracie. Not Tracy. You didn't even know my friggin' name!"

By comparison to just a few minutes ago, the room was now relatively quiet. Grace could feel at least a dozen pairs of eyes on them.

"Sit down, you're embarrassing me," Brandon whispered tightly. "Let me finish my beer and then we'll leave."

Grace could feel the rational, calm side of herself sliding into some dark abyss. She thought about how excited she'd been over tonight's date. About how she and Sarah had spent the better part of an hour trying to decide what Grace should wear. And how she hadn't eaten anything all day. And the humiliation she'd felt when Felix had figured out she'd been stood up. And how Brandon let his friend Doug make fun of Pop and Abuela . . .

"*I'm* embarrassing *you*? Brandon, I wouldn't go anywhere with you if you were the last man on earth!"

And then something happened that Grace hadn't *exactly* planned on. With a dramatic flair, she'd spun around to leave, causing her purse to knock over the pitcher of beer. Straight down the crotch of Daytona Beach's most eligible bachelor.

# 3

# Does Talking to a Plastic Alligator Mean You're Crazy?

She hadn't meant to do it. But somehow it would come back to bite her in the ass. Bad karma usually did. And while the person she would have really liked to douse in beer (baseball-cap-wearing Doug) only stood back with his mouth gaping open, seeing Brandon Farrell jump from his chair, his face silly with shock, had been extremely gratifying.

She could have offered to help dry him off (on the other hand, no—that wouldn't have been a good idea). Instead, she turned on her heel, and with her head held high, marched straight out the front door of the Wobbly Duck. Chairs had instantly slid to clear a path. No weaving her way through the tables this time. She might not have made much of an impression walking in, but she'd definitely made an impression walking out. Too bad it wasn't the impression she'd been going for.

Saturday evening traffic was still heavy. Grace turned on the radio, hoping to take her mind off the night's disastrous events.

"Welcome to the Track, Daytona Beach's hottest radio station! It's Saturday night and we're bringing you the best of the Speedway Gonzalez Show." This was followed by the familiar sound of an engine revving up in the background, the show's "theme music," so to speak.

"Hel-lo, speedsters! This is Speedway Gonzalez taking you *round* and *round* Day-to-na Beach," came the familiar obnoxious voice.

*Ugh!*

Speedway Gonzalez was Daytona's Beach's version of Tucker Max. He was obnoxious, chauvinistic, and just plain nasty. But it was also impossible to turn him off. Listening to his show was like rubbernecking on the radio.

"Today we're talking to Donna, who says her boyfriend isn't paying her enough attention."

Grace cringed. She'd heard this one before.

"So, Donna, tell me. Are you fat?"

"What?" came a confused female voice.

"You heard me, baby. Are you fat? Okay, so you are. Have you ever thought that's the reason your boyfriend has moved on?"

Grace rolled her car into her reserved parking spot behind the store just as Speedway was beginning to make mincemeat of poor Donna. Of course, it was no one's fault but Donna's. Everyone who called in to Speedway's show ended up sounding like an ass. Grace wondered if the whole thing wasn't just a big setup and the schmucks who called in nothing but wannabe actors trying to get discovered.

She switched off the radio. Florida Charlie's officially closed at nine p.m., which was in five minutes, but the Closed sign was already out. Long gone were the days they'd had to stay open late to finish ringing up all the last-minute sales.

She walked around to the front of the store and stood back, trying to inspect the place with an objective eye. A ten-foot hot pink flamingo in flashing neon stood on top of the building next to the giant aqua-colored Florida Charlie's sign. It was your typical tourist trap. Over five thousand square feet of wall-to-wall junk beckoning to wide-eyed children and their tired parents. Horny spring breakers need not enter. Florida Charlie's was strictly G rated. It was her grandfather's creation, given birth to some fifty years ago when Florida theme parks like Weeki Wachee and Silver Springs and Six Gun Territory had been booming attractions.

Grandpa O'Bryan had named the store after his only child, Charlie, and sold things like "mermaid-watching kits" and inflatable seahorses. They gave out free samples of fresh hand-squeezed orange juice and shipped citrus all over the States. But the shop's real appeal had been its quirkiness. Gramps had insisted the employees dress in costume. It didn't matter what the costume was, as long as it could be linked to something having to do with Florida. Billboards starting as far north as Virginia lined Highway 95, encouraging visitors to "Stop at the Flashing Flamingo!" Besides the must-have mermaid-watching kits and the prerequisite inflatable marine life, there was always something exotic on display. Currently, it was the infamous alligator tooth.

Her father had toiled alongside his father, and word of mouth, together with lots of blood, sweat, and tears (and all those billboards) had made Florida Charlie's a central Florida landmark. When Pop graduated high school, he went off to college in nearby Gainesville to attend the University of Florida. That's where he met Ana Alvarez, a Cuban emigrant from Miami majoring in elementary education. Pop had taken one look at Ana's big brown eyes and fallen head over heels in *amor* (unlike Grace, Pop *did* believe in love at first sight). They were married six months later, and after graduation, Mami (pronounced ma-mee, what all good children called their Cuban mothers) gave up a potential teaching career to work in the store alongside Pop and Grandpa O'Bryan. Soon after, Mami's widowed mother, Graciela Alvarez, fed up with the rising crime rate and horrific Miami traffic, came to Daytona Beach to live with her only daughter. Charlie Jr. was born a couple of years later, and three years after that, Grace had come along. Having Abuela in the house to help take care of two small children had made running a family business a lot easier.

When Gramps passed away, Pop inherited the store. Then two years ago, Pop had a heart attack. His doctor told him if he didn't slow down he wouldn't live to see sixty. Pop said he couldn't imagine putting Florida Charlie's into the hands of an outsider, but Charlie Jr. wasn't interested in the family business. Charlie was a tax attorney and in his seventh year at Lockett and Jones, Attorneys at Law, so the task had fallen on Grace. Pop still kept his finger in the pie, but Grace took over the day-to-day operations. As a kid she'd spent every possible free minute in the store. It had been like having her own personal playground. Despite the Richard Kasamatis of the world, Grace had been proud of Florida Charlie's.

But times had changed. Florida tourism was now synonymous with Disney World and Universal Studios. Places like Weeki Wachee and Silver Springs had managed to hang on, but Six Gun Territory, like so many other roadside attractions, had been hit by a silver bullet. The gun had been in the hands of a cute little mouse with a squeaky voice, but those were the facts. The shop wasn't so quirky anymore. It was now downright embarrassing. Pop still insisted on the billboards, but Grace had managed to convince him to let the employees wear the new standard outfit—khaki shorts or pants (if it was cold enough) and a bright aqua T-shirt with a Florida Charlie's insignia. The Florida Charlie's T-shirts had been Grace's idea. Although they weren't as popular as the Ron Jon Surf Shop T-shirts, they had been a mild success among tourists who were old enough to remember Florida Charlie's in its heyday.

But the revamping of the employee uniform was just the tip of the iceberg. As far as Grace was concerned, the entire store needed a major overhaul, with the exception of one thing: a standing eight-foot alligator that kept watch outside the double glass doors waiting to welcome tourists. And their MasterCards and Visas and American Expresses.

The alligator had been a staple at the shop as long as Grace could remember. Currently, he was wearing his Santa costume, complete with hat and white pom-pom. When she was five, Grace had nicknamed him "Gator Claus." No matter what time of the year it was, or what outfit he was decked out in, it was the name that had stuck, most likely since it was the costume he wore the longest. The Santa outfit went on November first and stayed on until January second. He was Gator Claus even when he was the Easter Bunny or wearing the Fourth of July Yankee Doodle costume Abuela had painstakingly sewn. The only holiday Gator Claus didn't do was Thanksgiving. Pop always noted a slack in sales whenever he wore the pilgrim costume. Apparently, giving thanks didn't put people in the spending mood.

Grace loved Gator Claus. Boyfriends came and went, but you could always count on a stationary eight-foot plastic alligator to be there when you needed him.

She looked up into Gator Claus's beady glass eyes. "What's a nice alligator like you doing in a place like this?"

No response.

Not that Grace was expecting one. Plastic alligators weren't real. Hence they didn't talk back. But every once in a while, if Grace concentrated very hard, she could swear Gator Claus was trying to communicate with her. The idea was unsettling. But there it was. Besides her belief in curses, it was the one other tiny blip on her logic radar.

"Yeah, I thought that was a pretty cheesy line."

Gator Claus stared down at her with a frozen, semisardonic half-snarl/half-smile on his face.

"Don't look at me like that! You would have walked out on Brandon too. And the beer thing was an accident. Although *Mal Genio* wishes she'd done it on purpose."

Silence.

"I'm half Cuban, half Irish. Can I help it if I got the bad temper gene? I was defending your honor, you ingrate! They laughed at you, you know. And Pop and his orange-head commercials. One of them even called Abuela a crazy old lady."

Gator Claus frowned.

*Finally*, a response.

"I know what you're going to say. I should have known better than to go to a bar named after a drunken bird." Grace sighed. "Why does this keep happening to me, Gator Claus? Am I picking the wrong guys? Or . . . do you think it's me? Do you think maybe I'm cursed?"

"Um, Grace?" a gravelly female voice asked. "Are you talking to the alligator again?"

Grace turned to see Penny Starr, the shop's assistant manager. Penny was tall and skinny with jet-black hair that came out of a box. She wore the shop's signature uniform—khaki shorts and aqua T-shirt. She tossed a half-smoked cigarette onto the asphalt and smashed it with the sole of her aqua high topped sneakers.

Penny was a crisis smoker. As far as Grace knew, this was Penny's first cigarette in six months.

"What's wrong?" Grace asked.

"I don't want to talk about it."

Grace raised a brow.

"Don't look at me like that. I'm not the one talking to a dead reptile."

"Gator Claus was never alive. He's plastic." Grace paused. "Penny, do you think talking to the alligator means I'm crazy?"

"No, but it definitely makes you weird. You'd only be crazy if you expected him to answer you." Penny's eyes narrowed. "You don't expect him to answer, do you?"

"Not exactly."

Penny took in Grace's dress and mud-caked stilettos. "I thought you had a hot date tonight."

"If you don't have to talk about it, then neither do I."

Penny rolled her eyes. "I closed the shop early. I didn't think you'd mind. We haven't had a customer in the last hour."

"You mean the world's largest alligator tooth isn't bringing them in by the carloads?"

"Actually, I had a few people ask to see it. They were kind of disappointed when I showed it to them."

"Isn't that a surprise."

"Your dad dropped by this evening right after you left. He told me he wanted the alligator tooth displayed up front in a glass case, by the cash registers."

"Sunscreen and visors go by the cash registers, Pen. They're our biggest sellers. Don't worry, I'll handle Pop."

"Okay," Penny said, but she looked unconvinced. "We're about to start the book club meeting. Sarah brought oatmeal cookies and Ellen brought vodka. We can raid the fresh-squeezed orange juice section and make screwdrivers."

"Sounds like a plan. What are we discussing tonight?"

"*The Great Gatsby*. Did you read it? It was on the list."

"I must have read it in high school. And I'm pretty certain I've seen the movie. Robert Redford, right?"

"High school for you was thirteen years ago. And watching the movie is *not* the same as reading the book. The movie version always sucks. Unless it's like *Gone With the Wind* or *The Wizard of Oz* or something."

"Can't we pretend I read it? Just for tonight?"

"I won't tell on you. But Ellen might figure it out."

Ellen Ames taught English at Daytona State College. She was forever trying to get them to figure out the theme or the recurring motifs of a book. Ellen could talk about theme for hours.

Grace just liked to go around in a circle and have everyone give the book a thumbs-up or thumbs-down.

She opened the front door to the store and was welcomed by a blast of delicious cold air-conditioning. Pop insisted on keeping the store's thermostat at seventy degrees. The temperature outside was probably only in the low seventies, not untypical for early November in central Florida, but the humidity was still high. The air-conditioning felt like heaven.

"Pen, do you ever wish it would like . . . snow or something?"

Penny gave her an odd look. "What's with you tonight?"

"I'll tell you if you tell me why you've started smoking again."

"I already told you, I don't want to talk about it."

"That means we don't have anything to talk about then. Right?"

"Right."

Grace bit back a retort. The thing was, she *did* want to talk about it. Spilling your guts to Gator Claus was only partially liberating. Sometimes it was nice to actually get a real response.

They snaked their way through the T-shirt racks to the back of the store where Sarah and Ellen were setting up folding chairs in the Hemingway corner. At least, that's what Pop liked to call it. In reality, it was a mismatched little section filled with books mostly featuring anything to do with Florida—from cooking to architecture to the history of the space shuttle. But the corner's crowning glory was an entire row of novels written by Hemingway. Ernest might not have been born in the sunshine state but he was Pop's favorite author. Pop could quote from *The Old Man and the Sea* as easily as Grace could quote Carrie from *Sex and the City*. As far as Grace was concerned, the Hemingway corner was two hundred square feet of wasted space. Tourists weren't looking to stop on their way to Disney and buy a book about Florida or a novel they were forced to read in high school.

They wanted cheap T-shirts, sunscreen, and hats. But trying to convince Pop of that was like trying to keep your hair from frizzing in the middle of a July afternoon.

Sarah was popping a cookie in her mouth when she spotted Grace. "I thought you had a hot date," she said, her voice muffled by crumbs. Sarah Douglas née Riley had been Grace's best friend since the first day of first grade at St. Bernadette's Catholic School, where they'd had the honorary distinction of being the tallest and the shortest girl in class. They'd been in Girl Scouts together, had plucked each other's eyebrows for the first time, and had been college roommates at Florida State. Grace had also been Sarah's maid of honor two years ago at her wedding to Craig the Cad, as well as the first person to know of their impending divorce. Sarah was an interior designer and always looked perfect, even now with her mouth stuffed full of high-calorie baked goods.

Ellen wrinkled her nose. "Does it smell like beer in here?"

"That would be me." Grace grabbed a handful of the oatmeal cookies. "Brandon spilled beer on the dress." She gave Sarah an apologetic smile. "Sorry, I'll have it dry-cleaned."

Sarah's blue eyes widened. "He spilled beer on you? I thought you were going to Chez Louis!"

"She doesn't want to talk about it," Penny said.

Grace stuffed two cookies into her mouth.

There was an awkward silence before Ellen said, "Maybe we should just start the book club meeting. I've been looking forward to discussing *The Great Gatsby* all month."

The Florida Charlie's book club had been formed three years ago after Grace decided she and Penny needed to inject some culture into their otherwise glamorous life of selling plastic seashells. The addition of Sarah was a given. And Ellen, whom Grace and Sarah had both known since high school, was an obvious match for the group. They'd started out with seven members. Then last year, Ellen (who had somehow taken over as their unspoken leader) switched the focus off popular book club selections to traditional literary classics. "How can we understand literature if we don't have a proper foundation?" she'd said. Gradually, the three other members had dropped out and now it was just the four of them.

They each took a seat. Ellen pulled a legal pad from her satchel and balanced it across her lap. Ellen always insisted on taking notes. She claimed it enhanced the book club experience. "Penny, would you like to—"

"I hated the book," Penny blurted.

Ellen looked like she'd just been smacked up the side of her head with a two-by-four. "How can you hate it? It's considered one of the most beautiful pieces of literature!"

"By who? A bunch of dried-up old men? You asked what I thought of it and I told you. Isn't that the purpose of the club? To discuss what we did and didn't like?"

Ellen frowned. "All right," she conceded. "But you just can't say you hate it. You have to tell us *exactly* why you didn't like it. And be specific in your examples."

Grace sighed. This was Ellen going into English teacher mode again.

"Okay, I'll be specific. I hated the ending," Penny said.

"It had to end that way!" Ellen said. "Fitzgerald had no choice."

"Sure he did. Old Daisy could have been the one who ended up with a bullet instead of that sad sack Gatsby. Man, what a loser."

"I'm with Penny," said Sarah. "All that production just to impress a woman like Daisy? She's the kind of twit who gives women a bad name."

"But don't you *see*? That's the whole tragedy of it! Gatsby's love for Daisy drove him to ruin. Fitzgerald was trying to make a correlation between Gatsby's dream of Daisy and the corruption of society." Ellen began scribbling in her notepad. "What did you think of the book, Grace?"

A fuzzy image of Robert Redford in a white tuxedo popped into Grace's head. "I have to agree with Penny and Sarah. Gatsby was a loser. But he sure knew how to dress."

Ellen stopped writing. "What do you mean?"

Sarah gave Grace a warning look.

"Um, you know, there was all that great description about his clothes. He had great style. Isn't that why they called him the Great Gatsby?"

Sarah started to giggle.

"You didn't read the book, did you?" Ellen said. "You're going off the movie version. Just like you did in September when we discussed *The Last of the Mohicans*."

"I already admitted I didn't read *The Last of the Mohicans*," Grace said, starting to feel testy. How many times was Ellen going to bring that up? "Sorry, but two hours of watching Daniel Day-Lewis without his shirt on was a lot better way to spend a night than reading that boring book. So maybe I did see the movie version of *The Great Gatsby*, but I promise you, I read the book too." She nudged Sarah's crossed legs with the edge of her muddy stilettos. "We read it in Mrs. Schumaker's class, back in eleventh grade, didn't we?"

"That was the week of swim team tryouts so I think you read the CliffsNotes instead," Sarah said.

Grace blinked. "Oh, yeah, I remember now."

Ellen slapped the legal pad against her knee, startling them all. In another lifetime, Ellen would have made a terrific nun. "What's the point of a having a book club if we aren't really going to read the books?"

"I've read some of the books," Grace said hotly. "Like *Little Women*. I loved that book!" She'd also loved the movie version starring Wynona Ryder and Christian Bale. But how Jo could have turned down Laurie's proposal still puzzled her.

"Maybe we aren't reading the right books," Sarah suggested gently.

"We could read *Wuthering Heights* again," said Ellen. "That was one we all agreed we liked." *Wuthering Heights* was Ellen's favorite book, mainly because she thought Heathcliff was the perfect romantic hero. Personally, Grace found Heathcliff to be a little on the psycho side.

Penny stood. "While you guys discuss this, I'm just going to step outside for a minute."

"So you can smoke?" Grace said.

"Pen! You're not smoking again, are you?" asked Sarah. "What happened?"

"I knew I smelled cigarettes in here," Ellen said, sniffling delicately.

"I thought you said you smelled beer," Grace said.

"That too."

The last crisis that had caused Penny to take up smoking was when Butch had bought his brand-new Harley motorcycle. Butch was Penny's on-again, off-again boyfriend of the past two years. "What's going on with Butch?" Grace asked.

"I don't want to talk about it," Penny chanted.

"You two aren't breaking up again, are you?" Sarah asked.

"The only thing I want to talk about right now is *The Great Gatsby*. Because I read it," Penny declared smugly.

"Well, I want to talk about anything but *The Great Gatsby*," Grace shot back.

"Okay, so maybe *The Great Gatsby* and *The Last of the Mohicans* are a bit passé," admitted Ellen. "I was just trying to inject a little intellectual stimulation into our Saturday nights."

"I don't know about you, Ellen, but I need a different kind of stimulation on my Saturday nights," Grace said.

Sarah sighed. "Me too."

"We could always meet on Thursdays," Penny suggested.

"Look at us! We're four reasonably attractive, intelligent, single—" Grace looked at Sarah. "*Almost* single women, and what are we doing on a Saturday night at"—she paused to glance at her wristwatch— "nine thirty p.m.? We're at a book club meeting. What does that say about us?"

"That we're losers?" Ellen said.

"I've thought about that. But all four of us? I refuse to believe it. It's *got* to be the men we're dating." She stood and began to pace the Hemingway corner. Little bits of mud fell off her shoes, dirtying the floor, but Grace didn't care. She'd mop it up later. "I spent all day looking forward to my date with Brandon. I even borrowed a dress from Sarah." She stopped and gave Sarah a pointed look. "Which was totally sweet of you, but don't *ever* let me borrow anything from you again. You wear a petite, for God's sake!" She resumed her pacing. "During my lunch hour I got a mani and a pedi and purposely didn't eat anything all day just so I could look good tonight, and for what? To be stood up at Chez Louis where *guess who* is the manager? Felix Barberi!"

Sarah's mouth dropped open. "You ran into Felix tonight? No wonder you don't want to talk about it."

"For someone who doesn't want to talk about it, she sure is talking about it," Penny muttered.

"Get this. Felix is worried that his cheating on me damaged my self-esteem."

"What?" Ellen gasped. "He did *not* say that!"

"Oh, it gets better." Grace spent the next fifteen minutes filling them in on the night's activities, including showing them her chipped tooth.

The three of them looked stunned. Then Penny started to giggle, which made Sarah laugh, and even Ellen smiled really big.

Grace had to admit, if you weren't the one it had all happened to, it might seem kind of funny.

Ellen was the first one to get serious again. "You really don't notice the tooth unless you point it out. Just don't show your mother. My mom still goes crazy over the fact that she spent five thousand bucks fixing my teeth and I never wore my retainer."

"Trust me, my mom won't find out, because first thing Monday morning I'm getting this thing filled or capped or whatever they have to do. It's nothing but a bad reminder of one of the worst nights of my life."

Sarah shook her head like she couldn't believe it. "Brandon always seemed so sweet in Zumba class."

"Brandon Farrell might look good on the outside, but on the inside? Ha! If he were a book, you wouldn't get past the first page."

"Instead of spending our Saturday nights talking about books, we should talk about the men we've gone out with. I guarantee you it'd be a whole lot more interesting," Sarah said with a laugh.

Grace blinked. "Sarah, you're a genius!" She waved her hand at Ellen's notepad. "Write this down: Brandon Farrell, thirty-two years old. Brown hair, brown eyes, investment banker. Never been married."

Ellen jotted it down. "What's this for?"

"It's Brandon's stats. He's our first critique."

"Critique on what?" Ellen asked.

Grace smiled at the little group. "Ladies, I propose that we follow Sarah's most excellent suggestion and turn our book club into a boyfriend club."

For a few seconds, no one said anything.

Finally Penny shook her head. "I think talking to Gator Claus has helped loosen a few screws in your head."

"A boyfriend club? What purpose would that serve?" Ellen asked.

"Do you know how many hours I've spent jumping around, sweating to Gloria Estefan and the Miami Sound Machine? If I hear '*Come on shake your body baby do the Conga*' one more time I'm going to puke."

Sarah giggled. "Darlene does love that one," she said, referring to their Zumba instructor's penchant for eighties hits. "But two months of Zumba class have really paid off. Your legs look better now than they did in high school."

Grace thought briefly about Rosie Dimples' cheesy opening line. "Thanks, but you're missing the point. Daytona Beach's most eligible bachelor or not, if I had known what a creep Brandon Farrell was I would have never given him the time of day. Don't you see how empowering this will be?" Grace said, her voice rising with enthusiasm. "We're taking control of our destinies! If Speedway Gonzalez can get on the air every morning and belittle the women of Daytona Beach, then we can get a club together and get back some of the power jerks like him take away from us."

"I hate Speedway," Ellen said. "He's nothing but a misogynistic pig. My friend Janine, who teaches psychology, says he must have deep unresolved mommy issues."

"Between the four of us, we know . . . what?" said Grace. "At least a dozen more single women? Think of all the men we've dated collectively! We could build a dossier on these guys. You don't run out and buy a book without reading a review or getting a recommendation, do you?"

"Sometimes I go by the cover," Sarah admitted. "But I always read the first couple of pages too."

"Wouldn't it be awesome to meet some guy and know in advance what kind of boyfriend he'll be? To know whether it'll be worth going out with him or not?" Grace persisted.

Penny tossed down the rest of her screwdriver. "Butch is quitting his job at the repair shop to tour the country on his Harley."

She met Grace's gaze head-on. "And he wants me to go with him."

"Are you going to do it?" Sarah asked.

"I'm thirty-two years old. I have a car loan and four credit cards on which I'm shuffling minimum payments. Butch says I should sell my car and all my furniture and we can live off the road."

"It sounds kind of romantic," Ellen said wistfully.

Penny reached for the last oatmeal cookie. "You don't think it's crazy?" she asked Grace.

If Penny went on the road with Butch then she wouldn't be working at the store. Penny had been at Florida Charlie's ever since she'd arrived in Daytona Beach after moving from Minnesota almost fifteen years ago. Grace had never considered the idea of Penny quitting before. She tried to imagine what the shop would be like without Penny. Some days the only thing that kept Grace sane was Penny's sarcasm.

"You have at least a month's paid vacation coming. And I would hold your job. You could take a leave of absence, if you wanted to do it, like . . . on a trial run," Grace said.

Penny seemed to think about it for a few seconds. "Next month is December, and the tourists will start coming down for the holidays. And then before you know it, it'll be February and that means Speed Week, and I couldn't leave you in a lurch like that. Besides, this just shows me that Butch isn't ready to settle down. And frankly, I am. Maybe it's best this way. We can make a clean break, you know?"

Grace couldn't help but feel a selfish rush of relief. But if Butch were truly the right man for Penny, wouldn't he care about what she wanted too?

Sarah made them all another round of screwdrivers. "I always thought you and Butch would be forever."

"Yeah, well, that's what I thought about you and Craig."

"The cad," Grace added, because that's what they'd all called him for so long now the nickname had stuck.

"I think Grace is on to something," Ellen said. "Maybe this boyfriend club *is* what we need to empower us. I know my friend Janine would totally be on board."

Grace raised her drink in the air. "Ladies, may I propose a toast? I officially call the first boyfriend of the month club meeting to order."

"Hear, hear," Penny said.

And with that, they all chugged down their drinks.

"Now," Grace said, "back to Brandon Farrell . . ."

# 4

# La Lechuga y el Tomate

Grace walked into St. Bernadette's Catholic Church, dipped her fingers into the holy water, and made a hasty sign of the cross. She slipped into the left side of the third pew from the front, the same pew the O'Bryan clan sat in every Sunday at noon. The clan consisted of herself, Pop, Mami, Abuela, and Grace's brother, Charlie. Grace supposed you really couldn't call a family of five a clan, but if the definition of the word included "tightly knit group who poked into one another's business all the time," then the O'Bryans definitely qualified. Only today, their clan seemed to have added a member.

Grace zeroed in on the tall, willowy, twentysomething standing next to her brother on the opposite end of the pew. "Who's the redhead?" Grace whispered to her mother in Spanish. Growing up in a bilingual household had its advantages.

Abuela, who was sitting on the other side of Mami, leaned over. "You're late," she scolded.

"Just by a minute. Father Donnelly must have started early." Grace blew a conciliatory kiss in Abuela's direction. Abuela caught the air kiss and pressed it to her thin cheek.

"Her name is Phoebe and she's a lawyer at Charlie's firm. Apparently, they've been dating almost two months now," said her mother. "You'd have met her if you were here on time."

"Must be serious if he brought her to Mass."

Her mother raised a skeptical brow, then turned her attention back to Father Donnelly and the Penitential Rite. Ana Alvarez O'Bryan took the Mass seriously. And she expected her daughter to as well.

Charlie's redhead caught Grace staring at her and smiled. It was a hopeful, friendly "please like me" kind of smile. Grace mentally sighed and smiled back at Charlie's newest soon-to-be-ex-girlfriend. This one must have it bad—sucking up to the family at Sunday Mass. Not that Grace blamed her. To most women her brother would seem like a catch. Charlie was a thirty-three-year-old handsome, straight, single attorney. He was also self-centered and a bit of a mama's boy, but it took most women at least three months to figure that part out. Charlie had another month before Phoebe called it quits. Which she would. Because they always did. Charlie made sure of it.

Maybe this time, though, things would be different. She tried to catch Charlie's eye, but he kept his gaze straight ahead. Charlie could go to Vegas and leave a millionaire; his poker face was that good. But Grace knew her brother better than anyone. One look at him and Grace would know if Phoebe was the one or not.

She sent up a silent prayer to St. Anthony. *Please, St. Anthony, let Charlie find a nice girl and settle down. Not so much for him—because, honestly, I'm not sure he deserves it—but because it would really make Abuela and Mami happy.*

Technically, St. Anthony was the patron saint of lost items. Grace figured lost causes was close enough, and if ever there was a lost cause, it was the hope that Charlie would settle down. When in doubt which saint to pray to, St. Anthony was Abuela's go-to guy. Grace figured it couldn't hurt.

It wasn't till Grace got in line to receive Communion that she noticed Sarah sitting by herself in the front pew. Ever since Sarah and Craig had split, Sarah had been going to church with her family again, but they went to eight a.m. Mass, which Abuela labeled barbaric. Only chickens and old people are up that early, Abuela said. Abuela, who was eighty-two, didn't count herself a member of either group.

Grace caught Sarah's gaze on her way back to her seat. Sarah hadn't gotten up to receive Communion, which was unusual. Maybe Sarah had stopped taking Communion because of the divorce. Something about that didn't sit well with Grace.

"Why didn't you take Communion?" Grace asked her the second they were both outside the church.

"Who named you head of the Communion police?"

"Is it because of the divorce? Did you go to Confession and Father Donnelly told you you can't have Communion anymore? Have you thought about an annulment?"

Father Donnelly was a nice man, but he was a Catholic priest first and he played strictly by the rules. Grace herself had avoided confession for at least three years now. Not that she'd committed any biggies. No murder or theft or coveting anybody's anything for her. But she was tired of repeating the same banal sins over and over. And the sins that were bigger, she had no intention of telling Father Donnelly. Those were between her and God. Besides, confession was supposed to make you feel better. Only in Grace's case she always ended up feeling worse about herself.

"It's called reconciliation now. And it's supposed to be private."

"The creep *cheated* on you, Sarah. What are you supposed to do? Forgive and forget? Surely the Church has to make an allowance for stuff like that."

"Father Donnelly hasn't said a word to me, so you can retract your claws. I didn't take Communion because I didn't want to."

Before Grace could respond, Sarah pointed to Phoebe. "Who's the Amazon with Charles in Charge?"

Grace followed Sarah's line of vision to see Abuela introducing Phoebe to Father Donnelly, who was heartily pumping her hand up and down. Judging by the gleam in Father Donnelly's eyes, he looked like he was already mentally scheduling Phoebe and Charlie's wedding Mass.

"Don't change the subject," Grace said. "We were talking about your divorce from Craig."

"Did someone just say donuts?" Grace turned to find Charlie standing behind her. "I could down a few dozen right now." He patted his flat stomach. "I'm starving." Charlie's metabolism was legendary, a thing of disgusting beauty. Grace studied her brother's face. What she needed to know, she figured out in two seconds. Poor Phoebe. She was a goner. The only thing Charlie was in love with was a chocolate-glazed Krispy Kreme.

"Have you no shame?" she asked her brother.

"What do I have to be ashamed about?" He reached over and tousled the hair on top of Sarah's head the way he did every time he saw her. "Hey, squirt. What's shakin'?"

Charlie had called Sarah squirt ever since Grace could remember, but the nickname hadn't fit Sarah since they'd graduated parochial school. Sarah might be vertically challenged, but she was the epitome of elegance. Kind of like Grace Kelly but with just the right amount of curves.

Sarah's traditional response to Charlie's "What's shakin'?" was always "Wouldn't you like to find out?" But before she could say it, Grace interrupted them. "Charlie, when did you start bringing your girlfriends to Mass?"

He looked startled. "Who said Phoebe was my girlfriend?"

"Are you sleeping with her?" Grace asked.

Charlie didn't even blink. "Nope."

"Okay, wrong question. Are you having sex with her?"

"Isn't that a little indelicate considering where we're at?"

"That means yes. So if you're having sex with her and you've brought her to Mass to meet the family, then she's your girlfriend. Jeez, Charlie! When are you going to grow up? I haven't even met her and I like her already. And now you've dragged the whole family into it, and then in approximately one month, when she breaks up with you because you're acting like a total ass hat, Abuela and Mami are going to be really disappointed."

Charlie had the look of someone who was being unfairly attacked. "For your information, I didn't bring Phoebe to Mass. She asked me what I was doing today and I told her I spent Sunday afternoons with my family. First Mass, then supper at the house. When we got here, she was waiting outside. What was I supposed to do? Ignore her? Then after Abuela found out we knew each other, she insisted Phoebe sit with us. I was ambushed!"

Sarah chuckled. "I like how this girl works. You have my permission to marry her, Charles."

Charlie shot Sarah a warning look. "Not funny," he said.

"Yes, it is," Sarah replied.

"Stop it you two. Charlie is right. This isn't funny."

Sarah's smile vanished. "Sorry." She turned to Charlie. "What's wrong with you? The girl is gorgeous and she's obviously *way* into you. Give her a break. Maybe she's the one, only you're too stupid to give her a chance." Sarah stomped off toward the parish hall. "I don't know about you two, but I need a donut!"

Charlie stared at Sarah's retreating back.

"Don't take it personally," Grace said. "It's this divorce from Craig."

The mention of Craig's name made a muscle on the side of Charlie's face twitch. "What's that bastard done now?" he asked. Grace couldn't help but find his brotherly affection for Sarah touching.

"Nothing. At least, I hope nothing. I think Sarah still blames herself for the marriage falling apart, and it's eating her up. You know Sarah. She's a perfectionist."

"Who's up for donuts?" Pop came up and placed an arm around Grace's shoulder. "And speaking of food, how's my To-mato this morning?"

Tomato was the affectionate nickname Abuela had given Grace as a little girl. Abuela gave everyone nicknames. The names were usually based on a physical trait. For instance, the neighbor next door, Mr. Abernathy, was tall and pigeon-toed, so he became the *pato flaco*, or the skinny duck. But sometimes the nicknames were based on personality quirks. Even earlier than when Charlie had christened Grace *Mal Genio*, Abuela had given her two grandchildren the titles of *Lechuga y Tomate*, Let-tuce and Tomato. Charlie was the Lettuce, cool and crisp. And Grace was the Tomato because, well . . . because she was the op-posite of that. Pop had stolen the nickname the second it had come out of Abuela's mouth.

"Pop, I need to talk to you today. In private."

"No one is eating donuts when I have a huge dinner waiting at home. Especially not you," Mami said to Pop. "Remember your high blood pressure." Whenever Mami reminded Pop of his high blood pressure it always made his face go red.

Abuela had her arm linked around Phoebe's like they were already the best of friends. Abuela liked everybody. Except Fidel Castro, of course. But he didn't count. "Won't this be nice! A big family dinner with both my grandchildren."

Charlie introduced Grace to Phoebe. She was in her first year at the law firm and Charlie was her mentor. Grace almost snick-ered at the mentor part. She really hoped Charlie was telling the truth about his relationship with Phoebe. Sleeping with someone you worked with was never a good career move.

"I'm so glad to finally meet Charlie's family!" Phoebe gushed.

"He's always talking about you and your parents and the store and your wonderful *abuelita*."

"Gracielita," said Abuela, "go find Sarah and invite her to dinner. It's been too long since she's eaten at the house." She patted Phoebe on the arm. "Why don't we go back inside the church and light a candle to the Virgin? I have a special intention I've just thought of." Abuela caught Grace's gaze and winked.

Grace gave Charlie an "I-told-you-so look."

"I'll go find Sarah," Charlie muttered. "The more the merrier."

Grace could only shake her head at her brother's naivety. If Charlie thought there was safety in numbers, then he didn't know much about women.

Grace opened the door to the den to find Pop rifling through the shelves, trying to find some family photos that Phoebe had insisted on seeing (Sarah was right—this Phoebe was good). It was the first time since they'd been at the house that Grace had found an opportunity to talk to her father alone.

Pamphlets with pictures of Big Ben and the Eiffel Tower were strewn over the desk in the center of the room. Her parents' thirty-fifth wedding anniversary was in April. To celebrate, they were going on their first trip to Europe. Pop pulled out a photo album. "Look what I found, Tomato. Your high school album!"

"I think we should open the store on Sundays," Grace blurted. No sense in beating about the bush.

Pop smiled like he'd heard this a thousand times before. Which he had. "We aren't opening the shop on Sunday. It's a family business, and Sunday is a family day."

"I get that. But it's also a lost day in revenue. People travel on Sundays, Pop. And they stop and spend money. Only they don't spend money at Florida Charlie's because it isn't open. You wouldn't have to be at the store. Lots of the kids we hire would love extra money. We could pay them time and half if that would make you feel better."

"What if something goes wrong? What if we need a manager on site? That would mean you or Penny or your mother or I would have to go in and take care of the crisis." He shook his head. "We've discussed this before and my answer is still the same."

Grace bit back a frustrated reply and opted for a more tactful approach. "Pop, you pay me to manage the store, and as the manager, I feel that it's in the business's best interests to open on Sunday. How about if I draw up a plan that would show some projected revenue figures? I could train Marty or one of the other senior cashiers to handle any emergency that might come up. We could do a trial run. Maybe open one Sunday a month and see how it goes?"

Pop flipped open the photo album. "Remember this? It's your senior prom."

"Yeah, I remember. Lots of fun. So how about it, Pop?"

"I'll think about it."

Grace knew exactly what "I'll think about it" meant. It meant no.

"Speaking of the store," Pop said, "I stopped by yesterday. Grace, honey, I thought I told you I wanted that alligator tooth up front where the customers can see it. We spent a lot of money advertising that tooth. Folks driving down on vacation see the billboards on the highway, get all excited about it, then come into the store to find that the tooth is stuck somewhere in the back. No hoopla, no fanfare, no nuthin. Remember, presentation is everything. My dad taught me that."

"Pop," Grace said gently, "I just don't think people are *into* that kind of stuff anymore. People stop at the store to buy T-shirts, and sunscreen, and hats."

Pop placed his hand on the small of her back and led her out of the den and into the dining room where the rest of the family and Sarah and Phoebe were already seated. "It's Sunday, and we don't talk business on Sunday, right?"

"Right," Grace repeated, knowing there was no point in arguing further. If Charlie said something, though, then maybe Pop would listen. Grace thought about the best way to approach her brother. Charlie wasn't interested in the family business as a career, but Grace knew he didn't want to see Florida Charlie's go down the drain. If Grace asked Charlie, he would offer to help. But Charlie was so busy with his job that he was always making promises he never followed up on. This time though, he was just going to have to make time. Grace would have to impress upon him the seriousness of the situation.

Pop took his customary seat at the head of the table, opposite Mami. Grace sat next to Abuela, and Charlie sat across from them, in between Sarah and Phoebe.

Mami passed around the *arroz con pollo* while Phoebe entertained them with a story that involved Charlie and a client from the firm. The way Phoebe told it made Charlie sound like the Clarence Darrow of tax attorneys. Mami and Pop listened proudly, while Sarah pretended to be impressed (Grace knew *that* was an act). Grace didn't think she'd ever seen Charlie look so miserable.

"These are the best *tostones* I've ever had!" Phoebe said, "Thank you, Mrs. O'Bryan, for having me over today."

"You're very welcome," Mami said, catching Grace's eye. Grace tried not to laugh.

Mami was a fabulous cook, but Abuela, who was fabulous herself (just not in the kitchen) had made the *tostones*. As usual they were dry as a rock, but no one in the family would ever think of saying anything to Abuela about it. The fact that Phoebe had singled out the *tostones* to compliment either meant that Phoebe didn't know much about Cuban food or she was just really brown nosing. Grace would guess it was a solid combination of both.

Abuela leaned over and whispered, "What do you think of her?"

"She seems nice."

"She's not the one," Abuela whispered back. "I had hoped . . . maybe there was something. But no."

Grace just nodded, because there wasn't anything else to say really. She wondered how long it had taken Abuela to figure it out. Probably less time than it had taken Grace. Abuela might be eighty-two but she didn't miss anything.

"What about you, Gracielita? When are you going to bring someone home to Sunday dinner?" Abuela asked, her eyes bright.

"When I find someone as terrific as Pop."

Mami, overhearing this, smiled at Grace.

Abuela reached for Grace's hand and covered it with her own. "You've already met him."

"What? No, Abuela, I'm not dating anyone right now."

Grace tried to lift her hand to resume eating, but Abuela tightened her grip. "You've already met him, *mi amor*, trust me. I've seen it."

A shiver ran down Grace's spine. Abuela had never talked like this before. Grace had told Brandon's obnoxious friend Doug that her grandmother dabbled in *brujería*, but it was a lie, of course. Abuela herself scoffed at all that Latin mumbo jumbo. Occasionally, Abuela would do something crazy, like throw buckets of water out the front door at the stroke of midnight on New Year's (to toss out evil spirits), but that was done in the spirit of fun. The only exception to this was Abuela's belief in the well-placed curse. Abuela wore a black onyx around her neck—an *azabache*—to ward off the *mal ojo*, or evil eye. But deep down, Grace suspected the only reason Abuela wore the *azabache* was because her own mother had given it to her, not because she attributed any special powers to it. But gazing at her clear brown eyes right now, Grace could tell Abuela was one hundred percent, drop-dead serious about what she'd just said.

"I had a dream," Abuela said stubbornly. "You've met him, Gracielita, you just wait and see."

Grace laughed nervously.

Mami set her fork down. "What's wrong with your mouth?" she asked, frowning.

*Crap.* Grace shrugged like she didn't understand what Mami was getting at.

"You don't normally laugh with your mouth closed," Mami continued. "Is there something wrong with your teeth? Do you have a toothache?"

"Tomato takes after me. Never had a cavity in her life," Pop said. "She has a beautiful set of teeth. Cost me five grand."

Sarah smiled impishly from across the table.

Later, after dinner, she and Sarah were alone in the kitchen, drying dishes.

"Why didn't you just show everyone your chipped tooth? You have to admit, the whole thing is kind of funny." Sarah automatically placed the large salad bowl in the top cabinet above the dishwasher. Sarah had been eating meals at Grace's house since first grade and was probably as familiar with the kitchen as anyone in the O'Bryan family.

"Funny to you maybe."

"Show me again," Sarah prompted.

Grace smiled widely.

"It's hardly noticeable, unless you know exactly where to look for it."

"Know where to look for what?" Charlie asked, sauntering into the kitchen. He reached inside the refrigerator, pulled out a couple of beers, and automatically offered one to Sarah.

Sarah pulled off the tab and took a sip. "Grace chipped her bottom tooth the other night. But don't tell your parents, on account of all the money they spent on braces."

"What am I, chopped liver?" Grace asked, motioning to the beer in Sarah's hand.

Charlie pulled another beer from the fridge and gave it to Grace. "Let me see your chipped tooth," he urged.

She opened her mouth. "So where's Phoebe? Trying on Mami's wedding dress?"

"What did you do to the tooth? Nibble on a rock? And I already told you, Phoebe's not my girlfriend." He took a sip of his beer. "She left five minutes ago," he added.

"Grace chipped her tooth trying to open a shrink-wrapped tampon," Sarah said.

Charlie made a man face. "Too much information."

"You're the one who wanted to know."

"I'm sorry," Grace said. "I shouldn't have egged Phoebe on. It's just . . . guys like you, Charlie . . . Well, you're my brother and I love you, but sometimes you can be a big shit."

"I'm going to have a talk with her tomorrow after work and straighten things out. Okay?"

Grace supposed he looked sincere enough. "Okay."

Sarah took a few more sips of her beer, then poured the rest in the sink. "Speaking of work, I need to go. I'm meeting the Dragon first thing in the morning and I still haven't found the right swatch for her living room couch. She's into pastel florals." Sarah shuddered. The Dragon was Sarah's newest client.

"What's wrong with florals?" Grace asked.

"The house is a Mediterranean Revival," she said, as if that explained it. She gave Grace a peck on the cheek. "Call me tomorrow after you leave the dentist's office. I want to know what Dr. Fred says when he hears how you chipped your tooth."

Charlie waited till Sarah left before he said, "Personally, if it were me, I wouldn't be telling Dr. Fred how you chipped your tooth. I'd make something up."

"Charlie, can we talk?" At the look on his face, she added, "It's not about Phoebe."

"Outside," he said, motioning to the back door.

It was late afternoon, almost evening, and the weather had cooled off significantly. It was finally beginning to feel like November. Grace grabbed a light cotton blanket from the wicker basket her mother kept by the door and draped it around her shoulders, then followed her brother to the wooden deck overlooking the backyard. She picked the Adirondack chair closest to the pool and settled in for a not-so-cozy brother-sister chat.

"I want you to convince Pop to let me open the store on Sundays."

"That's what you brought me out here to talk about?" Grace couldn't tell whether Charlie looked disappointed or relieved.

"I told you, I'm not going to harp on you about Phoebe anymore."

"Pop isn't going to open the store on Sundays."

"He will if you tell him the store is in trouble."

Charlie's gaze shot to her face. "Is it?"

"The economy is in a slump. People who are lucky enough to go on vacation aren't interested in stopping to see the world's largest alligator tooth. If you took the time to look at the books like you used to, you'd know that revenues have been steadily dropping for a long time now."

"What's Pop's take on that?"

"He's got his head buried in the sand. And now he and Mami are planning their big trip to Europe and I don't want to be the one to rain on their parade. Which reminds me, you *are* going to help me with Abuela, aren't you? We're going to have to take turns spending the night here. She can't stay alone." Abuela was hardly fragile, but Grace didn't think anyone would rest easy worrying about Abuela accidentally falling at night on her way to the bathroom or something.

Charlie looked insulted. "Of course I'm going to help." He took a sip of his beer. "I want to talk to you about something too. I'm thinking about moving."

Grace stilled. "But I thought you're about to make partner."

"The firm is opening a branch in Miami and they want me to head it. It won't happen for another six months, so I'll be here to help with Abuela."

"It doesn't sound like you're *thinking* about it. It sounds like you've already made up your mind."

He shrugged. "I didn't actively seek it. But it's a good opportunity. I'd be an idiot to turn it down. And there's nothing keeping me here in Daytona. Besides the family, of course. With the hours I've been keeping at the firm, you'll probably see me just as much as you do now. I'll come up on weekends some, and holidays too."

The only time they consistently saw each other anymore was on Sundays. And that was only because Mami and Pop insisted they keep the family Mass and supper tradition. But Charlie was fooling himself if he thought he'd be able to make the nearly five-hour drive from Miami to Daytona Beach more than a few times a year. Not with the kind of hours he kept.

"Do Mami and Pop know?"

"You're the first person I've told. Outside the firm."

"What does Phoebe think about it?"

"I told you, she's not a factor." He shifted around in his chair. "Look, even though it's none of your beeswax, I'm going to tell you what went down because you're my sister and I don't want you to think I'm an asshole. Phoebe and I went out for drinks a couple of times. Everyone in the office does. One time I got a little drunk and yeah, we kissed. End of story. It was stupid, I know. But she's a junior associate; I'm not about to get involved with her. Obviously, she thinks it's more than it was, but I swear, I never led her on. She has a boyfriend, for God's sake."

"And you kissed her anyway?"

"He's an out-of-town boyfriend."

"Are all men as delusional as you?"

"What's that supposed to mean?"

Grace thought about the boyfriend club and shook her head. "Nothing."

"Look, I'm sorry the store has fallen on your shoulders. I'll take a look at the finances and see if there's anything I can suggest."

"Thanks." She leaned over and kissed her brother on the cheek. "Since you're in such a generous mood, how about you do me another favor?"

He narrowed his eyes at her. "Like what?"

"It's Sarah. She's been so down lately."

"Like you said before, that's natural. She's going through a divorce."

"Isn't there some nice guy you can fix her up with? Just for dinner or something? I'd do it, but unfortunately my nice-guy list is severely limited. Like zero."

"Sorry, but so is mine."

"I'm just afraid she might get back with Craig. And it would be for all the wrong reasons."

"Not gonna happen. Sarah's stubborn. And unforgiving. She won't take him back. Not ever."

"How do you know?"

"She's been your best friend for, what? Twenty-five years? I might be delusional but every once in a while I pay attention. No worries. She's not getting back with Craig. Sarah's not the forgive-and-forget type."

It was true. For as long as Grace had known her, Sarah had never taken shit from anyone. Except Grace. Sarah wasn't stubborn and unforgiving with Grace. In the twenty-five years she and Sarah had been best friends, they'd gone through plenty of rough times. Yet they'd always forgiven each other the transgressions that went along with the territory. Although . . . there was one thing that Sarah might not forgive. But Grace didn't want to think about that, because . . . what was the point? It was over. Sarah was getting a divorce from Craig and that's what mattered. Soon, Sarah would be free to find someone else. Someone who loved her the way she deserved to be loved.

"You're right. I'm feeling much better now." She stood and followed Charlie back into the kitchen.

Grace watched as her brother opened the fridge and began to attack the leftovers they'd put away only an hour ago. Charlie might be insensitive on occasion, but he was her brother, and deep down he was a good guy. Six months from now he might be in Miami and their Sunday family get-togethers would be a thing of the past. And no matter what Penny said about not quitting her job, if Butch were to play his cards right, Grace could see Penny sitting behind Butch on the backseat of his bike with a big grin on her face as the two of them rode off into the sunset.

She'd still have Sarah, of course. And Ellen, and Mami, and Pop, and Abuela. But life wouldn't be the same without Charlie and Penny around.

# 5

# Dr. Joe

Monday morning, exactly one minute after eight, Grace was on the phone with her dentist. A pert, female voice that Grace didn't recognize answered. "Sunshine Smiles, how may I help you?"

"Is Tanya there?"

"Tanya no longer works at the front desk. I'm Melanie, the new receptionist."

Tanya didn't work at Sunshine Smiles anymore? Tanya had worked for Dr. Fred ever since Grace could remember. "What happened to Tanya?"

"Ma'am, I have two other calls on hold. How can I help you?"

"Oh, well . . . the strangest thing happened to me the other night." Grace couldn't help but chuckle.

"Ma'am, do you need to make an appointment?"

"Um, yes. Preferably today. Maybe even this morning if you could work me in. I'm Grace O'Bryan. I've been a patient at Sunshine Smiles forever."

"I'm afraid we only see dental emergencies on a same-day basis. What sort of problem are you having?"

"I chipped my tooth."

"Are you in pain?"

"Does emotional pain count?" Grace laughed, fully expecting Melanie to laugh along with her. "You'll never believe—"

"No, ma'am, I'm afraid emotional pain doesn't count."

Grace instantly sobered. Okay, so Melanie wasn't interested in her funny story. Point taken. Melanie at Sunshine Smiles was a very busy person. Grace suddenly felt like one of those clueless women who went on and on without ever getting to the point.

"Are you having any trouble eating or swallowing? Any active bleeding?"

"Bleeding? No, of course not."

"We can see you a week from tomorrow. How about ten a.m.?"

"Don't you have anything sooner?"

"I'm sorry, but we're totally booked. If the chipped tooth isn't causing you any pain or difficulty, then it's more of a cosmetic problem."

*Cosmetic problem?* Was Melanie insinuating that Grace was vain?

"Now that you mention it, I have had some pain. Yes, it's causing me terrible pain. Horrible, horrible pain. I'm in agony," Grace said.

There was a pause. "I see. Can you hold please?"

"Sure."

Grace tried not to feel guilty. It was just a teeny weeny itsy bitsy lie. In fact, it was so insignificant that if she still went to Confession, she would never dream of wasting Father Donnelly's time on it. Maybe a chipped tooth wasn't a life-or-death issue, but she hadn't lied when she said it was causing her emotional pain. She hadn't fully smiled since Saturday night. Didn't Melanie realize how hard it was to laugh with your mouth closed? So maybe it was more of a cosmetic issue than a true dental emergency, but Tanya would have understood and gotten her in right away. Tanya would have laughed at Grace's little joke. Apparently this Melanie was humorless. How could Dr. Fred have hired her?

Melanie came back on the line. "We can work you in with the rest of the emergencies after three. Do you think you can stand the agony until then?"

"I guess I'll have to. Thanks!" Then, remembering that she was supposed to be in terrible pain, Grace added with a slight moan, "Thank you, I really appreciate it."

"You're welcome," Melanie said curtly before hanging up.

The rest of the day passed quickly. Mondays were usually slow at the store, but there was inventory to do and it was Penny's day off. Grace worked through lunch, then handed the reins off to Marty. Marty Kovak was nineteen and had worked at the store since his sophomore year in high school. Besides being a senior cashier, he also did most of the stocking. Marty had an undisguised crush on Grace, which amused Penny to no end. Grace had never encouraged the crush, but it was hard not to be sweet to Marty when he stared back at her with his big brown puppy-dog eyes. Grace showed Marty her tooth and told him the story of how she chipped it (it just didn't seem indelicate telling Marty about the tampon) and Marty had laughed appropriately, confirming what Grace already knew. Melanie the Nazi receptionist had zip sense of humor.

Dr. Fred's office was near the beach, so Grace had to cross the bridge, and because it was midafternoon, traffic was steady. She rolled into the parking lot to Sunshine Smiles at exactly ten minutes past three. Melanie, had said *after* three, so it wasn't like Grace was late. Not technically.

Melanie was startlingly attractive. With a full set of pouty lips and a body that looked good even in scrubs. "Any change in insurance or medical information since you were here last?" she asked Grace.

Grace shook her head.

"How about change in address?"

"Nope."

"Have a seat and we'll call you as soon as Dr. Joe can see you," Melanie said.

"Dr. Joe?"

"Didn't you get the letter? Dr. Fred retired last month and Dr. Joe took over his practice. Dr. Fred sent a letter out to all his patients explaining the whole thing." She glanced at her computer screen. "I thought you said you hadn't changed your address. You're supposed to notify us if you move, you know."

Grace remembered receiving a letter from Sunshine Smiles, but she'd assumed it was a reminder to schedule a cleaning, so she'd tossed it unopened into her mail-to-be-dealt-with-later pile. "Um, no, no . . . I'm still at the same address. I did receive the letter, it just must have slipped my mind."

"Don't worry, you'll like Dr. Joe. Our patients have been giving him extremely high marks." She handed Grace a sheet of paper. "Dr. Joe would appreciate it if you'd fill out this patient satisfaction survey after your procedure today. Our goal is to score perfect tens."

Grace tucked the paper into her bag and scanned the reception area looking for a seat. There must have been a lot of emergency cases because the place was packed, although no one looked like they were in danger of bleeding to death or anything. Still, Grace had a feeling that her "emergency" was pretty far down the totem pole, which meant she was probably in for a long wait. Good thing Dr. Fred always kept the best magazines in his waiting room. But after a few minutes of searching, all Grace could find that was readable was a two-month-old copy of *Southern Living*. Where were all the *People* magazines? They'd been replaced with *Newsweek*, and *Time*, and *National Geographic*, and magazines on extreme sports like mountain climbing and glacial skiing. Who was interested in that? Didn't this Dr. Joe know there were no mountains or snow in Florida?

The *National Geographic*s weren't so bad, but Grace preferred learning about the exotic on the Discovery Channel. Everyone knew that magazines in a dentist's office were supposed to be mindless fluff. Speaking of which, Dr. Fred had installed a state-of-the-art forty-eight-inch plasma-screen TV in the waiting room last year. But the only things on the walls now were photographs of sailboats, which, Grace had to admit, were pretty. But you could only stare at a photo for so long.

Grace went up to the reception desk. "What happened to the big TV?" she asked Melanie.

"Dr. Joe feels that *we*, as a society, tend to watch too much television. He wants to set a good example for his younger patients."

The way Melanie said Dr. Joe's name was like he was some sort of saint. Melanie pointed out the newly remodeled children's area of the waiting room. There was a small plastic playground and several miniature tables with coloring books and crayons. Nice for the kiddies, Grace supposed, but apparently Dr. Joe intended to bore his adult patients into comas. Maybe it was some new kind of dental pre-anesthesia.

She found a spot near the water fountain and spent the next two hours watching the clock on the wall and thinking about what they would do to her tooth. Fixing it wouldn't involve drilling, would it? Grace shuddered. That hadn't occurred to her until now. She hated the sound of the drill. She should have brought a book to pass the time. But now that her book club was officially defunct, there wasn't anything she needed to read. She was the last person left in the waiting room when they finally called her name.

A young woman wearing royal blue scrubs who identified herself as Tiffany led her to a room in the back. She instructed Grace to sit in the padded dental chair. Grace had never seen Tiffany before. Where were all of Dr. Fred's regular staff?

"So you chipped your tooth, huh?" Tiffany said.

"I know it's not life-or-death. I guess you could say it's more like a cosmetic dental emergency," Grace said, waiting to get chastised by the assistant. She opened her mouth to show Tiffany.

"Yeah, I see what you mean," Tiffany said, studying the chipped tooth.

"You can? So you agree, this is an emergency?"

"Not an emergency exactly, but I'd want to get it fixed as soon as possible too," Tiffany confided.

Finally! Someone at Sunshine Smiles was on Grace O'Bryan's side.

"This isn't going to involve drilling, is it?"

Tiffany looked like she was used to hearing that question. "I don't believe so, but I'll let Dr. Joe explain the procedure. Don't worry! He's brilliant. He's got a lot of interesting theories on pain management. You're going to love him."

Brilliant? Grace didn't think she'd ever heard that word linked to a dentist before. If Melanie had made Dr. Joe sound like a saint, Tiffany made him sound like Albert Einstein. Grace began to feel uneasy. Like Melanie, Tiffany was also young and attractive. Tanya, Dr. Fred's longtime receptionist was in her late fifties. Just this past summer when Grace had come in for a cleaning she and Tanya had talked about Tanya's eldest daughter, Ruth, who was going through a difficult divorce. Tanya had confided in Grace that she was helping out Ruth financially. Tanya was too young to retire, and jobs weren't so easy to come by at her age. It was clear Dr. Joe liked to surround himself with pretty young things who found him "brilliant." Had he sent Tanya packing because she didn't fit in with the rest of his "new-and-improved" staff?

"Tiffany, is Connie still here? She's the hygienist who cleans my teeth. She's been with Dr. Fred for over twenty years."

"Connie? Oh yeah, I remember her. She left a few days after I started working here."

*Left?* Who left a job after twenty years? Dr. Joe was no saint.

He was more like the Hugh Hefner of teeth! Chipped tooth or not, Grace had her standards. She wasn't about to give the man who'd given the axe to both Tanya and Connie her business. How could sweet, loveable Dr. Fred with his cute, grandfatherly ways and his excellent waiting room magazines have left his practice to this . . . this Dr. Joe character?

"I've changed my mind. This isn't really an emergency." Grace sat up and swung her legs over the side of the chair. "I really hate to keep Dr. Joe in the office so late for something this trivial. So I think I'll just—"

"Trying to sneak out of my chair?"

Grace froze. She'd heard that voice before.

A man wearing maroon-colored scrubs took the folder from Tiffany's hands. Tall, broad shoulders, slightly mussed-up hair, and the prettiest blue eyes Grace had ever seen.

*Dr. Joe was Rosie Dimples?*

He extended his hand. "I'm Joe Rosenblum. It's nice to meet you . . ." He glanced at the top of her folder, "Ms. O'Bryan."

Grace had no choice but to shake his hand. "You can call me Grace," she squeaked.

He smiled. It was a professional smile. Fast, compact, with no real warmth behind it. Exactly like his handshake. Didn't he recognize her? If he did, he gave no indication.

"I hear you chipped a tooth."

"That's right. It happened *Saturday night*," she emphasized, hoping that would jar his memory.

"Let's take a look." He sat on a stool and pushed some buttons that made the head of her chair go all the way back. He examined the tooth, running the edge of his gloved finger over it. Oddly, the motion sent a shiver down her spine. Must be her nerves. "And this chipped tooth is causing you terrible pain?" he asked.

"Well, not exactly. But it does feel strange, you know? Like after you get your teeth cleaned and you can feel all the ridges behind your bottom teeth with your tongue?" She demonstrated to show him what she meant. "And you can't help but do it all day long, because it feels so . . . so . . . ."

"Weird?" he supplied.

Grace nodded.

He smiled again. Just the teeniest bit but enough to make his dimples pop out. Dr. Joe really was awfully pretty. Then Grace remembered she'd already decided she didn't like him.

"We have a few options," he began. "You can leave the tooth as is. I promise you, you're probably the only one who's noticed it. But . . . since the pain is so terrible you might not want to consider that." Grace could feel her face go hot. Not only did Melanie have no sense of humor, she also had a big mouth. "Another option is to bond the tooth. That would require filling in the gap with some composite material. Or we could place a cap over it."

"I definitely want to get it fixed," Grace said.

"Then I say we go with the easiest solution. That would be the bonding. I have to warn you, the area we're filling is pretty small and is susceptible to getting chipped again if you're not careful."

"As long as it doesn't involve drilling."

"No drilling. Got it."

"So could you do the bonding thing now? Or do I have to come back?"

"We can do it now." His gaze caught hers. "Unless you've changed your mind?" Grace must have looked confused because he said, "When I came in it looked like you were going for a fast escape."

"Oh, *that*. Well, I was just feeling a little . . . uneasy."

"It's normal to feel uneasy at the dentist's office."

"It's just that I'm used to Dr. Fred. He's been my dentist since I was four."

"Completely understandable." He began giving Tiffany instructions, talking about which color material best matched her natural tooth shade, things like that. Grace closed her eyes and tried to relax, but an image of Dr. Joe at the Wobbly Duck kept popping into her mind. Despite the muddy clothes he'd had on that night, she'd recognized him instantly. He had to recognize her too, but by the way he was acting you'd think they were total strangers. "Once we bond the tooth you'll have to be careful not to abuse the surface. So no more opening beer bottles with your teeth."

Grace's eyes flew open. "*What?*"

"That was just a little dental humor," Dr. Joe said, deadpan.

Dental humor, her ass. The beer analogy was no coincidence. He knew exactly who she was!

"So how did you chip it?" he asked.

She'd been so focused on getting the tooth fixed she'd forgotten to come up with a plausible answer for that particular question. She could always tell Dr. Joe the truth. *I chipped it trying to unwrap a shrink-wrapped tampon!* She'd told Marty and he'd found it hysterically funny. But Marty was a kid. Despite the fact that Dr. Joe was a health care professional, she couldn't help but think of him as a man first, dentist second. He'd probably have the same reaction as Charlie. Too much information.

"Um, I'm not exactly sure."

"You seem tense," he said. "I've found that some of my patients respond well to music." He flipped the switch on a silver panel to his right. A slow easy-listening jazz tune began to strum through the air. It was Diana Krall's "The Look of Love."

Mood music? Was he serious? Grace's spine went rigid. Dr. Joe's "theories" on pain management didn't involve substituting music for good old-fashioned drugs, did it?

"You're going to give me Novocain, right? Because I have to warn you, I have a really low pain threshold."

"You won't need an anesthetic for this procedure."

"But—"

"I promise, Grace. This isn't going to hurt."

Something in the way he said it made her relax. "I bet you say that to all your patients," she mumbled.

He looked like he was about to smile. Instead, he cleared his throat and went back to conferring with Tiffany.

Had she sounded too flirty? She certainly wasn't *trying* to flirt with Dr. Joe. Grace crossed her ankles and took a deep breath. It occurred to her that the standard Florida Charlie's uniform of khaki shorts meant she was showing a lot of leg. Rosie Dimples had seemed pretty fascinated with her legs. But Dr. Joe hadn't even taken a peek. *The girl of his dreams?* Ha! Men were so full of crap. Enough of this parrying back and forth.

"You seem really familiar, Dr. Joe. Have we met before?"

He smiled. It was the professional smile again, the one Grace had decided she didn't like. "I was just thinking the same thing about you."

She could "remind" him they'd met Saturday night at the Wobbly Duck, where he'd tried to pick her up with his cheesy lines. She'd like to see him squirm out of that one! But what if he commented about her dumping the beer in Brandon's crotch? It had been an accident, but he probably didn't know that.

"Maybe I'm confusing you with someone else," Grace finally said. The truth was she'd love nothing better than to forget Saturday night. She needed to concentrate on the matter at hand. Which was her chipped tooth and getting it fixed. "Before you start working on my tooth, do you mind if I ask how much experience you have at this kind of thing?"

"Didn't you get the letter?" Tiffany asked. "It contained Dr. Joe's complete resume." Tiffany looked up at Dr. Joe and smiled. Only an idiot wouldn't see that she was totally besotted. Probably the real reason Dr. Joe wasn't acknowledging his encounter with Grace was because he had something going on with Tiffany and he didn't want her to know he'd been trying to two-time her.

"Of course I read the letter," Grace lied. "So sorry. Go on with whatever you were going to do."

Dr. Joe hesitated. "The bonding isn't a complicated procedure, but if you prefer to get a second opinion, I understand."

He was giving her the perfect out. She should take it and walk out the door. None of what went down with Tanya and Connie sat well with her. On the other hand, she'd made such a fuss about this being an "emergency," and he and his staff had stayed late to accommodate her. It would be rude to just walk out on him. If she'd bothered to open the letter, she'd have known about the transition, so most of this was really her own fault.

She would let Dr. Joe fix her tooth today and she'd switch dentists first thing tomorrow morning. She'd find out where Tanya had gone and bring her business there.

"I think you'll be okay, I mean, yes, please do the bonding procedure," Grace said.

He placed something in her mouth to keep it open, then filled the tooth with the composite material. When he was finished he instructed Tiffany to place a light over Grace's tooth.

"This will help it dry," he explained. "Just a few more minutes and we'll be done."

Out of the corner of her eye, Grace watched as Dr. Joe wrote in her chart. Tiffany removed the light and he pulled out the thingamajig from her mouth. He spent what seemed like a couple of minutes looking at her tooth, then handed her a mirror. "What do you think?"

"That's it? Aren't I supposed to rinse and spit or something?"

Dr. Joe almost smiled again. "Not necessary."

Grace studied her bottom tooth in the mirror. She looked like her old self again. Before the disastrous date with Brandon Farrell. She had to admit, Dr. Joe did fine work. "It looks good," she said. "Now I can smile again." To demonstrate she grinned a few times. "So, I'm all done?"

"Just see Melanie on your way out." He began writing in her chart again. He didn't say anything else, so Grace assumed she'd been dismissed.

"Okay, well, thank you. It was nice *meeting* you."

"It was nice meeting you too, Grace," he said without looking up. Dr. Joe, the Lothario dentist, was some actor.

She grabbed her bag and started for the door.

"Don't forget to fill out your patient satisfaction survey," Tiffany said. "Everyone who turns one in gets entered in a raffle to win a forty-eight-inch plasma-screen TV."

So that's where the waiting room plasma-screen TV went. What a scam! Dr. Joe wanted perfect tens on the patient satisfaction survey, huh? Well, too bad. He was going to be disappointed.

She wrote out a check for her portion of the bill and handed it to Melanie, then waited for the receipt to print out. "If you don't mind, I'm just going to take a minute to fill out this survey," Grace said, scooting down to a private area of the counter.

Grace unfolded the paper and began to read. There were eight questions and adjacent to each question was a row of bubbles marked one to ten. One was the lowest score and ten the highest.

1. *Ease of scheduling an appointment.* Melanie had certainly made her feel like an idiot when she'd called, cutting Grace off before she could finish a story. But . . . it would be unfair of Grace to give them a low mark on this one. Not when she'd gotten in the same day she'd called. Begrudgingly, she darkened in the circle next to the ten.

2. *Staff Courtesy.* Aha! She began to go for the five, then stopped. Melanie hadn't been rude to her. Not really. She just hadn't laughed at any of Grace's little jokes. Grace had even lied about the pain from her chipped tooth. Melanie had known

about the lie, of course, but she'd still worked Grace into the schedule. And Tiffany had been more than pleasant and professional. Well, crud. She'd have to give them a ten here as well.

*3. Satisfaction with work performed.* Grace sighed and marked in the circle next to the ten.

Of course Dr. Joe and his staff were getting all tens. The survey was rigged! She skimmed through the rest of the questions until she got to the bottom.

*Please let us know if you have any further comments or suggestions.*

Boy, did she have "further" comments. Her pen began to fly over the paper.

*Dear Dr. Joe,*

*I think you did a good job on my tooth. Thank you for that. And you're right. It didn't hurt a bit. Tiffany is a doll. Very pleasant and professional. Melanie has zero sense of humor but she seems to be doing an adequate job at the reception desk and she did work me into your schedule today, so I can't blast her. However, I wanted you to know that after today, I will no longer be a patient at Sunshine Smiles and I think it's important for you to know why (I have placed the reasons in bullet form for easier reading).*

*• Whose big idea was it to get rid of Tanya? (I can only assume it was yours). When I first came here as a patient (twenty-six years ago!) my mother had to drag me through the door. For some reason (gee, I wonder why) I was afraid of the dentist. I sat in the waiting room and listened to the far-off noise of the drill and began to make up all sorts of crazy scenarios in*

*my head (most of which involved some sort of torture). It was Tanya who first put me at ease. She gave me a comic book and although I couldn't read yet, the pictures made me laugh, which helped take my mind off all those scary noises. Over the years, Tanya was always there with her bright smile, quick wit, and immense patience. Getting rid of Tanya is like getting rid of the heart and soul of Sunshine Smiles. To quote the famous Mr. Knightley, "Badly done," Dr. Joe!*

*• See comments from bullet point number one. Same goes for Connie.*

*• Last but not least, your waiting room magazines suck. Dr. Fred understood that nervous patients need mindless distractions such as* People *and* Cosmo. *And the big plasma-screen TV that you're now raffling off? That needs to go back in the waiting room. Who are you to decide "we" are watching too much television?*

*Sincerely,*
*Your ex-patient,*
*Grace O'Bryan*

*P.S. Like I said, you did do a good job on my tooth, so once again, thank you for that and for staying late to accommodate me.*

There. That ought to do it. She folded the sheet in half and dropped it into the box on the counter.

Melanie handed Grace her receipt. "It looks like you had a lot to say. Dr. Joe personally reads each and every one of those surveys. He really tries to respond to his patients' needs."

"Well, that's great," Grace said. She walked out to the parking lot and clicked the unlock button on her automatic car door opener. There was no reason to feel guilty about the things she'd written. She'd paid to get her tooth fixed. It wasn't as if Dr. Joe and his staff had stayed late to do her a personal favor. Plus, she'd given him his perfect tens, hadn't she?

So maybe he wouldn't be crazy about her comments in the free text section, but he deserved to know why she wasn't coming back. As the manager of a business herself, she understood the value of customer relations. It was important to know why a customer wasn't satisfied. Otherwise, how could you fix the problem?

# 6

# My Good Opinion, Once Lost, Is Probably Lost Forever

"What looks good?" Ellen asked, despite the fact she always ordered the same thing whenever they went to Luigi's, which was every Wednesday at noon.

The food wasn't great, but it was inexpensive and the service was quick. Plus it was centrally located so no one had to drive too far from work, which was especially convenient today because it was raining. And not just cats and dogs. It was raining lizards, frogs, and anything else that could creep out from the nearest palmetto bush. Daytona Beach was about to get its first serious cold front of the season. Pasta, in Grace's opinion, was an excellent comfort food to counteract the foul weather.

"I only have an hour tops," said Sarah. "I need to meet with my drapery lady this afternoon. The Dragon wants her house done by the holidays."

"Who is this dragon-woman?" Penny asked, fidgeting in her seat. If she got desperate enough she just might brave the rain to go outside and smoke the cigarette she was obviously craving.

"My newest client. Just moved here from south Florida. Lots of bucks but not a lot of taste."

"Well, don't run off before we get a chance to iron out the details of our new club." Grace plucked a hot crispy breadstick from the basket. The food at Luigi's might be so-so, but the breadsticks were excellent. "If I ever get stranded on a desert island, I want an unlimited amount of breadsticks from Luigi's. And chocolate ice cream." Although how she'd keep the ice cream from melting on a desert island, Grace had no idea. So she'd better not get stranded on one.

"My friend Janine definitely wants to join, and there are at least three other faculty members at the college who are interested," Ellen said.

"I thought this boyfriend club was a joke," Sarah said. "We aren't really going through with it, are we?"

"Of course we are," Grace said. "It's going to empower us!"

"At Grace's request, I've started our own private Yahoo! group," Ellen continued. "I'll take notes at each of the meetings and place them under the file section. That way we can resource our reviews."

Penny froze midway to stuffing a breadstick in her mouth. "Reviews?"

Ellen reached into her bag to pull out the familiar yellow legal pad. She flipped through a few pages until she got to the one she wanted. "We only have two so far, but they're both doozies. See?" She passed the legal pad around the table.

"Why does it have 'Peter Pan' in caps next to Felix's name?" Sarah asked.

"That was my idea," Grace said. "Since this was originally a book club, I thought it might be fun to give the guys we review an equivalent in the literary world. Felix Barberi is charming, egotistical, and childlike. Classic Peter Pan."

"Only, Peter Pan is likeable," Penny said. "And he didn't cheat on Wendy."

"Technically, Wendy is more mother figure than lover." Ellen's eyes glazed over like they did whenever they discussed a book.

"True," said Grace. "I'll have to give it some more thought."

"What about Brandon? Who's he?" Sarah asked.

"I haven't got him matched up yet, but I'm thinking about it," Grace said.

Ellen made a notation in her pad. "Back to the Yahoo! site. I sent out an invite to each of you, so don't forget to check your e-mail. We're going to have a meeting this Saturday. That's okay, isn't it?" she asked Grace. "I thought we'd keep meeting at the store like we've been doing."

"But we just met last week," protested Sarah.

"It's just for this one time to get things rolling while the idea is still fresh in our heads, then we'll meet once a month, like we did with the book club."

"I think that's a fabulous idea!" Grace said. "And afterward, we can go out for drinks."

"I'm all for the drinks part," Penny said.

"Me too," said Sarah. "But why do we have to set up a Yahoo! site?"

"The Yahoo! site will enable us to access reviews twenty-four seven," explained Ellen. "We're providing our members with information that they otherwise might not be able to get until it's too late." The waiter came by to refill their breadstick basket. Ellen ordered the vegetarian lasagna; no surprise there. Grace hadn't had time to look at the menu yet, although she had the thing memorized. The waiter jokingly asked if she just wanted breadsticks for lunch and Grace laughed.

"Hey! You got your tooth fixed." Ellen leaned across the table. "Open up and let us see."

Grace smiled big.

"Nice," Sarah muttered, trying to look delicate while talking with her mouth full of breadstick and somehow succeeding.

"Dr. Fred does good work," Ellen said.

"Dr. Fred retired last month. There's a new dentist at Sunshine Smiles." Grace took a sip of her diet Coke. "He hit on me Saturday night at the Wobbly Duck."

Ellen looked confused. "Dr. Fred was at the Wobbly Duck?"

"No, dummy, his replacement, *Dr. Joe.* Apparently he and Brandon play on opposing rugby teams."

Sarah started laughing.

"Shut up! He's not like a normal dentist. He's . . . well, he's pretty hot."

"Did *Dr. Joe* hit on you before or after you dumped the beer on Brandon's lap?" Penny asked.

"Before. Besides, I already told you, that was an accident."

"Maybe it was an accident for Grace. But I think *Mal Genio* knew exactly what was going on," Penny said.

"Don't you think talking about Grace like she has a split personality is a little creepy?" Ellen asked.

"Not as creepy as her talking to the alligator," Penny said.

"You're still talking to the alligator?" Ellen shook her head. "There are doctors who can help with that, you know."

"I think it's cute," Sarah said. "I wish I had an alligator I could talk to."

"Sorry," said Grace. "Gator Claus is all mine."

"So Dr. Fred's replacement is a hot rugby player." Ellen wiggled her jaw from side to side. "I think I feel a toothache coming on."

"That must have been awkward," Penny said. "Him working on your tooth after trying to pick you up at a bar."

"Not for Dr. Joe. He acted like he'd never seen me before. But I *know* he recognized me. He gave an award-winning performance, that's for sure."

"So he's a hot rugby player dentist creep," Ellen said. "Who should we classify him as?"

"Technically, I've never gone out with him, so I don't think we should do a review."

"I guess that's only fair," Ellen reluctantly agreed.

"Seriously? I just don't know about this whole boyfriend club," Sarah said. "It smacks of disgruntlement."

Ellen turned in her chair to give Sarah her full attention. "You of all people should be totally behind this. What if you'd known that Craig was a philandering two-timer? Would you still have married him? Would you even have gone out with him?"

Grace held her breath. She should have known the subject of Craig's infidelity would come up. Wasn't that the purpose of the club? To "out" the losers in the dating community?

Sarah's face went pale. "We're not doing a file or whatever you call it on Craig."

"But—"

"Read my lips, Ellen. I'm not discussing Craig in this boyfriend club. Not now. Not ever. Frankly, I'm not sure that I even want to be a part of it, to tell you the truth."

"Okay, okay, I didn't mean to upset you. Whatever you want. We never have to mention Craig at all. But you *have* to come. You just have to, or it won't be the same." Ellen looked to Grace for support.

"Sarah, if you don't want us to do the club, then just say so and we won't. Not if it makes you this uncomfortable," Grace said. And she meant it. No amount of empowerment was worth alienating Sarah from their group.

The three of them watched as Sarah struggled to come up with an answer.

"All right," Sarah said finally. "We can do the club and I'll come to the meetings. But Craig is off limits. Got it?"

"Sure! No problem. You'll see, Sarah, it's going to be great." Grace's cell phone went off. She decided to ignore it and let it go to voice mail.

Ten seconds later, Penny's phone rang.

"Sure, Mr. O. We'll be right there." Penny snapped her phone shut. "Your dad needs us back at work. He says . . . He said the shop is about to flood!"

. . .

Grace and Penny had driven together to the restaurant, so they zipped back to Florida Charlie's in Grace's car. Ellen and Sarah stayed to pay the bill and have the food boxed up, but they were probably only minutes behind. The second they'd heard something was wrong at the store, they'd insisted on following to see what they could do to help. The front parking lot to the store was empty and the Closed sign was displayed on the door.

"What's going on?" Grace asked, her heart thumping wildly. "Is anyone hurt?"

Mami was closing out the registers. Abuela held Gator Claus's Santa hat in her hand. Both of them looked too calm for any real disaster to be occurring.

"This costume is getting old. I think the alligator needs a new Christmas look," Abuela said, pointing to the loose pom-pom on the hat. "What do you think, Gracielita? Should I make the alligator into an elf?"

"*What*? An *elf*? No, Abuela, leave the alligator the way he is."

Grace did a quick survey of her surroundings. Things looked perfectly fine to her, until she spotted her father in the Hemingway corner.

Water dripped from the ceiling down into a large plastic bucket. The bookshelves that had previously made a faux wall were now pushed alongside the real wall. Other than her parents and Abuela, the place was empty.

"Where are the cashiers? And Marty?" Penny asked. "He's supposed to be cleaning out the stockroom."

"I closed the store and sent everyone home when we discovered the leak," Pop said. "Good thing your mother and I decided to stop by today."

"Pop, please tell me you didn't move those bookshelves yourself."

"It was either that or let the water ruin the books."

"What about your back?"

"What about my back? I'm strong as a bull! You're beginning to sound just like your mother."

Grace took a second to think. The leak was a setback, no doubt about it. But it wasn't the disaster she'd been expecting. "Okay, the situation isn't so bad. We don't even have to close the store. I can rig up some sort of a barrier here until the roof gets fixed."

"That's a no-go, Tomato. For one thing, we can't have customers getting rained on. Florida Charlie's has an image to live up to. Folks drive down on their vacation, see our billboards and get all excited about the store. Word of mouth is what made us what we are, and if we aren't one hundred percent, then we shouldn't open." He winked at her. "This will be a good opportunity to get that alligator tooth display done up right."

Grace grit her teeth. Pop wasn't going to be satisfied until the alligator tooth was done up in a gold-encrusted shrine. She studied the leak in the ceiling. "Pen, can you check the back storeroom and see if we have more buckets?"

Penny came back a couple of minutes later with a large plastic tub. "This might be better than a bucket."

"Good choice," Grace said, swapping out the tub for the nearly full bucket. If the rain didn't stop soon, this was going to be an exhausting process.

The bell on the front door chimed, signaling a customer.

"Sorry, we're closed," Grace heard her mother say. After a minute or so, Abuela called out. "Gracielita! Come quick."

*Now what?*

Grace, Penny, and her father all ran to the front of the store to find her mother holding a vase with what looked like at least a dozen red roses. "These were just delivered for you." Mami thrust the vase in Grace's hands.

"I didn't know you were seeing anyone," Pop said. "Who's the lucky fella?"

"And why haven't we met him yet?" Mami added.

"I told you," Abuela said. "It's the man I saw in my dreams. He's the one who sent them!"

Ellen and Sarah chose that exact moment to walk through the door.

"I thought the place was under water," Ellen said, sounding put out to discover it wasn't as bad as they'd first thought.

"Forget about the roof. Look what Grace just got." Penny counted each rose one by one under her breath. "Eighteen long-stemmed roses. From Benson's!"

Benson's was a seriously overpriced flower shop located on the beach. Grace had never gotten anything from Benson's before.

"Why eighteen? Why not a dozen?" Ellen asked. "Does it mean something?" Everyone turned to look at her. "You know how different flowers signify different things? Like yellow roses mean friendship. Everyone knows red means romance, but what does the eighteen mean?"

"That he's not cheap?" Penny said.

"How about we find out who the *he* in question is?" Sarah asked.

Grace pulled the card from the plastic holder and read to herself.

*Grace,*

*I know I can never make up for my reprehensible behavior Saturday night, but I wanted you to know how sorry I am. You're a terrific girl and I'll always regret that I blew it with you.*

*Brandon*

"So?" Penny asked. "Who are the roses from?"

"Brandon Farrell."

"How romantic!" Abuela said. "He must really like you, Gracielita."

Sarah didn't say anything. Not that Sarah had to say anything for Grace to know what she was thinking. It was obvious Sarah was impressed. But Sarah hadn't been there Saturday night. Brandon Farrell's bad behavior couldn't be wiped out by a few expensive flowers. Especially ones with thorns.

"It's no big deal," Grace said, mostly for her parents' and Abuela's benefit. "I went out with him and he has a lot of money. He probably sends roses to all his dates."

"Yeah, but why eighteen?" Ellen asked again.

Grace shoved the note inside the pocket of her khaki pants. "Will you *stop* with the eighteen already? Not everything has to have a hidden meaning."

Penny pulled out her BlackBerry. "I'll start looking up numbers to roofing companies."

Grace threw Penny a smile, grateful for the change in subject. She patted her father on the back. "Pop, why don't you and Mami take Abuela home? Penny and I will stay here and come up with a plan." She could see by the expression on his face that he wanted to stay and help. "You made me manager so you wouldn't have to worry about stuff like this. I have it under control."

"Grace is right, Charlie. Let her handle this," said Mami. "Remember your blood pressure!"

Pop looked like he was about to bust an artery. "Okay, but I'm just a phone call away if you need me. And don't forget to double check the lock on the doors when you close up." Pop always told Grace to double check the locks. It was a habit he couldn't seem to grow out of. Grace was used to it so she just nodded.

Mami shuffled Pop and Abuela out the door but not before Grace could grab the Santa hat from Abuela's hand. "I think the hat looks fine the way it is. Maybe you can make the alligator something new for Valentine's Day," Grace suggested. She'd never been crazy about the Cupid costume Gator Claus was forced to wear. It looked too . . . feminine. And Gator Claus was definitely all male.

"There's a roofer who can come out tomorrow. That is, if it's not raining," Penny said, punching numbers into her BlackBerry. "I'll call a few more companies so we can get more estimates."

"Thanks, Pen." What would Grace do without Penny? "And when you're finished with that, call up all the employees and tell them that tomorrow we'll be open for business as usual."

"But I thought your dad said we should close the store until the roof gets fixed."

"I know what he said, but every day we're closed is a drop in revenue. Don't worry, I'll handle Pop. I'm going to put up the alligator tooth display right where he wants it. He'll be so happy he won't care what I do."

Penny looked doubtful, but she went back to looking up numbers in her BlackBerry. Grace walked Sarah and Ellen out to their cars. Ellen handed her the takeout boxes with their lunch.

"Thanks for rushing over here," Grace said.

"Of course," Sarah said. "I love Florida Charlie's."

Ellen nodded in agreement. "This place is special. It would be terrible if anything happened to the store."

Grace stood under the porch area and watched as they drove off. It was still raining, although it appeared to be letting up some, so maybe things wouldn't be so bad after all. Grace repositioned the Santa hat back on Gator Claus's head.

"The roses don't mean anything, you know," she said, strategically laying the pom-pom to land next to Gator Claus's jawline. Somehow it made him look jollier this way. Less . . . reptilelike.

"He probably has an account at Benson's the same way he has an account at Chez Louis. He probably gets roses on discount, he buys so many. Besides, it doesn't matter. Nothing in this world is going to change my mind about Brandon Farrell, so he might as well be dead to me."

Gator Claus's expression turned smug.

"Don't look at me like that or I might let Abuela have her way with you. You don't know it, but you're just a few yards of green felt away from becoming an elf."

The smug look immediately disappeared.

Thursday at Florida Charlie's was business as usual. Which meant it was slow in the morning, picked up around lunchtime, and then died down by late afternoon. The rain stopped and two roofing companies came out to give estimates. Both agreed nothing short of a new roof would fix the problem. One company offered to do a quick patch up job at a reasonable price, but they couldn't guarantee how long it would last. Grace decided to consult Charlie before doing anything.

"Did Pop okay this?" Charlie asked, inspecting the makeshift rope-off job Grace had done around the Hemingway corner. Although it wasn't raining anymore, she didn't want to take a chance it would start up again.

"Have you had a chance to look over the store's finances?" she countered.

"So Pop didn't okay it. I hope you know what you're doing. And no, I haven't had a chance to look over the numbers yet. Work has been a bitch."

"Tell me about it."

"You don't have to work here, you know. Pop would understand."

"Right."

Charlie had the grace to look embarrassed. He stuck his hands in the pockets of his tan trench coat. Underneath he wore a fancy looking gray wool suit. He looked every inch the successful attorney that he was, and Grace was proud of him. But at the same time, she couldn't help but be envious. Charlie had had no problem telling their father that a career at Florida Charlie's hadn't been for him. So it had been up to Grace to come through. Felix was wrong when he'd said Grace hated working for her father. She didn't hate it. She just didn't love it. But if she didn't work at Florida Charlie's, what would she do?

"I'll look over the figures tonight," Charlie said.

"How's the Phoebe situation?"

"There is no situation. I told you, it was no big deal. We talked. She was cool."

Grace remembered the look on Phoebe's face during dinner. If Charlie had been dessert, Phoebe would have gobbled him up in one bite.

"So what should I do about the roof?"

"Off the top of my head, I'd say get the quick patch-up done, then we'll worry about getting a new roof later. I'll look into the insurance policy but I'm pretty sure it doesn't cover normal wear and tear."

"Okay, that's what I was thinking."

As soon as Charlie left, Grace took off for her Thursday evening Zumba class.

Sarah met her at the entrance to the gym. "What are you going to do when you see Brandon?" she asked.

"Absolutely nothing. Just because Brandon Farrell sent me roses from Benson's doesn't mean anything."

Sarah rolled her eyes.

"Okay, so maybe I'm a little nervous," Grace admitted. But it was only because of the awkwardness of the situation.

In the end, her worrying was for nothing. Brandon never

showed up to Zumba class, which only confirmed Grace's opinion of him as a wuss. He could spend a hundred bucks on roses, but he was too much of a coward to face her in person.

It was better this way. Now she could go to Zumba class and not have to worry about what he might say to her or what she might say to him. Daytona Beach wasn't a large city, but it was big enough that she could likely avoid him if she wanted to. Probably forever.

# 7

# Hopelessly Attractive Men

It was the first official meeting of the boyfriend club. Besides the four of them, Ellen's friend Janine was present, along with five other women who worked at the college, making a total of ten members. Ellen passed around her legal pad to get the new members' e-mail addresses. They were meeting in the Hemingway corner, like they normally did. In the past, when the club had focused on books, the Hemingway corner had seemed inspirational. Strangely, even although the focus of the club was now men, it still seemed appropriate.

A roofing company had come out yesterday and done a patch-up job, so Grace wasn't worried about the roof leaking if it should happen to rain again. Yesterday, as predicted, a cold front rolled in, dipping temperatures into the forties. For the first time this season, the heat was on in the store. Grace wore a leather skirt that fell to mid-thigh with her knee-length high-heeled boots and a black turtleneck. She'd pulled her hair back into a high ponytail, giving her a fun sort of retro sixties look. She hadn't realized until she'd started getting dressed for the evening how much she was looking forward to tonight.

"I'd like to take this opportunity to welcome all of you," Grace began. "The purpose of this club is to educate and empower one another. Between us, we've probably dated a lot of eligible men here in town—"

"And some ineligible ones too!" a woman with curly red hair blurted.

Everyone laughed politely.

"Exactly," Grace said. "For practical purposes, I think we should limit our discussions to one boyfriend per meeting. Two, if we have time. And afterward, we can go to Coco's for drinks, because this should also be fun! Now, I suggest that we begin by going around the room and introducing ourselves."

After they'd made their introductions, Ellen stood, her trusty legal pad in hand. "I'll start with a recap from last week. I've already made a file for our first two reviews. Those members who join tonight can access them online once they accept the invitation I send out." She cleared her throat and swept her gaze over the little group causing everyone to still. Grace had to admit, Ellen was good at working a room. "Our first review was Felix Barberi, aka Peter Pan."

"*Cheating* Peter Pan," Grace clarified.

At the confused looks on the new members' faces, Ellen went on to explain the classification system.

Several of the women mumbled their appreciation.

"That's so clever!" Janine said.

"I thought of that," Grace said, feeling quite proud of herself. "Although we're pretty sure Peter Pan isn't a true literary comparison for Felix Barberi. We're still working out the kinks in the system."

"I won't go over everything we said last week, because you can read the reviews for yourselves, but I can tell you it isn't pretty," Ellen said. "Who would like to begin tonight's discussion?"

Stacey, the woman with the curly red hair, raised her hand. "I'd like to talk about my ex—Chris Sullivan." She paused. "Does anyone know him?"

Penny shifted in her seat. "It's not the Chris Sullivan who works at Bob's Automotive Parts, is it?" At the questioning look on Grace's face, Penny said, "He's friends with Butch."

"That's him," Stacey said. "I dated him for almost two months. Then I found out he was married."

Everyone moaned.

"Maybe he's more of a work acquaintance than a friend, really," Penny rushed to add.

"It all started back in June when I took my Volvo in for an overhaul," Stacey explained. "She's fifteen years old and very delicate. Volvos are solid cars but they need an expert touch. Chris was the only mechanic who knew how to work on her. He understood her. He was . . . well, he was wonderful. He had her engine running so smoothly she almost purred."

Ellen began scribbling like a fiend.

Grace checked out the expressions on the other women's faces. No one seemed to read anything strange in Stacey's comments. *Get your mind out of the gutter, Grace!*

Stacey's voice began to quiver. "He was so handsome that I nearly swooned every time I looked at him. At first, I resisted the attraction. But he wasn't wearing a wedding ring and I thought maybe it was time to take the initiative in my love life, so I did something very unlike me. I asked him out."

"He was going Hando Commando," Ellen said, shaking her head in disgust.

"Married men who don't wear their wedding rings are despicable! How is a girl supposed to know who's been caught and tagged?" Janine said.

"Maybe he has an allergy. Or maybe he doesn't wear it because he's a mechanic and he gets grease all over his hands?" Penny suggested, but no one paid her any attention.

"After that first date, I sensed something mysterious about him, and after a couple of weeks, I was convinced he was definitely hiding something. But by then it was too late. I was already head over heels in love. Then one day, out of the blue, he told me he was married and going back to his wife."

"I think Chris and his wife were legally separated for a while," Penny said. One of the women turned to glare at her. "Not that it's an excuse for not telling Stacey the whole truth!" she added defensively.

"That was six months ago, and now I have major trust issues." Stacey reached inside her purse to get a Kleenex to wipe at her sniffles.

"Have you tried therapy?" Sarah asked.

"Why should I go to therapy? He's the one who needs therapy!"

"'*I had not intended to love him*,'" Ellen recited dramatically.

"What?" Stacey asked, looking confused.

"It's a quote. From Charlotte Brontë's classic, *Jane Eyre*. Don't you see, Stacey? You were duped, just like poor Jane. This is a classic case of a Mr. Rochester if ever I saw one," Ellen said.

Stacey nodded. "Exactly!"

"I love that book," one of the women said.

"Yes, it's a wonderful story, to be sure." Ellen pushed her reading glasses up her nose. "Although not as brilliant as her sister Emily's *Wuthering Heights*. Nothing can compare to that."

Penny leaned over and whispered to Grace, "I hope she doesn't start in on Heathcliff. We'll never make it to Coco's before it closes if Ellen starts expounding on the most romantic hero of all time."

But blessedly, Ellen kept to the program. She went on to describe other similarities between Stacey and Chris's doomed relationship and that of Jane and Mr. Rochester. Occasionally, other members would make a comment, but since no one knew the book as well as Ellen, no one could really add much of value. Grace had wanted to point out that, in the end, Mr. Rochester and Jane *did* eventually get together, but since Grace hadn't read the book and was strictly going off the cable movie adaption, she was afraid maybe the Hollywood version had fudged the literary ending and she didn't want to incur Ellen's wrath. By the time Ellen was through dissecting *Jane Eyre*, it was almost eleven.

"I think that about wraps it up for tonight," Grace said, bringing the meeting to a close. "How about we set up a standard date for the first Saturday of each month?"

The group unanimously approved. Grace and Penny locked up the store, and the ten of them headed to Coco's, an upscale bar located on the beach. The place was crowded so it was standing-room only, but one of the servers was a student of Ellen's and she managed to get them a table. They'd just ordered their drinks, when another server came over with two chilled bottles of Dom Perignon.

Sarah stared at the bottles wistfully. "You have the wrong table."

The server pointed to the bar area. "Compliments of the gentleman."

They all craned their heads to get a look. Grace nearly fell out of her seat when she recognized who the "gentleman" was. Brandon Farrell stood with his back to her, talking to another man. To Grace's relief, his friend Doug didn't appear to be with him.

"We don't want it," Grace said. "Take it back."

"The hell we don't!" Ellen reached for a bottle. "We'll need ten glasses, please."

"We're *not* accepting the champagne," Grace repeated.

"But I've never had Dom Perignon," Penny said.

The server looked torn. "The guy said if you take the bottles, he'll give me a fifty dollar tip."

"That settles it. We don't want him to lose his tip, do we, Grace?" Ellen said.

The rest of the table looked at the bottles with lust in their eyes. There was no way she could send back the champagne without seeming like a huge party pooper.

"We'll take the bottles. But I'm not going to have any," Grace declared.

He uncorked the champagne and poured them each a glass. Grace wished she had the willpower to resist, but like Penny, she'd never tasted Dom Perignon.

"Maybe I'll try a tiny sip. But I'm not going to like it."

The champagne was delicious. All bubbly and smooth as it trickled down her throat. She drained her glass. All right, so maybe she liked it a little.

"How much do you think this cost?" Penny asked.

"Too much."

"Isn't someone going to go over and thank him?" Stacey asked.

"Nope."

"He must really like you," Sarah said. "First the roses from Benson's, now this. Maybe you should give him another chance, Grace."

Some expensive roses and overpriced champagne and he had her friends eating out of the palm of his hand. Grace should have added "diabolical" to the list of qualities on his boyfriend review. She should get Ellen to add it to his file on the Yahoo! site.

After they finished the champagne, the waiter brought them their original drink orders. The lime in the rum and coke mixture of Grace's Cuba Libre tasted too tart after the smooth Dom. Grace tried to hold it in as long as possible, but her bladder felt ready to burst. Unfortunately the only way to the restroom was to walk by the bar.

She stood and smoothed out her skirt.

"I'll go with you," Sarah said, sensing Grace's discomfort. "There's safety in numbers."

Grace managed to elude Brandon on her way to the bathroom, but he was waiting for her the second she stepped back out of the door.

"Hello, Grace," he said, sounding nervous. Well, good. He should be nervous! He smiled at Sarah and she smiled back at him.

"Did you follow me here?" Grace asked.

"Of course I did. I was hoping we could talk."

"I know you followed me to the bathroom; I meant did you follow me here to Coco's?"

He looked amused. "If you mean, am I stalking you? The answer is no. It was just luck that you walked in the door."

"I think I'll let you two talk in private," Sarah said, making quick tracks back to their table. Grace reached out to stop her but Sarah was too quick.

"So who are your friends?" he asked. "Did they like the champagne?"

"It's my . . . book club. And of course they liked it. They friggin' loved it. I'm sure they'd like to canonize you about now."

He looked pleased with himself. "Did you get the flowers?"

"You shouldn't have done that either."

He didn't look so pleased anymore. "Damn it, Grace, what do I have to do to make it up to you? Would you feel better if I let you pour a bottle of the Dom over my head?"

"The beer was an accident. But I wouldn't mind draining a bottle of Dom over your head."

"Wait right here." Brandon went over to the bar and said something to the bartender.

Did he think she was an idiot? No way was he coming back with a bottle of hundred-dollar-plus champagne just so she could waste it by pouring it over his skull.

But that's exactly what he did.

"Here you go," he said handing her an opened bottle of the

champagne. "Not to be a snob or anything, but if a woman is going to dump alcohol on me, I'd prefer it be something I actually like to drink. The beer at the Duck leaves a lot to be desired."

She playfully raised the bottle above his head. "I'm going to do it," she said, which of course she wasn't. But it was interesting to see how far he'd let this little charade go on.

"Go for it," he shot back. He stood there, grinning at her.

"Is this a trick to get me arrested?"

"Why would I want to get you arrested?"

"I don't know. Payback for the Wobbly Duck?"

"I'm trying to get you to go out with me again, not get you thrown in the slammer."

She couldn't help herself. She smiled.

Hopelessly attracted to hopelessly attractive men . . .

*Wait a minute.*

What was wrong with her? He'd stood her up. He'd let his friends make fun of her parents' store and then basically gone Neanderthal. She lowered the bottle. The old Grace might have given in. The old Grace might have swooned at the flowers and the champagne and his pretty face. But this was the new Grace. The empowered Grace! And she wasn't going to fall for any of it.

"Okay, you're sorry. I get it and I accept your apology. But I thought I made myself clear. I'm never going out with you again."

"Never is a long time, Grace."

"Well, at least you know my name now."

A pained expression crossed his face but he didn't apologize again. He pulled out his wallet and handed her a card. "If you change your mind, call me. I'd really like a second chance. But I'm not going to beg."

She took the card, even though she never intended to use it, because not to would have seemed childish and grudgelike, and walked past him back to her table.

"Thanks a lot, Benedict Arnold," she said to Sarah.

"I thought you could use a moment alone," Sarah said. "He was always so nice in Zumba class. And he seems sorry enough."

"You're tipsy on his overpriced champagne. You keep saying how nice and how sweet he is, but we're not in Zumba class anymore, Dorothy. You weren't there to witness the horror that was our date. Honestly, Sarah, whose side are you on?"

"Do you really have to ask?"

Grace lost her frown. Ever since the first day of first grade, Sarah had always been on Grace's side. She'd been there through every single one of the Richard Kasamatis in her life. Could Grace say the same thing back? "Sorry. I didn't mean to snap at you."

"Is that more Dom?" Ellen asked, pointing to the bottle in Grace's hands. "Because if it is, hand it over."

Grace had forgotten she was still clutching the champagne. She handed the bottle to Ellen, who divided the contents into ten glasses. Grace raised her flute. "Ladies, join me in a toast. No matter how contrite or rich or good-looking Brandon Farrell might be, trust me on this: I'm never, and I repeat, *never* going out with him again."

Maybe if she said it enough times, she'd actually start believing it.

# 8

# Lettuce Is a Simple Vegetable

The next day was Sunday and the weather turned warm again. Grace went to Mass with the family as usual, then later, they all met back at the house for supper. The only difference from last week was that this time there was no Phoebe. Abuela seemed resigned, Mami disappointed, and Pop distracted. Around seven, Grace kissed the folks good-bye, then drove back to her place. Charlie followed in his car.

Grace lived in a twenty-year-old two-story stucco Spanish-style town house. She'd bought the place a year ago, and in that time she'd torn up the original carpet and replaced it with wooden floors, painted the downstairs a creamy sage that Sarah had suggested since green was Grace's favorite color, and retiled the kitchen. She loved everything about this little house.

They settled themselves on her living room couch. Charlie pulled his Mac out of the computer bag and began punching buttons. "Sorry it's taken me so long to get this done." He angled the screen so Grace could follow along with him. "I've gone through all the financials from the store, as well as the personal stuff. Mami and Pop are okay. They've paid off the house and have done a good job saving. No worries there." She waited for the dreaded *but* she could sense in Charlie's tone. "And actually, the store itself isn't in bad shape."

"Really?"

"You sound surprised."

"It's just . . . business has seemed so slow lately. Revenues aren't what they used to be." In the two years since Grace had taken over as manager she'd seen sales slowly decline.

"Sales are down, you're right about that. But that's not the problem. The store has still managed to squeak by in the black every month. But Pop has had to dip into the business reserves for unexpected expenses, which means there's not a lot left for an emergency."

"Like a new roof."

"Exactly. You know the Cracker Barrel restaurant they built off the next exit? It's doing pretty good. Hell, they all are. There's a motel going up right next to it. And I happen to know for a fact there are more companies looking to buy property off the highway. Florida Charlie's is sitting on some prime real estate."

Grace froze. "Are you saying what I *think* you're saying?"

"Don't freak. I'm just saying Pop shouldn't rule out selling the land. The building's old. At least fifty years. I've heard you say a hundred times the bathrooms need remodeling. And now there's the roof. Without a renovation, the property is decreasing in value." He met her gaze. "I'll be honest, the roof repair is going to strain the store's finances to the point that a few bad months will put us in the red. It's only a matter of time after that before Pop has to end up selling anyway."

"What about a loan?"

"That's an option, but it would mean putting the property up for collateral. I don't know if the business is worth doing that. That would be Pop's call." He hesitated. "There's nothing wrong with jumping off a sinking ship, Grace."

"You know what that would make me, Charlie? A rat."

"Selling the store could be a good thing. Mami and Pop have enough money saved that they can enjoy their retirement. And the money they'd make would be icing on the proverbial cake. And you could do what you want. I know it hasn't been easy for you stuck at the store."

"It isn't all bad."

"Don't romanticize it. How many times have you told me you wished you could quit and do something else?"

"I just can't break Pop's heart like that."

"So you'll do what? Wait till he's dead, then sell the place? You'll spend half your life miserable doing something you don't want? No one asked you to be a damn martyr, Grace."

The sudden vehemence in his voice made her sit up straight. It wasn't like Charlie to be so passionate about anything. "What's with you?"

He raked his hand through his dark hair. "Sorry, work has been complicated lately."

"It isn't Phoebe, is it?"

"I already told you, she's not a problem."

"Is it the Miami thing?"

"Yeah, it's the Miami thing." But Grace wasn't convinced. There was no use prodding him, though. Grace could see in his eyes that he'd shut down. He glanced at his watch. "I have an early morning appointment and I still have a shitload of work I need to get done."

"You work too much, Charlie," Grace said, feeling a little sad for him. She could understand why Mami and Abuela wanted to see him happily settled down with a nice girl. Charlie needed balance in his life.

"At least it's work I want to do, Grace."

*Touché.*

His expression softened. "Florida Charlie's had a good run in its day, but it's a dinosaur. It's the big companies that have taken over Florida tourism that will survive. Better to go out when you still have some dignity, right?"

What could Grace say to that?

She walked him to the door, hugged him good-bye, and watched as he drove off.

*Sell off Florida Charlie's?* Grace had never once considered it. She'd always assumed the store would be there forever. That her children and even her grandchildren would nod to Gator Claus (maybe even share a word or two with him), walk through the double glass doors, and feel the same way about the store that she'd felt when she was six. But Charlie was right when he said she didn't envision herself as the manager at Florida Charlie's indefinitely, and certainly not for the half a lifetime he had implied.

Still, how could her brother sit there calmly and talk about selling off the store like it was a used car? Charlie had a way of seeing things too simply. The store didn't make money, so sell it off. No emotion involved. Well, Grace wasn't built that way. Abuela had been right all those years ago when she'd named them the Lettuce and the Tomato. The lettuce was a simple vegetable. Uncomplicated. But the tomato? It wasn't even sure what it was. It looked like a vegetable, but inside it was a fruit.

Grace sighed. Sometimes she wished she could be the lettuce.

Thinking about Charlie's idea made her head throb. Maybe she should take a couple of Tylenol and go to bed. But it was too early to go to sleep. Grace scoured her refrigerator for something sweet but all she could come up with was a tub of nearly empty Cool Whip. She didn't want to think about the future of the store or even her own future. She just wanted to sit on her couch and eat ice cream. Preferably a whole lot of it. She grabbed her car keys and headed to Publix.

The grocery store was bustling for a Sunday night. It was the weekend before Thanksgiving and shoppers were trying to get a leg up before the last-minute rush. Grace dodged the crowded food aisles and made her way to the frozen dairy section. She could go straight for the big guns and get the Moose Tracks—creamy vanilla ice cream mixed with chocolate and peanut butter. But the mint chocolate chip had its appeal too.

Which to choose? Of course, she could always get both . . .

"I prefer pistachio, myself," said a familiar male voice.

# 9

# Just Joe

Grace turned to find Rosie Dimples aka Dr. Joe leaning against his shopping cart. He wore above-the-knee nylon basketball shorts and a T-shirt. Maybe he'd just come from the gym. Grace squelched the urge to reach out and smooth an errant lock of hair off his forehead.

"There's no chocolate in pistachio ice cream," she said.

"What is it with women and chocolate?"

*It's the universal substitute for sex, dummy.* She wondered what Dr. Joe would say to that. He'd probably volunteer to fill in for the ice cream.

"It's one of our daily food groups," she said instead.

He smiled. "How's the tooth holding up, Grace?"

So he remembered her name. Had he read her patient satisfaction survey? Melanie claimed he personally read each one. Tomorrow it would be a week since she'd been to his office. Surely he'd read it by now. Which reminded her, she really did need to investigate where Tanya had gone to work so she could find a new dentist. She'd planned to do it right away, but with all the roof drama going on at the store, she'd forgotten. Technically, she supposed, she was still Dr. Joe's patient.

"The tooth is holding up great. Thanks for asking, Dr. Joe."

"The patients find it easier to call me Dr. Joe rather than Dr. Rosenblum. But outside the office, it's just plain Joe."

There was nothing plain about this Joe, that was for sure. He seemed friendly enough too. Almost too friendly. There was no way he had read her patient satisfaction survey. Melanie was so full of it. She probably read them herself and only showed him the good ones to pump up his ego.

A woman with a cart full of baby items tried to slide between them. Joe pushed his cart off to the side to let her pass. You could tell a lot about a person by the items in their grocery cart. What did a hottie like Dr. Joe have in his? Probably a lot of pretentious, overpriced health food items. She tried to discreetly peek at the contents inside his cart.

"Are you checking out my turkey, Grace?"

"*What?*"

"Do you think my turkey is too big?" He pointed to the large frozen turkey that took up nearly half his cart.

She narrowed her eyes at him. He had to realize his double entendre, although the expression on his face seemed innocent enough. "That depends. How many people do you plan to feed with your big turkey?"

"Just me, my mom, and a few friends."

Grace looked at the tag around the wrapper. "This is a twenty-five-pound turkey. You could feed half of Daytona Beach with this."

"Really?" He looked alarmed.

"Not exactly, but it's way more than you need. Unless you want to eat turkey leftovers until Christmas. The rule of thumb is about one pound per person."

"I don't even really like turkey all that much," he said.

"Then I suggest you go with a smaller version."

He pulled a list out of the back pocket of his shorts and handed it to Grace. "This is the menu I came up with, along with the list of ingredients. Would you mind taking a look at it and telling me what you think? That is ... if I'm not keeping you from something."

She studied the list. "You're not planning to make all this yourself, are you? You said your mom is coming to dinner? Is she going to help cook?"

"The only thing my mother knows how to cook is hot water."

Grace found that impossible to believe. Whose mother didn't cook? Of course, Abuela didn't cook. Or not well, anyway. How Mami had become so talented in the kitchen was puzzling. But then Mami couldn't sew the way Abuela did. "So did your dad do all the cooking when you were growing up?"

"I don't think my dad could manage even the hot water."

Grace frowned. "Will he be at dinner too?"

"He'll be spending Thanksgiving with his newest girlfriend down in Boca Raton."

"Oh." Grace looked at the list again. She rummaged through her purse and pulled out a pen and began crossing off items. "You don't need four different types of vegetables, but you do need both mashed potatoes and sweet potato casserole, even though they're both starches. That's a given for Thanksgiving. Are you going to stuff the turkey?"

"Stuff it with what?"

"Never mind. Just don't forget to take out the insides before you cook it."

"The insides?"

"It's probably not too late to have this catered, you know."

"Where's the fun in that?"

"You're going to give me nightmares. Visions of exploding turkey gizzards are dancing in my head right now."

He looked puzzled but laughed anyway. "You seem to know a lot about this stuff. Maybe you can help me figure out what to buy. If you're not busy," he said again.

She should say no, go do your own grocery shopping. But he'd been nice enough to stay late to fix her tooth. Grace was no Martha Stewart, but it appeared she knew more than he did and the least she could do was help him out. Although it still irked her that he pretended not to remember where they'd first met. And there was also the slight flirtation going on between them. Or was that her imagination?

*Are you checking out my turkey, Grace?*

He wished.

This was one area where Dr. Joe knew *exactly* what he was doing.

"Okay, I'll help you out. On one condition. You admit that you know where you met me. *Before* I came to your office."

"Is this a deal breaker?"

"Yep."

Then he grinned and the dimples came out full force, like some secret weapon he held in reserve. "Do you really think I don't remember our first meeting?"

"Isn't that what you said in your office? That I looked familiar but you couldn't *quite* remember where you knew me from?"

The look on his face said *busted.*

"Look," he said, "I've had the practice for less than a month and I'm still trying to navigate my way around. I'm a single guy with an office full of women, half of whom are single as well. There's a line that can't be crossed. If I'd admitted where I'd met you in front of Tiffany that day, she might have gotten the wrong impression about me. Not to mention how unprofessional the whole thing was. Trying to pick up one of my own patients in a bar, even though at the time I had no idea that's what you were. I'm trying hard to keep my private life outside the office."

Grace supposed that was Dr. Joe's delicate way of saying that half the women in his office were after him and he didn't know how to handle it. Poor baby! Grace could almost feel sorry for him. But she wasn't buying it. It was his fault he'd gotten rid of Tanya and Connie and replaced his office staff with a live version of *Beverly Hills, 90210.*

"So where *exactly* did we meet, Dr. Joe?"

"I already told you, it's just Joe."

Grace crossed her arms over her chest and waited.

He sighed. "Turn around."

"Why?"

"Because I asked you to. Please."

She reluctantly did a three-sixty.

"You're right, I should have noticed your ass first. Do you need more? Because even though I ended up getting really trashed that night I can still remember the dress you wore. It was black and only came up to about—"

"Okay, okay, I'm convinced!" She laughed.

He grinned back at her. Whatever else Joe was, and she was beginning to suspect *player* was way up there on the list, she couldn't help but feel a bit fascinated. Coupled with the fact that he seemed genuinely confused about Thanksgiving dinner, she decided to take pity on him. It was the holiday season. Do unto others and all that. Father Donnelly would be proud of her. She took off down the aisle, list in hand. "Come on, we've got some power shopping to do."

The first thing she did was replace the turkey with a fifteen pounder. "This is a perfect size. If a couple more people show up, you'll still have plenty and you can send home leftovers." Next, they went to the fresh produce section, where Grace picked out onions and celery and items for a fresh salad. "You do know how to make a salad, right?"

"Sure. Just chop everything up and throw it in a bowl."

She picked up a bag of prewashed greens and pointed to the bottom. "You see here where it says 'ready to eat'? Ignore that. Wash it in cold water, then drain it well."

"Why does it say 'ready to eat' if it isn't?"

"I'm sure it's perfectly fine the way it is, but I took microbiology in college, which I'm sure you did too. Scariest class ever."

He nodded. "Got it." He began rummaging through the tomato bin. "So you took microbiology? What did you major in?"

"I ended up in business administration, but I experimented a little first."

He held up a bright red tomato. "How's this?"

"Too ripe. It'll never last till Thursday. Go for something a little firmer."

They continued shopping in a comfortable fashion, going up and down the aisles, filling the cart with the rest of the items from his list. Grace noticed the frequent looks the other female shoppers threw first at Joe, and then at her. *Get in line. He's got an entire office of women after him!* Still, it was sort of fun to be the object of other women's envy. Joe didn't seem to notice. Or maybe he was so used to it that he simply tuned it out.

She helped him unload the items from his cart onto the sliding counter and watched as he paid the cashier. Not because she was of any use to him anymore, but he kept making small talk and there didn't seem to be a point in the conversation where she could ease away gracefully. They had just exited the supermarket when he snapped his fingers. "I forgot something." He handed her his keys. "It's the black Range Rover parked in front. I'll meet you there in a second."

She had all the groceries loaded into the back of his SUV by the time he returned. "I didn't mean for you to load all this stuff yourself," he said.

"It's no problem."

He handed her a grocery bag. "You forgot your ice cream. My treat."

She looked inside the bag. There were five cartons, all different varieties with chocolate being an ingredient. "Thanks, but this is a bit excessive, don't you think?"

"Consider it my way of paying you back. I would have been in serious trouble in there without you."

Grace thought he was still in serious trouble, but Thanksgiving dinner was his problem, not hers. "All right, well, have a happy Thanksgiving."

She made a move toward her car, which happened to be conveniently parked next to his, when he called out, "Hey, Grace, who's Mr. Knightley?"

She froze. "Um . . . he's a character from *Emma*."

At the blank expression on Joe's face, she added, "It's a Jane Austen novel."

"Ah! Okay." He shook his head like he should have known. "Thanks. I've been wondering about that." Then he got into his Range Rover, waved good-bye and drove off.

# 10

# Badly Done, Grace

Okay, so he'd read her patient satisfaction survey. No big deal. Grace dished out a healthy portion of ice cream and settled onto her couch to watch a movie. Joe was gorgeous. And sexy. And actually kind of funny. But he'd also let Tanya go and she could never forgive him for that. She flipped through the channels with the remote, hoping to find a movie as stimulating as the Moose Tracks ice cream.

*Who's Mr. Knightley?*

It was pretty sneaky of him the way he dropped that bombshell. He could have asked her that question at any point during their little grocery expedition, but he'd saved it till the last moment. Like a punch line. Grace felt like he'd bounced a ball in her court and was waiting for it to be returned. Only Grace wasn't sure exactly where she wanted the ball to land.

She couldn't find a movie she wanted to watch, but there was a "reality" show with people eating bugs and it was too fascinating to turn off. Grace wondered if the bugs were real. And if they were, how much the chumps on the screen were being paid to eat them. She took a big bite of the ice cream and watched as one of the contestants ate some kind of sea anemone. Whatever it was, it looked slimy enough. Good thing Grace had a cast-iron stomach.

*Who's Mr. Knightley?*

Where had she placed that letter from Sunshine Smiles? The one that outlined Joe's "resume"? She might actually get a kick out of reading it.

Grace set down her ice cream and rummaged through her desk to find the to-be-dealt-with-later pile of her mail. Most of it was store ads. She tossed those in the trash and kept digging until she found an envelope from Sunshine Smiles dated almost two months ago.

It was a two-page letter from Dr. Fred. He was retiring and wanted to thank the many loyal patients he'd been privileged to serve over the years and hoped they would continue to patronize the new dentist who had taken over his practice, Dr. Joseph Rosenblum. Blah, blah, blah.

Grace took the letter back to the couch, along with her bowl of ice cream, and sat down to finish reading. Joe was raised in south Florida where he attended a high school with a preppy sounding name. Then it was on to the University of Florida where he did his undergraduate degree and dental school, graduating summa cum laude both times.

After graduation he'd fulfilled a childhood dream and—

*Entered the Peace Corps?*

She set the bowl of ice cream down on her coffee table and continued reading. He'd helped provide dental care to the poor and underprivileged in a remote area of Guatemala. After two years in the Peace Corps, he fulfilled another dream of his and took a year off to "explore" the world. He'd surfed in Australia, climbed mountains in eastern Asia, and went scuba diving off the coast of Panama.

Now, he'd returned to his beloved home state of Florida to begin his practice of dentistry. Dr. Fred was certain that his patients would find Dr. Rosenblum every bit as competent and professional as his credentials implied. He was also fluent in three foreign languages, including, of course . . . Spanish.

No wonder Melanie and Tiffany were all gaga over him.

Dr. Joe Rosenblum: Renaissance man!

The only thing left for him to do besides run with the bulls in Pamplona was cure gum disease.

Grace didn't know whether to be impressed or disgusted. Nobody was this perfect. And who wrote this kind of stuff about themselves, anyway? Then she remembered the letter wasn't from Joe; it was from Dr. Fred. So technically Joe wasn't bragging on himself, but still, he would have had to approve the contents, wouldn't he?

She set her attention back to the letter. Dr. Fred explained other changes in personnel. *Aha!* Here it was. The bit about Tanya being let go. Dr. Fred's niece, Melanie (*Melanie was Dr. Fred's niece?*), was taking over the front desk duties since Tanya was now promoted to office manager.

*What?*

Tanya was now the office manager at Sunshine Smiles?

Why hadn't Grace been told this important information?

A few other office staff had decided to retire along with Dr. Fred. Connie's husband had been transferred to Tampa, so she'd relocated with him.

*Well, for Pete's sake . . .*

The brief resumes of the additional professional staff were provided. The letter ended once again with Dr. Fred's sincere thanks for almost forty years of practice and the hope that his patients remained in good dental health. He signed the letter with the salutation, *Don't forget to smile! Dr. Fred.*

Grace could feel the ice cream curdle in her stomach. Why had she assumed Tanya had been fired? True, on the phone Melanie hadn't been forthcoming with Tanya's whereabouts. Add that to Melanie's sinister-sounding voice, it was almost logical that anyone with half a brain would put two and two together and come up with the same conclusion.

Only . . . it wasn't logical.

Not really.

Grace had let her imagination run away—like, all the way to China.

Had she wanted to think the worst of Joe because her ego had been bruised when he hadn't acknowledged that he knew her? She'd already assumed Tanya had been fired way before she'd ever sat in the dental chair, so that couldn't be it. But . . . if Grace was being honest, Joe's cool detachment while he'd fixed her tooth had lent fuel to the fire.

If she'd just read Dr. Fred's letter like she was supposed to, then none of this would have happened.

*Badly done, Dr. Joe.*

More like badly done, Grace.

What must Joe think of her comments in the patient satisfaction survey? He certainly hadn't seemed angry with her tonight. He'd seemed . . . friendly, flirty.

*Who's Mr. Knightley?*

Joe might have graduated summa cum laude and climbed mountains, but he hadn't read Austen. At least, not *Emma*. Of course, Grace hadn't read *Emma*, either, but the movie version starring Gwyneth Paltrow and Jeremy Northam was outstanding.

Her doorbell rang. It was almost ten. Most likely it was Sarah or Penny. Since tomorrow was a workday, Ellen would be in bed by now curled up with a book—probably rereading *Wuthering Heights* for the thousandth time. Or maybe it was Charlie coming back to tell her that his idea to sell the store sucked. She folded up the letter and placed it on her coffee table. She'd worry about Dr. Joe later.

If Grace didn't know the man standing on her porch she would have immediately slammed the door shut in his face. He had shoulder-length dark hair pulled back in a ponytail and wore a bandanna over the top of his head. Sporting a neck tattoo and dressed entirely in black leather, he was six foot four and, although on the thin side, he looked tough enough to eat nails. And screws and bolts and anything else you could throw at him. It was Darren Montgomery, better known to friends and family as Butch. And he was as sweet as a pussycat. If he liked you. Which, luckily for Grace, Butch did.

"Sorry to come by without calling first, but I need to talk to you about something important," he said.

Grace stepped aside and waved him in. Seeing Butch on her doorstep was unusual. The only time Butch had been to her house was when he'd helped with the move-in. And then there was the time he'd come over with Penny for dinner, but that was it.

"Want something to drink?" Grace asked. "A bowl of ice cream, maybe?"

Butch glanced at the half eaten bowl of rapidly melting Moose Tracks. "No, thanks." He sat on the couch and pulled a tiny box out of the pocket of his leather jacket. "I wanted to show you this." He flipped open the lid. Inside was a thin platinum band with a very pretty, very shiny diamond in the center. It wasn't big—probably only about a quarter of a carat—but it was elegant, and not something she would have expected Butch to select.

"Butch, it's beautiful! Penny's gonna flip."

"So you approve? Penny's only got the one aunt in Minnesota. You're the closest thing she has to family here."

Grace felt herself choke up. "Butch, are you asking my permission to ask Penny to marry you?"

He grinned sheepishly. "Yeah, I guess I am. Kind of corny, huh?"

"Not corny at all. And I approve. One thousand percent!"

He looked relieved. "We won't have much except what we can carry on our bikes. We'll camp when the weather is warm.

But I have a little nest egg, so every once in a while we can splurge and get a hotel. We'll go hiking and swimming and—"

"Camp? You mean you're still serious about this bike thing?"

"Well . . . sure. Penny doesn't want to go on the bike tour because she wants me to make a commitment. We can get married right after Christmas. Forty-eight states in three hundred and sixty-five days. It'll be a year she'll never forget."

"And then what?"

"Bob says he'll rehire me whenever, so I know I'll have a job waiting for me." His dark eyes lowered. "I know you can't hold Penny's job indefinitely, but—"

"As long as I'm the manager at Florida Charlie's, Penny will always have a job." Now didn't seem the time to warn Butch that a year from now Florida Charlie's might be leveled to the ground.

"Thanks, babe." Butch grinned. "That's exactly what I wanted to hear. I think it will nudge along my cause."

"When do you plan to pop the big question?"

"I convinced Penny to come down to Cocoa Beach to my parents' for Thanksgiving. I figure after we eat, I'll take Penny for a walk on the beach and propose then."

"That sounds very romantic, Butch."

"Hey, I'm a romantic guy. I just didn't know it until now." He stood and gave Grace a bear hug. "Thanks again. I should have done this a year ago, you know?"

Grace nodded, too numb to do much else. Butch didn't seem to notice. He saw himself out the door and waved good-bye.

A wedding after Christmas, with Penny leaving soon after that.

It was only a month away . . .

It wasn't that Grace hadn't thought about it ever since Penny had mentioned Butch's road trip idea. But lately, Grace had been convinced Penny would stick to her guns and refuse to go. The engagement ring changed everything, though. Butch was right. This was the commitment Penny was waiting for. And Grace was genuinely thrilled for her. It wasn't that Penny was irreplaceable. Marty could probably do most of the assistant manager duties. But Penny was . . . Penny. She kept Grace grounded. She made going to Florida Charlie's fun. She had a great way with the customers. And with Pop. Work would be miserable without Penny. Grace didn't want to think about it.

She took the bowl of melted ice cream and dumped it down the sink, then opened the refrigerator freezer. This called for a fresh bowl. Or maybe two. She stared at the five cartons of ice cream. At the time it had seemed like overkill, but now she wasn't sure it would be enough.

# 11

# The Way to a Man's Heart
# Is Through Flan

The next two days were torture. Grace cringed every time she thought of Joe reading her patient satisfaction survey. But that was nothing compared to working alongside Penny and having to pretend not to know about the engagement ring. Considering that Penny mentioned the Thanksgiving trip to Butch's parents' at least every other hour, it was getting more and more difficult to keep a poker face. She asked Grace's advice on what she should wear to dinner. Or whether she should even go at all since Butch was leaving after the first of the year, and really, what was the use of schmoozing his parents if their relationship was going nowhere?

Grace tried to be upbeat, but the truth was, only part of her was happy. Why couldn't Penny and Butch get married and things stay exactly the way they were? The more she thought along those lines, the more she wondered what was *wrong* with her. Shouldn't she be one hundred percent happy for Penny? Instead, all Grace could think about was herself. She was a selfish cow, that's what she was.

She couldn't do anything about the way she was feeling. Feelings couldn't be helped. But she could do something about Joe. At the very least, she owed him an apology for accusing him of firing Tanya and Connie. Only she wasn't sure exactly how to go about it. A simple "I'm sorry, can I be your patient again?" letter seemed too trite. So, Tuesday after work she stopped by her parents' house.

Abuela was in the kitchen, sipping on a *café con leche* and watching Univision, the Spanish television station. It was the only TV Abuela watched, with the exception of *Dancing with the Stars* and *CSI*. And not just the original *CSI*. Abuela watched all the spin-offs as well. As far as Grace was concerned, Abuela knew way too much about collecting DNA evidence.

"Abuela, I need some advice."

Abuela managed to keep one eye on the screen and gaze at Grace at the same time. "What's the problem, *mi amor?*"

"I need to apologize to someone. I was thinking maybe a nice card or—"

"Man or woman?"

Grace hesitated. "Man."

"The one who sent you the beautiful flowers?"

"No, not that man."

She now had Abuela's full attention. "There's *two* of them?" Abuela's forehead scrunched up. "I only saw one in my dream. And he definitely had flowers in his hand."

"It's not like that. I'm not romantically involved with this man. Or with the other one either," she stressed.

Abuela chuckled. "That's what you think."

"No, honestly, I just really messed up with him and I owe him an apology."

"So tell him you're sorry."

Grace bit her bottom lip. "It's not that simple—"

"Do you know what your problem is, Gracielita? You make everything too complicated."

"No, I don't."

"And you're stubborn too."

That's exactly what Charlie had said about Sarah. But no one was as stubborn as Sarah.

"Flan," Abuela blurted, cutting through Grace's thoughts. "The way to a man's heart is through his stomach. When your *abuelo* Pedro was courting me, my mother used to make him flan. He couldn't resist it. Make him a flan and he'll throw himself at your feet."

Grace didn't want Joe at her feet, but maybe Abuela was on to something. She didn't remember seeing dessert on Joe's grocery list. A flan would make a nice addition to his Thanksgiving dinner. She could bring it to his office tomorrow afternoon, offer up her apology, and they'd be even.

"Good idea." Grace looked around the pristine kitchen. "Where's Mami?"

"Your parents went down to the church to help distribute the Thanksgiving food giveaway. Go ahead and make one. Your mother won't mind. Just make sure to clean the kitchen before you leave."

Grace had seen her mother make countless flans in her lifetime. But she'd never actually made one herself. "You know what's funny, Abuela?"

Before Grace could finish, Abuela said, "Eggs, sugar, evaporated milk . . ." When Grace didn't do anything, Abuela shooed her with her hand. "You know what goes inside!"

Grace began pulling out the familiar ingredients. She set the stove for medium heat, then dumped two cups of sugar into a skillet.

"The secret to a good flan is to make enough syrup so that the custard doesn't stick. Did you put in sufficient sugar?" Abuela asked.

"I think so."

Abuela chuckled at something on the screen. "This show is stupid. But it makes me laugh, and I don't have to think so hard when I watch it."

Growing up in a bilingual household, Grace had taken her knowledge of Spanish for granted. When she spoke English, she thought in English, and when she spoke Spanish, she thought in Spanish. But Abuela had learned English as a grown woman. There were certain sounds that were difficult for her to make, like the *y* sound in yellow. Grace found herself thinking of Joe and his "resume." Exactly how fluent was his Spanish? she wondered. Grace had been to Mexico a few times, but to resort areas like Cancún and Acapulco. She'd seen the poverty, though. It was hard to miss. What was Guatemala like? And what had inspired Joe to go there right after dental school, at a time when he was probably anxious to start making money? He was a mystery, that was for sure.

"Give it a shake," Abuela said, pointing to the stove.

Grace gave the skillet a jiggle. Watching the sugar melt was her favorite part, the transformation from solid to liquid as the white crystals morphed into a lovely brown liquid caramel, all gooey and hot. As a child the temptation to stick her finger in the syrup had always gotten her a whack on the bottom. But it had been worth it each time.

"You'd better get the rest going or all you're going to have is a sticky brown mess." Abuela might not be the best cook herself, but she certainly seemed to know how to direct.

Grace placed the remaining ingredients into a blender and whirled them together. She took a second to sniff the frothy liquid. The smell of vanilla wafted up, enveloping her in familiar comfort. She got out the pan her mother used to bake the flan, set it on the counter and frowned. Something was missing. . . .

"You need to make a *baño de Maria*. So that the flan doesn't stick to the pan," Abuela said.

Of course. Grace got out a large rectangular pan and filled it with an inch of hot water, then set it aside.

"Did you preheat the oven?" Abuela asked.

"Yep." She'd done that first thing. She wasn't totally incompetent. She could make *arroz con pollo*, but that was pretty much the only Cuban dish she knew how to make. Maybe she should get Mami to teach her how to make some staples, like *ropa vieja* and *picadillo*. Grace stored that away as one of her New Year's resolutions.

Once the sugar melted, Grace poured the caramel mixture from the skillet into a Bundt pan, quickly swirling it around to evenly distribute it. Satisfied the entire pan was coated in the caramel, she set it aside to let it cool. Abuela glanced at her out of the corner of her eye, then went back to watching her show. After the caramel had set, Grace poured the liquid flan mixture on top, then placed the Bundt pan inside the larger pan filled with hot water and put the whole thing in the oven.

There! That wasn't so hard.

"Don't forget to cool it well before placing it in the refrigerator," Abuela said. "But when you're ready to flip it, make sure it's been at room temperature first. Do you have a plate to serve it in?"

Grace nodded. "Thanks, Abuela."

"For what? You already knew how to make a flan."

# 12

# I'll Take What's Behind Door Number One, Please

Wednesday was busy. The Thanksgiving holiday exodus into Florida had backed up southbound traffic on I-95, which meant tourists were stopping at the store. Florida Charlie's hadn't seen this much business since last February during Speed Week. Grace was supposed to get off work at three, but it wasn't until almost five that she was able to sneak away. She dashed home, took the flan out of the fridge, and drove to Sunshine Smiles. There was no time to ease the flan out of the pan so Grace would just have to give it to Joe as is and explain to him how to flip it.

She parked alongside the building and carefully lifted the pan out of the passenger seat, then glanced around the parking lot. The place was empty except for two cars, neither of which were a black Range Rover. She was too late. Joe must have already left for the day. Grace felt a ping of disappointment. Which was silly. The flan would keep. She could bring it to Joe on Monday and he could share it with his office staff. Except she had to admit, she'd been looking forward to seeing him again. Not because she was anxious to apologize and eat crow. Who would look forward to that? But she'd be lying to herself if she didn't admit she was attracted to him. In a completely superficial way, of course.

And even though she had no intention of doing anything about that attraction, it never hurt to look.

Since she'd driven all the way over, she should check to make sure Joe wasn't in the office. Besides, she could leave the flan with one of his staff. Surely they had a fridge inside their break room. She had her hand on the office door, when it opened from the other side, bringing her face-to-face with Tanya. The older woman's eyes lit up in recognition.

"Grace, it's so nice to see you!" Tanya hugged her. "What are you doing here? You didn't have an appointment, did you? Melanie and I were about to close up."

Grace looked beyond Tanya to see Melanie standing in the doorway with a large wicker basket in her hands.

"I ran into Dr. Joe at Publix on Sunday and he mentioned he was cooking Thanksgiving dinner. So I made him a flan."

"How nice," Tanya said, but Grace thought she detected a trace of knowing humor beneath the words.

"That makes six dozen cookies, three cakes, four dozen brownies, one torte, and a flan," Melanie said. She took the pan from Grace's hands and placed it inside the basket. "Dr. Joe's patients have been very generous this holiday. I'll make sure he gets it."

Patients were bringing Joe baked goods? Apparently, the office staff weren't the only ones enamored of good ol' Dr. Joe. Tanya must think Grace had some sort of crush on him. Well, she would just disabuse her of that notion this instant.

"The flan is more of an apology than a holiday gift. I thought, well . . ." There was absolutely *no* delicate way of saying this. "I thought Dr. Joe had fired you," she said to Tanya. "So I called him out on it in my patient satisfaction survey."

Tanya looked taken aback. "Why would you think that?"

Melanie frowned. "You didn't give Dr. Joe all tens? *Everyone* gives Dr. Joe straight tens."

"The firing thing was a misunderstanding. Or rather . . . I

jumped to the wrong conclusion. And I actually *did* give Dr. Joe and the staff all tens. It was the free text portion of the survey where I blasted him."

Tanya chuckled. "You didn't read Dr. Fred's letter, did you? I'm sorry, but Joe's gone for the day. Why don't you drop the flan off at his house?" Tanya plucked the wicker basket from Melanie's hands and gave it to Grace. "As a matter of fact, you can bring him the whole basket while you're at it."

"Hey! I was going to give that to Joe myself," Melanie said.

"I know, sweetie, but this way you'll have time to make your Pilates class," said Tanya.

Melanie looked genuinely torn. *Dr. Joe or Pilates?* Grace had to admit, Melanie knew how to work those pouty lips. Watching Melanie mull over the choice was fascinating. Grace wondered how much collagen implants cost these days.

"You're right," Melanie said finally. "I'd hate to miss Pilates class the night before Thanksgiving. Got to get a head start on working off all those carbs." She said good-bye to Tanya and took off in her car.

Tanya wrote Joe's address down on a slip of paper and handed it to Grace.

"Doesn't showing up at his house uninvited cross the line in the patient-dentist relationship?" Grace asked.

"Ordinarily I wouldn't give out his home address," Tanya said, "but I've known you for a long time, so I know you're not some crazy stalker." She smiled at her own joke. "Poor Joe was worried all day over this dinner. He'll be relieved to know dessert is a done deal." Tanya hesitated a moment and added, "You'll be doing Joe a big favor. I'd do it myself, but I'm on my way to babysit my grandkids and I don't want to be late." She looked like she was going to say something more, but then changed her mind. Grace had the distinct impression the something more involved Melanie.

. . .

She might not be a crazed stalker, but she still felt uneasy standing in front of Joe's two-story stucco townhouse. The ironic part was that he only lived a half mile from her place. No wonder she'd bumped into him at her Publix. It was his Publix too. The small front yard was neatly manicured but bare of shrubs or flowers. There was a ten-speed bicycle on the front porch and Grace could see his Range Rover tucked inside the otherwise empty garage. She rang the bell and hoped that Tanya was right about Joe not minding a surprise visit from one of his patients.

He didn't look surprised to see her. He looked relieved.

"I come bearing gifts." Grace handed him the basket. "There's a flan—that's from me—six dozen cookies, three cakes, four dozen brownies, and a torte." She frowned. "Or is it three tortes and a cake?"

"Thank God." He waved her inside.

The living room was an exact replica of hers, except it looked like it still had the original carpet and the walls were painted the same boring beige color that had once adorned the walls of Grace's town house. The only furniture was a leather couch and a plasma-screen TV. Joe could use some much needed decorating advice from Sarah. Maybe she'd give him her card and do them both a favor.

She gave the TV a double take. "A little hypocritical, don't you think? What with your 'no television in the waiting room' policy?"

He shrugged, but he didn't seem embarrassed getting caught. "Monday night football," he said, as if that explained everything.

"So is it normal for you to get a house call from a patient? You seem like you were expecting me."

"Tanya called to tell me you were on your way. Listen, I really appreciate it." Something in his voice told her that the favor extended to more than just delivering dessert.

It wasn't hard to figure out the reason Tanya had practically insisted Grace deliver the basket of baked goods herself. Grace wondered if Joe appreciated the way Tanya was looking out for him.

"Poor Dr. Joe. What are you going to do about Melanie's big crush on you?"

"Just Joe," he reminded her. "And the hell if I know. I can't very well fire her. She's Dr. Fred's niece."

"I know. I finally got around to reading the letter. You're practically a saint."

The friendly expression in his eyes died.

What was wrong with her? She'd come here to apologize, not pick a fight. Why was it so hard for her to admit she'd been wrong about him? She thought about what Abuela had said about her stubbornness.

"Sorry, I didn't mean that. And I'm sorry I accused you of firing Tanya. I thought maybe a nice flan might make my apology seem more sincere. Plus, I thought you might be able to use it for your Thanksgiving party tomorrow."

She looked over at the small kitchen area to the right. The turkey, still wrapped in its original plastic, sat on the countertop. It was surrounded by what appeared to be some of the ingredients he'd bought at the grocery store on Sunday.

"Joe, please tell me that turkey hasn't been sitting on your counter for the past four days."

"Was I supposed to refrigerate it?"

"Um . . ."

He laughed. "I took microbiology, remember? I just took it out of the fridge a few minutes ago to prep it. Or clean it. I'm not sure which, but I know I'm supposed to do *something* to it."

He was all friendly again and Grace let out an unconscious sigh of relief that he'd accepted her apology, as well as for the fact that he hadn't let the turkey become a salmonella breeding ground. It would be near impossible to find another turkey this size so close to Thanksgiving.

He looked inside the basket. "How did you know flan was my favorite?" Before she could respond, he asked, "Does it need to go in the fridge? I'll be honest on this one, I have no idea."

"Actually, it needs to be flipped first, then refrigerated again. I can do it while I'm here, if you'd like. I'd meant to do it before coming over but I was running late."

He eyed her Florida Charlie's T-shirt and her khaki shorts and sneakers but he didn't say anything. Might as well get this out of the way.

"Yes, you've probably figured out by now that I work at Florida Charlie's. And before you make any wisecracks, let me tell you that my parents own the store. My dad is the one-and-only Florida Charlie himself."

Instead of laughing, Joe looked impressed. "No kidding. We used to stop there on the way to my dad's condo in St. Augustine. I thought it was just about the coolest place on earth. Is the alligator still around?"

"Yep, he's still around." It was silly, but she couldn't help but be pleased that Joe remembered Gator Claus. "The shop hasn't changed much in fifty years." *Which is part of the problem,* Grace thought. "You should stop by sometime. I'll throw in a free Florida Charlie's T-shirt, seeing that you're my dentist and all."

Joe placed the baked goods on the kitchen countertop next to the cans of green beans and whole kernel corn. "I thought you fired me in your patient satisfaction survey. By the way, you'll be happy to know that I've now got *People* and *Cosmo* in the waiting room. But I refuse to subscribe to the *National Enquirer.*"

She had been wondering when he was going to bring up the patient satisfaction survey.

*Really?* He'd taken her seriously about the magazines? Grace couldn't help but be pleased.

"You know, supposedly the *National Enquirer* is pretty accurate most of the time. And in my defense, I did give you all tens. I only blasted you in the free text portion because I thought you'd fired Tanya."

"Why did you think that?"

"I jumped to a wrong conclusion based on something Melanie said. I know, it was totally unfair. Sorry."

"Do you do that a lot?"

"What?"

"Jump to wrong conclusions." Joe leaned against the counter and crossed his arms over his chest. It was a good look for him. Confident. Sexy. In control.

Grace cleared her throat. "Not normally, no." At least, she didn't think she did. "And . . . I'm sorry for firing you. So are we good? Will you still be my dentist?" She fluttered her eyelashes at him hoping he would laugh.

"I don't think it would be a good idea to keep you on as a patient, Grace."

She hadn't expected that.

"Oh. Right. I can see—"

"Like I told you at the grocery store, I don't date my office staff. And I don't date my patients either."

"You want to go *out* with me?"

He raised a brow at her incredulousness. "I thought I made what I wanted pretty clear a couple of weeks ago at the Wobbly Duck."

Grace snorted. "I don't think what you wanted that night could be called a *date*."

"Okay . . . fair enough. But unless I'm getting my signals crossed," he paused, "and I don't think I am, I'd say you're pretty interested too. We can do this any way you want. We can start off as friends and meet for coffee, or we can take it up a notch and do dinner and a movie, or we can cut to the chase and have a few hours of hot, sweaty sex. I'll be honest, I'd like all three of those, but it's your call."

For a moment she was speechless. She felt like a game-show contestant with Joe as the smarmy master of ceremonies offering her the choice of three different doors. Door number one: friends. Door number two: more than friends. Door number three: a *lot* more than friends.

Joe was right. She was attracted to him. She'd already admitted that to herself. But the warning bell in the pit of her stomach didn't just ding whenever she was around Joe; it clanged. *Hopelessly attracted to hopelessly attractive men.* What was the point of the boyfriend club if not to learn from her previous mistakes?

"The hot, sweaty sex sounds lovely, but I'm afraid I'm going to have to pass. As for dinner and a movie, that's a date, and I'll be honest, Joe, I don't think that's going to work out between us."

"Why not?"

"Well, for one, you're too good-looking."

He blinked, clearly nonplussed, and Grace felt a twinge of satisfaction that she'd left him momentarily speechless.

"And that's a problem, because . . .?"

The fact that he didn't deny he knew he was good-looking actually scored a few points in his favor. False modesty was one thing, but out-and-out denial of the obvious, especially when the obvious stared at him in the mirror each morning, would only fuel the argument she was about to hit him with.

"It's a problem because in the past I've let appearances taint my other relationships. I've let guys like you get away with crap just because you have a pretty mug. But if I take away that face of yours I'm left with one indisputable known fact about you. You're disingenuous. Are you also nice? Yeah, I'll give you that. Smart, most definitely. But you're also full of shit, and I don't feel like starting another relationship where all I do is shovel."

"Wow. Tell me what you really think of me, Grace."

Had she gone too far? Grace O'Bryan, ballbuster. But she wasn't telling him this to achieve any feelings of self-righteous feminine superiority. When all was said and done, she kind of liked him. And she wanted to be honest.

"*'What's a nice pair of legs like yours doing in a place like this?'*" she mocked. "My personal favorite though, and excuse me if I'm paraphrasing, is *'I meet the girl of my dreams and she's meeting someone else.'* I'm curious, Joe, how many other girls have you said that to?"

"I wanted to get laid, Grace. I don't think I'm the only guy in America who's guilty of that."

She didn't say anything and neither did he. But then he smiled and she smiled and they ended up laughing.

"All right, considering our first meet, I'll buy the disingenuous bit. But are you going to hold that against me forever?"

"Not at all. I find the idea of being your friend kind of intriguing. So I pick the friends and coffee option."

"I guess I walked right into that one."

"You told me to pick."

"How about the friends and a beer option?" He nudged his head in the direction of the kitchen counter. "I could use some friendly help right about now."

"Domestic or imported?"

He opened the fridge. "Domestic. Sam Adams, to be exact."

"Okay. But I don't peel potatoes."

Joe found a suitable plate for the flan and Grace flipped it the way she'd seen Mami do a million times. The syrup spread slowly, making a halo around the custard. Grace couldn't help but be pleased. It looked as good as the flans Mami made.

Joe swirled his finger around the edge of the plate and took a taste of the syrup. "Nice."

"It's my first flan," Grace told him. "My *abuela*—that means grandmother—showed me how to make one. Although why I haven't made one until now is beyond me. I'm thirty years old."

"I know what *abuela* means."

That's right. He spoke three foreign languages fluently. Guatemala. The Peace Corps. Surfing in Australia. Landing on the moon. *Oops*, he hadn't done that last one yet.

"It's impressive, really, everything you've achieved. The Peace Corps, traveling around the world," she said sincerely. "Can I ask you a question? Why dental school?"

"You mean why not medicine?"

She nodded. He'd obviously been asked that question before.

"I can't stand the sight of blood."

The idea of the man standing next to her being afraid of blood made her laugh. "I might buy that if I hadn't seen you right after a rugby game. It's like the most violent game ever. Plus, I know for a fact that you see blood as a dentist. And probably a lot grosser things too."

He grinned like he'd just gotten caught. "My dad's a doctor. The hours suck. I picked dental school in part because I work Monday through Thursday, eight to five, Fridays eight to noon. Not so philanthropic, huh?"

"I think it's nice what you did in the Peace Corps, helping people who needed it."

"It's not like I was out there doing brain surgery."

"Hey, you were filling cavities, right? A person needs their teeth. How else are they going to eat? Which reminds me . . ." She waved her hand over the ingredients spread over the kitchen counter. "Where do you want to start?"

In the end, she did peel potatoes, but Joe chopped onions, so Grace figured they were even. She helped him wash and prep the turkey and laughed at the look of astonishment on his face when she pulled the neck and the giblets out of the cavity.

Another beer and a takeout pizza later, Grace stood and

raised her arms above her head, stifling a yawn. "I think you're pretty well set here. And as stimulating as the company's been, I need to hit my bed. Tomorrow's a big day. I have to be at my parents' in time to see the Macy's Thanksgiving Day Parade on TV. It's a family tradition. My mom makes breakfast and we *ooh* and *ah* at the floats."

Joe smiled. "Sounds like fun." He walked her to her car and the whole thing felt ridiculously like a date.

"Maybe we can do the coffee thing sometime, if you still want to," she said.

"I'd like that." He looked like he was going to kiss her. But he didn't. And she was relieved he wasn't going there. And disappointed at the same time.

*Make up your mind, Grace.*

"How about next Saturday? We can do coffee. After we do dinner." He looked smug, like he'd been ultra clever working in the dinner part.

She shouldn't reward him for his sneakiness. But friends could have dinner too. She was going to say yes when she remembered next Saturday was the first Saturday of the month. "That's my . . . book club night."

"Your book club meets on Saturday night?"

"It's kind of a social thing too."

"How about Friday then?"

"Okay. But it's just friends," she reminded him.

"Sure. We'll have a real friendly dinner."

There was nothing in his tone that implied anything to the contrary, but Grace still suspected that somehow she'd been tricked into picking door number two.

An image of what lay behind door number three popped into Grace's head. She instantly wiped it out.

# 13

# Bad Karma JuJu

For the first time in thirty-some years, the O'Bryan Macy's Thanksgiving Day Parade tradition was broken. Charlie worked Thanksgiving morning and most of the early afternoon, barely making it in time to sit down for Thanksgiving dinner. Mami and Abuela clearly disapproved of his working through a holiday, but neither of them said anything. Pop grumbled a bit, but then Charlie told a joke and everyone laughed and that was that. Score one for the Lettuce!

The next day Charlie came to the house to help Pop decorate. Pop loved Christmas lights, the more the better. By the time they were done the place looked like the house from *National Lampoon's Christmas Vacation* movie. Abuela and Mami had gone out to power shop and Grace was putting the finishing touches on the nine-foot artificial Christmas tree in the living room.

Charlie detoured through the kitchen and came back out into the living room with a soda in his hand. "It's hot as hell out there. Are you sure this is Thanksgiving weekend? I thought a cold front was supposed to come in."

"It went down to fifty last night and now it's back up to the mid-eighties. But that's Florida. And it's only going to be warmer down in Miami, you know."

"You haven't said anything about my moving to Mami or Pop, have you?" The way he said it reminded Grace of when they were kids. Charlie would inevitably do something he shouldn't have and Grace would threaten to tattle on him. She never did, of course, and Charlie would get away with whatever it was he'd done. Charlie never tattled on Grace either, but somehow whatever she'd done wrong would find its way back to Pop or Mami and Grace would get in trouble. The same system that worked beautifully for Charlie failed Grace each and every time. Go figure.

"Miami is your news to tell, not mine," Grace said.

He took a sip of his soda. "I wasn't going to say anything until I had the details ironed out, but I think I have a solution for the store problem."

"Oh, yeah. What?"

He shook his head. "Not until it's solid."

Later that day, Grace went in to work. Black Friday had never been slow at Florida Charlie's, but this year it was busier than normal, which was a nice surprise. It also took Grace's mind off Penny and the engagement ring. She only thought about it a couple of times in between handling customers or going into the back storeroom to replenish the T-shirt inventory. The world's largest alligator tooth now sat in a glass display case in the front of the store, exactly where Pop wanted it. Grace had to admit the kids (and a lot of adults) got a big kick out of it. Maybe Pop had been right about the presentation thing.

On Saturday, business eased back to normal, so Grace left at noon and met Sarah for lunch at Luigi's. Grace thought about telling Sarah about her "friends" date with Joe, but Sarah seemed so depressed it would have been insensitive, since Sarah's romantic life was basically down the toilet. The hard part was not telling Sarah about Penny's big upcoming news. But she didn't want to steal Penny's thunder or have to make Sarah promise to pretend that she didn't already know about the engagement when Penny whipped out her ring to show them.

Bright and early on Monday, Grace pulled up to Florida Charlie's with two cups of Starbucks coffee.

"Well, Gator Claus, pretty soon it's just going to be you and me around here."

Gator Claus looked down at the coffee with a wolfish gleam in his eye.

"Sorry, I didn't get you any. Maybe next time, dude." Grace took a deep breath, opened the door to the store, and plastered a great big smile on her face.

Penny was in the office, sorting through a stack of mail. She glanced up, spotted the coffee and moaned in appreciation. "You're a goddess."

Grace waited for the big announcement, but Penny continued tossing mail in the trash while she downed the coffee. She read the return address on one of the envelopes and laid it on Grace's desk. "This one looks like a formal estimate from one of the roofing companies. Have you decided what you're going to do?"

"Charlie and I have been talking, but I haven't approached Pop yet. How was Thanksgiving?"

Why wasn't Penny jumping up and down and showing off her ring? It's what Grace would be doing.

"Thanksgiving was nice."

"Just nice?"

"Butch's aunt and uncle from Ocala came over. Butch's mom kept stuffing food down my throat because she said I was too skinny, and I thought I was going to explode. One of the cousins drank too much and passed out on the bed I was supposed to sleep in, so I ended up on an air mattress in the family room, which was actually kind of nice because I got the room to myself. You know," she shrugged, "typical family holiday get-together."

Penny said that last part casually, but Grace knew family get-togethers were both exciting and stressful for Penny. Primarily because Penny didn't have much of a family to begin with. Her mother had taken off shortly after Penny was born and left her in the care of an elderly aunt. "Mom" lived in a religious commune somewhere in Texas and only contacted Penny when she wanted money. Penny's father had always been an unknown entity.

"Where did Butch sleep?"

"In his old room, with his brother." Penny tossed the last piece of mail into the trash and took a long sip of her coffee. "His parents are fundamentalist Christians and they don't believe in sex before marriage."

"I thought fundamentalist Christians didn't believe in drinking alcohol either."

"I guess some of the fundamentals get hazy around the holidays."

Grace smiled. "My parents would never go for sleeping in the same bedroom before marriage either. It's like they don't want to know you're having sex, so by giving you separate rooms it makes them feel better."

It was also about respecting their values, and Grace got it. She would never want to do anything that would make her parents or Abuela uneasy. In her experience, it was just best not to mention the sex thing at all, like it didn't exist.

"So we drove back up on Saturday," Penny continued, "and I helped Butch pack some of his stuff and yesterday he hit the road on his grand adventure."

"But what about—" Grace took the coffee cup from Penny's hands and set it on the desk. She flipped Penny's left hand over. There was no ring. "What about your engagement?"

Penny pulled her hand away. She didn't look surprised that Grace had known about the ring. "He asked. I said no. End of story."

"But why? I thought that's what you wanted!"

"To hop behind Butch on his motorcycle and traipse all over the country like a couple of gypsies? The ring was just Butch's way of trying to get me to go along with his agenda. But he doesn't want to compromise and I don't want to be that woman who finds out five years after she's married that she and her husband want different things. I don't want to end up like Sarah and marry the wrong guy."

"But Butch is the *right* guy and you know it."

"He's not the right guy if he doesn't want to settle down and have kids. Not for me, he isn't."

"But—"

"No *buts* about it. And I really . . . I really don't want to talk about this anymore. Okay? And please, don't mention this to Ellen and Sarah. The less I have to think about it, the better."

Grace wanted to protest again but she knew Penny well enough to know it would do no good. "All right," Grace agreed, feeling strangely let down.

Never in a million years would she have guessed this outcome. She'd come into work today expecting to squeal over Penny's ring and start making wedding plans. Now there wasn't going to be a wedding. And Penny was still going to work at Florida Charlie's, which, of course, was awesome for Grace. But Grace didn't feel awesome and she couldn't stamp out the niggling sensation that somehow, because she'd been pouting about losing Penny, she'd inadvertently put out some bad karma into the universe for her.

It was a disturbing thought.

## 14

# The Most Dangerous Kind of Man Is One Who Actually Listens to You

A real cold front came in on Friday, which gave Grace a wider selection of what to wear for her dinner and coffee with Joe. He'd called to confirm but he hadn't mentioned where they were going, although she didn't think it was anywhere too fancy, so she put on her most flattering jeans, coupled with a long-sleeved white T-shirt, a funky neck scarf that Sarah had given her for her last birthday, and a short-waisted tan jacket. Joe wore jeans too, only he looked better in his than Grace did in hers, she thought not too begrudgingly. He opened the car door for her, but other than that he didn't seem to be on date mode. They drove to a small seafood restaurant twenty miles north of town that Grace had never heard of.

"It's a hole-in-the-wall, but they make great hush puppies here," Joe said.

Grace ordered grilled scallops and Joe ordered the fried catfish and a bottle of wine.

"Do you eat here a lot?" Grace asked.

"I used to come here as a kid. My dad discovered this place."

"How long have your parents been divorced?"

"Since I was ten." Before she could ask, he said, "I'm thirty-two, so you do the math."

"Any brothers or sisters?"

"A couple of half sisters from my dad's second wife, but they're six and eight. We aren't close."

She found out his father was a surgeon. Joe saw him a couple of times a year, and although he didn't go into details she got the impression their relationship was strained. Joe's mother never remarried and Joe was her only child. Grace didn't ask what his mother did for a living, only because it seemed from the bits of information Joe dropped about her that she spent her time torn between being a professional shopper, a world traveler, or a spa reviewer. Either Joe's mother was independently wealthy or she'd scored big in her divorce settlement against Joe's father.

He asked about her family and she told him all about them and their Sunday ritual of Mass followed by supper. He laughed when she told him about the different nicknames Abuela gave everyone.

"I have a nickname for you too," Grace said.

"Oh, yeah?" Joe leaned forward in his seat.

"Rosie Dimples."

It clearly wasn't what he expected, so she explained how she'd come to think of it the night they'd met at the Wobbly Duck.

"The guys on the rugby team call me Rosie. But the dimples part?" He shook his head.

"Hoping for something more macho?"

"Maybe." He started to smile, then realizing that would make his dimples pop out, pretended to look serious. They both ended up laughing. "So do you think your *abuela* would like me?"

Abuela would love him. She'd take one look at those dimples of his, then he'd open his mouth and start speaking Spanish, and she'd be a goner. She speared a scallop off her plate. "I don't know. Are you Catholic?"

He made a face, like he wasn't, and Grace decided the conversation was running too close to the sort of interrogative banter that made up a date, so she changed the subject. "That night we met at the Wobbly Duck. Did you, um . . . did you see me leave the bar?"

"You mean did I see you dump that pitcher of beer over Farrell's lap? Yeah, I think everyone saw that."

"That wasn't me. Well, it *was* me, but it was an accident. Not that I didn't want to do it on purpose," she added. "At least a side of me wanted to do it on purpose. I have this really bad temper, you see. My family even has a name for it. *Mal Genio*. It means—"

"Bad Angry One?"

"Not exactly. My brother gave me the name. He meant to call me Bad-Tempered One."

Joe grinned. "Well, *Mal Genio*, on purpose or not, I'm sure Farrell deserved it. The guy's an asshole."

She liked how easily Joe worked her family nickname into their conversation, and how perfect his accent sounded when he said it. *Joe Rosenblum: Renaissance Man*. It hadn't been too far from the truth.

"So you and Brandon are rugby rivals?"

"You could say that," he said in a careful tone. "I've known him since college." Joe's gaze sharpened. "There's nothing going on between you and Farrell, is there?"

"Between Brandon and me? We've had one date. You were there. You saw how fantastic it ended."

He visibly relaxed. "He's not what he seems to be, Grace." And with that cryptic statement left hanging in the air, he excused himself to the restroom.

Grace downed the rest of her wine. What did Joe mean? That Brandon was two-faced? That he was exactly what she'd accused Joe of being? Disingenuous? It was almost like the pot calling the kettle black.

Maybe she shouldn't worry about it. She was never going out with Brandon again so what did it matter? She should enjoy the evening for what it was and not overanalyze everything.

Grace settled back in her seat and took another look around the restaurant. It was small, basically just a narrow room with a wall of windows that faced the ocean, but Joe had been right about the food being excellent. She glanced out the window. The lights from the restaurant and the surrounding businesses illuminated the dark shoreline. She wondered if Joe would suggest a walk along the beach. Which, on second thought, seemed too romantic for a friends date.

A familiar laugh made her turn her head from the window. A few tables over, a woman with blonde hair sat with her back to Grace. Grace hadn't noticed her before because Joe had blocked her view of the other tables, but now with his seat empty, Grace could almost make out the woman's features. The woman laughed again and Grace stiffened.

*Good Lord.* What was Sarah doing here? With *him*?

Grace set down her napkin and marched straight over to Sarah's table. "Well, hello, you two."

Sarah almost dropped her water glass. "What are you doing here?"

"I was just about to ask you the same thing." She tried for a polite smile, but under the circumstances, it was damn near impossible. "Hello, Craig."

Grace hadn't seen Sarah's almost-ex in six months, but he looked the same as always—cleanly shaven, his light brown hair impeccably groomed. Like one of those models who posed for the photo that came inside a store-bought frame, the one you slipped out and tossed in the trash before you put in the real picture.

"Hello, Grace." Craig Douglas didn't smile back. But he didn't look hostile either. If anything, he seemed resigned to Grace's anger.

"I'm here having dinner," Grace said in answer to Sarah's earlier question, but what she really wanted to say was, *What are you doing here with this creep? Laughing and acting like you're on a date?* She wished she had the *huevos* to actually say it. But the last thing she wanted was to embarrass Sarah or bring her more grief. Lord knows that if Sarah was thinking of getting back with Craig, then the grief would come soon enough. She wanted to trust Sarah's judgment on this, she really did, but Sarah didn't know all the facts.

Grace felt Joe slip up behind her. There was no choice but to make introductions. Joe was friendly, but not overly friendly. He was astute enough to feel the tension in the air, which probably confused him, although it pleased Grace that he was able to read her vibe so well.

Joe placed his palm against Grace's lower back. It was an intimate gesture. One that felt strangely comforting too. "The waiter wants to know if we want dessert."

"I'm full, but thanks."

Joe said his good-byes and left to take care of the check.

"I hope you two know what you're doing," Grace said before walking away.

"So what was that about?" Joe asked once they were in the car.

"That was my best friend. And her soon to be ex-husband."

"Ex-husband, huh?"

"Yeah, they looked pretty cozy to me too."

He didn't say anything more, which was good, because Grace wasn't in the mood to talk. They were almost to the Daytona Beach city limits when he asked if she wanted to stop for the coffee part of their date.

"How about something stronger?" Grace said.

Joe pulled into the parking lot of an unfamiliar bar. It took her a minute to realize it was the bar near the Wobbly Duck that he'd invited her to the night they'd met. They sat in a booth near the back which, under different circumstances, might have been romantic, but there was a different buzz in the air between them and once again, Grace found herself grateful that Joe seemed sensitive to her mood. She'd gone out with guys before who were social idiots and it had been a huge turnoff.

Joe ordered a beer and Grace ordered a white wine. Grace took one sip of her Chardonnay and blurted, "Craig cheated on Sarah. And it's my fault."

"How is it your fault?" He lowered his gaze. "Unless—"

"God no!" Grace shuddered.

"Well, okay, good. Not that I thought . . . I mean . . ." He shook his head as if to clear it. "So how is it your fault?"

"It's my fault because I should have seen it coming. I should have warned her about him. About the type of guy he is."

"Because you're psychic?" he said sarcastically.

Grace fiddled with the edge of her wineglass. "Because he cheated on her before they were married. And I knew about it and I never told her."

Grace went on to tell him the whole sordid story, how a week before the wedding she'd stopped by Craig's apartment one Saturday morning on her way to the store to talk to him about Sarah's surprise bachelorette party, only to have the door answered by an attractive brunette wearing nothing but a T-shirt and pink underwear. Craig had insisted Carla was nothing but an old friend who had crashed on his couch the night before, but Grace wasn't stupid.

"I thought about telling Sarah, but Craig promised me he'd tell her himself. And I thought . . . maybe it was best that way. To hear it from him, you know?"

Joe nodded.

"And I kept waiting for her say something, but she never did. I tried to tell her the night of the rehearsal dinner, but we were all having a good time . . . and I guess I really wanted to believe him when he told me that nothing had happened between him and Carla.

"Sarah seemed happy enough the first year they were married. Not ecstatic or anything, but I never saw them fight. And I thought, okay, it all worked out for the best and it would be crappy of me to rock the boat by telling her something that didn't matter anymore. Then six months ago she walked into their house to find her husband in bed with guess who."

Joe's face tightened. "That must have been rough."

Grace felt sick to her stomach whenever she remembered Sarah's frantic phone call telling Grace what she'd discovered. Sarah had been inconsolable. "I've been cheated on too, so I kind of knew how Sarah felt, although my situation was way different."

She told Joe about walking in on Felix and his exotic dancer and about Felix's penchant for Céline Dion. Joe tried not to laugh but he couldn't help himself.

"You couldn't have been serious about this guy."

"For a while I thought Felix might be the one. But it was my pride that was hurt more than anything. And . . . it left me thinking maybe I'm a bad judge of character. At least where men are concerned." She looked him in the eye. "What about you? Have you ever been cheated on?"

He shook his head but he didn't meet her gaze, and she wondered if there was something he wasn't saying. Maybe because he hadn't been a victim himself, there wasn't anything he could add to this part of the conversation.

"If Sarah had found out Craig had cheated on her before the marriage, I *know* she would have called the wedding off. She's going through this divorce because I was too big a coward to do what I should have done and warn my best friend off her rat-cheating fiancé. And now she's all hush-hush with me about stuff and she's having dinner with him out in the middle of nowhere, like she doesn't want to get caught."

"She's a big girl, Grace. If she wants to get back with him, then that's her decision. She already knows he's cheated on her."

"Yeah, but she doesn't know that he's cheated on her at least *twice*, and right before the wedding. With the same woman. That's a pattern, Joe. And I can't let her go back into this marriage without telling her what I know."

"How's she going to take that?"

"Not good."

*Sarah's stubborn and unforgiving.* She could hear Charlie's voice say it over and over in her head.

"Sarah has a lot of pride. She's been my best friend for twenty-five years and . . . it's like I made a fool out of her. At least, that's the way she's going to see it." Hot tears blurred her vision. "Sorry," she said, wiping the wet from her eyes.

"Don't be sorry," Joe said. He looked conflicted, like he didn't know what else to do or say. Crying did that to most guys. But he didn't try to brush it off with a joke or change the subject because he felt uncomfortable.

"You're right, though. You have to tell her," he said eventually. "She might be angry at first, but she'll be even angrier if she finds out on her own."

She tried to pay for their drinks, since he'd paid for dinner, but he was faster with his wallet than she was with hers.

It wasn't till her head hit the pillow that she realized she'd never confided the Craig story to anyone before Joe. Not to Ellen, and not even to Penny. Joe was a good listener, a rare trait in a man. It occurred to her that the last half of their "date," the part in which they'd connected like real friends, was more intimate than the superficial flirting they'd done at the restaurant.

Later that night she woke up from a dream that had seemed so real, she'd been startled and, if she was being honest with herself, disappointed to discover that it wasn't.

"Well, shit," she muttered, punching her pillow back into shape. How was she ever going to be just friends with Joe if she couldn't get that "hours of hot, sweaty sex" thing out of her head?

# 15

# Players, Like Rakes, Amuse More in Literature Than They Do in Real Life

"Get a load of this." Penny shoved a piece of paper under Grace's nose. At the top of the sheet in bold type was the header: *Join Daytona Beach's fastest growing female network*: *The Boyfriend of the Month Club*. The line below gave the time and location of their next meeting, which was tonight. In exactly fifteen minutes, to be precise.

"Where did you get this?" Grace asked.

Penny pointed to the front of the store, singling out a woman in her late thirties who looked busy examining the alligator tooth display. "She wanted to know if she was in the right place. She said she found it on the bulletin board in the women's locker room at her gym."

Grace studied the flyer. "One of Ellen's friends from the college must have put these up."

"Grace . . . I'm kind of with Sarah on this. I went along with this boyfriend club because it seemed fun, but honestly, I thought it was just for one night, maybe two at the most."

They watched as a trio of women entered the store and asked Marty for directions to the club meeting. Marty guided them to the Hemingway corner. A minute later, another woman came in carrying a couple of bottles of wine and a box of paper cups. "Does your dad know about the meetings?" Penny asked.

"He knew about the book club meetings."

"But we aren't here discussing books. You have to admit, at the last meeting, that chick who went off on her ex—what was her name?"

"Stacey"

"Yeah, her. She seemed kind of unstable. When it was just the four of us, it was fine, but I don't think it's a good idea to let strangers in the store after hours. And we *definitely* shouldn't let them bring in alcohol."

"Don't sweat it, Pen. There's probably only going to be a few extra women. And I'll make an announcement about the alcohol." Grace was dying to ask her if she'd heard from Butch, but the last time Grace had brought him up, Penny had gotten tight-lipped and then slipped out for a smoke.

The few extra women turned out to be a lot more. There were only fifteen folding chairs in the storeroom, so Grace and Penny had to drag out the benches from the employee break room. They also had to push back the bookshelves to make room for all the seating. The second Ellen walked in the store, Grace grabbed her elbow and took her to the side.

"Have you seen this?" She showed Ellen the flyer.

"Isn't it great? Janine did those during her lunch hour."

"Ellen, there're at least thirty women here tonight."

"That's fantastic!"

"Where am I supposed to put them all?"

Ellen frowned. "I didn't think about that. We might need to bring extra folding chairs."

"No more flyers. And no more members. This is too much," Grace said, seeing the wisdom in Penny's admonition.

"Okay, you're right. I guess statistically, I can make do with thirty."

"What's that supposed to mean?"

Ellen opened her satchel, but instead of the familiar yellow legal pad, she pulled out a laptop. "To save time, I'm going to type up the reviews directly into a word processing program, then upload them into the Yahoo! file. Wait till you see the most exciting part."

Grace peered at the document on the screen. She recognized it immediately. It was Ellen's dissertation for the master's degree she'd received a few years ago: "Undressing the Romantic Hero in Popular Literature." Grace remembered proofing the paper for Ellen. Despite the sexy title, it was dullsville. Undressing hadn't been meant literally, Ellen explained, after Grace had grumbled about the paper not living up to the title. It was a metaphor for delving deeper into literary archetypes.

"What's so exciting about your research paper?"

Ellen's eyes took on a familiar excited gleam. "I'm going to take it beyond the boundaries of this thesis. I've developed a program that takes the data from my paper and uses it to compare and contrast the characteristics of well-known literary figures against the characteristics of real live men. It's like when you compared Felix to Peter Pan, and I compared Stacey's ex, Chris, to Mr. Rochester, only this will be more objective."

Grace thought about it a second. "That sounds kind of fun."

"It'll be a lot more than *fun*. It's a predictor for how good a boyfriend candidate will be. Let me show you." She brought up Felix's file. "The key words we agreed upon for Felix were charming, egotistical, and childlike. Which, if left by themselves, would make Felix a classic Peter Pan."

"Right," said Grace.

"But we also agreed that Felix didn't fit the Peter Pan mold. So I did some more analysis and realized we didn't have enough descriptors. Three isn't enough to give us an objective match. It's the fourth descriptor that brings it all together. But even that won't work unless the descriptor isn't a tight enough word."

"What do you mean?"

"There are a lot of different words that can be used to describe the same thing. For instance, your Felix—"

"Please don't call him *my* Felix. He was *everybody's* Felix."

"Exactly!" Ellen pointed to the computer screen but all Grace could see were a bunch of adjectives jumping out at her. "Correct me if I'm wrong, but when you first met Felix he was funny and charming and he swept you off your feet. Felix is the modern contemporary of what used to be called a rake."

Player equals rake. Yeah, that was Felix all right. "Go on."

"So I went through a list of famous literary rakes, and voilà! It was so obvious. Felix is Henry Crawford from *Mansfield Park*! Remember the time right before you caught Felix in bed with his hoochie girl? You told me something was off. That Felix was acting weird. It's like Fanny Price in *Mansfield Park*. She knew Henry Crawford was up to no good, she just didn't have the proof until he ran off with Maria Bertram. Although actually, she was Maria Rushworth when that happened, but you get my meaning."

"Which is? Honestly, Ellen, you've lost me."

"Felix's fourth descriptor word isn't cheater, although he's that too. But a better word to describe him is self-indulgent, which is different. The two of you had opposing work schedules. Felix stayed up late every night to close the restaurant and you got up early every morning to go into work and open the store, which made it hard for the two of you to find time to be together. And then you were out of town for a few days and instead of dealing with it, he took his selfish pleasure where he could because he simply couldn't help himself, like a little kid who couldn't wait for his dessert. Felix is exactly like Henry Crawford in *Mansfield Park*. One of Jane Austen's more interesting villains, I think, but nevertheless, there you have it."

Grace let it all sink in. For once, Ellen was really onto something.

"Wow! Ellen, you're a genius. I totally remember that horrible scene where Fanny walks in on Henry Crawford and her half sister. Or what is it, her cousin? Anyway, you're right. It was *exactly* like when I caught Felix in bed with his stripper. Felix is a Henry Crawford!"

"Grace, that's the movie version of *Mansfield Park*, not the book. Jane Austen would never have written something so vulgar as to have her heroine catch someone in *the act*. But I'm not going to scold you for confusing the two. Not tonight anyway, because I'm simply in too good a mood. This revelation is going to allow us to use my research to help women avoid players like Felix Barberi. *Some* members of the English department thought my thesis was self-indulgent. But tell me this: how often can you say that a graduate thesis paper on literature can have a real-world practical purpose? I'm thinking about working up a description for a class. Who knows? Maybe they'll let me teach it next semester." Ellen glanced at her watch. "Time to start the meeting! Would you like to address the room, or should I?"

"Um, I think you should open the meeting, since we've got this new program in play. I could never explain it half as well as you. And can you tell everyone no alcohol, please? Penny and I don't think it's a good idea to bring it into the store."

"You're no fun," Ellen said, but she was still beaming from talk of her computer program, so Grace knew she didn't really mean it.

Grace took a seat next to Penny. Ellen stood and clapped her hands to get everyone's attention. Grace envisioned Ellen going through the same motions in front of her classroom and couldn't help smiling.

"On behalf of the founding members, I'd like to welcome all of you tonight," Ellen said, addressing the group. "May I have a show of hands if you're new this evening?"

She pulled out the yellow legal pad (Grace just knew she couldn't get rid of it all together) and passed it to the woman sitting to her left. "It looks like we have almost twenty new members. When this comes your way, please write down your name, your contact information, and most important, your e-mail address. Within the next twenty-four hours you'll receive an Evite to join our Yahoo! group. This is how you can access the files."

Just then the door opened and Sarah came running in, conveniently late, most likely because she didn't want to deal with any of Grace's questions about her little tête-à-tête with Craig last night. Grace had thought about calling her a dozen times today, but she had no idea how to begin. *Oh, by the way, Sarah, before you take your husband back, let me tell you a little story.* The thought of it made Grace woozy. But Joe was right; she had to tell Sarah the truth. She just had to find the right time and the nerve to go along with it.

Ellen went on to explain how the meeting would be run. Since the group was getting larger, someone suggested that instead of Ellen writing down every review, that members take the initiative and write their own reviews to add to the files.

"That way, we'll have lots of information up at once. Like a databank," Janine said.

"Excellent suggestion!" Ellen said. "More data means more material to work with." She singled Grace out. "What do you think, Grace? Since, technically, this is your club."

"Sounds good to me," Grace said.

Ellen nodded, pleased. "All right then, why don't we go around the room and introduce ourselves?" After the introductions were completed, Ellen opened the computer files on Brandon and Felix and read the information out loud. Grace noticed that a few of the women were drinking from paper cups. Ellen had forgotten to make the no-alcohol announcement. Grace stood to tell the group herself, when a curvy brunette with glasses interrupted her to take the floor.

"Hello, everyone, my name is Jessica and I'm sick and tired of dating losers."

"Hello, Jessica!" the crowd yelled back in the same tone of an AA meeting. This produced some intense giggling in the room.

Grace had to admit, it was funny.

Ellen began punching keys on her laptop. "Go ahead, Jessica, tell us about your latest boyfriend."

"His name is Douglas J. Kirkpatrick, *the third*, and I've got plenty to say about him."

Someone in the crowd moaned. "I've dated him too. You go first, and if there's anything you've missed, I'll fill them in on it."

Jessica went on to give a detailed description of Doug. He was average looking, but he had lots of money and was charming and Jessica was thrilled that he'd singled her out from the other women at the bar where they'd met.

He sounded eerily familiar. Grace raised her hand. "Does this Doug like to wear a baseball cap and play rugby by any chance?"

"So you've dated him too! Man, this guy gets around, huh?"

"Not him, but a friend of his. Go on," she urged Jessica.

"After about a month of some very *intense* dating, if you know what I mean, he tells me we have to lay low for a few weeks because he's up for a promotion at his accounting firm. Did I mention he's a CPA? Says he has to put in all these hours to impress his boss. When he stopped calling all together, I got suspicious, so I began following him around. Just to collect the evidence before I confronted him. He was smart, I'll give him that. It took weeks to finally confirm what I knew all along: that he was dating the boss's daughter." Jessica paused long enough to retrieve a cup stashed beneath her folding chair and take a fortifying sip of whatever was inside. "So I walked in on them in the middle of a cozy dinner in some swanky restaurant on the beach, and guess what that asshole did next? He filed a restraining order against me!"

To call Doug an asshole was almost a euphemism. Still, Grace wondered what Doug's side of the story might be.

"What we need now are four key words to describe this creep," Ellen said, her tone all business. "From the description you've given us, I would say: charming, smart, ambitious, vengeful. Would you agree?"

Jessica took another sip from her cup and nodded.

"Okay, then let's see what we have." With a great flourish, Ellen made a show of hitting the final key on her computer. She gasped and looked over at Jessica in concern. "He's an Iago!" she declared. She deepened her voice. "'Demand me nothing. What you know, you know. From this time forth I never will speak word.'"

"Is Ellen quoting Shakespeare?" Penny whispered to Grace.

"I think so," Grace whispered back. "*Othello*, right? Kenneth Branagh, Laurence Fishburne. It was on cable a few weeks ago. Great flick."

Jessica looked confused. "Iago? You mean, like the parrot from the Disney movie *Aladdin*?"

"No! Iago from Shakespeare's *Othello*," Ellen snapped, clearly horrified by the parrot reference.

The woman sitting next to Jessica shook her head. "Iago from *Othello*! It's a good thing you got away from this guy when you did, sweetie. The whole thing could have ended in tragedy."

The women began murmuring in agreement.

*Got away from him?* Hadn't they heard the part about the restraining order?

Jessica went on to talk more about Doug. After a while, some of the women began getting out of their seats to use the bathroom or to stand up and stretch. Ellen noticed the shift in energy. "I think we have more than enough information on this Doug

Kirkpatrick character. Thank you, Jessica." Jessica looked miffed by the interruption, but she sat down. "We have time for one more review," Ellen said, looking around the circle of chairs. "Who's next?"

The woman sitting on the other side of Grace stood up. "Hello, everyone. I'm Karina," she said softly.

"Hel-lo, Karina!" the group shouted.

"My last boyfriend was Matt Lakowski." Her brown eyes darted around the room, waiting for someone to comment. When no one did, Karina let out a visible sigh of relief. "He's . . . well, he's pretty terrific, actually."

"Stats?" Ellen asked.

"Oh, um, he's thirty-four, divorced, and has a four-year-old son, Matty Jr. He's a wonderful father." She looked around the room again and Grace smiled at her in encouragement. "We dated for about six months before I broke up with him." Karina spent the next twenty minutes extolling Matt Lakowski's virtues.

"I don't get it," Ellen said. "So far, key words here are patient, kind, intelligent, honest. Why did you dump him?"

"The thing is . . . I thought I could do better. Matt's a terrific guy, but he isn't too exciting. His idea of a good time is renting a movie and making microwave popcorn." Karina looked like she was about to cry. "I was wrong, though. He's perfect. I'll never meet anyone like him ever again."

"Why don't you just get back with him?" Penny asked.

"I tried. But he told me that our breakup hurt too much. And that he didn't want to subject Matty Jr. to another failed relationship. He's a terrific father, did I tell you that?"

"Yes, yes, you already mentioned that," Ellen said, frowning down at her computer screen.

"I only brought him up because, well, he's such a great guy. He deserves the best. And if any of you are lucky enough to ever go out with him, I hope you don't blow it the way I did."

"I've got it!" announced Ellen. "We were missing the key word, which in this case is *dull*. Your Matthew is a Colonel Brandon, from Jane Austen's *Sense and Sensibility*. He didn't have his own child, but there's the whole paternal thing he does with his ward's illegitimate baby, or was it *his* baby? I can never remember since I don't particularly like that book."

Karina appeared insulted. "I never said Matthew was dull."

"The definition of dull is 'not too exciting,'" Ellen said.

Grace waited for Ellen to start quoting Jane Austen. But she didn't. Since Ellen didn't like *Sense and Sensibility*, she probably didn't know it well enough to quote by heart.

"All righty," said Ellen. "We have a great start here. So far we have five reviews, but we need more, so upload, upload, upload! I'll read each one carefully to select the proper descriptor words, then put them into my program to come up with a match. I encourage each and every one of you to read these reviews. Memorize them. Information is power, ladies. If we don't use what we know, then we only have ourselves to blame for heartache." She snapped her laptop shut. "So, who's up for Coco's?"

Grace made certain to catch Ellen alone once the meeting had broken up. "Ellen, don't forget, no more alcohol. Maybe you can put an announcement on the Yahoo! site."

"Sure, no problem." She lowered her voice. "Can you believe Jessica thought Iago was a bird from some Disney flick? What are they teaching in high schools nowadays? Wait, don't answer. I know exactly what they're *not* teaching in high schools." She sighed. "I'd love to stay and help clean, but I need to get to Coco's ASAP to reserve a table. You're coming, right?"

"Sure," Grace said, surveying the small mess left by the group. No one had bothered to put away their folding chairs, and there was still the matter of getting the shelves of the Hemingway corner back where they belonged. Penny and Sarah stayed to help.

"Is it just me, or is Ellen having way too much fun with this whole thing?" Sarah asked. "And I mean way too much fun not in a good sense. By the way," she said, giving Grace a look that said enough about Ellen and on to you, "you were right. Your dentist is hot. You have to tell us what's going on! Are you two going out?"

"What dentist? The one who tried to pick Grace up at the Wobbly Duck then pretended not to know her?" asked Penny. "And I agree about Ellen. This whole computer program thing of hers is wacko."

"You know Ellen," Grace said. "Intense is her middle name. But we're all having fun, right? So what's the harm? I kind of think the computer thing is cool. She's even figured out a way that she can use this for a class." She folded up a chair and leaned it against a stack of books. "And for the record, Dr. Joe and I are just friends. That's it."

"How good-looking is this guy?" Penny asked Sarah.

"On a scale of one to ten, eleven."

"Twelve," Grace chimed in and they all laughed. They tried to get her to talk about Joe, but Grace kept steering the conversation back to the club and eventually Sarah and Penny got tired of asking questions that were being ignored.

Once the store was back in order, Grace turned out the lights and locked up. "Should we take our own cars or ride together?"

"Take our own cars," Penny said. "I have a feeling I'm going to want to cut out early and I don't want to hold anyone back."

"Before we head to Coco's, I want to tell you guys something," Sarah said. Although she'd addressed both of them, her focus was on Grace. "Craig and I are definitely going through with the divorce. As a matter of fact, it'll be final at the end of the month. That's what dinner last night was about. We were working out some last-minute details. He's getting remarried on New Year's Day and I'm truly at peace with the whole thing."

Grace thought she'd heard wrong. "How can he be getting remarried so soon?"

"He's marrying Carla."

"The *ho* he cheated with?" Penny said.

"They're in love. They have been for a while, and honestly, like I said, I'm okay with it. Craig and I are going to remain friends." Sarah's voice sounded flat.

*Friends?*

Grace was ecstatic that Sarah and Craig weren't getting back together, but for Sarah to be okay with Craig marrying the woman he'd cheated with just days after their own divorce was final, seemed all wrong to her.

Penny gave Sarah a hug. "If you're okay with it, then I'm okay with it."

Grace gave Sarah a hug too, because it seemed like the thing to do, but it felt wooden. The upside to all this was that now there was no need for Grace to tell Sarah about Craig cheating on her before the wedding. It certainly let Grace off the hook. But something here was very un-Sarah-like. How could Sarah be so blasé about the man she loved being in love with another woman?

If Grace were the type to misquote Shakespeare, she'd say something was definitely rotten in Daytona Beach.

# 16

# In Vain Have I Struggled, My Feelings Will Not Be Denied

Chez Louis looked spectacular decked out in Christmas finery. Twinkling white lights and fresh evergreen garlands hung above the windows. The warm yeasty smell of freshly baked bread made Grace's stomach rumble. This time she wasn't leaving Chez Louis until she'd had at least half a loaf just for herself. Maybe that's what she'd have for dinner tonight. *A bottle of white wine and a loaf of bread, please.*

She adjusted the collar to her red jacket and patiently waited for Felix to notice her. He was absorbed with the ledger in front of him when he automatically began the customary greeting. "Welcome to Chez—" He looked up, stopped mid-sentence, and broke out into a grin.

"Hey, Felix." Or maybe she should call him Henry. Grace wondered what Felix would make of his comparison to a nineteenth-century libertine like Henry Crawford. Who knows? Maybe he'd be flattered.

"Grace, you look . . . you look wonderful."

She wasn't wearing anything as sexy as the black dress she'd had on for her last visit to Chez Louis, but she felt comfortably chic in the tailored cream-colored pants and brown leather ankle boots.

"Thanks."

"I was hoping you'd stop by again."

"I didn't *stop by*, Felix. I have a reservation. Or rather, my brother does. Try Charlie O'Bryan."

Felix's face paled at the mention of Charlie's name. "Is he with you?" He sounded as if he expected Charlie to pounce on him at any second. Which Grace had to admit was funny, because even though Charlie was certainly manly enough, Grace couldn't picture him beating up anyone outside of a conference room.

"Don't worry, Felix. Charlie wanted to kick your sorry behind after the way you cheated on me, but I told him it wasn't that big a deal."

Felix winced. "Grace, if I could take that night back, I would. I don't know what got into me."

She knew exactly what "got into him." The funny thing was, Grace suddenly realized she wasn't sorry she'd caught Felix cheating on her. If anything, she was grateful. There was no telling how much time Grace would have wasted on their relationship if she hadn't had a solid reason to break up with him. Felix wasn't the right man for her, just like Henry Crawford hadn't been the right man for Fanny Price in *Mansfield Park*. She had Ellen's theory on literary archetypes to thank for her realization. She'd told Ellen her boyfriend theory had been genius, but Grace hadn't truly appreciated it until this moment.

"Felix, I think it all worked out for the best between us."

He frowned, like he hadn't expected that.

"Can you please show me to my table?"

He scanned the ledger in front of him. "I'm sorry, Grace, but Charlie doesn't have a reservation and we're—"

"Yeah, yeah, I know. You're booked." Grace thought back to their conversation this morning. She could have sworn Charlie said Chez Louis. They were meeting to discuss Charlie's big idea to save the store. Grace had thought about asking him to change up the location, but why should she avoid Daytona Beach's hottest new restaurant just because Felix was the manager? Especially now that she'd put their history in a new perspective.

"Can you try Mark Lockett or Andrea Jones? They're the partners at Charlie's law firm. Sometimes the secretary makes a reservation under their name."

Felix rechecked the ledger. "Actually, there *is* a reservation under Mark Lockett's name, but it's for three."

Charlie had mentioned there was someone he'd been conferring with about the store, someone who wanted to help, but he hadn't given Grace a name.

"That's us. We're supposed to be meeting a third party."

Felix snapped his fingers at a hostess. "Please seat Ms. O'Bryan right away. There will be two more guests as well." He leaned over and whispered in Grace's ear, "Call me. We have a lot to talk about."

Felix couldn't seriously believe Grace would actually call him. She pretended she didn't hear him. She followed the hostess to her table, then sat back in her chair to admire the view. The tables were covered with crisply starched linen cloths. Lit tapers surrounded by freshly cut flowers made up the centerpieces. The sweet but sad sound of violin music played in the background. The atmosphere was beautifully elegant and she couldn't help but wonder how her date with Brandon might have ended if they'd started out here instead of the Wobbly Duck.

She was perusing the wine list when the hostess seated a man in the chair across from her. Grace did a double take. "You've got the wrong table."

Brandon Farrell smiled apologetically. "There's no mistake, Grace. I'm sorry. I thought Charlie told you."

"Told me what?"

"That I'd be meeting you for dinner tonight."

"Charlie told me we were meeting with someone who wanted to *help* the store."

"I *do* want to help. Look, the least you can do is hear me out." Brandon hailed a server and ordered the most expensive bottle of wine on the menu, along with a Seven and Seven. "But first I want to explain something. That night at the Wobbly Duck, I had an epiphany."

Grace struggled not to roll her eyes.

"Doug and I have known each other since prep school and I knew he could be a jerk, but I didn't realize until that night what an asshole he is. Which makes me an even bigger asshole because I've sucked up to him all my life. I've always been that guy who wants everyone to like him. The guy who doesn't want to make waves. Dumping that pitcher of beer on my lap is the best thing anyone's ever done for me, so thank you for that, Grace."

"You're welcome." Any second now, Ashton Kutcher was going to jump out of the potted fern to her left and tell her she'd just been Punk'd.

"You don't believe me."

Brandon's drink and the bottle of wine arrived. Grace waited till they were alone again before saying, "It's not that I don't believe you, Brandon. You've already apologized and I've already accepted it. I *get* all that. I just don't get what you want from me now."

"I thought I just made it clear. I want another chance."

"Brandon—"

"I know what you're thinking. Poor little spoiled rich boy who works for his daddy. But it's not like that. My parents are good people. They didn't raise me to be a conceited moron. I achieved that all on my own. My mother would scalp me alive if she knew how I'd treated you that night at the Duck."

She had to admit, Brandon sounded sincere. And there were

the roses and the champagne to consider. If this was some sort of scam, it bordered on the Machiavellian.

"You want another chance? Okay. You probably have about ten minutes before my brother shows up, so go ahead, Brandon. Wow me."

"You mean . . . now? Here?" He glanced around the restaurant.

"Sure. Dazzle me. Tell me in fifty words or less why I should go out with you again."

"All right. I accept the challenge." He threw back his drink. "I know this is going to sound corny, but I've thought of nothing but you since that night at the Wobbly Duck. You practically saved my life! I could have choked to death, but you were willing to do the Heimlich on me even though I was behaving like a total ass. Grace," he said, reaching out to take her hand, "you make me want to be a better man."

Grace pressed her lips together.

"What? Was that more than fifty words?"

"Brandon, you do know that last line is from the movie *As Good As It Gets*, right?"

"*Damn.* I was hoping you hadn't seen it." Then he smiled and Grace had to admit, it had the desired effect he was going for. She couldn't help but laugh.

"What's so funny?"

"A week ago, I would never have believed it if you'd told me I was going to be sitting in Chez Louis eating dinner with you. I could resist the roses and even the Dom Perignon, but quoting Jack Nicholson is the final straw. I give up!"

"Does this mean you'll go out with me again?"

"Maybe. I don't know. Why don't we start back at square one and see how it goes."

"Fair enough." He picked up his drink and held it in the air, waiting. Grace raised her wine and they clinked glasses. "I'm glad we're friends again. You have no idea how much I've missed Zumba class these past few weeks."

When had Brandon become so funny?

"You pretty much sucked."

"The strange thing is, even though the reason I joined was because of you, I actually ended up liking it."

"Really? You joined because of me and you couldn't even remember my name?"

"I knew your name. But I was upset, and I admit . . . more than a little drunk on cheap beer and my own self-importance that night."

"Darlene will be thrilled to have you back in class. She misses you terribly. You were her one great challenge."

He laughed and Grace was reminded of how handsome he was. They spent the next few minutes talking about food. Brandon had an opinion on every dish on the menu, so Grace decided to let him order for her. She'd just taken a bite of their appetizer, a heavenly garlic-laden, butter-soaked escargot, when her cell phone buzzed. "Charlie, where are you?"

"Something came up at work and I'm going to have to ditch the meeting. Sorry, I feel bad about this. Is Farrell there yet?"

"He's here."

"Then he can fill you in on what we've talked about. Be nice to him, Grace. Farrell's on our side."

"Yeah, yeah." Grace snapped her phone shut. "Charlie can't make it," she told Brandon. She narrowed her eyes at him. "The two of you didn't plan this, did you?"

"You think I convinced your brother to lure you here to Chez Louis, then had him bail just so I could have you alone for dinner? That's a lot of work, don't you think? You're cute, but you're not . . ." He paused, then smiled. "*Yeah*, you're that cute."

Once upon a time she would have been flattered by his flirtation. But he seemed more friendly than serious, and she had to admit, she was beginning to like Brandon. She thought about how Joe had called Brandon an asshole. Brandon had called himself that too. But he'd also apologized for his bad behavior and all that appeared to be behind them now. Grace was a big girl. She didn't need Joe Rosenblum telling her how to think. She could make up her own mind where Brandon Farrell was concerned.

"I had no idea Charlie was your brother until he approached me last week about the store," Brandon said.

"How do you two know each other?"

"Our bank does business with his firm. He's a sharp guy."

"I agree. So let's cut to the chase. What's the deal? And make it simple."

Brandon looked impressed by her bluntness. "I'm part of a group of private investors who are interested in highway real estate. But we're not looking to turn around the land any time soon, so my proposition is this: Let my investment group buy Florida Charlie's. The store can stay as is for a guaranteed minimum of three years, with you as manager, if you'd like. We'll take responsibility for everything. At the end of the three-year term we'll either put the land up for sale or reconsider extending the time frame."

Grace felt her jaw drop. *This* was her brother's big idea to "save" Florida Charlie's?

"So what do you say, Grace? Everyone wins here. Your parents get a payout right away, and Florida Charlie's and your job stay intact for three years with no worries about making payroll or repairs on a building that, quite frankly—according to what Charlie tells me—is falling apart."

*What did she say?*

She had a lot to say.

But she'd promised Charlie she'd play nice tonight. On the other hand, Charlie wasn't here, so screw him.

Grace tried to rally *Mal Genio* to do something. Say something. Anything at all.

But the truth was . . . she wasn't angry. Because the more she thought about it, the more Brandon made sense, and once she was able to process that, all she could feel was sadness. Sadness that Charlie could be so cavalier about the whole deal that he couldn't even bother showing up to tell her about it himself. Sadness that the store her parents loved so much wouldn't be around for Grace's children to see. And most of all, strangely enough, sadness for herself.

"I appreciate you meeting with me," she told Brandon. "But I honestly don't think my father will go for that."

"That's what Charlie said, but if the two of you together convince him it's for the best, maybe you can get him to consider it." He leaned forward and lowered his voice. "If the business continues on the downward trend it's on, eventually your father will have to sell. The options might not be so good then."

# 17

# I Haven't the Least Idea
# of Loving Him, Or Anyone
# Else for That Matter

It was the Wednesday before Christmas and Luigi's was packed. Grace was the last one out of the four of them to arrive. "Did you order breadsticks?" she asked Sarah.

"Of course we did," Sarah said. "Don't worry, they should be here any minute so you can get your carb fix."

"How was the mall?" Penny asked.

Grace and Penny were splitting managerial duties at the shop today. Grace had taken the morning off to do some last-minute Christmas shopping and the afternoon would be Penny's turn.

"Ghastly. But I'm done shopping, so I can now officially enjoy the holidays."

"I have finals to grade, *then* I'll start my shopping, and I have absolutely no idea what to get my mother this year. I've never been so behind before," Ellen grumbled.

The waiter took their orders and left a basket of hot breadsticks.

"There's a kiosk near the food court where they're selling silk scarves. I bought Abuela two of them. You should check it out," she advised Ellen.

"What did you get Charlie?" Sarah asked.

"From me? He's getting a lump of coal."

She told them about Charlie's idea to sell the store and about her dinner with Brandon and how Charlie had been a no-show.

Sarah tossed her napkin across the table in disgust. "I can't believe Charlie could be so cold about this."

"Do you think your dad will go for it?" Penny asked.

"No, but . . ." Grace shrugged. "Charlie seems pretty confident. I convinced him to wait until after the holidays to approach Pop with the offer."

No one said anything for a minute.

"I finally finished the Dragon's house," Sarah said, trying to sound upbeat. "There's a couple of pieces on back order that won't come in until after the first of the year, but otherwise, it's pretty much done."

"Is it horrible looking?" Ellen asked.

"*Nothing* I decorate is horrible. The house is a real stunner, despite the floral couch in the living room. She's throwing a big housewarming party after the holidays to show it off." She paused. "She found out my divorce is almost final and she wants me to meet her *doctor son*. Which reminds me, in celebration of my upcoming divorce and spending the rest of my life being fixed up with men that no one else wants to date, I'm throwing a New Year's Eve divorce party. My place. Just the four of us."

"Her son's a doctor? You should go for it," Ellen said.

Sarah took a sip of her water. "What do you think, Grace?"

"Definitely!" Grace urged.

Sarah smiled brightly. "You're right. Maybe he won't be so bad after all."

"That's the spirit! So what are we going to do at this New Year's Eve party?" Grace asked. "Should I bring something?"

"Just your sweet self. We're going to eat chocolate fondue and drink cold champagne and watch chick flicks."

"Sounds good," said Ellen. "I'm in."

"Me too," said Penny.

"How was it being forced to have dinner with Brandon Farrell?" Sarah asked. "Did you want to stab him with a fork?" Her face got a funny look on it. "Grace, you *didn't* stab him with a fork, did you?"

"*Mal Genio* behaved beautifully. And . . . actually, we had a good time." This was met by a stunned silence that made Grace laugh. "I know, hard to believe." She went into more detail about the dinner, including Brandon's explanation of how he'd let himself be led by evil Doug, aka Iago.

"That's such a weird coincidence how both Brandon and his friend Doug were reviewed in our boyfriend club. Don't you think?" Sarah asked.

"It just goes to show how few eligible men there are in this town," Grace said. "Oh, and Felix wants me to call him."

"You're not, are you?" Ellen asked.

"He's *got* to be on drugs," Penny muttered.

"The only reason I'd ever call Felix Barberi is to make a reservation at Chez Louis. Which, by the way, you totally need if you ever plan to go there. Despite the ridiculous prices, the place has really taken off."

"So now what? The two of you are, like, friends?" Penny asked.

"Who? Me and Felix, or me and Brandon?" Before Penny could clarify, Grace continued. "Felix and I will never be friends, but yeah, I guess Brandon wants to be friends. Actually, he wants to go out again. Which, believe it or not, I'm considering. So the moral of the story is never say never. He even told me that walking out on our date was the best thing any one has ever done for him."

She tried to conjure up an image of Brandon at the Wobbly Duck, but strangely enough a vision of Joe and what lay behind that door number three of his popped into her head instead. "Get this. Brandon said I 'make him want to be a better man.' " Grace made air quotes with her fingers for the last part.

Penny and Sarah giggled.

Ellen, who'd been uncharacteristically quiet up until now, let out a large gasp. She laid down her fork and reached into her bag to pull out her iPhone.

"I told you Brandon was a nice guy," Sarah said. "So he's a follower, not a leader. The fact that he knows he's screwed up and tried so hard to make it up to you shows a lot of character."

"And anyone who can quote Jack Nicholson can't be that bad," Penny added.

Ellen cleared her throat and began reading from her iPhone screen. "'I have been a selfish being all my life, in practice, though not in principle. As a child I was taught what was right, but I was not taught to correct my temper. I was given good principles, but left to follow them in pride and conceit.'"

Grace moaned. "Ellen, are you reading *Pride and Prejudice* to us?"

"'By you, I was properly humbled. I came to you without a doubt of my reception. You showed me how insufficient were all my pretensions to please a woman worthy of being pleased.'"

"Ellen, please stop. You're scaring me," Grace said.

"You're scaring all of us," Penny muttered.

"Grace! Don't you see?" Ellen cried. "Brandon Farrell is Mr. Darcy! Number one: He's rich and handsome and seems unattainable. Number two: You have a crush on him from afar and he finally asks you out, but he disses you on the date, and you tell him you wouldn't go out with him again if he was the last man on earth. Number three: He tries to apologize in the form of flowers and champagne, but you don't buy it. Finally, and here's the really good part, he offers to help your family by buying the business and you begin to see him in a different light." She sat back in her chair and crossed her arms in triumph. "If *that* isn't a classic case of a Mr. Darcy, then what is?"

"I hate to say it, but I think Ellen is on to something," Penny said.

"No wonder we could never classify him before," Sarah said. "We didn't have all the facts. Ellen's right. He's your Mr. Darcy!"

"Brandon's offer to buy Florida Charlie's isn't some altruistic gesture," Grace pointed out. "He plans to make money off it."

"Yeah, but it's a genuine solution to the problem," Ellen said. "And by helping out the store, he's helping you out. Right?"

"Okay, I admit it, at first I was really into Brandon, but that was before our date. Now, I think he's probably potential good friend material. Honestly, I'm not interested in anyone right now."

"Women have been making speeches like that for centuries and then *bam*! They end up married to the guy they said they only liked as a friend. As far as I'm concerned, *he's* your Mr. Darcy and I'll never be convinced otherwise," Ellen said.

# 18

# The Way to a Woman's Heart Is Through Her Stuffed Alligator

"What do you think, Gator Claus, is Brandon Farrell my Mr. Darcy?"

Grace watched carefully for any change of expression on the alligator's face. The idea of Brandon being her Mr. Darcy was so ludicrous Grace wanted to laugh. But it hadn't just been Ellen who'd thought it. Penny and Sarah were on board too, which made Grace wonder if maybe, just maybe, as ridiculous as it all sounded, Ellen might be on to something.

"One day, you're going to answer me. I can wait. I'm pretty patient, although—"

"Grace?"

She stiffened. There was that voice again. Had he heard her talking to the alligator? God, she hoped not, because she really wasn't sure how to explain that one. She turned around. Joe wore a set of dark blue scrubs with a U of F sweatshirt over the top.

"Aren't you supposed to be drilling into people's mouths or something else equally sadistic?"

"You really have a problem with the drill, don't you?"

"Who doesn't? Well, except maybe people who are into *that*, but I'm not one of them."

"Too bad."

"Poor Dr. Joe. All fun and no work."

"Call me Dr. Joe again and I'll think you were serious about being just friends."

There was a directness in Joe's gaze that made Grace feel awfully warm despite the cool fifty-degree temperature outside.

"What are you doing here?" Grace asked.

"I was in the neighborhood and thought I'd stop by for that free T-shirt you promised."

*In the neighborhood?* It seemed highly unlikely he'd be eating lunch in the vicinity of Florida Charlie's in the middle of a workday. With traffic, it was at least a thirty-minute drive from his office just one way.

"Thanks again for the other night. All that stuff going on with Sarah? It really helped to talk it out."

"Have you told her yet?"

"No, and I'm not going to. She and Craig are definitely getting a divorce, so it kind of takes me off the hook."

"Maybe you should tell her anyway." Was that disapproval she heard in his voice?

"What for? It would only hurt her feelings, and she's in a bad enough place as it is." Before he could respond, she opened the front door to the store and waved him inside. "You really want a T-shirt? Come on in and I'll set you up."

They had just entered the store when a well-dressed middle-aged woman came up to Grace. "Excuse me, do you work here?"

It always amused Grace that people would ask that question, considering that she had on the Florida Charlie's uniform, but she always chalked it up to politeness.

"How can I help you?" Grace asked.

"I'll just wait over here," Joe said, making tracks for the alligator tooth display.

"I was wondering if you have any Hiawatha dolls?" The woman frowned. "Or maybe I'm not calling them by the right name?"

"I'm not sure I know what you're referring to," Grace said. "Can you describe it?"

"It's an Indian doll, or rather I guess you'd call them Native American now, but the doll was about six or maybe seven inches tall with long braids." The woman smiled ruefully. "When I was a little girl we used to come down to the beach every summer and we'd stop here at Florida Charlie's. My mother would let all us kids pick one treat from the store. One summer, I think I was about five, I picked out the Hiawatha doll, but she was too pricey. I spent the rest of that vacation begging my parents to buy me the doll."

She chuckled, in the way that adults did whenever they remembered something obnoxious they did as kids. "Mother said if I was a good girl, she'd think about it. Well, let me tell you, I was a *very* good girl, so on the way back to Atlanta—that's where I was raised—we stopped here again and she bought me the doll."

Grace could sense there was more to the story, so she smiled and waited patiently.

"We weren't in the car ten minutes before my sister, who was four at the time, decided she wanted to hold the doll. Of course I said no. She'd already picked her treat from Florida Charlie's, so why should I share my doll with her? We started to tussle in the back seat—that was before you had to wear seat belts—and Daddy started yelling for us to stop because he couldn't pay attention to the road. But my sister and I kept fighting, and even my brothers were getting into it. So Mother just turned around, plucked that doll out of my hands, and tossed her out the car window onto the highway."

Grace gasped. "That's awful," she said, smiling in sympathy.

"That was my mother," the woman said affectionately. "She told me if I couldn't share, then I didn't deserve the doll. I cried all the way home, but I never fought with my sister in the car again." Her eyes took on a faraway look. "I wish I knew where I could get one of those dolls. I've tried eBay but I've never seen one. I know it sounds silly. I'm fifty years old, but I swore if I ever saw a doll like that again, I'd buy one."

"I'm sorry I can't help you," Grace said. "I think I remember the doll you're talking about, but we haven't sold anything like that in a long time."

The woman looked disappointed but resigned. "Thanks, anyway." She strolled to the back of the store, to the Hemingway corner. Grace was still thinking about the woman's story when Joe approached her.

"That alligator tooth is pretty cool."

She studied him a moment to see if he was being sarcastic. But he wasn't.

Grace walked him through the T-shirt aisles. "Take your pick. We have the standard Florida Charlie's T-shirt that features a sketch of the front of the store, complete with Gator—um . . . complete with the alligator up front. That comes in every color you can imagine, including hot pink. But I don't think that's your color."

"No, it's not."

"Then, there's the more artsy fartsy version that features the seagulls in the background. Those we carry in muted pastels."

"Pass."

"And then finally, we have my favorite. The montage look. In one corner we have the alligator dressed in his patriotic Yankee Doodle summer outfit, the Florida Charlie's logo on the opposite side, the store image in another corner, and a mermaid at the bottom. In honor of one of our past bestsellers, the infamous mermaid-watching kit."

"I actually had one of those," Joe told her.

"A mermaid-watching kit? You're kidding."

"I think I was about six or seven at the time. We were on our way to the condo and my dad bought me one. I spent the next two weeks trying to hunt down a real honest to goodness mermaid. The old man loved it. It kept me out of his hair all vacation."

The correlation between the woman's story and Joe's made Grace smile. She was glad Joe's story had a somewhat happier ending.

"It was my childhood dream to be a mermaid in the show at Weeki Wachee," Grace confided. "But I couldn't hold my breath long enough." She found his size in the montage T-shirt and handed it to him. "Enjoy."

"Thanks," he said, tucking the rolled-up T-shirt under his arm. "If you're not too busy, would you mind showing me around? I've always wanted to get an inside look at the famous Florida Charlie's."

Why not? Business was usually slow this time of day. She guided him back to the front of the store.

"Like anything else, in order to understand it, you need to start at the beginning. In case you hadn't noticed, the place is set up like an old-fashioned general store with a sort of *Ripley's Believe it or Not* feel to it. Grandpa O'Bryan, that's my pop's dad, loved that place. We'd stop there whenever we went to St. Augustine. Charlie and I used to wander through the rooms for hours."

"My favorite was always the mirrors."

"Me too! Sometimes Sarah would come along with us. She'd stand in front of the mirror that made her look tall and I'd stand in front of the mirror that made me look short and Charlie would make fun of us. We tried to take pictures with our Polaroid but the flash always ruined the effect."

Marty interrupted them to ask Grace a question about a sunscreen shipment. He threw Joe an uneasy look and Grace introduced them. Joe shook Marty's hand and asked him about his job at the store and after a few minutes Marty was all smiles.

"Okay, so, to the left here is the citrus shop." She introduced Joe to Stella, Florida Charlie's oldest employee. "Stella has been at Florida Charlie's since our inception fifty years ago."

"I started working here when I was two," Stella said.

Joe chuckled appropriately.

"Stella works Monday through Friday, nine to two, and is our number one orange girl."

"That's Florida Charlie slang for the person who gets stuck trying to get the tourists to buy oranges," Stella explained upon seeing the confusion on Joe's face.

"Besides the hourly wage, the orange girl or guy gets a commission for anything they sell, but it's not easy work," Grace said. "All our orange juice is hand squeezed. Pop insists on it. So when you're not actively selling, you're squeezing."

"It's not so bad unless a tour bus stops. If you've been slacking instead of squeezing, then you'll be in trouble. Not that I ever slack off," Stella confided. "Everyone who comes in the store gets a free sample. Want one?" She offered Joe a small paper cup filled with orange juice. "Or do you prefer grapefruit?"

"I'll take the orange juice." Joe drained it in one swallow. "Thanks, it's delicious."

"Then, of course, you have to explain to people why the oranges cost so much when they can get them cheaper at the grocery store. So there's the spiel on how all the oranges come from local groves and they're packaged in these great crates, and we can ship them anywhere and what a wonderful gift they make and that there's a money-back guarantee. That kind of thing," Stella said. "Would you like to hear it?"

Joe looked at Grace with a smile that asked, *Didn't I just hear the spiel?* He ended up buying four of the most expensive gift arrangements and when he was bent over the counter, writing in the names and addresses of where he wanted them sent, Stella mouthed "wowza" over his head. Grace wasn't sure if Stella referred to the pricey sale she'd just made, or to Joe himself. The oranges were a terrific gift but he was doing it to be a nice guy and to impress Grace. And it was working. *Big time.*

They moved on to the hat and flip-flop aisles. Grace was about to show Joe the back section of the store, when he stopped, transfixed like a little kid who'd just entered Disney World for the first time.

"Those aren't what I think they are, are they?" He pointed to a row of funny-looking machines.

"Yep. Mold-A-Rama machines." Grace had always thought they looked like something right out of an old TV episode of *Star Trek*. "There aren't a lot of places left that still have them, but Florida Charlie's is one of them," she said proudly.

Joe fished inside the pocket of his scrub pants for change. He walked up and down, staring at the machines like he couldn't decide which one to try.

"This one makes some very nasty-looking alligators," Grace said. "And of course, we have the space shuttle machine, and this one makes dinosaurs, and this one does flamingos. And—"

"I want a dinosaur. A T. rex."

"Got two bucks?"

"I could have sworn these cost a quarter when I was a kid. Fifty cents, tops."

"Inflation," Grace said with a shrug.

Despite complaining of the cost, Joe eagerly plunked his change into the machine. The Power Forward button came on and the mold snapped together. Grace got a kick out of watching the looks on the faces of people who remembered Mold-A-Rama machines from their childhood. They looked exactly like Joe did right now, both stunned and excited. The machine made the familiar whirring sound as the liquid wax poured through the tube and into the mold. A couple of minutes later, a palm-sized, gold-colored T. rex plopped down into the sliding glass chamber. Joe bent to retrieve it.

"Careful, it's hot," Grace warned.

He picked it up anyway and brought it up to his nose. "It even smells like summer vacation."

She showed him all the different kinds of beach towels and

hats and the entire aisle of sunscreen and lotions available. He seemed impressed by the variety but he didn't show much interest again until they got to the Hemingway corner. She explained Pop's fascination with the writer and Joe picked up a couple of books and read the backs. He tucked one of them under his arm. He'd picked *The Old Man and the Sea.*

"That's Pop's favorite."

"I don't ever remember reading it," he said.

"I've never read it either. It's kind of a guy book."

She finished the tour by showing him her office.

"What does that lead to?" he asked, indicating a door across the hallway.

"That's the museum. It's what we call the storage room that holds all our outdated bestselling and not-so-bestselling junk."

She hadn't been in the room in forever, but based on Joe's reaction to the Mold-A-Rama machines, he might get a kick out of it. She opened the door and flipped on the light.

"Holy shit," Joe muttered. "Look at all this stuff." It was four hundred square feet of ceiling-to-floor shelves jammed with products from bygone eras.

"Mami—that's what I call my Mom—catalogued all this. It's all in order, from the date the product was originally sold. I bet we even have a mermaid-watching kit here." Grace searched for the most likely aisle to find it on. "Yep. Right here." She pulled one down. Inside a clear plastic cellophane bag was the "kit": a child-sized scuba mask and breathing tube, an underwater magnifying glass, and a book on mermaid lore. "These were specially prepared for the store," Grace explained. "We stopped selling them in the mid-eighties, so you probably got one of the last ones."

"How long have you worked here?" he asked, clearly impressed with her knowledge of the inventory.

"All my life. I was practically raised at Florida Charlie's. Officially, I started drawing a paycheck at fifteen. First I was a cashier, then I worked my way up to orange girl. I was pretty good at that. After I went off to college, I worked here during the summers, and then when I graduated I came on full-time, mostly as Pop's Girl Friday. For the past eight years, I've been the store's main buyer. That's the person who buys all the stuff you see here. I bet I've been to more trade shows than you've filled cavities. I also helped develop ads, filled in as manager, that kind of thing. Then, a couple of years ago, after my dad had a heart attack, I took over everything."

"Sounds like a great job."

That startled Grace. "It can be. Sometimes."

He looked like he was about to say something when her attention was drawn to a shrink-wrapped doll on the counter to her right. "Good grief!" She reached for the doll and brushed the dust off the plastic. "C'mon," she said, grabbing Joe by the hand. "I think she's still here."

Joe didn't ask questions. He followed Grace to the front of the store where the woman she'd spoken to earlier was waiting in line for Marty to ring up her purchases. "Ma'am, is this the doll you were talking about?" Grace showed her the package.

"That's her!" The woman took the doll in her hands and turned her over in amazement. "Where do you have these?"

"It was in the back, in a storage room full of old products."

"Can I buy it?"

"Actually, it's not in the store's computer system, but since you remember her, you can have her, free of charge."

"Oh! Thank you. Thank you so much! My sister . . . she's . . . she's going to love this."

Joe waited till the woman left the store. "What was that about?"

"Customer relations," Grace said, thinking about the expression on the woman's face when she talked about her sister. There was another story there, Grace was certain of it. Funny, if Joe hadn't stopped by the store today, Grace wouldn't have had a reason to check out the "museum" and the woman wouldn't have gotten her doll. It was like the two events were intertwined somehow.

"Would you mind ringing this up for me?" he asked, holding up the book. "I wish I could stay longer but I need to get back to work."

"It's a freebie." Joe began to protest. "No, really, you spent a small fortune in oranges. Take the book," she said.

"Customer relations?"

"You got it."

"So what are you doing New Year's Eve? Because I've been invited to a party and I'd like you to go with me." There was no pretense that this was a friends anything. It was a date, pure and simple.

She almost said yes. And then she remembered Sarah's party. "I'm sorry, but I already have plans. I'm going to Sarah's for New Year's Eve. It's an all-girl thing. Chocolate fondue and champagne and chick flicks. Sarah's divorce will be final right after Christmas, and even though she's come to terms with it, it's still going to be a sucky time for her. I'm her best friend, so I have to go."

He nodded like he understood, but deep down she wondered if he thought he was being blown off. Grace walked him back to the store's entrance just as Pop and Mami and Abuela came through the front doors. They'd been out shopping, Mami explained, and Pop had insisted they stop by.

"So, Tomato, how's business been today?" Pop asked.

Joe smiled at her. *Tomato?*

*Ha. Ha. Yes, Tomato*, her expression said. She smiled back at him and it felt like they'd just shared a secret joke.

"Business has been okay," she said. She introduced Joe to the family.

"So you're the guy who took over for Dr. Fred, huh? Nice of you to stop by the shop." Pop shook his hand and when he saw Joe had a copy of *The Old Man and the Sea*, his face lit up and the two of them talked Hemingway for a few minutes. Then Joe spoke in Spanish to Mami and Abuela and Grace thought both of them might melt into puddles right there on the floor.

Later, after Joe left with his T-shirt and his book and his wax T. rex safely wrapped up in tissue paper, Abuela made a point of finding out more about him. "He's so handsome! And he seems like a very nice young man."

Grace thought about the past hour Joe had just spent in the store. It felt more like a date than any date she'd ever been on. Men had bought her flowers, candy, and now even bottles of Dom Perignon, but no one had ever wooed her like Joe. If she thought his interest in the store had been strictly for her benefit, then it wouldn't have made such an impact. But he'd been genuinely charmed by Florida Charlie's and that, in turn, had charmed *her*. It was the most potent aphrodisiac Grace had ever encountered. She'd told the girls she wasn't interested in anyone, but she couldn't lie to herself anymore. She was interested in Joe.

"Abuela, do you . . . do you remember telling me about the dream? About my future husband?"

"Of course I remember."

Grace waited for Abuela to say something. "Oh," Abuela said, after a few seconds. "You want to know if your dentist friend is the one I saw in the dream?"

"Well, just for fun. I mean, I don't really—"

"Is he the one who sent you the flowers?"

Grace shook her head no.

"I'm sorry, Gracielita, he's not the one. But he might make a nice husband for your friend Ellen."

# 19

# What Are Men to Champagne and Chocolate?

The chocolate fondue was sinful. The champagne wasn't Dom Perignon but it was cold and bubbly and delicious. And the company was, without doubt, the very best. It should have been a recipe for a successful New Year's Eve party. So why was Grace miserable? It wasn't that she didn't love her friends. But New Year's Eve was meant for glittery cocktail dresses and handsome men dressed in tuxedos and waiters carrying trays of exotic hors d'oeuvres while a band played the kind of stuff Michael Bublé sang in the background.

Grace speared a fat strawberry onto a skewer, dipped it into the dark, velvety mixture, and wondered if a chocolate-covered strawberry still counted as a fruit serving or if it rolled over into the dessert category.

"This is so much better than sex," Ellen said, pulling a chocolate-covered marshmallow out of the fondue pot.

"Nothing is better than sex," Penny muttered. "Except maybe a cigarette." Before anyone could say anything, Penny put both hands up in surrender. "Which I'm giving up! Again. It's my New Year's resolution."

Ellen stuffed the chocolate marshmallow in her mouth. "I'm going on a diet. Starting tomorrow. Or rather, the day after tomorrow, since I plan to continue eating until well after midnight."

"I'm going to journal," Sarah said. "A lot of books on divorce therapy recommend it."

"What about you, Grace?" Penny asked. "What's your New Year's resolution?"

"I don't know. There are so many things I need to improve on, it's a little daunting trying to narrow it down to just one or two. I know I want to learn to cook. But not that fancy stuff on TV. I want to cook what Mami makes, so that I can pass it down to my own kids. If I ever have any, that is." She waited till the chocolate hardened on her strawberry before she took a nibble. "Ellen, tell us who you've been having mediocre sex with, so I can cross him off my potential boyfriend list."

Sarah and Penny started giggling.

Grace smiled. "You didn't think I was going to let that comment slide, did you? I love chocolate-covered marshmallows as much as the next girl, but better than sex? I don't think so."

Of the four of them, Ellen was the most secretive about her love life, but she now looked resigned to the fact that she was going to have to talk.

"You remember I told you about the IT guy who was revamping all the computers on campus? I went out with him a few times."

"Ellen, I'm shocked!" Sarah said. "A *few* times? And you gave it up that easily? What happened to your ten-date rule?"

"The ten-date rule is only good if you actually go out ten times. I haven't had more than four consecutive dates with the same guy in almost three years."

"That's because you're not giving it up fast enough," Penny said.

"Was it that bad?" Sarah asked.

Ellen reached for another marshmallow. "He was all right. But he certainly wasn't—"

"Heathcliff!" the three of them shouted.

"Honestly, Ellen," Grace said, "if you're going to have a crush on a fantasy hero, why him?"

"I have to agree with Grace," said Sarah. "What's the fascination? Because I don't get it. He's, like . . . sadistic."

"I know Heathcliff isn't perfect," Ellen said. "But nobody is, not *even* Mr. Darcy, which Grace would know all about since she has her own live version of him." Grace started to protest but Ellen made a *shut it, you* gesture with her thumb and four fingers.

"You want to know what I love so much about Heathcliff? It's not Heathcliff himself; you're right when you say he's over-the-top. What I love about *Wuthering Heights* is the unbelievable passion that he and Catherine shared. The feeling that there's someone out there who is so utterly perfect for you, and you alone, that you feel that you're actually *that person*. It's like when Catherine says, 'Whatever our souls are made of, his and mine are the same.'" Ellen paused. "Who wouldn't want that? Even the title of the book tells it like it is. *Wuthering Heights*. Wild crazy passion. That's what I want. And honestly, I'd rather be single for the rest of my life if I can't have that kind of love."

"Shit." Sarah looked dazed by Ellen's stirring speech. "And all this time I thought the title only referred to that creepy old estate. I need to read *Wuthering Heights* again!"

"I need to read it for the first time," Grace said. And this time they all laughed, except for Penny, who had something suspiciously like tears in her eyes. Penny, who never cried for anything.

"Pen! What's wrong?" Sarah asked.

"Butch asked me to marry him." She looked at Grace, who encouraged her on with a smile. She was glad Penny was finally going to confide in Sarah and Ellen about Butch's proposal.

"Penny!" Ellen squealed.

"I turned him down."

"*What?*" Ellen and Sarah said in unison.

Sarah shook her head. "I thought you loved Butch!"

"I do love him," Penny said. "It's just . . ." She shrugged and looked away.

Grace knew how hard it was for Penny to talk about her feelings. But she suddenly understood why Penny had turned down Butch's proposal. It didn't have anything to do with any bad karma Grace might have accidentally leaked out into the universe.

"Penny wants the big gesture, the grand passion. She wants . . . well, she wants Heathcliff," Grace said.

Penny nodded. "Not Heathcliff, exactly, but Grace is right. I want Butch to be so crazy about me that he couldn't imagine living without me. I don't want to be that chick who gives her boyfriend the 'propose or else' ultimatum, which is exactly how the whole thing went down."

"Every woman wants a grand passion in her life," Ellen said wistfully.

Penny blinked away the tears from her eyes. "Speaking of passion, what's going on with you and the dentist?" she asked Grace. "Have you gone out with him again?"

Penny was changing the subject, the way she did whenever she couldn't handle whatever was going on. It was no use trying to redirect the conversation back to Butch. Penny would talk about it again when she was ready, and not a second sooner. End of story.

"When did Grace go out with the dentist?" Ellen asked, frowning. "The one who pretended he didn't know her after trying to pick her up the Wobbly Duck?"

"You're not the only one who can keep secrets," Grace told Ellen. "Only it's not a secret because it's not a big deal. Joe and I have decided to keep it on a strictly friends basis. Going out for coffee, a casual dinner, that sort of thing." She decided to omit the fact that he'd asked her out for tonight. And that she'd wanted to say yes.

"So . . . what do we want to watch next?" Sarah asked in an overly cheery voice. "There's *Sleepless in Seattle*—"

"They don't meet till the end," Penny said.

"How about we just watch the ball drop? It's almost midnight," Grace suggested.

"Already?" Sarah glanced at the clock. "Tonight has gone by so fast!"

*Not fast enough.*

Grace lanced another strawberry. Not that she regretted her decision to turn down Joe's invitation. Sarah needed the support of her friends, and since Grace was her best friend, it would have been totally traitorous of her not to be here. But she still couldn't help wondering if Joe had asked someone else to the party.

Sarah kept flipping stations until a view of Times Square popped on the screen. The crowd looked happy and a little drunk and a whole lot cold. It was cold in central Florida tonight too. At least cold enough for the natives to feel the bite. Which meant it was probably in the forties.

Ten . . . nine . . ." the crowd in Times Square chanted.

"Hold on! We need more champagne," Ellen said. She went around the room, refilling their flutes.

Sarah raised her glass in the air. Her blue eyes looked misty. "A toast. To old friends."

"Two . . . one . . . Happy New Year!" the announcer yelled. And everyone in Times Square began kissing everyone, and all Grace could think of was who was Joe kissing right now. She set down her champagne without tasting it.

Sarah grabbed her in a hug, and soon all four of them were hugging, and now even Sarah was crying. Only the tears weren't happy ones, and Grace couldn't help but feel her own eyes water up. At this rate, they'd all end up having to buy stock in Kleenex.

n't worry about you?" Grace wanted to throttle her. How she *not* worry about her? "Say you'll come. Everyone will sappointed if you don't show up."

Maybe," Sarah said. She waited at the door while Grace med up the engine to her car and waved her off.

t was twelve thirty, too early for most people to be leaving New Year's Eve party, so the streets of Daytona were mostly ear. Every once in a while the sound of a distant firecracker roke through the silence in her car.

Why had she left Sarah's? She wasn't sleepy. Not by a long shot. As if on autopilot her car drove down the street that led to her neighborhood, but instead of driving to her house she went to Joe's. There were no lights on inside his town house and his Range Rover wasn't in the open garage.

Grace banged her head against the steering wheel. "Stupid! What did you think? Because you'd turned him down he didn't go to the party? He probably took a date. A really hot date. He's probably bringing her home tonight and *she* won't want to just be friends and—"

A knock on the car window made her jump.

*Crap!*

Joe opened the door and looked past her to the empty passenger seat. "Who are you talking to?"

"I . . . I was singing along to the radio."

He glanced at the unlit dashboard. "Are you okay? It's cold. Let's go inside."

He ushered her into his town house and flipped on a light.

"Where did you come from?" she asked. "I thought you were going to a party tonight."

"The party was just a mile down the road. I've had a few beers and I didn't want to chance being pulled over. So I walked home. I'll get my car in the morning."

"Oh, that makes sense." She tugged on the end of her sweater

"It's not about Craig," Sarah said, snit. want him to be happy. But Penny got me tl I want a grand passion in my life too."

"I know, sweetie," Ellen said, rubbing S sighed. "Another New Year, another year of bei.

"Well now, that's just damn morose," Sarah sa tears away in an angry gesture. "And I refuse to al. be depressed, even though I think New Year's Eve i the most depressing holiday there is!"

"'Auld Lang Syne' is the worst song *ever*," Grace sa.

"I agree," Penny said. "Whatever it means, it sucks."

"Okay, now that the sad stuff is out of the way, which did we decide on?" Sarah asked, looking like she hadn'. been crying less than a minute ago.

Sarah had an incredible way of compartmentalizing her fe ings. Ten minutes of feeling down and getting all those bad emc tions out and she was good to go. But Grace couldn't function like that.

"I say we blind pick," said Ellen. She closed her eyes and reached for the pile of DVDs and pulled out *The Philadelphia Story*.

"Excellent selection," said Penny. "Cary Grant, Jimmy Stewart. What could be better?"

Grace got up and stretched her arms above her head. "I think I'm going to call it a night. Tomorrow or rather today is a holy day of obligation and we're doing the family Mass thing to be followed by the traditional O'Bryan New Year's Day brunch, which you're all invited to, by the way." Penny was a definite yes, Ellen was planning to sleep in, and Sarah didn't commit one way or the other.

Grace gave Sarah another hug on her way out the door. "Come by the house. *Please*. We've avoided it all night, but the fact is Craig is getting married today and you shouldn't be alone."

"Don't worry about me. I'll be fine."

in a nervous gesture. Was Joe drunk? He didn't seem drunk. He didn't even seem tipsy. "I was just driving by and thought I'd wish you a Happy New Year," she explained. "Then I saw that your car wasn't here and I was just about to leave, when you . . . you know, snuck up on me again."

"I'm glad I didn't miss you."

"Yeah, me too."

There was a book facedown on his couch. It was the copy of *The Old Man and the Sea* that he'd bought at the store.

"So how was the party?" she asked, trying to sound casual. She couldn't meet his eyes. What must he think of her, showing up at his place this time of the night? She knew what she would think if the situation had been reversed.

"It was all right. How was Sarah's party?"

"It wasn't really a party. Like I said, it was just a girl thing."

"It's good," Joe said, following her gaze to the book. "You can borrow it if you'd like. Since you've never read it."

"Thanks. Yeah, maybe I'll do that."

They stood there for a few seconds, not saying anything. He wore jeans and a white button-down shirt with a black blazer and loafers, no socks. His hair looked like it needed a trim, and she was reminded of her first impression of him. An older version of a preppy, brooding Abercrombie and Fitch model.

"So, Happy New Year," she said.

"I thought it was customary to kiss someone when you wish them a Happy New Year."

"Oh, yeah . . . sure." She stretched up and gave him a peck on the cheek.

He looked unimpressed. Insulted, almost.

"What?"

"I'm not your damn brother, Grace."

He didn't sound angry, more like frustrated. It was startling to realize that she, on the other hand, *was* angry.

She was angry at Sarah. Although for what, Grace had no idea, but there it was. Finally out in the open, pulled from somewhere inside her subconscious, and she didn't even know she was feeling it until this very moment. There was something not right about Sarah's divorce. But she didn't trust Grace enough to confide in her about it.

She was angry at Joe too. Because he was beautiful and smart and funny and she wanted to find just *one* thing wrong with him. Just one thing that would put them on an even playing field. And because he'd known from the start that whatever there was between them wasn't just friendship.

But mostly she was angry with herself. Because she wanted Joe. Even if he wasn't the one, according to Abuela's dream. And, silly as it sounded, because she didn't believe in any of that woo-woo stuff, some part of her sensed that Abuela was right. Joe wasn't the guy she was supposed to end up with. And she'd never made love with anyone where the possibility hadn't at least existed that he *could* be the one.

"Who did you take to the party tonight?" She hated how insecure she sounded, but she had to know.

"I asked the only girl I wanted to take. She shot me down."

Her heart stopped. Or maybe it was her lungs. She wasn't sure.

"No, she didn't." Grace reached up and wrapped her arms around his neck and took all the anger and confusion and suppressed lust she'd been feeling and channeled it into a kiss.

Like everything else Joe did, it was perfect. The summa cum laude of kisses. It was tongues and moans and bodies pressing up against each other. It was the kiss every girl dreamed of whenever she fantasized about the guy who was supposed to sweep her off her feet. Rhett kissing Scarlett by the roadside. Mark Darcy kissing Bridget Jones in the middle of a snowy London street.

He began walking her backward, his kisses turning her from a solid into a warm liquid caramel, all bubbly and hot and easy to slide around, just like the sugar in her flan. Since the layout of his place was exactly like hers, her body automatically understood where they were going.

They tumbled onto the bed. Joe reached over and turned on a light. Grace thought about asking him to turn it off, but she didin't want to come across as a prude. So what if she had some cellulite on the back of her thighs? No one was perfect . . .

He slipped her sweater over her head and began to nuzzle her breasts through her thin camisole.

"Joe?" she asked, stunned that she still had a voice left.

"Hmmm?"

"Before we . . . before we do this, can I ask you a question?"

"Nightstand," he muttered, his mouth hovering over her breast. "Condoms are in the top drawer."

"That's great. But it's not the question."

He looked excited, hungry, nervous. A combination of all three. She liked knowing she wasn't the only one who felt conflicted.

"I'll tell you anything. I'll *do* anything. As long as it doesn't involve getting out of this bed." He got rid of her camisole next and started in on her jeans.

"Tell me one thing that's wrong with you."

He laughed painfully. "Grace, I'm far from perfect. Stick around and you'll discover that on your own."

"You see, that's like the *most* perfect answer you could give. Modesty is a huge turn on," she said, tugging his shirt loose from his pants. She didn't want to be the only one naked.

"You want a flaw? I'm impatient as hell."

"I don't know if that really qualifies—"

"Grace," he said, beginning to sound desperate, "you're beautiful, but sometimes you talk too much."

She started to say something, but then he kissed her again and she thought Joe was right. Sometimes she did talk too much.

Grace woke up to the sound of a car engine. She opened her eyes. Joe was still asleep. Blissfully, peacefully, sound asleep. According to the clock on the nightstand it was almost eleven thirty. She had fifteen minutes, tops, to leave and still make it to Mass in time. Carefully, she slid out from beneath his arm and gathered her clothes off the floor.

Should she wake him up before she left? It seemed rude not to say good-bye. But they'd just fallen asleep a few hours ago, and he looked so, well . . . worn out. Joe hadn't exaggerated about the "hours of hot, sweaty sex."

She tiptoed to the kitchen, found a caffeinated sports drink in the refrigerator, a blank sheet of paper, and a pen. She'd never been in this situation before and a simple "thanks and see you later" didn't seem sufficient. She took a few sips of the drink, thought about it some, and began writing.

*Dear Joe,*

*Because you place such importance on satisfaction surveys, I thought I'd fill one out regarding last night's activities. In case you're looking for feedback in order to improve future performances (pun intended).*

*Foreplay: 10*

*A note of general interest: When using your mouth, you might want to be a tad more careful during bathing suit season. Luckily, that's not for a few more months because I'm fairly certain that I'm now the proud owner of a hickie on my left inner thigh. Not that I'm complaining, because the events surrounding my acquiring that particular little love bite were, to say the least, spectacular. Really. There are no words to describe it. They don't teach you that kind of oral technique in dental school, do they?*

*Actual Consummation: (please note there are three separate scores here because I believe that each separate consummated act deserves its own individual mark).*

*8, 9, 10*

*I know you have a thing about tens, but honestly, eight is a perfectly respectable score. Better than respectable, actually.*

*Now, for a confession about encounter number two. Will I reveal a lack of sexual sophistication, or of my former partners (not that there have been that many), to admit that I've never actually tried that position before last night? To be honest, I really didn't think it could be done.*

*As for encounter number three. It was . . . lovely.*

*Afterplay (the definition of this should be self-evident): General overall score: 10.*

*Can I just say that you make the best grilled cheese sandwich I've ever had? And that you look drop-dead gorgeous in your boxers while cooking it?*

*Oh, and one more thing. I'm happy to report that I did find something wrong with you. Joe, has no one ever told you before that you snore? Don't worry, it's not some big obnoxious noise, more like a gentle purring kind of whirl. I just thought I'd mention it, in case it ever comes up again. Then you have a legitimate fault you can lay claim to.*

*Sincerely,*
*Grace.*


*P.S. Since you expressed concern earlier in our relationship regarding the size of your turkey, let me assure you that it's neither too big, nor too small. It is just right.*

# 20

# Clueless Is Not Just the Name of a Movie

"Grace, when are we going to talk to Pop about the offer?" Charlie was in her kitchen, snooping through the cupboards. Grace had approximately ten minutes to finish getting ready before Sarah arrived to pick her up.

"Don't you buy your own groceries?" Grace asked her brother. "You make at least four times what I do."

"It's more fun to mooch off you."

"I thought we agreed to wait until after the holidays to talk to Pop?" Grace said.

"We're already into the first week of January. What holiday are you waiting for?"

"I have to tell you, Charlie, I think it's a waste of time talking to Pop. He isn't going to go for it."

"He won't if you come in with that kind of attitude. Farrell made us a good offer. We should convince Pop to take it before it's too late."

Grace tried to ignore the sour sensation she got in her stomach every time she thought about talking to Pop about Charlie's idea to sell the store. "All right. But you do all the talking, and I'll just nod like a puppet."

Charlie opened her fridge. "When did you stop buying milk?"

Grace ignored him and slipped into her bedroom, threw off her bathrobe, and donned her new black dress. Some lipstick, a splash of perfume, and she looked as good as she could hope to. Tonight was the January boyfriend club meeting. Afterward, instead of going to Coco's with the girls, she was going out for a drink with Joe. She'd been at the mall, looking for something new to wear, and had found an exact replica of the little black dress Sarah had loaned her for her date with Brandon. Only this one was in Grace's size. No tugging on the hem for her tonight.

She walked back to the living area to find Charlie digging into her hidden stash of Oreos. "Where's the rest of the dress?"

"You like?" Grace couldn't resist doing a twirl around.

"Farrell said the two of you hit it off pretty well the other night at dinner. Anything I should know about? Because if you're dating him, I approve. Not of the dress. But the guy's okay. He's also loaded."

"Is money all you think about?"

"I would say money is number two on my list."

"Since we're talking sex, anyone special in your life, Charlie?"

"You're the one who looks like she's got that covered. Not that I want to hear about it, but is it Farrell? And if it's not, when do I meet him?"

The doorbell rang. Two seconds later Sarah walked in before anyone could answer, the way she always did. "Wow! That dress looks identical to the one I loaned you."

Charlie attempted to muss Sarah's hair but she dodged him. "You got a dress like that, squirt? How come I've never seen it?"

"Maybe because I've never been out on a date with you?"

"Not true. Your senior prom. I came home from school even though I'm sure there was something better going on. I got you an orchid for a corsage. Don't tell me you've forgotten? I'm heartbroken."

Sarah rolled her eyes. "That was a mercy date."

Grace stared at the two of them, torn between wanting to laugh and kick herself at her own stupidity. *Sarah and Charlie.* Why had she never seen it before?

"So turn around," Sarah ordered. Grace happily obliged. "I can't wait to see the look on his face when you walk out in that."

"Whose face?" Charlie asked. "Just so you know, I'm feeling very left out here, girls."

"Good thing there's a whole box of Oreos to console yourself with." Grace picked up her purse and headed for the door. "If you're going to stay to raid my refrigerator, please lock up."

"Don't come crying on my doorstep if you catch a cold on account of that dress!" Charlie yelled.

They were almost to the store when Grace broached the subject she'd been thinking about ever since Charlie had brought up senior prom.

"Sarah, what do you think of Charlie?"

Sarah kept her eyes on the road. "What do you mean?"

"He's cute, isn't he? Since he's my brother, I can never think of him objectively in those terms, but women always seem to go for him."

"He's all right, I guess."

*All right?* It wasn't exactly glowing praise. Grace tried another approach.

"Okay, remember in *Little Women*, how everyone thinks that Jo and Laurie are a sure thing? But in the end, it's Amy who ends up with Laurie. And there are tiny clues here and there, but you don't see it until all of a sudden, and then it becomes obvious that Amy and Laurie were meant to be together all along."

"What does *Little Women* have to do with Charlie?"

"I always thought that stupid grammar school shtick you and Charlie do was just a friendly throwback to when we were kids, but I don't know. Tonight I was watching his face, and I could have sworn—"

"Grace, that's *never* going to happen." The quiet intensity in Sarah's voice took Grace by surprise. If anything, she'd expected Sarah to laugh at the suggestion, not appear so adamantly against it.

"Why not?"

Sarah pulled into Grace's private parking spot behind the store and turned in her seat to face her. "Because it just isn't. I'm not Amy and Charlie isn't Laurie. Life doesn't work like that. We aren't characters from some novel. Ellen's got you brainwashed into believing that computer program crap of hers!"

Neither of them made a motion to get out of the car. They watched silently as car after car filed into the parking lot. How stupid and insensitive could Grace get? She knew Sarah was having a hard time with this divorce. Much as she hated to admit it, Sarah wasn't over Craig yet.

"It looks like there's going to be a big crowd again," Sarah said, her voice subdued.

"I told Ellen not to put up any more flyers. I hope she listened."

"Grace . . . why did you bring that up about Charlie and me?"

"I'm sorry, Sarah. I wasn't thinking. But you're my best friend, he's my brother. You're both single now and I thought, why not?"

"But why *now*? Why not five years ago?"

"I don't know, because I'm dense?" She laughed, expecting Sarah to laugh too. Only she didn't. "Maybe because the timing has never been right? You always had a boyfriend or Charlie was off in law school or something. And now I guess the timing is *really* messed up because even though you're free, Charlie's moving to Miami—"

"*What?*"

Grace sucked in a breath. She'd never broken Charlie's confidence before, but this was Sarah and she was going to find out anyway. "That's supposed to be a secret, but I'm sure Charlie won't care if you know. His firm is opening up an office in Miami and they want Charlie to head it. It's a good opportunity. But he hasn't told Mami and Pop yet, so don't say anything around the family."

"When is he leaving?"

"Not till May, I think. He promised me he'll still be here to help with Abuela when Mami and Pop go to Europe in April for their anniversary. Which I really hope he comes through on, because frankly, I'm tired of Charlie making promises he never keeps."

Sarah pulled the key out of the ignition. "I'm getting cold," she said. "Let's go inside."

Penny met them at the door. "It appears that our *membership committee* has been at it again," she grumbled. "Where are we going to put them all?"

There had to be at least fifty women in the store. Some of them were browsing through the aisles, looking at the merchandise. A small crowd had gathered in front of the Mold-A-Rama machines. "Does anyone have change?" Grace heard one of the women ask.

Grace slipped her heels off and she and Sarah and Penny moved another shelf out of the way to make more room in the Hemingway corner. "Maybe we should keep one of the cash registers open, in case anyone wants to buy something," Penny joked.

"How do we know someone isn't going to rip off the merchandise?" Sarah asked.

"Sarah has a point. There are a lot of strangers loose in the shop," Penny said.

Grace had never considered that before, but other than Ellen's friends from the college, Grace didn't know any of these women. She was going to have to put a stop to this now.

A minute later Ellen came flying down the aisles, her face

flushed, her glasses on top of her head. She had two computer bags, one looped over each shoulder. "I swear I didn't promote the club! We took down every flyer we could find."

"Then where did all these women come from?" Grace asked.

"Word of mouth?"

"I say we toss some of 'em out the door," Penny said.

"We can't do that," Ellen said, "it wouldn't be right."

"We're going to have to find another place to hold the meetings," Grace said.

"I'll start looking first thing Monday morning. I promise." Ellen eyed Grace's outfit. "Wow! You look great. I guess you're definitely going to Coco's tonight, huh?"

"Grace has got a hot date tonight," Penny said.

"With Mr. Darcy?"

"With the dentist," Sarah said.

"The dentist? I thought you two were keeping it casual. Just friends. Isn't that what you said New Year's Eve?"

"Get with the program. A lot has happened over the past week," Sarah said. "If you'd been to lunch at Luigi's on Wednesday, you would have heard all about Grace's New Year's Eve fireworks."

"Damn faculty meeting," Ellen muttered. She gave Grace one of her bags. "Here, give me a hand." She began pulling out the familiar items—her laptop and her yellow legal pad. "Going out with the dentist is a waste of time, Grace. The facts all point to Brandon being your Mr. Darcy."

She thought about what Sarah had said in the car, about Grace being brainwashed by Ellen's computer program. It's not that Grace believed it one hundred percent, because she didn't. It was an empowerment tool, and mostly for fun. But still . . . Ellen had been spot-on about Felix being a Henry Crawford. Grace wondered who Joe's literary equivalent would be.

"We'll see," she said humoring Ellen. "So why did you bring two computers?"

"Janine volunteered to take notes. That way I can concentrate on running the meeting." She paused. "Unless you'd like to do it. After all, it's your club."

It was true. Technically the idea for the club had been Grace's. But since Ellen was the one who knew all about the computer program, it made more sense for her to preside over the meetings. "No, you go ahead."

The meeting flowed the same way the last one did. They went around the room and all the members introduced themselves, which took up more time because of all the extra women. Grace shuffled uneasily in her chair.

With everything going on—Joe, the holidays, worrying about the future of the store—she'd forgotten to tell Pop about the meetings. Not that Grace thought Pop would mind, but having all these people in the store after hours was suddenly making Grace uneasy. Shoplifting was one concern, but what if someone slipped and fell and hurt themselves? Could they sue Florida Charlie's? She hadn't thought of that before.

A group of women were passing around a bottle of wine. Hadn't Ellen put a message up on the Yahoo! site asking women not to bring alcohol? Grace hadn't been to the site since their first meeting, but she was certain Ellen wouldn't have forgotten something that important.

Grace stood up to remind them of the no-liquor policy.

"Ah! Excellent!" Ellen cried. "Tell us about him, Grace."

Forty-nine-plus sets of eyes turned to stare at her.

"Tell you about who?"

"Your new boyfriend," Ellen said. "I asked for volunteers and you were the first one to stand up."

"Oh, I guess I wasn't paying attention. The reason I stood up was to make a no-alcohol announcement. I'm the manager here at Florida Charlie's and we can't have alcohol on the premises."

A light scattering of boos filled the air, some good-natured, some not.

"We brought alcohol to the last meeting," one woman said, making a hostile show of recorking her wine bottle.

"Yeah," echoed several others.

"I know, but I've decided that—"

"Who are *you* to decide?" someone asked. "Why don't we put it to a vote?"

The room began to buzz in agreement.

"I'm sorry, but this isn't a democracy," Grace said. "I'm the manager of the store and what I say goes." She looked to Ellen for support, but Ellen was typing something into her computer.

After a few seconds, Ellen looked up, sensed that something unpleasant was going on, and plastered a smile on her face. "Whatever Grace said, she's right."

*Whatever Grace said*? Obviously Ellen had been too preoccupied putting data into her computer to follow the conversation, but her decree mollified the women into silencing their objections.

"Thank you for your cooperation," Grace said. "It's just that—"

"*Yes, yes*, we get it. Now tell us about your boyfriend. Or sit down and let someone else have a turn," said a woman with short blond hair and glasses.

Grace stared at the woman. Of all the rude . . .

"I don't actually have a boyfriend, not at the moment. At least, I don't think of him as my boyfriend. We've just started seeing each other and—"

"Are you going to stand there and blabber all night or are you going to get to the point?" someone shouted. Grace thought she recognized the voice, although she couldn't be sure. Where was all this sudden animosity coming from? It couldn't all stem from her no-alcohol announcement, could it?

"All right, his name is Joe Rosenblum. He's . . . well, he's pretty terrific."

This was met with disbelieving laughter.

"Grace is in what I like to refer to as the 'honeymoon' phase of the relationship," Ellen explained to the crowd. "It's normal at this point to be unrealistically infatuated."

*Unrealistically infatuated?* Grace tried to keep her voice steady. "I know what you're all thinking. But the fact is, he's handsome, and kind, and funny, and smart and—"

"Boy, do you have it bad," someone yelled.

"This is actually quite good," said Ellen. "Remember, the purpose of the club isn't to bash the men we've dated; it's to provide reviews so that we can all benefit from each other's experiences. Let's say, a few months from now Grace and Joe are broken up and one of you decides to go out with him. It will be nice to know that he's a decent guy. Unless of course, Grace needs to amend his file. Okay, let's have some stats."

"I can provide those," came the familiar unwelcome voice. Grace recognized it now. She searched the group until she spotted the face she was looking for. It was Melanie, the Nazi receptionist from Sunshine Smiles.

"Melanie, what are you doing here?" Grace asked.

# 21

# Vanity Working on a Weak Head
# Produces Every Sort of Disaster

"Joining the club, of course," said Melanie, her Angelina Jolie lips looking moist and pouty. It *had* to be collagen implants. No one looked that good while they were scowling. Except maybe Angelina Jolie. Grace tried to think of a reason to refuse Melanie membership, but there wasn't any except for the fact that Grace didn't like her.

"May I go on?" Melanie asked.

The women all turned in their seats to hear Grace's response.

"By all means," Grace said. She grit her teeth and tried for a smile.

"Where was I? Joe is thirty-two, six foot two and a half, never been married, has light brown hair . . . only the brown is an illusion. When he's outside and it catches the sun, you see all these streaks of blond that really bring out his blue eyes. And he has a beautiful smile. Did I already tell you he's a dentist? When he smiles these absolutely gorgeous dimples pop out on his lower cheeks. He's a fabulous sportsman. He plays rugby. I believe his position is loose head prop. Or maybe it's tight head prop. I get those two confused." Melanie giggled like a little girl. "I've seen him play several times but I have to confess I'm not too sure what goes on other than a lot of running and bashing into one other!"

Six foot two and a half? *A half?* What had Melanie done? Measured him? And when had Melanie seen Joe play rugby? Grace had no clue what position Joe played, let alone what a loose head prop or a tight head prop was.

"Is there anything you'd like to add to that, Grace?" Ellen asked.

"Yeah, tell us more about Mr. Perfect," said a woman to Grace's right. This remark produced a few snickers.

"I never said he was perfect," Grace said. "Joe has his faults too."

Ellen began fiddling with her computer again. "Like what?"

"Like . . . you know, he snores, stuff like that."

Melanie gasped.

Sarah gave her a *what the hell?* kind of look.

Grace could only shrug helplessly.

"Snoring is more a personal habit than a characteristic," Ellen said, "and frankly, we'd probably have to put it down for the majority of men, so we'll ignore that one."

Grace had to admit to being more than just a little peeved right now. Why had she let herself be manipulated into reviewing Joe? And why had she felt the urge to one-up Melanie with the sort of detail about Joe that could only mean Grace had slept with him?

"Handsome, kind, funny, smart," Ellen said, oblivious to anything other than collecting data for her boyfriend project. "I'm afraid you're going to have to provide more information, Grace, because right now the man is coming out to be a mix between Brad Pitt and the Pope."

This produced a round of laughter. Grace could feel her face go hot.

"You want more information? Okay, here goes. Joe graduated summa cum laude from dental school, then joined the Peace Corps, where he was stationed in Guatemala. After providing dental care to the poor, he spent a year traveling the world. As Melanie has already said, he's an excellent sportsman, *and*, he cooked Thanksgiving dinner for his mother." Grace wanted to shout "Top that, Herr Melanie!" Only everything Grace had just told the group except for the part about Joe cooking Thanksgiving dinner could be gotten off Dr. Fred's letter, so it couldn't really be deemed personal.

"Too. Good. To. Be. True." Ellen said, typing away again. She paused, then looked up at Grace in concern. "Oh, no, it's just as I suspected. He's a Wickham."

"A what?"

"He's George Wickham, the villain from *Pride and Prejudice*."

The women began murmuring in agreement.

"No, he's not!"

If Ellen started quoting *Pride and Prejudice*, Grace wouldn't be responsible for what happened next.

"Grace," Ellen said gently, "don't you remember telling us he tried to pick you up at the Wobbly Duck? Only to pretend that he'd never seen you before when you went to his office practically the very next day? You yourself even said he was some kind of actor. I know you don't want to hear this, but what's the purpose of the club if we can't be honest? The signs are all there. On the surface, this guy seems perfect. Yet we know for a fact that he's capable of deceit. He's hiding something. The fact that he's overcompensated by all his other achievements means that whatever he's hiding is probably something pretty big."

Grace was too stunned to respond.

"In my experience these kind of guys are usually good for a couple of months, tops. Then the horns come out," said Janine.

"'Mr. Wickham is blessed with such happy manners as may ensure his making friends—whether he may be equally capable of retaining them, is less certain.' *Pride and Prejudice*," Ellen said, "in case anyone here doesn't recognize the quote."

*Argh!* Grace struggled to hold *Mal Genio* back. Any second now she was going to march over and whack Ellen over the head with that blasted computer of hers.

"Maybe Melanie can tell us more about him," another woman said. "Give us a different insight."

"Good idea," Ellen said. "So, Melanie, what exactly is your relationship with this man?"

"First off, I have to say I completely disagree with the Mr. Wickham characterization. Joe is a wonderful man," said Melanie.

Grace felt a moment's vindication. Maybe Melanie wasn't so bad after all.

"Technically, he's my boss. So initially we decided to keep it on a strictly friends level. Going out for coffee, a casual lunch, that sort of thing."

Ellen's gaze shot to Grace. It was almost the exact same phrase Grace had used at one time to describe her relationship with Joe.

"Maybe we've heard enough," Ellen said. "Thank you, Melanie, now—"

"Being that he's my boss, it's been a dilemma for sure," Melanie continued. "He's been dropping some pretty big hints about me leaving my job because I'm pretty sure he wants to bring the relationship up to the next level. Things have gotten kind of heated around the office, if you know what I mean. Of course," she gave Grace a pointed look, "I'm not the type to kiss and tell."

"What the hell is that supposed to mean?" Grace demanded.

Ellen started fluttering around in her chair like a bird with a broken wing. "Okay, I think that about wraps it up!"

"But I'm not finished," Melanie whined.

"I'm sorry, but we've already spent enough time on this guy," said Ellen. She threw Grace an apologetic look.

Sarah tugged on Grace's elbow. "Sit down," she whispered. "By arguing with Melanie, you're only making it worse."

Sarah was right, of course. Grace would deal with Melanie *and* Ellen later. In private. She slumped down in her seat.

Ellen looked relieved that there wasn't going to be a catfight. "I'm happy to report that besides the reviews we've done live during our meetings, we've had several members take the initiative and post their own reviews, bringing us to a whopping total of twenty-three."

The women all clapped at this good news. Except for Grace, who was still too mad to do much of anything except sit and fume.

"Which brings me to our next order of business. As you can see, our club is growing by leaps and bounds, and we've simply outgrown our current location. So next month, we'll be meeting somewhere new. Does anyone have any suggestions on where we should go?"

Grace had a suggestion as to where Ellen should go, but she'd keep it to herself for now.

A woman a few seats away from Grace raised her hand. "How about using a conference room at The Continental? That's the new high-rise hotel on the beach. My company had its annual business retreat there last week. Of course, they might charge us a fee, but maybe not if we had bar service." This last part was met with a large murmur of agreement from the crowd. "And there's a band every weekend night in the lounge, so it's perfect for those of us who want to socialize afterward."

"Excellent idea!" Ellen said. "Can I see a show of hands if you agree with moving the club meetings to The Continental?"

Grace was the first to shoot her arm up in the air. The rest of the room followed suit.

"It's unanimous then," Ellen said, beaming. "All righty, let's help fold up chairs and get this place back in order, then it's on to Coco's!"

Grace made sure she grabbed Ellen before she got out the door. "Ellen, can I talk to you?"

"Grace, isn't it fantastic? Now we can really grow the club! A conference room is just what we need. Do you think they have mics?"

"Ellen, how could you tell everyone about my meeting Joe at the Wobbly Duck? That was told to you in confidence!"

"No, it wasn't. I distinctly remember, we were at lunch at Luigi's and—"

"That's right, Ellen, we were at Luigi's. Just the four of us. I told my *friends*, not a bunch of strangers I've never met before."

Ellen considered this a moment. "I'm sorry. I can understand why you'd be upset about this. I tried to shut Melanie up because I could tell she was hurting your feelings. But don't you see? It only goes to prove how much of a discrepancy there is between our perceptions and reality. It's why we need this boyfriend club! Before you started getting emotionally involved with this guy, you saw there was something not right with him. But *now*? You should hear yourself, Grace! It's like he's some kind of saint."

Grace tried to think of something to defend herself with, but the irony was that Ellen actually had a point. Grace was beginning to sound exactly like Melanie and Tiffany.

"I only pointed out the obvious for your own good. Don't you remember how you felt after that first date with Brandon? You were so hurt. And with good reason! But then you saw another side of Brandon and found out he wasn't so bad. He might even be your—"

"If you tell me that Brandon is my Mr. Darcy one more time, I'm going to scream."

Ellen sniffed. "Grace, you know as well as I do that there's a flip side to every coin. You just haven't seen Joe's flip side yet, or rather *you have*, but you've chosen to ignore it. I hope I'm wrong. I hope he's not a Wickham. But it wouldn't be right for me to have this kind of information and not share it with someone I happen to care about a great deal. What kind of friend would I be then?"

How could Grace argue with that? Ellen was doing what she thought was right. She was looking out for Grace's best interests. Which was more than Grace had done for Sarah . . .

"Okay, I get it. But for the record, I think you're wrong about Joe. And in the future, I would appreciate it if what I say to you outside this club stays outside this club."

They gave each other a hug, then Ellen scurried away to round up a group for Coco's.

Joe wasn't a Wickham. He just couldn't be. Speaking of which, there he was at the entrance to the store, looking bewildered. Women were going out of their way to walk around him like he was some sort of germ. Being ignored by this many women was probably Joe's equivalent of *The Twilight Zone*.

Had he run into Melanie on her way out? Melanie had been one of the first women to leave, probably because she didn't want to speak to Grace, so maybe they'd managed to miss each other. Should she tell Joe what Melanie had said in tonight's meeting?

She snuck up behind him and tapped him on the shoulder. "Looking for someone?"

Grace got a kick out of seeing his reaction to her outfit. "Nice dress."

"Glad you remembered it. Although it's not the same one, actually."

She introduced Joe to Penny and he and Sarah made some friendly small talk as the four of them finished putting up the chairs left behind. Despite Ellen's announcement asking the members to clean up, the place had been left a mess.

"So how was the book club meeting?" Joe asked.

Penny and Sarah gave each other a look.

"It's not exactly a book club," Grace said. She wished she

didn't have to lie to him, but she couldn't tell him what the club was about. Not without going into a whole lot of stuff she didn't want to go into. So there was really no way to warn him about Melanie either. "It started out as a book club, but it's grown into more of a . . . women's empowerment group. But we also discuss books too." *Sort of.*

"Sounds cool. What book did you discuss tonight?"

*You.*

"Um, well . . . *Pride and Prejudice* was brought up."

"What is it with women and Jane Austen?"

"I'll tell you later," she said.

# 22

# My Good Opinion Is Restored

"I'll have the vegetarian lasagna, please." Ellen handed the waiter her unopened menu. He took the rest of their orders and left them a basket of breadsticks. Grace reached out and took one. She nibbled on the end, but instead of the warm, buttery, garlic sensation she was used to, it tasted more like cardboard.

"What's wrong?" Sarah asked Grace. "Why aren't you devouring the breadsticks?"

"Today's the day we approach Pop about selling Florida Charlie's."

"He's never going to go for it," Penny said.

"That's what I told Charlie but he says we have to try." While the idea of selling Florida Charlie's was still repugnant, the offer guaranteed the store another three years. That was something at least.

"When is this all taking place?" Ellen asked.

"Right after lunch. Brandon is meeting us at the store."

Sarah looked surprised. "Brandon's going to be there too?"

"Charlie thought if it was just the two of us, Pop could blow us off too easily. But with Brandon there, he'll be forced to listen to the deal. Pop is too polite to walk out on a stranger."

"True," Penny said. "That was smart of Charlie."

"Let's not talk about it," Grace said. "Let's talk about something else." Grace could now understand Penny's theories on avoidance. Just thinking about selling Florida Charlie's was enough to make her stomach turn.

"Well, you'll be happy to know that I have the go-ahead on The Continental for our next club meeting," Ellen said.

"That's good news," Penny said.

"*Very* good news," Grace agreed.

"I've booked a room for the first Saturday of every month, except for next month. I've switched the meeting to the second Saturday especially."

Penny began counting on her fingers. "That's Valentine's Day."

"I know," Ellen said. "Very apropos, don't you think?"

"But what if someone has a date?" Sarah asked.

"I think the point is that the women in this club won't be having dates on Valentine's Day," Penny said.

"Joe hasn't said anything yet, but I'm keeping my fingers crossed," Grace said. "So don't plan on my being there."

Sarah clapped her hands together. "Gracie, you're going to break your St. Valentine's Day Curse!"

Grace waited for Ellen to start in again with Joe being a Wickham, but thankfully Ellen kept her mouth shut. "Maybe," Grace said. "We'll see."

"I won't be at the boyfriend club meeting either," said Sarah. "That's the night the Dragon is having her housewarming party, and my attendance is mandatory. It's too bad that's the night of the club meeting, because I was actually hoping you all might come to the party. I'm dying to show you her house. I think it's my best work yet. The before-and-after pictures are going up on my website."

"Why don't we cancel the meeting? Or move it to another Saturday?" Grace suggested.

"We can't do that. This is a woman's empowerment group!"

Ellen said, waving a breadstick in the air for emphasis. "What better day to have a meeting than on a holiday that only serves to make women who don't have a man in their life feel like they're less-than?"

No one had a good argument for that, so Penny changed the subject. "Is the Dragon still trying to fix you up with her son?" she asked Sarah.

Sarah nodded.

"What does he look like?" Grace asked. "If you've decorated her house, you must have seen pictures of him."

"Oh, I've seen lots of pictures. He's about three feet tall, blue eyes, he's missing a front tooth—"

Ellen began choking on her breadstick. "He's . . . a . . . a mid-get?"

Grace gave Ellen a few hard thumps on the back. "Don't make me do the Heimlich on you," she warned. "After your performance at the boyfriend club Saturday night, I'd love nothing better than to put you in a half-Nelson."

Ellen took a big swig of water. Her face was beet red. "I'm okay," she croaked.

It reminded Grace of when Brandon had nearly choked on his beer at the Wobbly Duck. And thinking of Brandon reminded her once more of this afternoon's meeting with Pop. Cardboard or not, Grace stuffed a breadstick in her mouth.

Sarah was still giggling when she said, "Sorry, Ellen, I couldn't resist. I have no idea what the man looks like because I've only seen kiddie pictures."

"She doesn't have any other pictures of him up in the house?" Ellen asked.

"I've seen one from early high school. He had braces then. I know he likes to sail, because there are a lot of pictures of his boat, but that's it."

"You know what this means, don't you?" Ellen said.

"No, but I'm sure you're going to tell us," Grace said.

"She says she wants to fix Sarah up with her son, but what she really wants is control over his life. She doesn't have pictures of him as a grown man because, in her mind, he's still a little boy. *Her* little boy."

Penny rolled her eyes. "I thought Janine was the psychology expert."

"It doesn't take a degree in psychology to figure out an Oedipus complex."

"I think Ellen is right. This guy is bad news," Grace said. Not that Grace really agreed with Ellen's theory. Grace had been all for Sarah going out with the Dragon's son, but that was before her Charlie/Sarah brainstorm. Despite Sarah's protests to the contrary, Grace was still clinging to the slim hope that Charlie and Sarah might one day get together. Strange, but now that the idea had taken root, she couldn't get it out of her head.

"Don't call out the National Guard, but I think I actually agree with Ellen too," Sarah said.

"So what are you going to do?" Penny asked.

"I'm going to the party and I'm going to make nice with the Dragon and her son. And if he shows any interest in me, which I'm sure he won't because he's probably sick of his mother's interference and wants to meet me about as much as I want to meet him, I'll just tell him that I'm not over my ex yet."

"That's actually a pretty good idea," Grace said. "But that's not exactly true, is it? I mean, when do you think you'll be ready to move on and start dating?"

Penny raised her brows at Grace. No one at the table said anything.

Was she being insensitive again? It irked Grace to no end to think of Sarah pining away for Craig. If Sarah only knew the truth. She thought briefly of Joe's advice, about telling Sarah everything . . .

"What about you, Penny? Can I count on you to be at the meeting?" Ellen asked.

"Sure, I've got nothing better to do on Valentine's Day."

"Have you heard from Butch lately?" Grace asked.

"Nope. And I don't expect to either. Oh goodie," Penny said, spotting their waiter from across the room. "Our food's on the way."


Grace practiced her speech the entire drive back to the store while Penny critiqued. Even though Grace had told Charlie she was going to sit there and nod like a dummy, Pop would expect her to say something.

"Don't sound so nervous," Penny said. "Keep it short, simple. Besides, knowing Charlie, he'll probably take over and you won't have to say anything anyway. Lawyers love to hear themselves talk."

Penny was right. She probably wouldn't have to say much. And this was business. No reason to get all maudlin. Who knows? Pop might even be relieved by the offer.

*Ha.* Who was she fooling? Pop would never go for it.

She spotted Brandon's silver Jaguar in front of the store but there was no sign of Charlie's car. Technically they weren't meeting until one thirty. Hopefully Charlie wouldn't be late. There were about a dozen customers inside, three of them waiting in line at the citrus shop. Penny went to help Stella take orders. Grace found Brandon perusing the T-shirt aisles.

"I've never seen you in your official Florida Charlie's uniform," he said. "Very cute." He smiled and Grace got the impression he wanted to say something more but held back. On the off chance that Pop went for the deal, Brandon could very well end up being her boss. How weird would that be?

"I have to warn you, I'm still pretty sure my father is going to say no."

"I can be very persuasive, Grace."

Grace knew all about that persuasiveness firsthand. Maybe she was wrong and Pop *would* go for the deal, after all. Of course, it would take more than some long-stemmed roses and a few bottles of Dom Perignon to sway Pop, but still, it was probably wise not to underestimate Brandon.

The bell above the front door jingled and they both turned. Grace had hoped it was Charlie, but it wasn't.

"So here I am," Pop said. "What is it you and your brother wanted to talk to me about?" His face looked unusually ruddy.

Grace kissed her father on the cheek. "Did you just come from the gym? You look flushed."

"Nah, but I thought I'd head there after our talk. I promised your mother I'd walk two miles a day. New Year's resolution," he said, sounding more resigned than enthusiastic.

Grace introduced Pop to Brandon and the two of them shook hands.

"Maybe we can go ahead and start?" Brandon asked. "We can catch Charlie up later."

Pop gave Grace a *who the hell is this guy?* look.

"I'll explain everything in my office," Grace said, feeling nervous all over again. She ushered them inside and offered to make coffee. Brandon politely declined. Pop appeared impatient.

"Is the air-conditioning on?" Pop asked. "It's hot in here."

Grace checked the thermostat. It was set at seventy, as usual. "Do you want me to get a fan?"

"Nah, don't bother, let's just get down to it. What did you want to talk to me about?"

Grace glanced at her watch. It wasn't one thirty yet so she couldn't even blame Charlie for being late, but damn him anyway. This was his idea. How could he do all the talking if he wasn't here?

"Perhaps I should start, sir," Brandon said.

Pop took a handkerchief from his back pocket and wiped his forehead.

Brandon handed her father a business card. He began with a history of his investment group and then went into the current status of the local real estate market. Brandon was smooth and professional, but Pop didn't appear to be listening and Brandon noticed. "Sir, is there something wrong?"

"Other than the fact that it's hot as hell in here?"

Grace felt a moment's alarm. It wasn't like her father to use that tone of voice.

"Grace, maybe you should go get that fan," Brandon suggested.

"Of course." Grace rose from her chair and pulled out the box fan she kept in her office closet. She set the fan to high.

"That's better," Pop said, but he didn't look any better. If anything, he looked worse. Why was his face so red?

Brandon gave her a look that Grace couldn't read. "I think we should wait till your brother gets here before we go on."

"Good idea," Grace said.

Pop didn't say anything. Which wasn't like him.

"Pop, are you okay? Did you take your blood pressure medicine this morning?"

"Your father has high blood pressure?"

"I'm right here so you two can stop talking about me like I'm not. And yeah, I took my pills this morning. But I have to admit, I feel . . . dizzy. Must be this heat."

"Pop, maybe you should lie down."

He placed his palm against his cheek. "And my face feels numb . . ."

Brandon jumped from his chair. "Do you keep a blood pressure cuff in the office?" he asked Grace. "Or an AED machine?"

"A what?"

"Sir, let's get you down on the ground."

The scary part was that Pop didn't argue. He let Brandon ease him to the floor. "Grace," Brandon said in a low voice, "does your father have a history of heart attacks?"

*Oh my God.*

Grace snatched up the phone and dialed 911.

"The ambulance is on its way, Pop." She knelt next to her father and touched her hand over his forehead. It felt clammy.

"My chest . . ." he said. "It feels like I'm being . . . crushed."

"Sir, do you have any nitroglycerin tablets?" Brandon asked.

"At the house," Pop said between breaths.

Brandon looked Grace in the eye. "Do you keep aspirin in here?"

Grace ran to her desk, flung open the top drawer and handed the aspirin to Brandon. Between the two of them they were able to help Pop get down a pill.

Tears welled in Grace's eyes. "This is just like before," she whispered to Brandon. "He said the same thing before, about his chest . . ."

Brandon clasped Grace's hand and gave it a strong squeeze. "His breathing is a little heavy and his pulse is fast, but it's steady. I'm going to let the store employees know what's going on and get the customers to clear their cars out of the way so the ambulance can park as close as possible to the door. I'll be right back."

Thank God the paramedics arrived quickly. They checked Pop's vital signs, placed some oxygen on him, and transferred him to a stretcher.

"Can I go with him?" Grace asked.

"Sorry, ma'am, there's no room in the ambulance," one of the paramedics told her.

Brandon placed his hand on her elbow. "We'll follow them to the hospital in my car."

Penny and Stella and the rest of the store employees stood

back, wide-eyed, and watched as the EMS personnel pulled Pop through the store on the stretcher.

"Penny," Grace shouted on her way out the door. "Call Mami and Charlie and let them know what happened!"


"I hate hospitals," Grace said, putting her quarters into a coffee machine. A foam cup plopped right side up. A steady stream of questionable brown liquid shot directly inside, stopping a half inch short of the top. *How eerily precise,* Grace thought. Then she thought how weird it was that she'd be thinking of a coffee dispensing machine at all. But then she'd had a lot of time to think in the past four hours they'd spent in the ER waiting room. Like how lucky they were to still have Pop.

The thought that they'd almost lost him made Grace shudder. She handed Brandon the cup.

"Thanks. Are you sure you don't want it?"

"Sarah went to get Starbucks. I'll wait for the real thing."

He drained the coffee in a couple of gulps. Grace both grimaced and marveled at the fortitude of his stomach. Noticing her reaction, he said, "I used to live on worse stuff than this in college."

"Well, I owe you a *real* cup of coffee. And a lot more than that for all your help. You were great back there with Pop."

She still couldn't get over how efficiently Brandon had handled everything. And how he'd insisted on staying to keep Grace company through the ER wait. Grace had taken a CPR course after Pop's heart attack. Precious little good that had done. In her panic, she hadn't even remembered what an AED machine was. She thought back to how she'd walked out on her date with Brandon and then refused to accept his apology despite the flowers and the Dom Perignon. He'd made a big effort to win her over and she'd been unfair to him.

"I think you would have made a great doctor. You have a really nice bedside manner."

"That's what all the girls say."

Grace smiled. The night they'd had their business dinner at Chez Louis, she'd wondered how things might have gone between them if they'd never had that disastrous date at the Wobbly Duck. Now, she couldn't help but wonder how things might be if Joe wasn't in the picture.

*Brandon Farrell is your Mr. Darcy,* she heard Ellen's voice whisper in her ear. *And Joe is your Mr. Wickham.*

Grace's smile vanished. What a traitorous thought.

"Will you excuse me?" she said to Brandon. "I need to make a phone call."

"Actually, I need to get back to the office. Call me if anything changes in your dad's condition. Promise?"

Grace reached out impulsively to hug him. "Thanks again. You were terrific."

He looked embarrassed, but pleased. "No need to thank me. I'm just glad I was there to help."

She waited till he was gone to dial Joe on his private office line.

"Hey, we still on for tonight?" he asked.

"Joe . . . my dad's in the emergency room."

"Is he all right? What's going on?"

"At first, they thought he might be having a heart attack, but now they think maybe his blood pressure got too high, although they've ruled out a stroke. We were at the store and he was feeling dizzy, and—" She was going to tell him about Brandon and his role in the whole thing, then thought better of it. "Anyway, my mom and my brother are with him and the doctor just updated us. They're going to keep him overnight and run a few tests. The doctor says he's stable and that we can all go home, but I'm going to stay anyway."

"I can be there in fifteen minutes."

Grace felt a moment's panic. She'd hadn't expected that. For some reason, her throat refused to cooperate. The silence seemed to drag on forever, although in reality it couldn't have lasted more than a few seconds.

"Or not," he said.

"It's not that I don't want you here," she said. "It's just . . . my grandmother and Charlie and Sarah and Ellen and Penny are all here, and we're having to take turns going in to see him, so it's kind of a madhouse."

"Sure, I understand. It's a time for family. And close friends. Keep me posted, will you? And Grace, please call me if you need anything," he said before hanging up.

Grace thought about their phone call for the rest of the evening. Why hadn't she wanted Joe to come to the hospital? The girls knew Grace and Joe were dating. And Mami and Pop and even Abuela had already met him the day he'd come to Florida Charlie's. But she'd introduced him as a friend, not a boyfriend. If Joe were to come to the hospital, it would be like some sort of unspoken announcement. And the truth was, she just wasn't ready for that.

# 23

# It's Raining Men

"An anxiety attack? The hell it was," Pop grumbled for the hundredth time today. "I know a heart attack when I have one, and I was most definitely having a heart attack!"

He was lying on the living room couch, where Mami had insisted he stay at risk of death—by her own hands—if he dared exert himself. He'd been discharged from the hospital this morning after all his test results had come back negative. Most people would have been thrilled. Not Pop.

"Charlie, be grateful it was what it was," Mami said. "Now lean forward so I can fluff the pillows behind your head."

"Ana, did you not hear the man? He said I was a nutcase! All I can say is, thank God they let me out when they did if all those fancy tests and machines of theirs can't tell when a person is having a genuine heart attack. The damn place should be investigated for fraud."

"Pop, the doctor never said you were a nutcase," Grace said. She tried to halt a yawn from escaping, but it was impossible. She'd spent the night in the hospital waiting room, along with Mami and Charlie. They were all exhausted, although lack of sleep was only a partial reason. Most of the exhaustion came from trying to keep Pop calm.

"What do I have to be anxious about? My life is perfect. I have a beautiful wife, a successful son, a house, a business, and my own little Tomato who saved me from almost certain death yesterday."

"I didn't do anything other than call the ambulance, Pop. Brandon was the one who kept it all together."

"Nice young man," Pop said. He picked up the remote and began flipping channels. "Who was he again?"

"He's Charlie's friend."

"Is he trying to sell us something?"

"Uh, not exactly."

"In that case, you have my permission to marry him."

"Thanks, I'm sure he'll be thrilled to know that."

Grace rose from her chair and headed to the kitchen to find Charlie and Abuela walking through the door. They'd just come back from church, where Abuela had gone to light a candle for Pop.

"Now that I have the Virgin working on your father's recovery, I'm going to get some sleep," Abuela said, giving Grace a kiss on the cheek. "Good work yesterday, *mi amor*. You saved your father's life."

Grace would protest, but she'd already done it a dozen times since yesterday and Abuela refused to belittle Grace's part in getting Pop to the hospital. She waited till Abuela was gone. "So now what?" she asked Charlie.

"I don't know. What do you think? Wait till Pop feels better, then try again?"

"*Try again?* You weren't there. You didn't see how his face got all red and sweaty. It was awful!"

"You can't blame his anxiety attack on Farrell's offer. From what I hear, he never got around to actually mentioning it."

"You talked to Brandon?"

"He called me this morning to find out how Pop was doing.

I think he plans to call you later this afternoon." Charlie looked pleased.

"Brandon isn't the guy I went out with the other night, Charlie."

"*Damn.*"

"Back to Pop. I don't think we should bring up Brandon's offer again until we know the cause of this stress he's under."

Charlie raked a hand through his hair. "Okay, I'm going to leave this up to you. If you don't think Pop can handle it, then we'll drop the whole thing and let the store run its course."

Leave the whole thing up to her? It didn't seem fair that it would all fall on her shoulders. Option one: risk Pop's health by bringing up the offer and potentially stretch the store's life by another three years and ensure her family's financial security. Or option two: keep Pop in the dark about the offer and let the store continue on its downward slide.

Neither option seemed good.

Grace spied the familiar tan Toyota Corolla parked in front of her town house and moaned. She was in no mood to deal with whatever this might mean.

The second he saw her pull in the driveway, Felix hopped out of his car and jogged up to meet her.

"Felix, what are you doing here?"

"I was in the neighborhood and thought I'd stop by."

Grace raised a brow.

"Okay, so maybe I wasn't exactly in the neighborhood. I got tired of waiting for your phone call so I thought I'd take some action."

"Uh-huh." Grace fiddled with the keys to her town house. Would it be horribly rude to just walk past Felix and ignore him?

"Aren't you going to invite me in?"

"No."

"Grace, I've thought long and hard about what happened between us. I was an ass. An idiot. A moron. Like I said before, if I could take that night back, I would. Baby, I'm sorry. Please, will you give me another chance?"

Did Felix actually have *tears* in eyes? No way. But he definitely had his sad face on. The one that seemed genuine.

"Felix," she said, trying to gentle her voice, "thanks for the apology. I accept it because I think you truly couldn't help yourself, but maybe this is a lesson hard learned. The next time you have a girlfriend, don't cheat on her."

"That's it?" he asked incredulously. "You aren't even going to try? Baby, what we had was a once-in-a-lifetime love."

Grace had to bite into the inside of her cheek, otherwise the delirium caused by no sleep and Felix's outrageous remark was definitely going to make her start laughing. "Felix," she tried again, "we had a good thing for a while. The truth is, there's someone else now."

The sound of an approaching car made them both turn their heads. A sleek shiny silver jaguar parked behind Felix's dinged up Toyota. It was like she'd conjured the car, and the man stepping out of it, from thin air. She couldn't have scripted this better if she'd been the author herself.

"So you're really dating Farrell now, huh?"

"Well—"

"How am I supposed to compete with him?"

She should tell Felix the truth. That the man she was dating wasn't Brandon Farrell. But if he wanted to jump to conclusions, then who was she to correct him?

"You don't have to compete with anyone, Felix. You just have to keep your pecker in your pants."

Felix looked defeated. He reached out and hugged her. "If it doesn't work out with Farrell, you know where to find me."

Grace stiffened but she didn't reject the hug altogether. "Thanks, I'll keep it in mind."

Felix nodded to Brandon, who was tentatively making his way up her driveway. He looked unsure of whether to approach them or not, but Felix got in his Corolla and drove off, giving Brandon the unspoken permission he seemed to be looking for.

"Isn't he the manager at Chez Louis?" Brandon asked.

Grace nodded. "Also known as my cheating ex."

"Yeah?" Brandon frowned. "What did he want?"

"Believe it or not, he wanted me back. I said no." Brandon was dressed in jeans and a T-shirt and had a Publix bag in his hand. "What are you doing here?"

"Charlie called and told me you were on your way home. He gave me your address. Said you might be hungry. I hope you don't mind."

"Charlie told you that, huh?" It was sort of funny. Charlie playing matchmaker. Grace wondered what her brother would think of her attempt to get him and Sarah together.

There was a delicious greasy smell coming from the Publix bag. "It's fried chicken from the deli. And a tub of potato salad," he said, noting Grace's interest.

Despite being at her parents' house all day, Grace hadn't eaten anything. She'd been too tired. But she was suddenly ravenous. Her stomach made a loud, embarrassing grumbling sound.

"There's a movie marathon on cable tonight. *Bringing Up Baby* starts in ten minutes. Ever seen it?" he asked.

"Only every time it comes on TV. Katherine Hepburn and Cary Grant. It's a classic."

Brandon grinned. "I knew you'd love old movies."

Oddly enough, she wasn't so tired anymore. The idea of eating fried chicken and watching a movie with Brandon sounded strangely comforting. Maybe it was because he'd been with her during a traumatic event. It bonded them in a way that made their relationship unique.

Three months ago she'd been in the middle of the driest dating spell in her entire life. Now, three men wanted her.

"I'd love to invite you inside, but I need to tell you, Brandon, I'm sort of seeing someone right now. But if you're looking for a friend, then you definitely have one in me."

He looked mildly disappointed, but he smiled good-naturedly and the two of them watched *Bringing Up Baby* and scarfed down all the fried chicken in the box, and had such a good time, they decided to do it again next week.

# 24

# Lies, Sex, and Jane Austen

It was one p.m. on Friday, three weeks after the "attack," the generic term they'd been using to refer to whatever it was that had happened to Pop. Grace and Joe were eating lunch in her office. He sat in a chair across from her desk. She sat perched on the edge of said desk, her bare feet propped against his knees. It was her habit to sometimes pull off her sneakers if she was going to be in her office for an extended period of time.

Eight days and counting till Valentine's Day and Joe hadn't mentioned doing anything special. But they were spending a lot of time together and maybe he just assumed she'd know they would be going out. Although this weekend they'd be apart. Joe had a rugby tournament in Tampa tomorrow and he was already packed and ready to leave.

"I don't get it," he said, shaking his head. "How can chocolate be a substitute for sex?"

"Okay, I'll try to explain it again. You know how running releases endorphins and they make you all happy and relaxed? Well, eating chocolate is kind of like running," Grace said. "It releases some kind of magic drug into your system that makes you feel all tingly and happy inside." She pulled the banana peppers out of her Italian sub in disgust. "Did you tell them I didn't want banana peppers?"

"Sorry about that, I should have checked. Okay, I get the chocolate. Now explain the Jane Austen thing."

"It's also like chocolate, but for the brain. Women crave the kind of heroes she wrote about. Men like Mr. Darcy, and Mr. Knightley, and Captain Wentworth."

"You mean guys who aren't real."

"Consider it a kind of fantasy."

"Like *Playboy*?"

Grace giggled. "I've never heard of comparing Jane Austen to *Playboy*, but I guess it's not so far off."

"So your women's empowerment group is really a front for talking about sex?" he joked.

Grace had forgotten she'd told him they'd discussed Jane Austen at the "empowerment meeting." She hated lying to Joe about the boyfriend club. She really did. And more than anything she wanted to warn him about the extent of Melanie's infatuation, which, if you asked Grace, bordered on seriously delusional. But to do that would expose the exact nature of the club, and although Grace had no problem with that in general, she was pretty sure Joe *would* have a problem with the fact that he'd been the club's latest flavor of the month. Grace could still kick herself for being manipulated into critiquing him.

"Um, Joe, how's Melanie?"

He shrugged. "Fine, I guess."

"I mean, how's it going around the office? Does she still have a big crush on you?"

"It's under control." He sounded slightly annoyed.

*No, it's not under control,* she wanted to say. She thought back again to Ellen's ridiculous conclusion that Joe was a Wickham. Objectively speaking, maybe the descriptors pointed to a similarity, but there was no correlation in real life between the two men. Wickham was the womanizing equivalent to a category five hurricane. Like Wickham, Joe was handsome and charming, but he . . . well, Joe had joined the Peace Corps, for heaven's sake. That in itself totally blew Ellen's theory out of the water. Ellen didn't have the right descriptors for Joe. She just couldn't.

"So tell me again why you can't go to Tampa with me?" he asked, taking a bite of his sandwich.

"Because not all of us work half days on Friday."

He laid his sandwich on the desk and wrapped his hands around her ankles. "I can wait till you get off." He glanced at the closed door, then back at her. "Speaking of which, do you know what this position reminds me of?"

"It's not just this afternoon. I have to work tomorrow too. Penny's already covered enough Saturdays this past month." Grace slapped his hands away. "Don't even think about it," she said.

"Why not? I promise, it'll be fast."

Joe's idea of fast wasn't exactly shabby. For one wild moment, Grace actually considered it. There were places deep inside her that were more than just considering it. In the end though, she just couldn't.

"Because it would scar me for all eternity."

"Explain to me how an office quickie is going to ruin your life."

"This isn't just the place I work. It's Florida Charlie's, keeper of all my sweetest, most innocent girlhood dreams. It would be like doing it in church. And besides, I could never cheat on Gator Claus with him so close by." The last part slipped out of her mouth before she realized what she'd said. She watched his face for a reaction, but he didn't act as if she'd said anything out of the ordinary. "Um, Gator Claus is the nickname I call the stuffed alligator."

Joe nodded. "The one you talk to."

Grace almost fell off the desk. "You *know* about that?"

"I've seen you talk to him before."

"And you don't think it's . . . weird?"

"Maybe a little. But I like weird girls. The sex is always better."

Well, that was one perk Richard Kasamati's third-grade self couldn't have foreseen.

She smiled, but the truth was his response brought up a sore subject. She'd told him a little bit about the two serious boyfriends she'd had, but he'd never discussed any past girlfriends with her. Not that she wanted specifics. They'd discussed enough of each other's sexual history that Grace felt confident their relationship wasn't going to end with her on triple antibiotics.

But the fact that he never said anything about his past relationships, even when prompted, led her to believe that he'd been really hurt and just didn't want to talk about it. Or maybe he'd had lots of casual girlfriends and none of them stood out enough to mention. Grace didn't like the idea of Joe being hurt in love, but she preferred the former to the latter. How did the saying go? *People who have loved deeply once, are capable of loving deeply again.* Or something like that.

And speaking of feelings, what were hers, exactly? Was she in love with Joe? Technically they'd only been dating a little over a month, but time wasn't the constraint here. It didn't matter if she'd known him a couple of months or a couple of years; she either felt it or she didn't. She loved being with him, no question about that. The sex was great and they had a similar sense of humor. When she wasn't with him, she was thinking of him. It certainly seemed like love. But . . . there was something missing. She'd known it when Pop had been in the hospital and Joe had wanted to come to the emergency room to be with her and she'd made an excuse about there being too many people.

"How's your dad doing?" Joe asked. It was weird—no, she

didn't like that word—it was *uncanny* how he could read her mind.

"Finally coming to grips with the fact that it wasn't a heart attack and that it was stress related. He's going to a therapist. Some guy named Jim who's a retired marine. I think he primarily deals with ex-military types who suffer from post-traumatic stress disorder. A real man's man kind of shrink. So now, thanks to Jim, Pop is journaling and he and Mami are going to join a yoga class. You should have seen his face last Sunday at dinner when Abuela mentioned she's thinking of joining the class too."

Joe smiled politely and resumed eating his sandwich. He suddenly seemed uncharacteristically pensive and Grace thought it was as good a time as any to broach the subject that had been on her mind for a while. Since Pop's "attack," Brandon had returned to the Thursday night Zumba class. Grace had gone out with him a few times for coffee and lunch and he'd come over for what she considered their weekly movie and popcorn night, conveniently scheduled for a night when Joe was playing rugby. It was all strictly platonic, with the exception of the one night after class that Brandon had hinted heavily that they should take their relationship "up a notch." The expression had reminded Grace of what Melanie had said of her relationship with Joe. There was no reason to feel guilty about being friends with Brandon, except that she was keeping it from Joe, and that in and of itself told her that maybe there was something there she should explore. The whole thing was confusing.

"Remember when you told me Brandon Farrell wasn't what he seemed and that I shouldn't trust him?"

He frowned. "What made you think of him just now?"

"He was here when Pop had his attack."

"Here at the store?"

"Here in the office. He's part of an investment group that's interested in buying the store to eventually sell the land for commercial highway development. Charlie set the whole thing up and—"

Joe stilled. "You're selling Florida Charlie's?"

"Well, not exactly. Pop hasn't heard the official offer yet. Charlie and Brandon came up with the idea. The store has been in financial trouble for some time now. Didn't I tell you?"

"No, Grace," he said slowly. "You didn't."

"It's a long story, but Brandon never actually got to present the offer to Pop. And now, I just don't think it's a good idea. I don't want to stress Pop out any further."

"And?"

"I think you're wrong about Brandon. He seems like a really nice guy, Joe."

Joe laid his sandwich back on the desk. "Did this *really* nice guy make a pass at you?"

"No! It's just, I wanted you to know that he and I are friends. He was terrific with Pop, both here and then at the hospital . . ."

He couldn't hide the surprise from his face. Or the expression that followed it.

*Well, that was really stupid, Grace.*

Joe wrapped up his portion of uneaten sandwich and stuffed it into the takeout bag. "If you're not going to Tampa with me, then there's no need to wait around. I promised the guys I'd be at the hotel in time to get in a practice."

"That's it? You're just going to leave without talking about this?"

"What's there to talk about? Obviously we don't need to know every little thing about each other, do we?"

"I . . . No, I guess we don't. I just didn't want to hide anything from you."

She'd never seen Joe react like this. Why had she let it slip that Brandon had been present at the hospital? Had she wanted to make Joe jealous? A part of her couldn't help but feel a tiny feminine thrill, but mostly she was ashamed of herself. She hadn't meant to tell him about Brandon. Not like this. She couldn't have. She certainly wasn't trying to pick a fight with Joe. Yet that's how it must seem to him.

"I'm glad Farrell was such a rock for you in your time of need. But I already told you, the guy's bad news. You either trust me on that or you don't. That's your call." He gave her a hasty peck on the forehead. "I'll call you when I get back in town."

# 25

# Busted

Pop had been holed up in his den like a squirrel with a nut ever since they'd come home from Mass. It was the first Sunday in February and perfect Florida winter weather—a cool, crisp sixty-five degrees outside. Mami had given Grace the assignment of trying to get Pop to come outside and sit with the rest of the family on the deck, but Grace had her own agenda. She couldn't talk to Pop about Brandon's offer, lest that brought on another anxiety attack, and Lord knows no one wanted that to happen. But she needed to clear up the roof situation. She shuddered to think what would happen to the Hemingway corner during the next good rainfall.

The sun streamed in through the den window, picking up the gray in Pop's dark hair. He wore a new pair of reading glasses, a set of thin wire-rims that Mami had picked out because she said it didn't hide his beautiful green eyes. For a second, he looked exactly like Charlie—broad shouldered, confident. It was comforting to think that in about twenty-five years this is what her brother would look like. On the other hand, it made it impossible to believe that Pop had really suffered from something as vague-sounding as an anxiety attack.

Pop looked up and caught her staring at him.

"Mami says dinner will be ready in about thirty minutes."

Grace played with the doorknob, twisting it back and forth between her fingers. It was a nervous habit from her teenage years. "She says I'm supposed to tell you that you've been in here too long and that you need some fresh air."

"Tell your mother I'll be out in fifteen minutes."

"Are you busy? Because I need to talk to you about something."

Pop waved her in. "Close the door."

The last time Pop had asked her to close the door was when Grace had been caught sneaking out of the house in the middle of the night her senior year in high school. He hadn't yelled at her. Mami had taken care of that. Instead, they'd had a calm conversation about curfews, and trust, and respect, and in the end she'd been grounded for a week, which, though it had seemed harsh at the time, was lenient compared to Sarah's monthlong punishment of no car.

Grace was now feeling the same anxiety of the unknown that she'd felt all those years ago. And then she remembered she was the one who had sought Pop out, not the other way around. There was no reason for her to be nervous.

"Looking up travel information for your trip?" she asked, pointing to the computer screen.

He hesitated. "I'm glad you're here, Grace. There's something I want to talk to you about too."

"Okay. You go first."

He pulled off his glasses, carefully folded the arms inside, and made a production of placing them in the cloth eyeglass case. Grace had seen Pop pull of his reading glasses thousands of times, but he usually yanked them off in one move. Was Pop nervous too?

"Let me start by telling you that my father and I had to have this exact same talk."

"Don't sweat it, Pop. Mami already gave me the talk back in the fourth grade."

She expected Pop to laugh. But he didn't. Pop had *never* not laughed at any of Grace's jokes before. Not even the really bad ones.

"This is serious, Tomato."

"Oh." Grace sat on the edge of Pop's reading chair—a La-Z-Boy recliner he refused to get rid of despite its frayed condition. "Is it about the tests they ran on you in the hospital? Did . . . did they find something?"

Pop's face softened. "Nah, this has nothing to do with those tests. Although it does have something to do with my attack." He leaned back in his chair and crossed his arms over his chest. "Grace, do you remember the day the roof leaked and we had to close the store?"

"Funny you should bring up the roof leak, Pop, because—"

"Maybe I didn't make myself clear when I told you to keep the store closed till the repair was done."

Grace blinked. "But I was able to find a company that did a quick fix. I sent you the receipt." She leaned forward to see if she could make it out among the papers on his desk, but they appeared to be printouts of some kind, along with a leather notebook she'd never seen before. "They were able to do the patch-up job in a day, and the customers didn't seem to mind. I've contacted several companies for estimates and they all say the same thing. We need a new roof."

"I'm fully aware the store needs a new roof. There's some alternative financing that I'm considering, and once I've made a decision, I'll let you know which way I've decided to go."

She was relieved that Pop seemed to have the roof situation already under control, but Grace was beginning to feel uneasy about something, although she couldn't put her finger on what it was exactly.

"You know, Grace, when I had my heart attack two years ago—and that was a *real* heart attack—your mother convinced me to slow down. I admit, at the time I was putting in too many hours at the store, so she had a valid point. If it gave her peace of mind to think that by not going in to work every day it was somehow going to extend my life, then so be it."

Grace sat there and nodded. What was Pop trying to say?

"At first, I thought this anxiety thing was just some bull the doctors made up because they couldn't figure out what was really wrong with me. But Jim—that's my therapist, you've heard me talk about him, hell of a guy—he's got me thinking the docs are right." Pop shook his head. "Never thought I'd see the day I succumbed to some girly nerve problem, but there it is. I'm holding all this tension inside me. Jim says it's because I'm stewing about something that's not going right in my life. Well, what would that be? I said. I have the perfect life. So he had me write everything down in this." He picked up the leather journal. "All my thoughts, feelings, crap like that. And guess what? It's costing me a hundred bucks an hour to figure out I'm worried about the store." He ended with a disbelieving chuckle.

Grace cleared her throat. "What exactly are you worried about, Pop?"

"It's like this, Tomato. My father worked his tail off to make Florida Charlie's a success. Not just for himself, but because he wanted to hand down something of value to the next generation. I want to do the same for you and Charlie. I know Charlie's not interested in the store, but one day fifty percent of it will be his, just like fifty percent of it will be yours. I always knew when the two of you were kids that you'd be the one to carry on the business. Charlie never felt the same way about the store that you did. And that's okay." He picked up the spreadsheets. "I have to tell you, though, sweetheart, the business isn't the same as it was when I put it in your hands two years ago. That's partially my fault. I didn't train you well enough, I think."

Pop was blaming *her* for the decline in business? She'd worked her tail off to bring Florida Charlie's into the twenty-first century. Was it her fault the economy had taken a nosedive in the past few years? She thought about all the things she could bring up—decreased tourist dollars, rising competition. But they felt like empty excuses.

"What are you trying to tell me?"

"I'm trying to tell you the same thing my father said to me when I thought I knew more about the business than he did. I may be your father, Grace, but when I tell you something about the store, I expect you to listen. As long as my name's on the deed, I'll make the ultimate decisions."

In all the years Grace had worked for her father, she'd never heard this tone of voice from him. She felt her cheeks go warm. "You're right, Pop. I'm sorry. It won't happen again."

"Good. I've been going over the spreadsheets, trying to figure out where we've been losing revenue. Once I study these a bit closer, then I want to meet with you again and come up with some new strategies."

"Have . . . have you had a chance to look over the proposal I gave you? About keeping the store open on Sundays?"

"I have." He paused. "It's actually a well-thought-out plan, but I'd prefer to keep it as a last-minute resort. I feel confident we can keep the same hours we always have and still get back to where we were financially."

Grace fidgeted with a loose thread on the chair arm. She wasn't sure whether to get up and join the rest of the family outside or sit here and talk to Pop some more.

"So what was it you wanted to talk to me about?" Pop asked.

"It was the roof thing," she said.

He pulled his reading glasses out of the case and put them back on. "I'm glad we've had a chance to get this out in the open. Tell your mother I'll be done here in a few minutes, just as soon as I finish this row of figures."

"Sure, Pop." She took a look at him, head already bent over his desk again, punching numbers into an old fashioned handheld calculator.

She hadn't been chastised by her father.

She'd been brought down a notch or two by her boss.


After supper Grace drove home to find Joe's black Range Rover parked in her driveway. With Joe standing next to it. It occurred to Grace that Joe didn't have a key to her town house. She didn't have a key to his either. On the one hand, she was glad to see him. She'd hated the way they'd left things on Friday. But if he was in horny rugby player mode, then for the first time in their relationship he was going to be disappointed because they had some serious talking to do first.

"Hey," she said. "How was the tournament?"

"Second place." He kissed her on the cheek and wrapped her up in a hug, and any intention of refusing Joe anything went out the window. The truth was, if he pulled her inside, she'd probably follow, no questions asked. She'd never felt so powerless in a relationship before. It bothered her, no doubt about it. "I can't stay. I promised my mother I'd have dinner with her tonight."

"She's in town?"

"Just for a week or so."

She waited for him to ask her to join them, even though she'd already eaten, but he didn't. He had to know that she was expecting an invitation. Was this Joe's way of punishing her for finding out Brandon had been at the hospital during Pop's attack? Grace hoped not. It reeked of pettiness. And Joe wasn't like that. At least, Grace didn't think he was.

He tucked a loose strand of hair behind her ear. "I've thought about Friday afternoon all weekend long. I'm sorry, Grace. I was a jerk. You can be friends with anyone you want. Even Farrell."

"Thanks. I was waiting for your permission on that."

He grinned. "Are you always going to be a smart-ass?"

"I don't know. How long do you think we're going to be together?"

The instant she said it she wished she could take it back. But maybe it was good to give their relationship a push. She needed to see where it would land, even if it was someplace she didn't like.

"I was hoping we could take it slow and see where this goes," he said cautiously.

"Am I your girlfriend, Joe?"

He seemed taken aback by her question. "If you don't know the answer to that, Grace, then we're in trouble."

She sighed. "You have no reason to be jealous of Brandon Farrell."

He nodded like he already knew. "I don't want to talk about Farrell anymore. Let's talk about next weekend."

Valentine's Day. Grace's heart did a nervous flip.

"I thought maybe we'd go up to St. Augustine. I think it would be good for us to get away from here."

"An overnighter?"

"Sure. Can you leave after lunch on Friday?"

Next week was Speed Week, the countdown to the Daytona 500. Thousands of tourists would descend upon the city and it was Florida Charlie's busiest time of the year. It was an unwritten rule that everyone worked the weekend of the race. No exceptions.

But Grace had been working so hard, these past few months especially, and the results had been less than stellar. Pop had even insinuated that she was behind the store's recent decline in sales. Did it matter if she wasn't at the store for a couple of days?

She would work extra all week to make sure everything was in tip-top shape and she'd leave Penny in charge. Other than that, all Grace could be was an extra set of hands.

"I'd love to go to St. Augustine with you," she said, feeling herself grin ear to ear.

The St. Valentine's Day Curse was finally going to be lifted.

# 26

# A Tangled Web

Speed Week was crazy, as usual. Daytona Beach was overrun with tourists and Grace was thrilled for the extra business, but she was also exhausted. She'd spent the first half of the week working from opening until long after closing. Besides the regular managerial duties, she'd spent hours prepping the store in anticipation of her upcoming absence. At her insistence, they'd dropped the Cupid costume from Gator Claus's wardrobe and Abuela had come up with a very sharp NASCAR outfit for him to wear, complete with a checkered cap. Even Pop had approved. He noticed the hours Grace had been putting in and commented on it.

Grace hadn't planned to tell him about her weekend getaway with Joe, but she couldn't lie to Pop. Especially not about something that could affect the store.

"I'm going away for the weekend," Grace said. "I know Sunday is the big race and Saturday is going to be huge for the store, but I think everything is under control here."

Pop seemed a little taken aback at first. "All right," he said slowly. "If you say everything's under control at the store, then I have no problem with you taking off the weekend. But is there something I should know, Tomato? Or rather, *someone* I should know?" There wasn't so much disapproval in Pop's tone as disappointment. Why hadn't she told the family about Joe yet? Despite Abuela's dream and any niggling reservations in Grace's mind, it was past time she officially introduced Joe as her boyfriend to the O'Bryan clan.

"Actually, you've already met him. He's Dr. Fred's replacement at Sunshine Smiles."

Pop nodded like he remembered Joe. "The guy at the store."

"How about I bring him to supper on Sunday?"

"Good idea," Pop said.


It was now Friday, and as far as reputations went, Friday the thirteenth, Grace decided, had gotten the shaft. Who had proclaimed it an unlucky day? The weather was heavenly—a tart, crisp sixty degrees. Cool enough to wear jeans and boots and a light sweater, and comfortable enough to walk around all day and never feel anything other than absolutely perfect. But then, maybe she would have felt the same euphoria if it had been hot and muggy or raining or even snowing (although that would have been something). It was hard to tell, because the root cause of Grace's current happiness wasn't the weather.

She took one last look around the store. The aisles were neat, the inventory was full, and the cashiers were ready. Penny promised to call if there were any disasters, so at noon, feeling confident there was nothing left for her to do, Grace slipped off to her town house and packed her weekender. By two p.m, she and Joe were headed north on I-95 to St. Augustine.

Grace flipped on the radio, then leaned back in her seat to relax. Maybe she'd take a nap.

"Welcome to The Track, speedsters! It's Speedway Gonzalez taking you round and round Day-to-na Beach," said the voice on the radio. "We'll be live all day bringing you the latest in race events. Right now, we're at the bikini Jell-O wrestling match, and I don't know what's jiggling more: the girls or the Jell-O!" This was followed by a roar of obnoxious male laughter in the studio background. Speedster's minions were in top form.

Grace reached over to turn the dial.

"Leave it on," said Joe. "The guy's funny as hell."

"True," Grace said, "although not very politically correct."

Joe glanced at her out of the corner of his eye. "If you really find it offensive we can listen to something else."

It would be hypocritical to turn the dial, not when Grace listened to the show herself when she was alone in the car. And although she occasionally did laugh out loud, she wasn't proud of it. Listening to Speedway was like . . . catching a glimpse inside the enemy camp. Most times she listened more out of a sick curiosity than anything.

"Do men really think like this?" Grace asked. She could practically see the inside of Joe's brain churn, trying to figure out the best way to answer. "Be honest."

Joe shrugged. "No. And yes. It's like any parody or sarcasm, it's exaggerated, but there's always a kernel of truth hidden somewhere."

Grace couldn't argue with that. So they listened as Speedway went into detail on the contestants and gave a play-by-play account of the match. The show picked up momentum when he began taking callers.

"Can I just say that this whole Jell-O wrestling thing is a disgrace?" said a female voice.

"Who am I talking to?" Speedway asked.

"This is Loretta," said the caller.

"Loretta, aren't you the chick we turned away because you couldn't fit into the bikini the sponsor provided?"

"Absolutely not! I would never degrade myself in that way."

"So how would you degrade yourself?"

"I wouldn't do anything to degrade myself!" Loretta sputtered.

"Loretta, sweetheart, that's not what you said. You said you wouldn't degrade yourself in *that* way. Which implies . . ."

Joe turned down the volume. "Don't tell me that Loretta, or whatever her real name is, isn't getting her rocks off going one-on-one with Speedway."

"You think she's a fake?"

"More like a groupie."

Joe sounded so sure of himself that Grace couldn't help but play devil's advocate. "Maybe she's exactly what she claims to be. Maybe she's tired of hearing Speedway degrade women on the radio. Maybe, just maybe she wants to empower herself."

Joe threw her a look she couldn't interpret.

"What?"

"Don't be so naïve, Grace."

Something about this conversation didn't sit well with her. "Enlighten me, Joe."

"I'm just saying there are some women who like this kind of attention, and there are plenty of guys who are willing to give it to them."

"Like the kind of woman who walks into a rugby bar wearing a short dress?"

He sighed. "I thought we already hashed that out."

"So are you the kind of guy willing to *give them* this attention?"

Joe pulled his SUV into a rest stop and killed the engine. "I never claimed to be a saint." He turned in his seat to look at her. "Where is all this coming from?"

Good question. Grace could kick herself. This wasn't how she'd envisioned starting off her romantic weekend with Joe. She shouldn't let Speedway get under her skin. But she was tired, and her head was suddenly buzzing with visions of Melanie and her claim that Joe wanted to bring their relationship up to the "next level." Grace was certain Melanie's claim was bogus. Plus, there was the fact that Joe had made a point to tell Grace that he didn't mess around with his office staff. But Melanie was beautiful and she wanted Joe. What man wouldn't be tempted under the circumstances? Joe himself just admitted he was no saint. He was also no Felix Barberi, either. Grace didn't want to punish Joe for Felix's sins, but she also didn't want to be stupid.

"Joe, I think there's something important you should know. About Melanie. She's seriously obsessed with you."

"What is it with you and Melanie? Are you jealous of her?"

"No! Of course not."

"I already told you, she's not a problem." Joe was pensive a few seconds. "You say she's obsessed with me. Is there something you know that I don't?"

And here lay the crux of Grace's problem. Once you started lying, it led to more lies. If Ellen were here, she'd probably start quoting Shakespeare or Sir Walter Scott or somebody else equally irritating on the evils of deception. And she'd be right. Grace had to tell Joe about the club. But not this weekend . . .

"No, there's . . . nothing specific. I'm just speaking in general. Look, I'm sorry I brought up Melanie. I shouldn't have let Speedway's show ruin our drive up."

Joe took a minute to let it all sink in. "They're probably actors, anyway," he said.

Grace tried for a smile. "That's what I've always thought."

The tension caused by their little spat evaporated by the time they arrived in St. Augustine. They checked into a bed-and-breakfast on Sevilla Street, a restored late-nineteenth-century Victorian that Grace had always admired whenever she'd walked through the area surrounding the historic district. They spent the next two hours sightseeing, mulling their way through the crowds of tourists, many of them couples. St. Augustine, located between Daytona Beach and Jacksonville, was the nation's oldest European city. It was founded in the early sixteenth century by Spanish conquistadors and was the home of the Castillo de San Marcos—an old stone military fortress overlooking the water—as well as countless tourist offerings such as the Ripley's Believe It or Not Museum and Ponce de León's Fountain of Youth.

"How on earth did you get a room on Valentine's Day weekend on such short notice?" Grace remembered Joe had told her that his father owned a condo in St. Augustine and she had wondered why they weren't staying there. Not that she was complaining. The room at the bed-and-breakfast was charming, complete with a queen-sized poster bed, fireplace, and its own private patio.

"Who says it was on short notice?" They went into a side shop where Joe bought them a cotton candy to share. He stuffed his mouth with the pink sugary stuff, making him look like a big kid. "I made the reservation the day after New Year's Eve."

"Right," Grace said with a laugh. He had to be joking. Grace was almost certain Joe had never meant for them to last beyond that one night, let alone all the way to Valentine's Day.

He pretended to look hurt, but then he grinned and those dimples popped out and Grace decided she would believe anything he said when he smiled like that. Since they still had all of tomorrow, Joe said they would save the best for last. A morning visit to Ripley's, followed by the Spanish fort.

They ate dinner at a small restaurant near their bed-and-breakfast. The food was delicious and the atmosphere unhurried. Grace wore a long-sleeved red silk sheath, her black heels, and the Mikimoto pearls Mami and Pop had given her when she graduated from FSU. Joe wore dark linen slacks with a blue silk shirt open at the collar, a black blazer, and no tie. Grace was cognizant of the looks they received from the other patrons. It was similar to the ones they'd gotten that Sunday evening a few months earlier when they'd shopped together for Joe's

Thanksgiving feast. Only then, Grace had been amused by the stares. Tonight, she couldn't help but feel proud. Excited even. And maybe just a tad bit nervous. Although what she was nervous about, she had no idea. They didn't mention the Speedway show or Melanie again, and Grace was grateful for that, but they didn't talk about anything overly serious either.

After dinner, they took a horse-drawn carriage ride through town. The temperature had dipped into the forties but Joe had his arm around her the whole time so she stayed warm. By the time they got back to their room it was after eleven.

She sat on the edge of the bed, kicked off her heels and watched as Joe built up a fire. It was such a manly occupation, conjuring up images of caves and loincloths, that it made Grace giggle.

Joe turned and faced her. "Are you laughing at my fire?"

"Never," she said in a deep guttural voice. "Fire good."

Joe quickly caught on. "Fire better than good. Man make great fire." He joined her on the bed and gave her a slow, heated look. "Why woman still have dress on?"

Grace had no logical answer to that, so they dropped the caveman shtick along with their clothes and made love on the queen-sized bed in front of the blazing fire. Joe was sweet and slow and thoughtful, and Grace felt she'd never been happier. Afterward, they lay there for a few minutes not saying anything, both of them catching their breath. Then Joe pointed to the bedside clock. "Hey, it's official. Happy Valentine's Day."

It was ten minutes after midnight. The St. Valentine's Day Curse was broken!

"I have something for you." He slipped out of bed and padded his way to the closet.

"I thought I just got my present," Grace joked.

"This is one you can hold in your hand."

"I have something for you too." She grabbed his discarded

dress shirt and donned it, because she just couldn't prance around the room naked like he could. She pulled a box from her suitcase. "Here." She handed it to him. "You go first."

Joe ripped the paper off in one sweep. He stared down at the plastic shrink-wrapped bucket with the assorted paraphernalia inside. It was a child's toy, and now that he held it in his hands, she was struck with how ridiculous it looked.

"It's the last known mermaid-watching kit in existence," Grace said. Sure, Joe had liked it as a kid, but what would he do it with now?

"I love it," he said quietly.

"*Really?* I know it's kind of hokey, but it's actually a collector's item." She gave him a mock hard stare. "If I ever see it on eBay, I'm coming after you."

"I'd never do that," he said so solemnly that any anxiety she'd had over the present was instantly gone.

"Okay, my turn." She peeled off the paper to expose a plain white box. Inside was a pink wax mermaid. None of the Mold-A-Rama machines at Florida Charlie's made mermaids. "Where did you get this?" she asked.

"In Tampa, last weekend when I was there for the rugby match."

An image of Joe dressed in his rugby gear, most likely all muddy and sweaty, scouring through amusement parks to scope out Mold-A-Rama machines made her throat tighten. "It's the most romantic gift anyone's ever given me."

"Most girls would want jewelry or flowers. But I thought . . . Do you not see the irony here? You give me a mermaid watching kit and I give you this. It's like we're—"

"On the same page?"

He nodded. She snuggled up against him and stifled a yawn against his neck.

"I'm glad you decided to take the weekend off," Joe said.

"Me too." For a brief second she thought about Florida Charlie's. But everything had to be okay. Penny had promised she'd call if it wasn't.

"So you like this place? This bed-and-breakfast?"

"It's great." This time she couldn't stop the yawn. She let her fingers drift over his chest. In the next two seconds, she'd be asleep.

"I was worried maybe it wouldn't be as nice as it looked on the outside." He placed his hand over hers, the one that was making the lazy patterns over his skin, and stilled it. "I thought about taking you to my dad's condo."

It was an unfinished thought, one that made Grace suddenly alert.

"Why didn't you? Does your father have it rented out?"

"He doesn't rent it out. I have a key, but I've never used it."

"Why not?" she asked softly.

"I used to love that place when I was kid. Lots of windows. Right on the beach . . . My dad and I built this huge sand castle one summer. It took us an entire day. A local photographer took a picture of it and it showed up in the paper."

Although she couldn't see his face, she sensed him smile. She could also sense when the smile disappeared.

"I don't go there because that's where my father used to take his girlfriends."

"You mean, before he married your mother?"

"No, I mean *while* he was married to my mother."

Grace didn't know what to say.

"Of course, I didn't know that's what they were at the time. One summer, instead of coming up with us, my mom stayed back home to attend some charity event. I think they got in a fight about it, I'm not sure. I was only six or seven. So my dad and I got here and about an hour later this woman showed up. I thought she was the babysitter."

She could feel his heart beating with her palm. Oddly, it felt slow and steady. It was only her heart that was beating faster.

"Fucking bastard." He laughed, but it sounded more like a rusty growl.

Grace remembered the night she'd told him about Craig cheating on Sarah and how Felix had cheated on her. When she'd asked him if he'd ever been cheated on before, he'd answered no, but his expression had seemed off. She understood now. He'd been cheated on too, just not in the usual way.

"Apparently he had quite a reputation with the ladies. Especially among the ones who worked in his office."

Joe's firm insistence on keeping his private life separate from his professional life made more sense now. She could even understand why he hadn't wanted to acknowledge that he knew her in front of Tiffany. Not with the way she and Joe had first "met."

He shrugged. "He is what he is. I've accepted that and he and I are okay now. But I wanted you to know why I didn't take you to the condo. In case you thought . . . I don't know . . ."

There was something so incredibly vulnerable in his voice that Grace couldn't stand it anymore. Her heart felt like it was swelling, getting bigger and bigger while it pushed the rest of her organs off to the sides. She could hardly take a breath. She wanted to reach inside her chest and stop it, it hurt so much.

"Joe . . . I—" She shook her head, not sure of what she'd been about to say. So she kissed him instead. A deep, powerful, hungry kiss that she knew he'd respond to. And then he jumped her. Or maybe she jumped him. And this time he wasn't sweet and slow and thoughtful, and that was perfectly fine with her.


"This place is beautiful and creepy at the same time," Grace said.

They were inside the Spanish fort, gazing into one of the tiny holding rooms where prisoners had been housed during one of the many skirmishes over the fort's illustrious history. After a morning spent at the Ripley's Believe It or Not Museum, they had lunch at The Columbia restaurant, where Grace had pronounced the *ropa vieja* not nearly as good as her mother's. They'd made it to the fort just in time to see the last cannon demonstration of the day.

They climbed the steps to the observation deck, and when they reached the top, Joe kissed her. It was impulsive and Grace couldn't help but feel relieved. Although they'd had a nice enough day, Joe had seemed distant, which was unlike him, especially in light of last night's intimacy.

His cell phone went off. "It's my mother," he said, glancing at the screen.

Joe's mother had already called once this morning, during breakfast. Joe hadn't asked for privacy, so Grace had listened as they were eating. His end of the conversation had been basically a series of grunts. They spoke for a few minutes, with Joe once again giving noncommittal answers before he snapped the phone shut.

"Is she okay?" Grace asked.

"Everything's fine," he said.

They finished their tour of the fort and were walking back to the bed-and-breakfast when Joe's phone went off again. He looked at the screen and slipped his cell back in his pocket without answering.

"Is it your mom?" Grace asked, beginning to get worried.

Joe told her it wasn't. He placed his hand in hers and they walked back to the bed-and-breakfast. They had just walked into their room when she heard the pinging sound that meant he'd just received a text message.

What was with all the calls? Grace was dying to ask who it was, but if Joe wanted to share, then he would. A myriad of crazy thoughts flashed through Grace's mind. She wasn't jealous of Melanie, or anyone else for that matter, but still . . .

"I'll go run a bath," Grace said, slipping into the bathroom to allow him some privacy. When she came out a few minutes later to retrieve something out of her suitcase, Joe was packing his bag.

"Baby, I'm sorry, but we're going to have to cut the weekend short."

"Is your mother all right?"

"My mother's fine." He paused. "Let's just say there's some family drama going on that I have to take care of." She waited for him to expound but he didn't.

"Okay, I'll just gather up my stuff."

He reached out and pulled her in his arms. "Hey, this has nothing to do with us," he said, his voice all warm and husky. "I had a good weekend."

She smiled, relieved. "Me too."

"Tonight's not over. I'm going to drop you off at your place, go handle the Rosenblum version of 911, and come back. Although it will probably be late. Maybe around midnight, if that's okay."

"Not a problem. And Joe, don't worry. I understand. Family comes first."

# 27

# The Curse Strikes Again

Joe dropped her off at her town house, so Grace called Sarah and made plans to attend the Dragon's housewarming party. In a way, Grace was okay with the way things had turned out. She'd had her romantic getaway with Joe, but now that it had been cut short, she could support Sarah. She didn't once consider going to the boyfriend club meeting at The Continental. Penny and Ellen could handle things for one night.

Sarah said the Dragon was on the fussy side, so best to dress up. Grace didn't have time to think about what to wear, so she donned the same red silk sheath she'd worn to dinner the previous night in St. Augustine, which luckily had traveled well and hadn't wrinkled. Sarah wore a coral-colored cocktail dress shot through with gold metallic thread and matching gold belt. Her hair was twisted into a knot at the nape of her neck. She looked like she'd just walked out of a fashion magazine, all cool and elegant and sexy, and Grace couldn't help but feel how unfair it was that Craig was already remarried and here Sarah was starting over, going on a blind date of all things.

"Thanks for tagging along," Sarah said, turning her car onto a side street. "What did Joe say? He had a family crisis to take care of?"

"Something like that."

A man wearing an orange vest waved them forward to the next vacant spot along the grassy edge of the road. Grace estimated there must be over forty cars already parked. Brightly lit tiki torches lined both sides of the path leading to the front door.

"Parking attendants and everything. Very fancy," Grace said.

Just as they were about to step inside the house, Sarah grabbed her wrist. "Now be honest. Tell me if you hate it. Tell me if you think it's too fussy."

The house was a four-thousand-square-foot Mediterranean revival with a backyard view of the river. The floors were wall-to-wall polished Mexican tile. There were lots of leather pieces and dark woods, but it wasn't overdone. Everything seemed to serve a purpose, giving the home a minimalist feel befitting the architecture. The color scheme consisted of burnt orange, gold, and brown, making the home feel warm and inviting.

Sarah guided her to a small hallway off the foyer and into the formal living room. Three floor-to-ceiling picture windows looked out into a small courtyard patio with a bubbling fountain. In the center of the room was the infamous floral couch. A baby grand piano sat in one corner. Grace had to admit, it was a more feminine version of the rest of the house, but it all flowed beautifully. She knew Sarah was good, but this was artistry.

"It's beautiful!" Grace said. "It's you, but it's not. I mean, it's like the house decorated itself the way it should."

"Really? You like it?"

"No, I don't *like* it. I love it."

Sarah's face glowed at the compliment. Grace couldn't help a rush of envy. Sarah had known since high school what she'd wanted to do with her life. Charlie lived, breathed, and practically ate the law. Then there was Ellen, who would shrivel and die if she couldn't quote a legion of dead writers. Grace loved

Florida Charlie's, but being the manager of a tourist store wasn't exactly a calling.

"Sarah!" a deep female voice called, making them both turn.

"Nora Sherman, I presume," Grace muttered as she and Sarah watched the elegantly clad sixty-something woman walk into the room. The Dragon was shorter than Grace had imagined, but then with a nickname like the Dragon, Grace had also been expecting her to be green and have scales. She had lively blue eyes and thick brown hair styled in a pageboy. She also emitted a high energy to which Grace was immediately drawn.

"Mrs. Sherman, everything looks wonderful!" Sarah said.

Nora Sherman frowned at their empty hands. "Where are your drinks? Why don't you have drinks?" She hailed a tuxedo-clad server and demanded he bring them champagne at once. He instantly complied. Not that there was any doubt that he would. Nora Sherman had the air of someone who always got her way. Grace almost felt sorry for her doctor son. She also now knew why Sarah had given in on the floral couch. "That's much better." She gave Sarah a hug and smiled curiously at Grace. "And you brought a friend!"

Sarah made the introductions.

"Grace O'Bryan," the Dragon mused. "Why does that name seem familiar? Are you related to the Fort Lauderdale O'Bryans by any chance?"

"No, ma'am, just the Daytona Beach O'Bryans."

"You're not Jewish, are you? Have I seen you at Temple?"

"Um, no."

"Oh, well." She linked her arm through Grace's to pull her off to the side. "Has Sarah told you I'm fixing her up with my son?" Although Sarah was just a few feet away, she didn't bother lowering her voice.

"She's mentioned it."

"Do you have a boyfriend, Grace?" Then, before Grace could

answer, she said, "I don't know what's wrong with young people today! Take my son, a handsome, eligible doctor, and he's still single and seems perfectly content to stay that way. Which leaves me all the work of finding him a wife. When am I going to have grandchildren? What's there to live for if I don't have grandchildren? What's the purpose of this house, the purpose of all my money, if I can't spoil *someone* rotten?"

Grace could only nod, mesmerized by the Dragon's power. Poor Sarah. The Dragon might not let her leave tonight until the next generation of Sherman offspring was neatly tucked inside her uterus. Grace could hear her now: "But, sweetheart, the guests are already here!" A shotgun wedding and consummation all at once.

The Dragon dropped Grace's arm. "You two stay right here. Don't move a hair! Not one hair on those gorgeous heads of yours. I'm going to get Phillip right now."

"Why do I feel like we're stuck in a modern day version of *Fiddler on the Roof*?" Grace said once they were alone again.

"Just play nice, and when she's not looking, we can make a fast escape. Maybe we can even make the club meeting tonight. Ellen's been sharpening her laptop. Should be interesting."

Before Grace could respond, the Dragon was back, her arm looped around a surprisingly handsome man. Introductions were made. Dr. Phillip Sherman, cardiologist, mid-thirties, somewhere between medium and tall (which meant tall for Sarah), sandy brown hair, blue eyes. Phillip looked as embarrassed as he should be under the circumstances, and Grace couldn't help but instantly like him for it.

"I'll just leave you two young people alone." She tried to wave Grace out the door. "Let me show you what Sarah did upstairs in my bedroom."

Uncertain what to do, Grace looked to Sarah, who gave her the "leave and you die" stare. "Maybe later, Mrs. Sherman."

The Dragon frowned. "How about I bring a fresh round of champagne," she said, going after a waiter.

"We have about three minutes until she comes back with reinforcements," Phillip said, eliciting a relaxed smile from Sarah. "So . . . you're the decorating goddess my mother can't stop talking about."

"That's me," Sarah said, raising her champagne flute in mock salute.

"And I'm playing the role of best friend who's come along to chaperone," Grace added.

Phillip smiled, but along with the embarrassment there was also undisguised weariness in his eyes. "I love what you've done to the place," he said to Sarah. "The lobster bisque color you used in the family room really makes that north wall pop."

Sarah gave Phillip a discreet once-over that Grace immediately caught. "You think so? I almost told the painters to go entirely with the cream, but I wanted just a hint of something different."

"It's very subtle. Mother would never have thought of it herself."

Grace listened to the two of them talk. Phillip was an avid sailor as well as an amateur photographer. He'd taken all the sailboat pictures that Sarah had strategically placed throughout the house. Sarah kept throwing little smiles Grace's way and Grace politely smiled back.

"Here we are!" the Dragon said. Grace glanced at her watch. Her timing must be off. It had taken five minutes for the reinforcements. Nora had brought along another woman, maybe a couple of years younger than her and with a less animated air. "This is my sister, Lydia, who's visiting from Fort Lauderdale but I'm trying to convince her to move up here, and if she does— and she *will*, because I always get my way—she'll need a decorator. Sarah, darling, do you have your cards with you?"

Sarah pulled a business card from her clutch and handed it to the Dragon's sister, who smiled and thanked her. Grace was instantly mesmerized. There was something familiar about her but Grace was positive she'd never met her before tonight.

"Joe! Sweetheart, come here, come here!" Nora Sherman called to someone in the foyer. That's when Grace realized what was so familiar about Lydia's smile. *It was the dimples!*

"I have someone I want you to meet." She winked at Grace. "My nephew, who by the way is also single. Not an MD, he's a DDS." She whispered in Grace's ear, "Personally, a much better occupation for married life. None of those *terrible* overnight calls my poor Phillip has to take." Then in a louder voice, "You didn't know there'd be two of them, did you, Sarah! I have to say I'm surprised myself. Rarely do I have both my favorite men in the same place at the same time."

Grace turned to see Joe stroll into the room, hands in his pockets. He spotted her and, for a second, stopped in his tracks, but then he forced a smile and pushed ahead. This was the family drama that had cut their weekend short? Why hadn't he simply told her he had a familial obligation to attend his aunt's party? Grace would have understood. Especially after meeting the Dragon. There was no way anyone could say no to the woman.

"Here he is! My other beautiful boy!" Nora stood on tiptoe to give Joe a peck on the cheek, then made a hasty round of introductions.

This wasn't how Grace had imagined meeting Joe's family. Maybe this was a good thing, though. There was no time to be nervous or second guess what she'd worn. She moistened her lips and smiled. "We actually already know one another," Grace said.

"Really!" Nora's eyes widened. "Joe, are you holding out on us?" She turned to her sister. "Lydia! Why didn't you tell—"

"Grace is a patient of mine." Joe smiled again and Grace froze.

It was the same smile he'd given her in his office three months ago when he'd pretended he'd never met her before. Impersonal. Professional.

"Isn't that a coincidence? Not that Daytona Beach is that big, but still, what are the odds? Now that we have a happy four-some here, I say we leave the young people alone to do what they do best. Lydia and I are going to mingle with the old stodgy folks." The Dragon took her sister by the hand. Joe's mother smiled apologetically and let herself be dragged away.

Had Joe really just introduced Grace as one of his *patients*?

Sarah cleared her throat nervously, and Phillip looked on, confused, because he could tell something was happening, only he wasn't sure exactly what it was.

Grace set her champagne flute on a table and made fast tracks for the front door.

"I'll just follow her," she heard Sarah say.

But Joe caught up with Grace first. His hand touched her elbow. "Grace—"

She spun around. "Oh! It's my dentist, Dr. Rosenblum. Fancy meeting you here."

He winced at her sarcasm. "Let's go outside where we can talk."

"I can talk perfectly fine in here. Is there something constricting your larynx? Maybe you can get your cousin the doctor to fix it."

"Grace, please." He looked a suitable combination of guilty and miserable, giving Grace a modicum of satisfaction.

"I can't believe you," she said, hating how her voice came out all wobbly. Now wasn't the time to get soft. It was the time for *Mal Genio* to make an appearance. She should be mad. But she wasn't. She could feel the tears pooling behind her eyes. If she started crying, she'd never forgive herself.

"Let's go outside and talk. Please."

What was he going to say? I'm sorry, I panicked, please forgive me?

Grace felt herself soften. She could understand that.

Without asking for permission, he took her by the hand and led her through the house to the backyard, winding their way around the other guests. She was reminded of how earlier in the day she'd walked through the streets of St. Augustine like this, her hand in Joe's warm, confident grasp. Joe hadn't lied to her. He'd just left out the fact that the family emergency was a party. She could deal with that. Family situations were complicated. But the other part? The part where he'd basically pretended he didn't know her? She really hoped he had a good explanation for that.

They ended up on a narrow wooden dock, which was deserted and quiet and far enough away from the house that they would be assured privacy. The river was dark and still. For a second *Mal Genio* thought about pushing Joe into the water. Grace had to admit, it was tempting. But then she'd just have to jump in after him to make sure he didn't drown (although Joe was a perfectly fine swimmer), and she didn't want to ruin her dress.

"I'm sorry I didn't tell you about the party," he said. "My mother and my aunt have been on my case for the last week to attend, but I wanted to spend the weekend with you."

She'd been so stunned earlier that she hadn't noticed much. But now that the shock of seeing him had worn off, she could take in everything about him. He wore tan slacks and a black long-sleeved turtleneck and expensive-looking leather shoes. He'd come dressed to impress. Had he known his aunt might try to fix him up?

"Go on."

"Obviously, I had no intention of being here, but this afternoon my cousin called and asked me to come. And I couldn't say no to him, Grace. If Sarah had needed you, I mean really needed you, would you have said no to her?"

Grace sighed. She knew exactly what Joe was referring to. She could understand why he'd ditched their weekend, but it still didn't excuse his pretending she was nothing but a patient.

"Your aunt has no idea, does she? About Phillip?"

Joe looked surprised. "How did you know?"

"Sometimes a woman just senses this kind of stuff. Why doesn't he just tell her?"

"He plans to tonight. After the party."

"So what are you supposed to be? Backup?"

"Something like that."

"Nora's a smart woman. So she's a little pushy, but I like her. She doesn't seem the type to faint dead on the spot just because she finds out her son is gay." He didn't say anything. "Are the two of you close?"

"Like brothers."

"So how come you've never mentioned him before?"

"I haven't?"

"No, Joe, you haven't." A sudden wind rippled off the water, making Grace shiver. She rubbed her hands up and down her arms to warm herself. "You have a cousin who you're obviously close to, who lives here in town, and you've never talked about him, let alone introduced me to him. And instead of telling me why you had to cut the weekend short, you give me this cryptic excuse. And honestly, Joe? I'm okay with that because, like you said, we don't have to know every little thing about each other. Not right away anyway. And I get not wanting me to meet your family yet, because, I agree, it's a big deal and it has to be thought out. But Joe, if we'd run into my family at a restaurant, I sure as hell wouldn't have introduced you as my *dentist*."

"You might not remember, but the only time I've met your family, that's exactly how you introduced me."

"*What?* You mean that time you came to the store? That's not fair, Joe, we weren't together then."

"We'd already gone out, Grace. At least in my mind we had."

The friends dinner at the beach. She should have known Joe would have considered that a date. "The situation is different now."

"Why? Because it's *you*? In my defense, I was caught off guard."

"Okay, we can fix that. Let's go back into the house and you can introduce me to your mother again."

He shoved his hands in his pockets and looked out toward the water. "I know you think that sounds really simple, but believe me, my mother and my aunt will make a big deal about us. So unless you're ready to make a big deal about us too, I'd rather we wait."

"What do you mean, unless *I'm* ready?"

He turned and faced her. "Am I your boyfriend, Grace?"

"What kind of question is that?"

"It's the same one you asked me last week."

"Of course, you're my boyfriend! I don't go away for the weekend with just anyone, Joe."

This mollified him some. "I just think you need to dig deep inside and see if I'm what you really want."

"Is this because of Brandon? Because he was at the hospital the day my dad had his attack?"

"I've already told you, I'm not jealous of Farrell. But I admit, it would have been nice if you'd wanted me there."

"I'm sorry. It was nothing personal, Joe."

"Yeah, I know. Just family and close friends."

"That's not fair! You're upset because I didn't invite you to come to the hospital when we'd been dating less than two weeks at the time. And here you have this whole secret life I know nothing about. So let me ask *you*, Joe. Am I what *you* really want?"

"I thought so," he admitted. "But honestly? As great as we are together, it feels like there's something missing."

Grace was speechless. Was Joe breaking up with her? *She* was the wronged party here!

"Tell me, Grace. Have you told Sarah about her ex? Because she deserves to know the whole truth. The two of you will never be right until you do."

"Never be right? What are you now, a relationship expert?"

"Grace?" Sarah's voice called out from the edge of the dock. "I'm . . . I'm sorry to interrupt, but it's kind of an emergency."

Grace's heart stopped. "Is it Pop? Is he okay?"

"No, it's not your dad," Sarah rushed to reassure her. "It's the . . . club meeting. Penny called to tell us there's been a change in venue. The meeting is taking place at Florida Charlie's."

"But I thought it was going to be at The Continental!"

"Something got screwed up. Penny sounds really frantic."

*Shit.* What had Ellen done now?

"I have to go," she told Joe.

"You're ditching me because of your women's empowerment group?" he asked incredulously.

"It's more complicated than that." *A whole lot more complicated.* "Call me. Or I'll call you!" she yelled over her shoulder, already making her way back to the house. She didn't turn around and take one last sad look at Joe standing there on the dock. She wasn't going to do that. Because if she did, she might be tempted to run back, and apparently she had a fire to put out.

# 28

# Overbooked, Overwhelmed, and So, So Over It

"I'm sorry to drag you away from the party," Grace said to Sarah. They'd come together, so they'd left together. Taxi service in Daytona Beach was iffy at best.

"No big deal," Sarah said. "I told the Dragon you had a family emergency. She really likes you. Said you gave off good chutzpah. I think if things don't work out between me and Phillip, you'll be number one on her potential daughter-in-law list." Sarah's voice was flat. Had she overheard Joe and Grace arguing about her on the dock?

"Is she really that clueless?"

"Apparently so." Sarah sped up to pass a car. "How could you tell? About Phillip?"

"It was obvious he wasn't into either one of us, which wouldn't have meant anything, except he never once snuck a peek at your rack. And don't take this the wrong way, because you know I'm totally a straight girl, but even *I'm* drawn to your magnificent cleavage."

Sarah laughed, but it didn't sound right.

Grace shifted in her seat. There was no doubt by Sarah's strange mood that she'd overheard part of Grace and Joe's conversation. "How about you?"

"The first red flag was when he called the pink color I used in the family room 'lobster bisque,' which is the most *perfect* description ever, and I wish I'd thought of it. But the clincher was when he kept talking interior design. Not that straight guys don't do that once they find out what I do for a living, but Phillip actually has good taste. It was the final nail in the coffin. He's pretty cool. He wants me to decorate his office."

"That's great."

"What was going on between you and Joe? That's so weird how he turned up at the party. Who knew he and the Dragon were related?"

"Small world, huh?" Grace's emotions teetered between mad and wanting to cry on Sarah's shoulder. But she had to keep it together long enough to take care of the situation at Florida Charlie's. She could fall apart later.

Sarah threw her a long look. "Why didn't he introduce you as his girlfriend?"

"That's the beautiful part. He actually had the nerve to throw it all back on me."

She told Sarah how Joe had found out about Brandon being at the hospital the day of Pop's attack, and what he said about Grace needing to figure out what she wanted and how there was something "missing" in their relationship. She fought the tears threatening to pool up again.

"You know, Grace," Sarah said, "maybe Joe's right."

"*Et tu*, Sarah?"

Sarah sighed and the sound of it made Grace cringe because she knew exactly what was coming next. "I overheard Joe say that I deserve to know the whole truth. What was he talking about?"

"Sarah, this is kind of a bad time. Can we please talk about this later?"

"I want to talk about it now."

"But—"

"*Now*, Grace."

*Sarah's stubborn and unforgiving.*

Charlie was definitely right about the stubborn part. Joe said her relationship with Sarah would never be right until they got everything about Craig out in the open. He was wrong, though. If anything, it would create a chasm in their relationship, not bring them closer together. But Grace was tired of keeping the secret. Tired of walking on eggshells whenever the subject of Sarah's marriage came up.

Grace shut her eyes tight. Best to spill it all out at once before she lost her nerve. "Three days before your wedding, Craig cheated on you with Carla."

"How do you know that?" Sarah asked in a calmer voice than Grace would have expected.

Grace slowly opened her eyes. "Because I caught them."

There were no tears, no screaming. Only Sarah frowning, like she was thinking hard about something. "Go on."

Grace told her the whole sordid story. "He promised me he would tell you. And I thought, okay, if he's innocent, and nothing happened, then it would all be cool. And I kept waiting for you to say something, but you never did. And . . . I knew I couldn't keep it from you, and I was so mad that it was going to be *me* breaking your heart with that kind of news. So I pretended to myself that he'd told you and that it was nothing, and that's why you never said anything. Then at the reception, I had enough booze in me to work up the nerve to ask Craig if he'd told you about Carla, and the son-of-a-bitch said no. And I knew . . . *I knew* then that he'd lied to me. That he *had* slept with her and I should have found a way to tell you, no matter how happy you seemed. But by then it was too late. So all this time I've kept my mouth shut. And I could see that it wasn't the greatest marriage, but I thought maybe it was just, you know, a matter of the two of you adjusting. And then he cheated on you again and it's *my* fault because if I had told you about the first time, I don't think you would have ever married him." The tears that Grace had been holding back for the past hour now streamed down her cheeks.

"Wow. No wonder you hated Craig so much!" Sarah shook her head and laughed incredulously, like she'd just found the final piece to a puzzle that had eluded her for a long time.

*That was it?* This was all the reaction she was going to get? Maybe Grace was misinterpreting and it was hysterical laughter. That must be it. She'd pushed Sarah over the edge.

Sarah suddenly stopped laughing. "Grace," she said, alarmed. "Look at the parking lot."

Grace swiped the tears from her face and craned her neck to get a better view of what lay ahead. Florida Charlie's was overrun with cars. They circled to the back of the building, but there was a minivan parked in Grace's private spot.

Sarah made a face. "Of all the nerve! Can't they read? I'll drop you off in front and find a place to park across the street."

"Sarah, I'm . . . I'm so sorry."

"About what?"

*About what?* "What do you *think* I'm sorry about?"

"Oh. No worries, Grace. It's not your fault. I understand why you didn't want to tell me about Craig."

Grace had known Sarah long enough to know when she was being sincere. She really *didn't* blame Grace for not telling her. Grace felt an overwhelming rush of relief. "Boy, was Charlie ever wrong about you!"

"*Charlie?* What does he have to do with this?" The color drained from Sarah's face. "Did Charlie know Craig cheated on me before the wedding?"

"Of course not. The only person I ever told was Joe. But . . . Charlie and I did discuss you and Craig once. I was afraid you were going to take Craig back, but Charlie told me not to worry. He said you were stubborn and unforgiving, which obviously isn't the case because—"

"Charlie said I was *unforgiving*?"

"Yeah. What does he know, right?"

A car horn blasted, startling them both. Sarah glanced up at the rearview mirror. "There's a car sitting on my ass. You jump out and I'll meet you inside."

Grace got out of the car and hustled around to the front of the store. The hat to Gator Claus's new NASCAR outfit was missing. He also looked extremely unhappy. "Tell me about it," Grace muttered. She opened the doors to the sound of a dozen different conversations buzzing at once.

There must have been at least a hundred women in the store. Grace recognized a few of the regulars from former meetings, but there were a lot of new faces as well. It took her a few minutes before she spotted Penny.

"Thank God you're here!" Penny said.

"What happened? I thought the meeting was going to be at The Continental!"

Penny's eyes narrowed. "Ask Ellen about that one." She pointed to the Hemingway corner, where Ellen was setting up her laptop. "She and some of her sycophants swooped in before the store was closed and now I can't get them out. Should I have called the police?"

"The police? No! We can't call the cops on Ellen. Besides, it would draw too much attention to what's going on. I'll take care of it myself."

Grace marched up to Ellen and tapped her on the shoulder. "I need to talk to you in private." She pulled Ellen into her office and flicked on the light switch.

"I swear I didn't do this on purpose!" Ellen said, already on the defensive. "I got to the hotel early to set up, but they had our dates screwed up. And they had this big wedding reception going on and nobody would talk to me and finally the manager said that since it was Speed Week and also Valentine's Day, there was no way they could accommodate us because they'd over-booked. Then all these women started showing up. What was I supposed to do?"

"You're an English teacher. Do you not understand what the word *cancel* means?"

Ellen flushed. "I thought about it. I really did, but it's Valentine's Day, Grace! And these women *need* this meeting. Tonight of all nights, especially. You of all people remember how it feels to be alone on Valentine's Day." Ellen stilled. "Wait, what are you doing here? Aren't you supposed to be on a big romantic weekend with Joe?"

"It's . . . complicated."

"Oh, Grace, no! Not the St. Valentine's Day Curse again." Ellen grabbed her into a hug. "I'm so sorry!"

"So am I, Ellen, but it's not important right now. Explain to me how you ended up here at Florida Charlie's when I specifically told you no more meetings."

"Like I said, I couldn't let all these women down. I'd have had the meeting at my apartment but you know how small my place is. So I thought just one more meeting and I promise, we'll never have it here again. I honestly didn't think so many women would show up. The word has spread like wildfire. Can you imagine how many women still think the meeting is at The Continental? I bet we would have had twice this number!" Ellen ended in an excited rush.

"Okay," Grace said, trying to stay calm. "This is what we're going to do. You're going to make an announcement and tell them that the February meeting of the boyfriend club has been canceled."

"But since we're already here, I thought—"

"Don't *think*, Ellen. It's what's getting us in trouble. Go out there and tell them we'll make the March meeting a double-header, anything to placate them, then steer them all to Coco's."

Ellen looked like a kid whose lollipop had just been stolen. "All right, I guess it's the practical thing to do. I really am sorry, Grace. I didn't mean for this to happen. And I'm really sorry about Joe, too."

Grace stepped outside the office to find Penny waiting to talk to her. "I hate to bring you more bad news, but you're not going to believe what's happening. All those cars outside are making people think the store is still open. We have tourists stopping and wanting to buy stuff. I already closed out the cash registers and the only cashier left in the store is Marty. Grace, what do I do?"

Grace looked at the time. Officially, the shop closed fifteen minutes ago, but there were still customers! She wished Pop could be here to see this. On the other hand, no, she was definitely happy Pop wasn't here to see this. "As much as I'd love to keep selling, there's too much chaos in the store. Can you get Marty to man the door? He can divert away the tourists."

"What should he tell people?"

"He can say that it only *looks* like we're open because we're having . . . an employee meeting." Although this was the strangest group of "employees" Grace could have imagined. Women ranging in age from twenty to sixty were crammed standing room only in the Hemingway corner. They overflowed into the aisles and along the sides of the walls. Most of them were dressed for clubbing, which was probably in the plans for later tonight. Hopefully they would cooperate when they learned the boyfriend club meeting was canceled. Grace spotted Melanie a few aisles over. Great. Just the person she wanted to see.

Ellen made her way to the front of the room. She had to climb up on a chair to be seen. "May I have your attention, everyone!" It took a few shouts of admonishment from the crowd urging them to stop talking before it was quiet enough for Ellen to speak. "Thank you! I'd like to welcome all of you to the February boyfriend of the month club."

The women began to cheer.

A slightly-out-of-breath Sarah pushed her way through the crowd. "Where did all these women come from?"

All Grace could do was shake her head.

"Now," Ellen began, "I have some good news and some bad news. The good news is we now have over two hundred members on our Yahoo! site."

*Two hundred members?* Grace was dumbfounded. How had the club grown so large?

"Another piece of good news is that the reviews have been pouring in. Besides the men we've critiqued live during our meetings, we've had almost fifty more profiles added to the files. Good work, ladies!" Ellen cried, pumping her fist in the air like she was revving up the crowd at an Amway meeting.

She waited until the cheering died down to put on her sad face. "As you can see, due to unforeseen circumstances, we certainly aren't at The Continental tonight." This was met by some polite laughter. "I'd like to apologize for any inconvenience this might have caused."

Grace tried to catch Ellen's attention. When was she going to tell everyone the meeting was canceled?

"It should also be apparent that our club has grown in leaps and bounds and there simply isn't enough room to conduct a meeting here tonight, so unfortunately—"

"You're not canceling, are you?" someone shouted. "I hired a babysitter to come to this meeting. Do you know how expensive it is to get a sitter on Valentine's Day?" A low hiss of disgruntled mumbling could be heard throughout the store.

Ellen looked taken aback. "Of course, we're not *canceling*," she said. "But we're definitely cutting the meeting short."

"How short?" someone asked.

"We only have time for one review. A small one," Ellen said, avoiding Grace's glare. A dozen hands shot up in the air.

"I'm going to kill Ellen," Grace said, not bothering to lower her voice.

"You," Ellen said, pointing to a woman standing in the T-shirt aisle. "You're new, aren't you? Why don't you introduce yourself and tell us about your latest boyfriend."

"My name is Phoebe Cutter and I'm an attorney at Lockett and Jones."

"Hel-lo, Phoebe!" the crowd roared.

"Phoebe, why don't you come stand next to me so everyone can hear you better?" Ellen said.

"Grace, is that Charlie's Phoebe?" Sarah asked. "The one who came to dinner that Sunday after Mass?"

Grace watched the tall redhead make her way to the front of the crowd. "Yeah, but they never dated. Charlie told me they had a few drinks and he kissed her. End of story. She's probably going to diss on the boyfriend she tried to cheat on with Charlie."

Phoebe gave the crowd a shaky smile. "First, I want to thank you for the warm welcome. I've had a chance to read some of the reviews you ladies have posted on the Yahoo! site. It's your strength and honesty in telling it just like it is that has given me the courage to come here tonight. *Despite* what might be a hostile environment." Phoebe looked directly at Grace and Grace felt herself go cold. What on earth was she going to say?

"The past few months have been difficult for me," Phoebe said. "I've been sexually harassed by a man I work with. A man who has the power to get me fired on a whim."

The crowd quieted. Ellen began pounding away on her computer keys.

Sarah grabbed Grace's hand and squeezed it. Surely Sarah

didn't think Phoebe was talking about Charlie, did she? Grace turned to look at Sarah, but Sarah's gaze was glued straight ahead.

"It began innocently enough," Phoebe said. "We were both working late at the office every night, and one evening, we went out for drinks. I have a boyfriend, but he lives in Orlando, so we don't see each other during the week and, I admit, I was lonely. This man I work with . . . he kissed me. I told him I was involved with someone and I thought that was the end of it. But then the harassment started. He said he would get me fired if I didn't sleep with him." Phoebe sniffed and Ellen produced a Kleenex from her purse and handed it to her. Phoebe dabbed at her eyes. "Thank you. This whole thing has just been so . . . awful!"

"Did you sleep with him?" someone in the room shouted.

"No, but every day it gets harder."

Sarah's grip grew tight. How many attorneys at Lockett and Jones was Phoebe having drinks with? The similarity to Charlie's story was uncanny, except for the last part, of course. There was no way Phoebe was talking about Charlie. Grace held her breath.

"Weeding out the creeps from the dating pool is exactly what this club is about," Ellen said, her face tight with indignation. "Knowledge is power! Okay, Phoebe, lets have this loser's stats."

"His name is Charlie O'Bryan and—"

"You lying *bitch*!" Sarah yelled. Grace watched, her jaw agape, as Sarah pushed her way to the front of the room. "Take it back!"

Ellen's hands froze over the computer keyboard.

"I will not!" Phoebe said. "It's the truth!"

"Prove it," Sarah shot back.

"I don't have to prove anything!" Phoebe said. Despite the fact that Sarah only came up to Phoebe's chin, she looked so angry that Phoebe took an uncertain step back.

Grace overcame the shock of Sarah's unexpected outburst to edge her way through the packed room. She grabbed the laptop from Ellen's hands and snapped it shut. To Ellen's credit, she didn't protest.

"Okay, everyone, listen up! My name is Grace O'Bryan. I'm the manager of this store and I say this meeting is officially over, so everybody out!"

"Of course, she's trying to shut me up. Charlie O'Bryan is her brother!" Phoebe informed the crowd.

Some of the women began booing. Ellen implored them to settle down, but no one paid her any attention now. Over the rumble of female chattering, Grace heard a familiar deep voice yell, "Penny!"

It was Butch.

He was standing in the doorway, his dark eyes darting through the crowd. Grace could tell the instant Butch found Penny. His face split in a grin and he took off for the center of the store in a determined stride.

Women began coming at Grace from everywhere, some of them chastising her for refusing to let Phoebe speak. Most of them were angry that she'd cut the meeting short. Grace did her best to shake them off and headed toward Penny and Butch, who were now clutched in the tightest public embrace Grace had ever witnessed.

"What was I thinking?" Butch said. "Pen, I can't live without you. Not one more day!"

"I missed you so much!" Penny said, her voice thick with tears. "I'm going with you. Right now. This instant!"

Butch laughed and picked Penny up and swung her around just like they did in the movies, then he laid a great big kiss on her.

Grace cleared her throat. "Butch, I hate to interrupt this really awesome reunion, but I need your help."

Butch lowered Penny to the ground but kept his arms around her. "Big Butch is here and at your service. What do you need?"

"Can you help me clear this place out?" Grace asked.

Butch quickly surveyed the situation. "Your book club sure has grown."

"It's not a book club anymore. It's more like a . . . women's empowerment group," Penny explained.

Butch looked confused by the fancy title but he shrugged and placed his fingers in his mouth to produce a bloodcurdling whistle. Immediately the place quieted. "Listen up, ladies! Florida Charlie's is closed. You have five minutes to get your tushes out of here before I personally toss 'em out."

"I'd like to see you try!" a woman in the crowd shouted.

Butch identified the heckler and started after her. The woman took one look at Butch and went tearing out of the store. Not that Grace blamed her. Six foot four and clad entirely in black leather, Butch was imposing, to say the least. Within seconds, women began shoving at one another to reach the front door.

"Are you Grace O'Bryan, the club's founder?" a woman with short spiky black hair asked.

"That's me, but really, I don't have time to explain why we're canceling the rest of the meeting and—"

"My name is Shania Brown and I'm doing a piece on the club for my Internet column. Maybe you've heard of it? *What's Up, Daytona Beach?*"

"Your Internet column? Do you mean your blog? No, sorry, never heard of it."

"Really? Oh . . . well, you will," she said with a laugh. "Anyway, you'll be thrilled to know that I'm dedicating my Monday morning column entirely to your club." She pulled out a notebook. "Can you tell me about this Felix Barberi character? Is he real? Or is he a combination of different men that you've dated?"

"How do you know about Felix?"

"I read his file on the Yahoo! site."

"But that's only accessible by members!"

"I joined a few weeks ago."

Grace blinked. She had no idea it was that easy to get into the files.

"Look, Shania, I'm sorry, but I don't want to talk about the club. I have a feeling this is going to be our last meeting anyway."

Shania looked stricken. "But it can't be! Grace, I don't think you understand what you've started here. Once I write my article, boyfriend clubs are going to start springing up all over the country." Grace tried to walk away, but Shania got up in her face. "Can I at least have a comment on what it felt like to discover that your brother is going to have a rather unflattering file of his own?"

"That's ridiculous. There will be no such file. The woman is a liar."

Shania began scribbling in her pad.

"Hey! I didn't say you could quote me. Although it's true. Phoebe Cutter is just pissed because my brother wasn't interested in her. She even followed him to Mass one Sunday and had dinner with our family. Does *that* sound like a woman who's being forced into a relationship?"

"How long did Ms. Cutter and your brother date before the harassment began?"

"They didn't date!"

Shania's attention shifted from Grace to a movement at the front of the store. Grace turned to see two uniformed Daytona Beach police officers.

"Who's in charge here?" the taller of the two officers asked.

Grace identified herself as the store's manager.

The shorter officer took a swift look around the store. "This is a great place you have here."

"Thanks," Grace said. Anyone who liked Florida Charlie's was okay in her book. She glanced at his name tag. Lakowski. It seemed familiar.

"We had a call saying that there's a disturbance going on." Tall Officer looked around the shop. "Are all these women customers?"

"Who called in?" Grace asked.

"I did!" The woman whom Butch had run out of the store marched up to the officers. Red faced, she pushed a strand of hair from her eyes. "That man," she said, pointing to Butch, "assaulted me. I want him arrested!"

"I never laid a finger on you, Bubble Butt," Butch said in disgust.

"I do not have a big butt!" the woman screeched. She pulled a paper from her purse and flung it at Officer Lakowski. "I came here in good faith to attend a meeting. Then she"—she nodded at Grace—"got all in a huff because her brother was exposed as a sexual predator. She went all psycho on us and demanded we leave. She even called this goon in to toss us out."

The police officer studied the paper in his hand. Grace peered over his shoulder. It was the flyer that Janine had put out a couple of months ago.

"Ma'am," Officer Lakowski said to Grace, "can you explain what's going on here?"

"Well, it's like this. My friends and I used to have this book club. It was just four of us, and since my assistant manager and I often work until closing, it just made sense to hold the meetings here after work. A few months ago we changed the . . . the focus of the club, and our membership got of control. Tonight's meeting was supposed to be held at The Continental—that's the new hotel on the beach—but it all got screwed up and the meeting accidentally ended up here. But there are too many people, as you can see, so I was in the process of *politely* asking everyone to leave."

Officer Lakowski nodded, like he'd heard all this a thousand times before. "Then the meeting was held here with your permission?"

"Sort of."

"It's either a yes or a no," Tall Officer said.

"Yes, the meeting was held here with my permission." What was Grace supposed to say? That she hadn't given Ellen her consent? Wouldn't that get Ellen in trouble? Even though a vision of Ellen being dragged away in handcuffs almost brought a smile to her face, Grace didn't really want to see that happen.

"So then, these women have every right to stay here for the meeting. Is that correct?" Tall Officer concluded.

"No, that's what I've been trying to tell you. There *was* a meeting. But not anymore. I called it off."

Tall Officer took the flyer from Lakowski's hand. "Let me get this straight. You advertised this boyfriend club"—he paused, then shook his head as if to say *what the hell*—"got all these women here, then called it off when they started a *discussion* about your brother. When they refused to leave, you called Easy Rider over there to act as a bouncer."

"Hey!" Penny said, frowning at the officer in Butch's defense.

"Something like that," Grace admitted.

"And as the store's manager, you have the authority to give permission for the building's use?" Tall Officer asked.

"Yes. Definitely," Grace said. "But I also have the authority to ask them to leave."

"Okay, seems to me like this is pretty cut-and-dry." Tall Officer turned to the crowd. "Ladies, I'm going to have to ask you all to start filing out. Understand?"

No one seemed happy, but to Grace's relief, the women began exiting through the front door.

Marty came back inside looking frazzled. "Grace, I can't get the customers to understand that the store is closed."

Tall Officer looked at Grace. "Would you like to me handle the customers as well?"

Have Florida Charlie's customers told to leave by the police?

"No, I mean, the store *is* closed, but—"

"What about him?" Bubble Butt demanded, pointing to Butch. "Aren't you going to arrest him?"

"Ma'am," Officer Lakowski said, "it appears that he was acting as an agent for the manager of the building. Unless he actually physically assaulted you, then there's nothing we can do."

"He ran after me, but I was faster. God only knows what might have happened if he'd caught me!"

Butch snorted. "Yeah, you wish I'd caught you."

The woman lunged for Butch, who flung his arms up in the air to fend off the attack and, in doing so, accidentally hit Officer Lakowski in the jaw with his elbow. Lakowski went down, bringing an entire rack of T-shirts with him.

"That's it, buddy!" Tall Officer grabbed Butch and handcuffed him. "You're coming with us to headquarters for striking a police officer."

"But it was an accident!" Penny said. "He was only trying to defend himself."

One of the women who'd joined the group a couple of months ago ran to Officer Lakowski's side. "Oh my God, Matt. Are you hurt?" With her help, he sat up and rubbed his sore jaw.

"Karina! What are you doing here?" He looked torn between being happy to see her and leery.

"I'm a member of the club."

"It's Colonel Brandon!" someone shouted.

That's why Lakowski's name had seemed familiar. He was Karina's ex-boyfriend. The perfectly sweet, yet dull, Colonel Brandon.

Shania's head popped up above the crowd, like a scary jack-in-the-box. "Officer, how does it feel to know that you're one of the men the club has reviewed? Do you agree with the Colonel Brandon characterization?"

"*Who?* Ma'am, I have no idea what you're talking about," Officer Lakowski said.

Grace didn't wait to hear how Karina was going to explain that one. She ran after Penny, who was running after Tall Officer and Butch. They watched helplessly as Butch was placed in the backseat of the squad car. A few minutes later, Officer Lakowski joined them and they drove off.

A small crowd of people who appeared to be customers were still lingering by the front doors. Grace told them that the store was officially closed and hoped they would come back on Monday.

"You aren't open tomorrow?" one woman asked. "I thought everything was open the day of the race!"

Grace almost opened the doors to let them in, but it was all too chaotic still. Plus, she had to help Penny. Grace watched, frustrated, as the customers went off, grumbling to themselves all the way to their cars.

Penny had tears in her eyes. "I'm going to follow Butch and see if I can clear this up."

"I'm coming with you," Grace said.

"No," Penny said, wiping away her sniffles. Penny, crying twice in the same year. This was really something. "First, get the store cleared out and locked up. By the way, we had a record-breaking sales day today."

Well, there was some consolation in that, Grace supposed.

"Okay, you're right. You go be with Butch. I'll be down at police headquarters just as soon as I deal with a couple of things. Like breaking Ellen's laptop." Despite the gravity of the situation, Penny smiled. Grace gave her a hug and waved her off.

There were a few stragglers left in the store. Luckily, Phoebe wasn't one of them. She must have slithered out the door when

Grace wasn't paying attention, which was good because Grace was afraid if she saw her again she might strangle her. Grace shooed off the rest of the women and locked up so no one else could get inside. Marty had already righted the collapsed rack of T-shirts and Ellen and Sarah were putting the shelves back in order.

"Grace, I'm so sorry," Ellen said. "I can't believe what happened here tonight. I never *never* meant for it to go down like this!"

Grace sighed. "I know you didn't mean for all this to happen, Ellen, but now Butch is in jail and there's some crazy Shania person who wants to write an article on us. Have you ever heard of a blog called *What's Up, Daytona Beach?*"

"Heard of it? Grace, Shania's blog gets thousands of hits a day! Isn't it awesome? She's a little snarky but *totally* sympathetic to the female cause. Trust me, whatever she writes about us, it'll be favorable."

"Favorable for who?"

"What about this woman who slandered Charlie tonight?" Sarah demanded. "Are we going to let her get away with that?"

"Well, I hope you know I'm not going to write *that* review up for the files," Ellen said.

"Write it up for the files?" Sarah repeated in stunned disbelief. "Is that all you've got to say? Clearly the woman is missing brain cells!"

"Or in need of some strong medication," Ellen agreed quickly. "I never once believed her. Of course, Charlie is innocent!"

"I have to warn Charlie about her," Grace said. "Before any of this gets back to his firm." *Or to Mami and Pop.* Grace put her arm around Sarah and gave her a fast hug. "By the way, you were a real tiger tonight. If I didn't know better, I'd say you were Charlie's sister, the way you came to his defense. Thank you." She handed Sarah the keys to the store. "I need a favor. Can you and Ellen help Marty clean up this mess? I'd stay, but I have to go to police headquarters and help spring Butch."

"Don't worry," Sarah said, giving Ellen the stink eye. "Neither of us is leaving until this place is spic-and-span clean."

The police didn't release Butch until after one a.m. No charges were filed against him but it still seemed to Grace to be a very severe case of police bullying. And Colonel Brandon, aka Matt, had seemed so nice at first! The only good thing that had come out of tonight was that Butch had gone back with Penny to her apartment, and from the way the two of them had been making goo-goo eyes at each other, Grace would say that the Penny/Butch estrangement had definitely come to an end. Penny had gotten what she'd wanted. Butch had made the Grand Gesture, and Grace was truly happy for them.

She rolled her car into her empty driveway. No sign of Joe. He said he'd come over tonight, but that was before their one-on-one on the dock. She should call him, but it was late and she was exhausted and she didn't want to say anything she might later regret. But she did call Charlie. He needed to know the crap Phoebe was spewing about him. But Charlie didn't pick up, so Grace left him a message to call her back ASAP.

# 29

# Be Careful What You Ask St. Anthony For

The next morning Grace woke up to find a text message on her cell phone from Charlie. *Call me no matter what time you get this.* He must have heard about Phoebe and her little "announcement" last night. What else could be that urgent?

She called but his cell went directly to voice mail, irritating Grace to no end. It was just like Charlie to leave a cryptic message and then not be available. Nor was he at church, like he should have been.

No one seemed to think it was strange that Charlie was missing from Mass, but Mami was the first to comment on Grace's appearance. "Grace, honey, are you sick?" she asked on their way out of church.

"Is it pinkeye?" Pop asked. "That's contagious, Tomato. Might want to see the doctor first thing in the morning."

"Have you been crying?" Leave it to Abuela not to beat about the bush.

"I need to talk to you, Pop. You too, Mami and Abuela." It wasn't going to be easy to tell them about last night's brouhaha at the store. Pop would be angry, which wouldn't be good for his blood pressure. But the fact that the cops had been called to handle a disturbance at Florida Charlie's wasn't something she could keep from him.

"What's going on?" Pop said. "First Charlie, now you."

"First Charlie what?" Grace said.

"Your brother called us this morning," Mami said. "He's going to miss Mass and supper, but he'll be at the house later this evening. He said he had something very important to tell us. As a family."

*Great.* The Miami thing. Charlie had finally decided to break the news that he was moving, and it couldn't have come at a worse time. Pop would be mad about the incident at the store and Mami and Abuela would be sad over Charlie leaving town. A good time would be had by all.

"Does this something you have to tell us involve your new boyfriend?" Pop asked, winking at Grace. "He's coming over today for supper," he informed Mami and Abuela.

*Shit.* She'd forgotten she'd told Pop she'd invite Joe over.

Before Mami and Abuela could get too excited, Grace had to nip things in the bud. "Um, things are a little complicated."

"Complicated? How? In my day, if you went off for the weekend with someone you were practically engaged."

Grace could feel a trickle of sweat run down her back. She was thirty years old, damn it. "Times have changed, Pop."

"Obviously," he grumbled.

"Maybe he can come over some other time," Mami said diplomatically.

Grace threw her a grateful smile.

She was in the process of getting the dishes out of the cupboard when Abuela intercepted her. "You never answered my question, Gracielita. Why have you been crying?"

Half a bottle of eye drops and thirty minutes of cold cucumber compresses hadn't been enough to keep her eyes from looking like she'd spent ten minutes in an alley with Mike Tyson. She wished she could spare Abuela this latest romantic heartache, but the truth was Grace needed to talk to someone about Joe. She'd almost called Sarah this morning, but under the circumstances it seemed too tactless to boo-hoo on Sarah's shoulder, especially after the news Grace had dropped on her last night. And she certainly didn't want to interrupt Penny and Butch's reunion. As for Ellen? Grace was still so mad at her she wasn't sure she'd be able to keep from punching her in the nose the next time she saw her.

"It's the St. Valentine's Day Curse, Abuela. I think it's happened again."

"*Lo siento, mi amor.*" Abuela laid her palm against Grace's cheek. "But all couples fight. It will be all right. Remember, I saw it in my dream."

Grace tried for a smile because she didn't want to bring Abuela any unhappiness. No use telling her that the man she saw in her dream wasn't the man she was talking about.

Just as they were sitting down to supper, Grace's cell phone rang.

"Hey," said Joe.

"Hey, yourself."

"Was everything all right at the store?"

"Things got a little . . . crazy." Mami called Grace to the table. "Look, Joe, can I call you later?" She wanted to ask him how things went between his aunt and Phillip, but it seemed like a subject better brought up in person.

"Sure," he said, sounding disappointed. Which Grace took as a positive sign. At least Joe wanted to talk about the problem. Maybe it wasn't as bad as she thought. Maybe they could still salvage their relationship, whatever that was.

Pop was full of nervous energy. He gave Grace the lowdown on the yoga class that Jim, the manly therapist, had suggested he take to relieve the anxiety Pop hadn't even known he had. Hearing Pop talk about things like the lotus position and chanting a mantra made Grace laugh out loud, which was good, because Grace needed to laugh right now. Pop knew how to tell a story, that was for sure. Too bad Charlie wasn't here. He would love listening to this. But this was the way it was going to be from now on, just the four of them, with Charlie down in Miami. It was depressing to think how much she'd miss her brother.

After supper, she helped Mami clean the dishes. Pop was getting impatient. What was keeping Charlie? he asked. And then he started dropping not-so-subtle hints that whatever it was Grace needed to say, she might as well have at it.

Grace had wanted Charlie to be present when she told Pop about the boyfriend meeting. He needed to know what Pheobe was saying about him, plus Grace really needed some sibling moral support. But it was after five already, and Grace had only gotten three hours' sleep last night. She was exhausted. And Pop wasn't going to wait a second longer.

She waited till they were gathered in the living room to begin.

"I know you don't like talking about the store on Sundays, Pop, but what I have to say can't wait until tomorrow. Plus, this involves the whole family too, including Charlie. I wanted to wait until he was here, but I'm beginning to wonder if he's even going to show up, so I might as well get this off my chest."

Grace was met with three serious-looking faces. "So . . . you know how Sarah and Penny and Ellen and I had a book club that met at the store after hours?"

"Sure, you met in the Hemingway corner. Damn appropriate, if you ask me," said Pop.

"Don't cuss, Charlie," Mami admonished. "It's bad for your blood pressure."

"*Damn it*, Ana, can you think of something that *isn't* bad for my blood pressure? Because if you can, I'd sure as hell like to know what it is!"

Mami's jaw dropped and Abuela's eyes got big. Grace had heard her parents argue before, but she'd never seen Pop lose his cool over something so minor.

"Ever since I had my heart attack I've listened to you tell me what I can eat, what I can't eat, what time I should go to bed, when I should get up in the morning. Hell, if you could tell my bowels when to move, I'm sure you'd take charge of them too!" He gave Abuela an apologetic shrug. "*Perdóname*, Graciela," Pop said, apologizing to Abuela in perfect Spanish, "but I have to get this off my chest."

Abuela waved him on.

"I'm fifty-eight years old. I'm not a child and I sure as hell am not an old man. I appreciate the fact that you're looking out for me and I love you for it. But you're my *wife*, not my mother. So start acting like it."

Mami was still speechless. Abuela was now smiling. And Grace stood there, unsure what to do or say. One thing was certain: Jim the manly therapist had made quite an impression on Pop.

"All right," Mami said a minute or so later. "It's your life. Live it or *not* the way you want."

Pop got up from his chair, walked over to Mami, cupped her chin in his hand and gave her a big kiss on the lips. Mami's cheeks went red. "Glad we got that settled," Pop said. "Okay, Grace, so what about the book club?"

"Um . . ." She cleared her throat and tried to hide the smile witnessing Pop's kiss had produced. "A few months ago—back in November, to be exact—we decided to change things up. Instead of a book club, we made it a boyfriend club."

"A boyfriend club?" Mami said. "What's that?"

"It's similar to a book club, but instead of discussing and critiquing books, we . . . well, we did the same thing with men."

"You invited men to join your book club?" Pop asked, confused.

"No . . . we didn't invite men. We *critiqued* them. Like you would a book. You know? Thumbs-up, thumbs-down. Only . . . we were a little more creative than that."

Pop blinked.

"How clever!" Abuela said, clapping her hands together. "That must have been your idea, Gracielita."

"As a matter of fact, it was." Only Grace wasn't so sure how clever Pop was going to find it. "The first meeting was fine. It was just the four of us, plus a few friends of Ellen's from the college. But by December, membership had grown to about thirty—"

"You fit thirty women in the Hemingway corner?" Mami said. "I didn't think it could be done."

"We moved the bookshelves out of the way," Grace said.

Pop's right eyelid began to twitch. "Go on."

"And, well, some of the women brought alcohol with them."

Mami's head snapped up. "There was drinking in the store?"

"Just wine! For the most part . . . like you'd have at a book club meeting. And nobody actually got drunk." *Not that I ever found out about.* "Anyway, after that December meeting I told Ellen we couldn't have any more members. I was *very* firm with her on that. And no more alcohol. She promised she'd put a message about it on Yahoo!—it's an Internet site," Grace explained to Abuela. "That's where we posted the reviews."

"I know what Yahoo! is," Abuela said proudly. "I know what Google is too."

"Grace, why didn't you tell me about this before?" Pop asked.

"I didn't think it was that big of a deal. And I didn't want to burden you with something I could take care of myself. Especially with—you know . . ." She trailed lamely. She was going to make a reference to his high blood pressure, but then thought better of it.

Pop's mouth thinned, like he knew what Grace had been about to say.

"But somehow it all got messed up, and last month we had a ton more women show up and I told Ellen that was it, that we had to move the club meetings somewhere else. So she arranged for a room at The Continental, that new hotel in town, only there wasn't a room available and the meeting ended up at Florida Charlie's last night."

Pop was mad; he was trying not to show it, but he was. And she hadn't even told him the bad part yet.

She went on to tell them about last night's meeting. About all the women in the shop and about Shania Brown and her *What's Up, Daytona Beach?* blog. And even though Abuela knew what Yahoo! and Google were, she'd never heard of a blog, so Grace had to stop and explain it to her. She also explained how even though the Monday morning post was supposed to focus on the club, Grace was afraid that maybe, just *maybe*, Shania might mention the store, since the cops had been called.

Pop started to pace the living room floor. "Penny's boyfriend was hauled off to jail from *my* store?" Before Mami could say anything, he turned to her. "If I want to have a heart attack over this, Ana, then I'm going to bloody well have a heart attack!"

"Be my guest," Mami said. "I'll join you."

Grace cringed. "And something really bad happened last night."

"Worse than the police coming?" Pop roared.

"Phoebe was at last night's meeting. The girl who works with Charlie? The one who showed up at Mass and had supper with us a few months ago?"

"The pretty redhead," Mami said. "She was very nice."

Abuela nodded in agreement. "The one who liked my *tostones.*"

"Yeah, well . . . she accused Charlie of sexually harassing her. She said that—" Grace gulped, because this next part was going to be really hard to say, "She said that Charlie told her if she didn't sleep with him, then he was going to get her fired."

"That lying bitch!" Mami said. "She said this about *my* Charlie? And in public?"

"We're going to sue the pants off her!" Pop said. "Or rather, Charlie is."

"I don't think we should use the words 'Charlie' and 'pants off her' in the same sentence, Pop."

"Does Charlie know all this?" Mami asked.

"Not yet. I've tried calling him, but his cell phone goes directly to his voice mail."

The front door opened and Charlie walked into the living room with a grin on his face the likes of which Grace had never seen.

"Um, I can pretty much guarantee that Charlie is clueless about this," Grace said.

"Did you know that some woman at your law firm is claiming you *sexually* harassed her?" Pop yelled.

"I knew that Phoebe was up to no good," Abuela said. "Everyone knows my *tostones* are only mediocre and it's my *plátanos maduros* that are my specialty dish!"

"I know all about Phoebe and the lies she's been spreading," Charlie said, way too calmly. "I'm not worried."

"But Charlie," Mami said, "she could make trouble for you at the office!"

"Like I said, I'm not worried. I haven't done anything wrong." Charlie gave Mami a reassuring squeeze on her shoulder. "I don't want to talk about Phoebe anymore." He glanced around the room "Now, isn't anyone going to ask me where I've been?"

"At the office, working as usual?" Grace said.

"Nope."

He seemed so boyishly happy, like a little kid who'd just come home with a straight A report card and was dying to show it off to the proud family. Grace noticed that instead of his usual weekend wear of shorts or jeans, Charlie wore tan dress pants and a white button-down shirt. He also had on a black blazer. The shirt looked rumpled and he was tieless.

"Did you sleep in that outfit, by any chance?" Grace asked.

He smiled at her like she'd just stumbled on to a clue.

"What is it, Charlie? What did you want to tell us?" Mami asked.

"The reason I didn't go to Mass this morning was because I was in Vegas."

Pop's brows nearly crossed over themselves. "You went to Las Vegas? Was it last-minute business?"

"Did you hit a jackpot?" Abuela asked, excited.

"Not business, Pop. And yeah, Abuela, you could say I hit a jackpot. I got married this morning."

Grace heard herself screech, "You got *married*? In Las Vegas?"

*"Ave Maria!"* Abuela said. Her eyes shot up to the ceiling. "I knew the Virgin was listening!" She got up from her seat and wrapped Charlie up in a hug.

"Charlie," Pop said. His face was now pink. "Let me get this straight. You went to Vegas last night, met some girl, and *married her*?"

"Calm down, Charlie," Mami said, addressing Pop. "Remember your high blood pressure. And I *am* going to say something about it when I think I need to. Just try and stop me. But seriously, *cariño*, are you that clueless? Of course our son didn't marry some girl he just met. He married Sarah!"

"Sarah who?" Pop asked, confused.

"Yeah, Sarah who?" Grace chimed, because he simply couldn't mean *her* Sarah.

Charlie crossed the living room in three long strides to open the front door. Sarah, (*her* Sarah!) stood in the doorway wearing a simple cream-colored above-the-knee dress and the goofiest smile Grace had ever seen. Her blonde hair hung loose and straight to her shoulders. She wore the barest of makeup and

Grace could immediately sense that, like Charlie, Sarah hadn't slept last night, but she still looked beautiful. And . . . happy. Truly happy. In a way Grace had never seen her.

Before Sarah could put a toe over the threshold, Charlie swooped her up in his arms and carried her into the living room.

"Put me down!" Sarah laughed, her arms looped tightly around Charlie's neck.

"Never!" Charlie said with such vehemence that Grace almost didn't recognize him.

Mami and Abuela fell on Sarah and Charlie, crying, laughing, telling each other that they'd always known that Sarah was the one for Charlie. The whole time Charlie held Sarah in his arms, grinning, like a besotted idiot.

And Pop and Grace stood there, mouths gaping open, like everyone had known about Charlie and Sarah but them. Which, apparently, was the case.

Pop recovered first. "Put her down, Charlie. She's not going anywhere," he said.

Charlie reluctantly set Sarah on her feet. "She'd better not."

Sarah gave Charlie a smile that made Grace's eyes sting. Pop gave Sarah a big kiss and welcomed her to the family. And Sarah actually *blushed*.

*What was going on here?*

It was like someone had taken the real Sarah off to the pod people and replaced her with this version that Grace had never seen before.

"I'm sorry that we didn't tell anyone," Sarah said. "It all happened so fast! And since I can't get married in the Church, Charlie thought that Vegas was a simple solution."

Pop punched Charlie playfully in the shoulder. "You could have given us a heads-up!"

"Do your parents know?" Mami asked.

"We called them. They're our next stop," Charlie said.

"Not until we have some champagne first." Mami scurried off to the kitchen. "This calls for a celebration!" she cried over her shoulder.

"Have you eaten yet?" Abuela asked. "Of course you haven't. The airlines want to starve you now, probably so they can keep making the seats smaller. I'll go heat up the leftovers."

"Grace?" Sarah said shyly. Up until now, Grace hadn't said anything, only because, well, because she had no idea what to say.

"What happened?" Grace blurted. "I mean, when . . . when did . . ."

"When did I know that Sarah was the girl for me?" Charlie interrupted. "That would be about twenty-five years ago."

Now Sarah wore the same identical, stupid grin Charlie had been sporting. It was like the two of them had been drinking the same alien happy juice.

*"I'm serious,"* Grace said. "When did this happen?"

"Last night, after the club meeting, I went to Charlie's place," Sarah said. "I wanted to warn him about the stuff Phoebe was saying. And—"

"I've been in love with Sarah for a long time." Charlie put his arm around Sarah in a protective gesture. "After she told me about Phoebe, she confessed that listening to Phoebe disparage me at the club meeting brought out feelings that . . . well, that she never knew she had for me. So I finally told her how I felt. I asked her to marry me and she said yes, so I grabbed her and threw her on a plane to Vegas before she could change her mind."

"We had to buy a dress at the airport gift shop. He wouldn't even let me pack!" Sarah said.

*He won't even let you speak either.* Grace's head was buzzing. This was all too . . . much.

"Sarah was hoping that with the time difference we'd still be able to make it to Vegas in time for a Valentine's Day wedding, but the official date is February 15. I like it better. Less sappy, huh, squirt?" Charlie said.

Charlie was probably the only groom in history who called his bride squirt while looking like he wanted to jump her at the same time. Before today, Sarah always scoffed at the nickname, but now she practically glowed at the endearment. She gave Grace a watery smile. "I hope you're happy about this."

*Happy?* Of course Grace was happy!

"Are you kidding? You're my sister-in-law. *Oh my God.* You're my sister-in-law!" She hugged her and the two of them started laughing. Because this was perfect. Charlie and Sarah. But still . . . it was so unexpected that Grace couldn't help but feel that they were leaving something out. "It's just so crazy! So impulsive. Sarah, it's just so *not* like you."

"There's no logic to love, sis," Charlie said.

Sarah smiled, but she didn't meet Grace's eyes.

Mami passed around the champagne and Pop made a toast to the couple's future happiness. Charlie kept his arm around Sarah the whole time, and Grace could plainly see that the two of them were in love. She looked around at the faces in the room. Nobody seemed anything less than totally thrilled by Charlie's impromptu nuptials.

The Lettuce scores a touchdown!

Grace instantly felt like a big weasel. What was wrong with her? Isn't this what she'd wanted? For Charlie and Sarah to get together? So why was she trying to find something wrong with a perfectly wonderful situation? Could it be that subconsciously Grace didn't want Sarah to be happy because Grace's love life was falling apart? Could she be *that* selfish?

*No.* She'd wanted Charlie and Sarah together. It was the whirlwind manner in which the whole thing had gone down that had Grace spooked, not the end result.

Abuela insisted that the newlyweds eat something, and after another hour of talking about how they'd always been meant to be together and how weird life turned out, and then drank some more champagne, they'd left to meet with Sarah's parents.

"This has been some day, huh, Pop?" Grace said.

Mami and Abuela were off in the kitchen, planning a reception for the new couple. She and Pop were alone in the living room for the first time today.

"It sure has." He didn't meet her eyes.

"I'm . . . I'm really sorry about all the stuff that happened at the store."

"Let me get this right. For the past few months—" He stopped and gave her a questioning look.

"Um, since November," Grace squeaked.

"For the last *four* months, you've conducted these boyfriend meetings at my store. Hundreds of women—"

"It wasn't hundreds," Grace rushed. "Except . . . maybe last night, it was," she admitted.

Pop closed his eyes. Grace could have sworn she heard him chanting something under his breath. "For the past four months, you've conducted these boyfriend meetings," he repeated in an eerily calm voice. "Unknown legions of women have trampled through my store after-hours, some of them bringing in alcohol, and last night the meeting got so out of hand that the police had to be called?"

It all sounded so horrible the way Pop said it. Grace swallowed hard. "I swear to you, Pop, it will never happen again."

"Oh, I know it won't." He shook his head and sighed. "You know I love you, Grace. More than anything, and that's why this is going to be hard as hell for me to say, but I just got to come out and say it. Tomato, you're fired."

# 30

# I Bet Jane Austen Was Fat

"Are you awake?" Ellen's voice crackled over the phone. "I'm driving in a dead zone so my connection might die, but Grace, you need to turn on the radio. Everyone's talking about us!"

Grace crawled out of her warm bed, her cell phone clutched to one ear. "What? Who's talking about us?"

"Speedway Gonzalez! He's talking about the boyfriend club on his radio show. I called in and—"

"Ellen, you're not making any sense. It actually sounded like you said you'd called in to Speedway's show. Hold on a sec."

First things first. She laid her cell phone down, shuffled to the bathroom, and brushed the gritty feel from her teeth. She wished she could make the pounding in her head disappear as easily, but that was going to require three Tylenol, a gallon of water, and, knowing from previous experience, at least twenty-four hours. Grace didn't do hangovers well.

Why had she drunk so much last night?

Well, there was Charlie and Sarah's unexpected news. That had been cause for celebration, even if it didn't make sense. So the champagne had been happy drinking. But the tequila shots she'd done by herself while watching late-night TV? Those had been the result of feeling sorry for herself.

Who got fired by their own father?

*Slackers who didn't listen to their boss and took their jobs for granted, that's who.*

"Okay, I'm back. Let's start at square one. Why would Speedway Gonzalez be talking about the boyfriend club?"

"Because of Shania's post on *What's Up, Daytona Beach?* Which is completely awesome, by the way. Shania is totally on our side. She loves the club! You have to read it."

The call-waiting on Grace's cell phone beeped. It was Penny. Grace put Ellen on hold. "What's up?"

"Have you had your morning coffee yet?"

"Is this about the Speedway thing?"

"Grace, it's bad. Look, I'm pulling into the store. We'll decide what to do when you get here. I tried calling Sarah but her cell keeps going to voice mail."

*That's because she and my brother are probably too busy screwing like rabbits.*

Coffee! Grace needed coffee. "Pen, I won't be going to the store this morning. Pop fired me last night."

"This isn't the time for jokes, Grace. I'll see you in fifteen," Penny said, and hung up.

Grace sighed and clicked the call-waiting back over to Ellen. "Okay, so why would Speedway be talking about us?"

"Because of Shania's blog!" Ellen said. "Go read it and call me back ASAP. My first class starts in forty minutes, but I'll have my cell on until then."

Grace put a pot of coffee on to brew, doctored her first cup of the day with plenty of half-and-half and Splenda, then sat in front of her desk and turned on her computer. She did a Google search for *What's Up, Daytona Beach?* and clicked on the link. Shania's blog jumped out in living Pepto Bismol hot pink. "Ugh!" Grace placed her hand up to shield her eyes from the screen until her vision adjusted. Then she took a big gulp of her coffee and began to read.

## Using the Power of Literary Archetypes to Determine Dating Compatibility
### *By Shania Brown*

Good grief. This sounded about as interesting as Ellen's thesis. No wonder Ellen was so excited about it. Grace popped the Tylenol in her mouth and chugged it down with another big gulp of coffee.

Dating in this day and age has become as dangerous as hunting for food must have been for early man. Twenty-first-century carnivores and herbivores disguised in their Armani suits and too-tight jeans crawl, snarl, and bite their way through the dating jungle while ill prepared gatherers haplessly stumble through the romance minefield.

While the odds of finding true love are heavily stacked against us, women right here in Daytona Beach are simply not content to leave it all to chance. Take Grace O'Bryan, the thirty-year-old never-been-married manager of central Florida tourist mecca Florida Charlie's. Just a few months ago, Grace was like every other woman battling out there in her quest for true love. But unlike her fellow sisters in the hunt, Grace decided to arm herself with the most powerful weapon available—information.

Similar to the format of today's popular book clubs, Grace established a much more practical group—a boyfriend club that meets once a month and allows women to discuss the men they've dated, building up "reviews" they post on a closed Yahoo! site.

But the boyfriend club takes it one step further.

Club cofounder, Ellen Ames, a professor of English at Daytona State College, author of "Undressing the Romantic Hero in Popular Literature," and web mistress for the club, has developed a simple computer program that matches up boyfriend profiles with well-known literary characters, giving a glimpse of just how likely your "happily ever after" might be. The experiment is in the beginning stages, but Ms. Ames hopes to compile enough data to expound on her original thesis and develop it into a book.

"It's really pretty simple," says Ms. Ames. "The key is to pull out the correct four 'descriptors' or key words from the critiques that can be placed into the program. I've done extensive research on the hundred most popular heroes and villains in well-known English literature, and have created a data bank using their personality traits."

Fascinating stuff, isn't it? I decided to give the club a try for myself. What sort of characters do we having running around Daytona Beach, you might ask? Let me give you a sneak peek.

Grace skimmed down to the next part and nearly choked on her coffee.

Meet Iago, the villain from Shakespeare's *Othello*. In real life he's actually D, an average-looking CPA who's climbing the company ladder by sleeping with the boss's daughter. He's been described as charming, smart, manipulative, and vengeful. Certainly not someone you'd want to meet in the corner of a dimly lit bar, right, ladies?

Then there's F, the maître d' of one of Daytona Beach's swankiest new French restaurants, who's been compared to the licentious Henry Crawford from Jane Austen's *Mansfield Park*. The critique on him alone is worth joining the club for. Frankly, I'd like to know if any man I'm considering dating can only get "inspired" by listening to Céline Dion's "My Heart Will Go On."

Not every comparison is negative, however. B, a well-known wealthy Daytona Beach bachelor, has been compared to perhaps the most famous romantic hero of all time—*Pride and Prejudice*'s very own Mr. Darcy. Only this Mr. Darcy plays rugby by day and is secretly into Zumba classes by night. Not that there's anything wrong with that . . .

And, last but not least, we can't have a Mr. Darcy running around Daytona Beach without his literary counterpart, none other than the villainous Mr. Wickham. Watch out for this one, ladies! Our modern-day Mr. W is J, a dentist who likes to pick up his conquests at raunchy bars with lines like, "What's a nice pair of legs like yours doing in a place like this?" I know how I'd answer that one.

There is one element to the experiment that needs refining. "Sometimes, we get two very different views of the same man," Ms. Ames said in her interview. "Which is to be expected, on occasion. But it's a variable I'm trying to iron out."

I was privy to an example of this during the February meeting when one member accused single local attorney C of sexual harassment. Another member jumped vehemently to his defense, creating a near riot that resulted in the police being called.

"There's a level of subjectivity that can't be completely ignored," Ms. Ames said of the encounter. "It's like a book or a movie review site. Why does the same book receive both five- and one-star reviews? It's because we can't take the emotion out of the experience. One woman's masterpiece is another woman's dregs. What the boyfriend club offers is information. It's up to the members to take it in and make up their own minds."

So there you have it. Internet dating and now boyfriend clubs. What's next?

Meetings currently take place the first Saturday of the month at nine p.m. at Florida Charlie's off I-95. But don't be late! Space is limited.

Grace stared at the screen in horror. The pounding in her head was nothing compared to the pounding in her chest. She speed dialed Ellen.

"Ellen," she said, trying not to yell into the phone, not out of courtesy for Ellen but because the noise would have hurt her head too much, "please explain how Shania's blog is being on our side."

"So you've read it?"

"She names names!"

"No, she doesn't, silly. She gives one little initial."

"Ellen, there's only one restaurant in town that fits the description of"—Grace paused to read her computer screen so she could quote it verbatim—"'Daytona Beach's swankiest new French restaurant,' and that would be Chez Louis. Do you really think that Felix isn't going to recognize himself? And what about Joe? Ellen, you had no permission to write up that file on Joe!"

"Grace, calm down. I know this tiff with Joe has you all upset. And I'm sorry about that file, but you have to admit, the facts do point to Joe being a Wickham. But as for Felix? I'm not the least bit sorry if anyone figures out who he is. Felix deserves to be exposed! He broke your heart, and now he's just going to have to pay for it."

"Pay for it? Ellen, this isn't about revenge, it's about . . . well, like we've been saying, it's about empowerment. Only I didn't want to empower all of Daytona Beach! You need to shut down that Yahoo! site."

"Shut it down? Why would we want to shut it down? Listen, I have to go. Speedway is back on the radio. Talk to you later!"

"Ellen, don't hang—"

Argh!

Grace turned on the radio.

"Welcome back to The Track, speedsters. This is the one and only Speedway Gonzalez taking you round and round Day-to-na Beach! So, for a quick recap. I thought we'd be doing our typical after-the-big-race show this morning and let you losers call in and lie about how much booty you scored last night. But all you duds want to talk about is this boyfriend club. Some local chick named Shania Brown— Yeah, how about that for a name. I bet she's fat. What do you think? Shania and her *What's Up, Daytona Beach?* blog are getting some big buzz. Well, I say nuthin' happens in Daytona without the Speedster putting in his two pesos' worth. Seems like some disgruntled chick— What's her name again? Oh yeah, Grace O'Bryan. I bet she's fat. What do you think? And Gracie, if you're out there listening, which I know you are, you're welcome to call in anytime, baby. Speedway is dying to talk to you."

*Yeah, like that's ever going to happen.*

"So, Grace decided to put together some women's empowerment group—and can I just say that's about the stupidest oxymoron there is. Ladies, listen up! You don't need to *get* power; you already have it. Just walk into any bar on Beach Street. I guarantee you the dude who's just spent the last two hours trying to get some chick wasted so he can get her in the sack isn't thinking, 'Man, I sure am glad I have all the power here!'

"So back to this boyfriend club. Seems Gracie was fed up with dating losers and decided to get back at some by reviewing the guys she's shagged. Toss in some more fat friends and we have a club. Whoa! I'm feeling the empowerment, how about you? Word is there's more than two hundred of them. And guess where they meet? Florida Charlie's!" Speedway chuckled. "About thirty minutes ago, Ellen Ames, the brainiac of this little empowerment group, called in and went one-on-one with the Speedster. The phones have been ringing off the hook ever since. Here's what she had so say."

*Oh no.* It was true. Grace hadn't heard wrong. What could Ellen be thinking? This was beyond awful. Grace turned up the volume.

"Hello? Hello? Is this Mr. Speedway?" Grace heard Ellen say.

"That's me, baby. So, Ellen, first things first. Are you fat?"

"I'm not going to fall for your stupid macho radio bull. I'm calling to set you straight about the boyfriend club."

"Okay, that means you're fat, but I'm not going to hold it against you."

To Ellen's credit, she didn't fall for Speedway's fat shtick. "You say that women are already empowered, but what you're talking about is sex—"

"You got something against sex, Ellen? It's because you're fat, right?"

"I'll tell you what I'm against, Speedway. I'm against guys like you who degrade women. The boyfriend club was developed to help women weed out the bad seeds in the dating game. You don't like the word empowerment? Okay, let's try this. The boyfriend club is about providing information that allows women to make better choices."

"Slow down, Ellen. All those big words are giving Speedway a headache."

"Oh? Sorry, I'll try to keep my words at five letters and under."

Speedway laughed. "I like you, Ellen."

There was a pause. *Oh, no.* Ellen had been doing so good up until now.

"Well, thank you," she said.

"What color panties are you wearing?" Speedway asked.

"Excuse me?"

"So you're not wearing panties, huh?"

"Of course I'm wearing panties! I'm an English teacher!"

Grace moaned. Ellen was about to be mashed into guacamole.

"Yeah?" Speedway's voice hitched with excitement. "Where at?"

*No, Ellen, don't tell him!*

"I teach English Composition and Appreciation of Poetry 1 at Daytona State College."

Grace slumped in her chair.

"Listen up, Ellen's students! Speedway is gonna give a hundred bucks to anyone who can tell me what color panties Ellen's wearing. But I'm going to need proof."

Ellen started to sputter.

Speedway's obnoxious chuckle made Grace cringe. "We're back live now, speedsters, and I still haven't gotten that proof I'm waiting for. Tell you what. I'll up the price to two hundred bucks. I want a photo of Ellen's panties. With her in 'em. And I want it bad!"

One of Speedway's sidekicks made a joke and they laughed.

"So, now that Speedway has talked to the chicks, let's get the male point of view. Who do I have on the line?"

"This is . . . Todd."

"All right, *Todd*, you got something to say? Let's hear it, dude."

"I happen to know Grace O'Bryan. I went out with her for almost six months. She's frigid, man."

*What?* Grace had never gone out with anyone named Todd!

"So you think the club is all about revenge, huh?" Speedway asked.

"Totally. She and her sorry pack of friends are nothing but a bunch of losers who can't get a date."

"You sound pretty pissed."

"Why shouldn't I be? She's a liar as well as a bitch."

"So which guy are you, Todd?"

"What do you mean?"

"Which of the guys Shania mentioned in her blog are you?"

"I'm not any of them!"

*Todd, my ass.* It was Felix. What a lying, cheating skunk. And to think, she'd actually been civil to him when he'd asked for her forgiveness!

"I'd say you're the dude who uses Céline Dion for Viagra. Am I right?" asked Speedway.

"No!"

"Let's see . . . that would be F, the maître d' at Daytona Beach's swankiest new French restaurant. My sources here tell me that's Chez Louis." Speedway started talking in a mocking French accent. "So, F, why the need to lie to Speedway? We're all friends here."

"I didn't lie and I'm not this F person. I already told you, my name is Todd." Felix sounded like he was on the verge of tears. What an idiot. Why didn't he just hang up?

"Dude, I'm hurt that you don't trust Speedway. How can I help you if you won't be honest?" There was some shuffling in the background. "Okay, speedsters, I got the lowdown. Brianna, who works here at the station, is friends with some chick who's in the club, and we've just gotten access to the Yahoo! site." There was a moment of silence, then, "Felix, my man! What's going on?" Speedway asked.

"I . . . I already told you, my name is Todd."

If Speedway had access to the Yahoo! site, then he was privy to *everyone's* file. And to their real names. Grace felt her lungs seize up.

"Felix, I'm reading your review right now, and I have to say, I'm impressed! Even I've never done a chick from the Topless-a-Go-Go. You must be some stud, huh?"

"Yeah, well, I've never gotten any complaints before."

*Oh my God.* Speedway had just tricked "Todd" into admitting to his real identity.

"And on Valentine's Day, with your girl catching you! That's cold, man. Really cold."

"She deserved it. Like I said, she was frigid."

"You mean she didn't put out enough? You don't think maybe she might have been turned off by your little Céline Dion obsession?"

"I already told you, that's not me!"

"What did I say about lying to me, dude?"

"Okay, you want to know the real reason Grace broke up with me? She's a gold digger, man. She would have come back to me in a flash if it wasn't for her new boyfriend, Brandon Farrell."

"Central Florida's most eligible bachelor? *That* Brandon Farrell?"

"The one and only. His family's loaded. How's a working guy supposed to compete with that?"

*What on earth?* Why would Felix think Grace was dating—

Grace let out a whoosh of air. Felix thought Grace was dating Brandon because that's what she'd let him think the afternoon he'd dropped by her town house. How was she ever going to explain this to Joe? *God, please, don't let Joe be listening to the radio!*

Speedway pretended to be sympathetic to Felix for a few minutes, then went back for the kill. After he finished chewing and spitting Felix out, he moved on to Doug, who was also stupid enough to call in to the show. Didn't you have to have *some* brains to pass the CPA exam?

Doug threatened to sue everyone involved. Shania, Grace, Speedway, and even her father, since he was the owner of Florida Charlie's and that's where the original slander occurred. He accused Jessica, the ex who had tainted his "good name," of being crazy and needing medication.

"And now, speedsters, I've been saving the best for last. So I get this chick who works at the station to tell me all about this Mr. Wickham character, since I'm not familiar with him. Seems like he's some bad mother player from a Jane Austen novel. And can I just say, what is it with chicks and Jane Austen, anyway? I bet she was fat. But that's another show." Speedway chuckled maliciously. "Okay, so back to J. A *dentist*? I mean, ladies, really? How low can you get?"

It was like the class bully had stolen her diary and was running around the playground shouting out her most secret thoughts to everyone. This was worse than when Richard Kasamati had done the awful orange-head imitation. Worse than finding Felix in bed with another woman. Worse than . . . worse than anything Grace could have ever imagined.

Should she call Joe and warn him? Grace glanced at her watch. It was already after eleven. He'd be seeing patients now. And what would she say, anyway? Tune in to the radio and listen in along with the rest of Daytona Beach while Speedway Gonzalez makes coleslaw out of you?

One of Speedway's cronies came on the air and did a few dentist jokes, all of which involved the punch line "open wide." Grace supposed this was Speedway's warmup for Joe.

*Please, please, please, Joe, don't call in to the show*!

Speedway tried his best to egg Joe into calling. But thank God Joe was too smart for that. And just when Grace thought maybe the damage could still be minimized, she heard a familiar female voice.

"Is this Speedway?"

"You're talking to him, baby. Who's this?"

"My name is Melanie. I'm Dr. Rosenblum's receptionist and I also happen to be a good friend of his."

"Melanie, first things first. Are you fat?"

"*What*? Of course not! I have a great figure. I do Pilates and everything."

Speedway chuckled evilly. Grace could almost feel his heart race over the radio, his excitement was so palpable. Melanie was about to be crushed into the celery seed that went into the coleslaw. Grace couldn't listen anymore. She turned off the radio, crawled into bed, and pulled the covers over her head.

# 31

# Sometimes the Tomato Just Wants to Be Alone

Someone was knocking on her door. Could it be Joe? And if it was, what would she say to him? Grace dragged herself out from under the covers. It was dark outside. She glanced at her clock. It was almost eight thirty. She mustered her courage and opened the front door, but it wasn't Joe. It was Brandon.

"Hey," she said, sounding weak and puny and pathetic. So much for being empowered.

"Grace, are you all right? I've been listening to the radio all day." Brandon walked into her town house with a pizza box in his hands. "I've tried calling but your cell phone keeps going to voice mail." He took in her makeup-less face and her puffy eyes and her baggy sweats. "You look like shit." He placed the pizza on her kitchen counter. "But this will make you feel better."

"I'm fine. Brandon, listen, I'm so sorry. This all started the night of the Wobbly Duck and—"

"I was an asshole that night, so I guess I had this boyfriend club review coming to me."

"You're . . . you're not angry at me?" Brandon had gotten off lightly compared to Felix and Doug and Joe, but he'd still had his moment in the sun.

"Hey, I'm Mr. Darcy, right?" He smiled weakly. "I admit, I'm embarrassed. But I know you never meant for all this to go public. It's that *damn* Speedway. This is all his fault."

Grace wished she could blame it on Speedway. But to be fair, she couldn't. He was just capitalizing on her stupidity. Although Brandon's attitude was surprisingly cavalier. Maybe Joe wasn't upset either. Maybe he hadn't even listened to the show . . .

"Grace, your father came to see me today. I know about you losing your job."

"Why did Pop—" There was only one reason for Pop to go see Brandon. He was taking Brandon up on his offer to buy the store. Never in a million years would she have believed this. Pop was selling Florida Charlie's!

"Brandon, I appreciate you coming over here. More than I can say. But I kind of just want to be alone right now."

"Grace, I want to help you." He placed his hands on her shoulders and drew her to him. "I want to be your rock."

"Um, that's awful sweet of you."

"Damn it! I'm not doing it to be sweet." He kissed her hard on the mouth. At first, it took Grace so off guard all she did was sag against him like a puppet whose strings had suddenly been snipped off. But she was feeling sorry for herself and he smelled so good (was that Dolce and Gabbana he had on?) she couldn't help but kiss him back. Just a little. Maybe it was time to see if there was actually anything between them. He felt her respond and slipped his tongue inside her mouth. It was . . . pleasant. After a couple of minutes, they came up for air.

Brandon looked pleased. "I don't want to take advantage of you while you're down, so I'd probably better leave before we get carried away."

"Yeah . . . good idea."

"Call me later. And if you need anything, anything at all—a shoulder to cry on, advice, ice cream, I'll be here in a flash." He gave her a long, lustful look, then hustled out the door.

Grace groaned. Brandon couldn't really have thought there was anything in that kiss, could he? Curiosity made her open the pizza box. It was pepperoni and anchovies, Grace's favorite. Brandon had a good memory.

The doorbell rang. What if it was Brandon coming back to kiss her again? She didn't think she could handle that.

Thank God, this time it was Penny. She marched inside, took one look at Grace, and demanded, "Why aren't you answering your phone?" She stuck her nose up in the air and sniffed. "Is that pizza?"

"Help yourself," Grace said. "Brandon brought it over, but I'm not hungry."

"Grace, your dad told me what happened. About him firing you and all. Are you okay?"

"I'm fine." Or about as fine as she could be, considering she had no job and was the laughingstock of Daytona Beach.

"It's been horrible at the store without you. And . . . I've been dying to talk to you." She lifted her left hand in the air to show Grace the engagement ring.

"Pen!" Grace swallowed her up into a hug and the two of them did a jerky dance around the living room. "I have to say, after last night I'm not surprised!"

"He was willing to give it all up for me, Grace! His big dream of touring the country on his bike. I couldn't do that to him. And now, I'm just so happy I could burst! We want to get married in early April on the beach, before it gets too hot. And afterward, we'll take off on his bike for our honeymoon. And of course, you'll be my maid of honor. Right?"

"Just as long as you don't make me wear some kind of goofy prom dress. Or black leather." Grace narrowed her eyes. "You're not wearing black at your wedding, are you, Pen?"

Penny laughed. "No black leather at the wedding. Although

I guess I'll be wearing a lot of it on our road trip. What do you think? Penny Starr, biker chick."

"You mean Penny Montgomery, biker chick."

Penny looked radiant. It was the same look Sarah had on her face last night when Charlie swooped her through the door. Four months ago, who would have thought that Penny would be practically giddy at the thought of joining Butch on his motorcycle trip? Four days ago, who would have thought that Sarah would agree to a whirlwind elopement in Vegas wearing an off-the-rack dress from an airport shop? Love was a funny thing. It could make you forget the stuff you thought was important . . .

"After the trip, we'll come back here and settle down. Your dad said he would keep my old job waiting for me."

Pop must have made the same arrangement with Brandon that he'd mentioned to Grace, to keep the store open for the next three years. Grace fervently hoped so. She wasn't ready to see Florida Charlie's leveled. Not yet. Not ever.

"What . . . what was Pop's reaction when you told him you were leaving?"

"He was great. He even offered to keep paying into my benefits so I'd still have health insurance while I'm off. He's a pretty terrific guy."

"Yeah, he is." And Grace had let him down, only she didn't want to think about that anymore. "Pen, I have something to tell you."

"About Ellen calling into the radio show? God, it was awful!"

"Felix called in too, pretending to be some guy named Todd."

"I know. We had the radio on all day in the office."

Grace moaned. "Was Pop listening too?"

"All the employees were. And this thing with Ellen's panties? Okay, at first, it was funny because, you know, Ellen *totally* deserved it. Anyone who's dumb enough to call into Speedway's show should know it isn't going to end well for them. But she got mobbed everywhere she went on campus and she had to cancel all her classes and now she's hiding out in her apartment."

Penny was right. It wasn't funny, but still . . .

"Doug can't really sue us, can he? Or the store?" Penny asked.

"Of course not. At least, I don't think so. I'll have to get Charlie to look into that. Which reminds me, you've heard about Sarah and Charlie, right?"

"Oh my God! Sarah came into the store today, and Grace, I swear, she's never looked happier, except for the fact she's worried about you. She's tried to call you all day."

If Sarah was so worried about her, then why hadn't she come to see her in person? She knew the way to Grace's town house better than anyone.

"You must be on cloud nine," Penny continued. "Charlie and Sarah married! Isn't it awesome?"

"You don't think it's too fast? I mean, she hasn't even been divorced two months."

Penny didn't meet Grace's gaze.

"What?"

"Grace, I think you should talk to Sarah."

"Why don't I like the sound of that?"

"I just think if you need reassurance about the relationship, then you should tell her what you've just told me. That's all," Penny said. Her expression turned serious. "So did you hear Speedway rag on Joe?"

"I listened as long as I could. Then Melanie got on the air and I had to turn it off."

"It was awful! It'll probably go down as the best of Speedway. You know those shows the station plays over and over? She gushed about Joe ad nauseum and, of course, Speedway called her fat and she started crying about how Joe was being unfairly treated by the media and she . . . she blamed *you* for all of it.

And I think Speedway sensed that she wasn't playing with a full deck and he tried to back off but it was too late. She practically had a nervous breakdown on the air."

"I guess Speedway has a conscience after all."

"Either that or he's afraid Melanie will jump off a cliff and he'll end up getting sued."

"We can only hope."

"At least you still have your sense of humor," Penny said.

"It's called survival by snark, Pen. You've been a good teacher."

"What are you going to do now? I mean, about a job?"

Grace shrugged. "I don't know. I'll figure something out."

"I *hate* how all this has turned out."

"You tried to warn me. You and Sarah. This boyfriend club was a bad idea." Grace took the pizza box and handed it to Penny. "Here, you and Butch go celebrate. I'll call you tomorrow and we'll start planning the wedding."

"Butch can take care of himself. Why don't I stay over? We could watch a movie. Or make frozen margaritas."

"Thanks, but I just want to go to sleep." Maybe she'd wake up to find it had all been a dream. Wouldn't that be lovely?

Only she couldn't go to sleep without talking to Joe. So after Penny left, she dialed his cell phone, but it went directly to his voice mail. He had to have heard Speedway's show, otherwise he would have called her by now. Which meant that the reason he hadn't called was because he didn't want to talk to her.

There was no way she could sleep now. And chocolate ice cream wasn't the answer either. So she got in her car and drove to the one place that somehow seemed logical, despite the illogic behind it. The one place that had always lifted her out of whatever funk she might be in.

She drove to Florida Charlie's.

. . .

Second to the Santa outfit, the new NASCAR costume was now Grace's favorite. Not everyone looked good in checkered black and white, but somehow Gator Claus managed to pull it off. His hat was still missing. She'd have to get him a new one. She might not be working at Florida Charlie's anymore, but that didn't mean she couldn't help Abuela with the costumes.

"I've really fucked things up this time, haven't I, Gator Claus?"

Gator Claus stared straight ahead, looking eerily . . . plastic.

"Sorry, I know how you hate it when I use profanity." She batted her eyelashes at him.

Nothing.

Now this was strange, and Grace didn't like it. Not one bit.

"I guess you've heard the news. It's true. I've been canned by Pop and probably dumped by Joe. But there's no need to give me the cold shoulder."

If this was how Gator Claus wanted to play it, so be it.

Grace pretended to be interested in a flyer taped to one of the double doors. On it was a picture of a lost dog named Sammy. The owners were offering a reward. She pulled the flyer off the door and held it under Gator Claus's snout. "You didn't have anything to do with Sammy's disappearance, did you?" If anything, this should get a rise from him.

For a second, she thought she saw a glimmer in his eye. Grace waited, but nothing happened. It must have been a trick of the light. Or maybe it was her imagination. She sighed and taped the flyer back in its original spot.

It would be strange not seeing Gator Claus every day, not walking through the doors of Florida Charlie's to see Stella and Marty and the rest of the staff.

She used her key to open the double doors and walked into the shop and flipped on the lights. It was over five thousand square feet of wall-to-wall junk. But it was beautiful junk, the kind of stuff kids liked to buy with their allowance money.

Maybe it would end up in the trash before vacation was over. Or maybe it would stay tucked away in a bottom drawer to be brought out every now and then. Or maybe it might be something you kept forever, if you were that kind of rare sentimental kid. But the point was, whether it was a Hiawatha doll or a wax dinosaur or an inflatable seahorse, the memory of it was tangled up inside your childhood. And childhood memories were the stuff that made us who we are. As a kid growing up in the store, she'd taken it all for granted but she'd still known this place was magical.

Subconsciously it's what Joe had taught her the day he'd come to the shop and they'd made the T. rex wax figurine. Florida Charlie's was more than just some cheesy tourist trap. And Grace had forgotten that. She'd tried to make it into a tourist version of Walmart. The truth was, Pop was right. She didn't deserve to be the manager of Florida Charlie's.

She locked up the store, checked the door one last time the way Pop would, and turned to say good-bye to Gator Claus.

But he never changed his expression, not once.

Gator Claus wasn't talking to her anymore. Maybe Penny was right. Maybe he never had.

# 32

# The Official Kiss-Off

Finding something appropriate to wear to Chez Louis was a challenge. There was the black dress, but that was sexy and she didn't want Brandon to get the wrong impression. Then there was the red dress she'd worn for her romantic dinner with Joe in St. Augustine and for the disastrous night afterward, but she couldn't bring herself to look at it, let alone wear it. In the end she settled on a pair of black slacks and a simple sweater with some chunky heels.

She hadn't wanted to go to Chez Louis but Brandon had insisted. Grace had spent all day rehearsing a five-minute speech on why they should stay just friends.

When they got to the restaurant they were greeted by a short, older gentleman sporting what sounded like a genuine French accent. He introduced himself as Pierre, the restaurant's maître d'. Out of the corner of her eye, she spotted Felix talking to one of the hostesses. He caught her gaze, then made a point of snubbing her by purposely turning his back to her.

Well, at least there was one positive thing that had come from the whole boyfriend club revelation: Felix wouldn't be trying to get back together with her anymore.

"How have you been?" Grace asked Brandon once they'd

been seated. "Has there been any more fallout from the club review?"

"The Zumba thing has been a big source of entertainment for my buddies. But like I said, I can handle it." The server brought them their drinks. "So what's going on with you and Joe Rosenblum?" he asked casually, but Grace could tell by the way he watched her expression that he was more than casually interested in her answer.

Oh no. Brandon was going to bring up the kiss. Grace tried to remember the opening to her speech.

"I haven't talked to Joe since Sunday. He's not returning my calls."

"The St. Valentine's Day Curse?"

Grace had forgotten she'd told Brandon about the Curse. It was funny, but she'd told him a lot of things over the past month. Stuff that she usually only told Sarah and Penny and Ellen. "I think I can pretty much take full credit this time."

"Joe's a good guy, Grace. Maybe in time, it'll all work out."

Now *this* was a surprise. Grace thought for sure that Brandon was about to make a case for himself. "Brandon, Joe told me once not to trust you."

His gaze sharpened. "He did?"

"He's wrong, of course. You're one of the most stand-up guys I know."

He didn't say anything for a minute. "What made you do it, Grace? The boyfriend club, I mean."

"I don't know. I told myself it was about empowerment. But it was more about venting." She thought about it a moment. "That's not true. I guess you could say it was also about revenge." It felt good to finally admit it out loud. She raised her drink in the air. "The truth will set you free."

Brandon smiled sympathetically. "Don't be so hard on yourself."

"Are you always this nice? Or just this nice to me?"

He picked up her hand and began playing with her fingers. She tried to feel something. A zing. A tingle. *Anything.* Her life would be so easy if she could fall in love with Brandon.

Grace froze.

Ellen was wrong. Brandon wasn't her Mr. Darcy. He was the *Laurie* to her Jo. The perpetual friend, the trusted confidante, the guy who *should* be right for you. Only he wasn't.

"Brandon—"

He squeezed her hand and let go. "You don't have to say it, Grace. I wanted it to be there because you're so damn perfect for me. But we're better off staying friends."

Relief swamped her. She thought back to the scene in the movie version of *Little Women* where Jo shot down Laurie. Brandon was taking this a lot better than Christian Bale had.

"So we're good?"

"We're better than good. These past few weeks have been terrific. I feel like I can tell you anything." He paused. "It's been a long time since I've had a friend I could trust."

"That means a lot to me, Brandon."

He nodded. "So . . . I've been thinking about your future. Your business future, that is. Now that you're not working for your father anymore, have you thought about what you're going to do?"

"I hear the Waffle House is hiring."

"I think I can do a little better for you than that." He pulled out his wallet and handed her a card.

"What's this?"

"My buddy at the Chamber of Commerce is looking for a new PR person. I told him about you, and with your background in tourism, he thinks you'd be terrific. He's expecting your call."

"Brandon, that's awfully sweet of you, but—"

"Damn it, Grace. I don't do anything to be *sweet.* I wouldn't have put my professional reputation on the line unless I thought you were right for the job."

She tucked the card away in her purse. "Thanks. I owe you."

"Good. Then you'll buy the wine for our next movie night." He looked like he was on the verge of saying something more, when his cell phone rang. It was a business call, so he excused himself and went to the lobby to continue his conversation in private.

The server brought a freshly baked loaf of bread with real butter. Grace had just cut into a slice when she saw Joe. He was with his mother, his aunt, and his cousin Phillip. The hostess seated them at a table on the opposite side of the restaurant, but Joe caught her gaze. He said something to his mother and made his way across the room. Before she had time to think, Grace stuffed a chunk of bread in her mouth in a nervous frenzy.

Joe wore a dark suit and a pale blue tie that brought out the color of his eyes. He looked beautiful, and Grace wanted to kick herself for not dressing up because she had a sinking feeling this might be the last time she ever saw him again.

"Hello, Grace."

She frantically tried to swallow the bread so she could speak. "Hello," she said, her mouth still stuffed with bread. *What was she doing?*

"How are you?" he asked cautiously. He seemed somber. Not friendly, but not mad either.

"I'm okay," she squeaked. "And you?"

"I'm fine." He looked across the room. "We're celebrating my mother's birthday."

"Please wish her a happy birthday from . . . me." Not that Joe's mother would have any clue who Grace was. Other than as his patient of course.

He seemed to catch on to her thoughts and shuffled from foot to foot. It was the first time Grace had ever seen Joe physically uncomfortable. "I saw Farrell outside on his cell phone. Are you two together now?"

"What? No! I mean, we're *here* together. But not like you think. Brandon is a good friend, Joe. I told you that. The stuff on the radio, what Felix said? That wasn't true. *Please*, you have to believe me on that."

He nodded, like he did believe her, and Grace felt a second's relief. At least that was one thing she didn't have to defend herself on.

"Do you mind if I sit down? Just for a few minutes?"

"Of course!" Grace gestured to the empty seat across from her.

"I'm sorry I haven't returned your calls. I meant to, but I'll be honest, I didn't know what to say."

She didn't know what to say either. Except that she was sorry and that she wished she could take it all back. "How did it go with your aunt and Phillip?"

Joe seemed surprised but pleased that she remembered his cousin's dilemma. "It was . . . You were right. She was great. It was a big relief. For everyone."

"I'm glad." She thought about the best way to apologize but there was no best way except to simply come right out and say it. "Joe, I'm sorry about the boyfriend club."

"You mean your women's empowerment group?" Finally. There was the anger she'd been expecting. "What made you do it, Grace?"

"It started out as petty revenge for a date gone bad. Then it grew into something I couldn't control. It was . . . it was stupid."

"Why would you tell a roomful of strangers—" He shook his head, clearly at a loss.

"Why would I tell a roomful of strangers a bunch of personal details about us? About you? In my defense, I only told them the good stuff, Joe. The bit about you trying to pick me up at the Wobbly Duck? I told that to Sarah and Ellen and Penny, and Ellen thought you were my Mr. Wickham, and so she put that in the review. And I did tell everyone you snored, but that was because Melanie got me riled up."

"That's how you knew about Melanie being out of control. She was actually a part of this club too?"

"I wanted to tell you, but . . ." Her voice faltered. "I have no excuse, really. Except I'm sorry."

He didn't say anything, but then he didn't have to. The look on his face told her what she needed to know. This was it. The end. If she'd hoped that there was a possibility that the two of them would be able to get past the events of the last few days, the expression in his eyes killed it. He wasn't angry anymore. He was blank. Devoid of any emotion. And that was probably the worst of all. Grace felt like the earth had just tilted beneath her feet. She wished she knew how to push it back into place again.

"I'm sorry too, Grace, because I think we could have had something terrific here." He cleared his throat. "And I'm sorry I didn't introduce you to my mother when I had the chance, but I think there's something you should know. Maybe, I don't know . . . maybe it'll help us both if I say this out loud."

He looked nervous again, which only made Grace more nervous. She could feel her palms go damp.

"You won't believe it, but my cousin Phillip has been seeing this counselor. This ex-marine type—"

"Don't tell me. Jim the manly therapist?"

"Seems he's a pretty popular guy. He's been helping Phillip come to terms with his sexuality and a few other things. Like standing up for himself, taking control of his life, that sort of stuff. And now, because he's been in therapy, Phillip himself thinks he's Dr. Phil. Literally."

Despite all that was happening, Grace couldn't help but smile. Joe smiled too. But it was a sad smile.

"And I told him what went down between us, and he gave me some insight that I actually think is spot-on."

"Like . . . what?"

"Well, considering the timing, our relationship was probably doomed from the start. You weren't in a good place to begin with, and that might have influenced things. I'll be honest, Grace, when I look back . . . at one point I thought . . . Well, it doesn't matter what I thought. But there was something missing. Something that kept me from taking that final emotional plunge." He stopped and shook his head. "Wow. I'm beginning to sound like a damn shrink."

*Something missing.* It was the second time Joe had said that. Grace had felt it too.

"So after talking to Phillip and thinking about it some, I think I've figured it out. I don't think you really ever gave me a chance, Grace. I knew things weren't right when I found out about Florida Charlie's being in trouble. You mentioned it in some offhand way, and when I wanted to talk about it, you brushed me off. But I know how you feel about that store. The idea of selling Florida Charlie's has got to be eating you up inside. Maybe I could have been a good sounding board, if you'd opened up to me."

"I told you about Craig cheating on Sarah. I've *never* told anyone that, Joe. Not even my closest friends."

He considered that a moment. "Would you have told me if we hadn't run into them at the restaurant that night? I think you were vulnerable, and you let your guard down. I don't think you would have confided in me otherwise." He lowered his voice. "I don't want the kind of relationships my dad falls into. It's not enough to be lovers. I want to be friends too. You were right when you accused me of being jealous of Farrell. It was obvious you had connected with him in a way you and I hadn't."

"Is this about the day at the hospital? Because, Joe—"

The sound of a man clearing his throat startled them both.

She looked up to see Brandon. How long had he been standing there? Not long, or surely either she or Joe would have noticed him before now. The two men exchanged a curt greeting. Joe went back to his table and that was that.

"I'm sorry," Brandon said. "Did I interrupt something?"

"Nothing I wasn't expecting." She looked over at Joe's table and Brandon followed her gaze, staring for what was longer than had to be considered polite.

"Are you okay?" Grace asked.

"Sure . . . sure." He shook his head as if to clear it. "I should be asking you that."

"I'll be all right." Considering everything that had happened, Joe was being incredibly nice. She'd lied to him. And even though she hadn't done it on purpose, the boyfriend club review had made him out to be some cold, calculating playboy schemer. It was a miracle he'd even bothered coming over to talk to her.

Brandon opened his menu. "What are you hungry for?"

"Honestly? I've lost my appetite. Sorry."

"I'm not hungry anymore either," he admitted.

"You want to come back to my place and watch a movie? We could make popcorn and drink cheap wine."

"Why not?" Brandon motioned for the server to bring their check. "That actually sounds pretty good right now." Grace was surprised at how easily Brandon had capitulated. He was probably just saying that to make her feel better. Despite what he'd said earlier, he really was awfully sweet.

Brandon pulled the car up to the front of the restaurant and opened the door for her. "So what movie are we going to watch?" he asked.

"Anything except *Titanic*. I'm not in the mood to get vested in another doomed relationship."

"Me either," said Brandon.

# 33

# Reconciliation Is the New Confession

It was five p.m. on Wednesday afternoon. And way past time to face the music. Had it only been three days since the firing/big announcement? Pop's car wasn't in the driveway and Grace had to admit she was relieved, big coward that she was. Mami was in the kitchen, mincing an onion. Thin cuts of steak lay marinating in garlic and lemon on a plate to the side. Mami was making *Bistec Palomillo*, Grace's favorite comfort food. She just wished she was hungry enough to want to eat.

"Where's Abuela?" she asked her mother after giving her a kiss on the cheek.

"Taking a nap." Mami smiled wistfully.

Grace was glad that it was just the two of them. There were times in a woman's life when, no matter how old she was, the person she needed most was her mother.

"Mami, what do you think about Charlie and Sarah? Honestly?"

Mami finished mincing the onion and wiped her hands on a dish towel. "Well, I wish they could have gotten married in the Church, with Father Donnelly saying the Mass and Charlie wearing a tuxedo and looking all handsome and Sarah in a proper wedding dress, but . . ." Mami shook her head. "It wouldn't guarantee that the marriage would last. I'm happy. I think this is the real thing."

"You don't think it's too soon after Sarah's divorce?"

"I think it wasn't soon enough. I don't think you should put a timetable on happiness."

So everyone had seen the Charlie/Sarah connection a *lot* sooner than Grace had. And here Sarah was supposed to be her best friend, the person whom she knew better than anyone. It seemed Grace didn't know Sarah at all. Not if Sarah had been harboring some secret love for Charlie all this time. As for Charlie . . . In retrospect, it made sense. There were tiny signs here and there that Grace had seen but chosen to ignore. Mainly because it was futile, Sarah being a married woman and all. But they'd been there.

"Is Pop really mad at me?" Grace asked.

"He'll get over it. He's mainly angry at himself."

"Why would Pop be angry at himself? He hasn't done anything."

"That's *exactly* why he's angry. He thinks he should have paid more attention to the store." Mami shrugged. "I think he's still a little angry at me too, for the constant hovering I've done the past couple of years. But he'll get over it."

"What do I do now?" Grace asked. It felt surreal, going to her mother for advice at age thirty the way she'd done when she was a little girl and had messed up something.

"About what? About your job? About the thing on the radio? Oh, I heard." Mami shook her head. "What were you thinking, starting up this boyfriend club?"

That was the million-dollar question, wasn't it?

"I honestly don't know." She thought about the way it had affected the people in her life. Like Charlie and Brandon. But most especially Joe. "What if Pop and I never get over this?"

"You mean, what if he stays mad at you forever?" Mami

smiled in the way mothers did when they thought their adult children were being silly. "Grace, your father worked for his father for the first ten years of our marriage. Do you really believe they never fought? Your grandfather fired your father at least three times before you were even born."

Grace was stunned. "Why haven't I heard that before?"

"Working with family is never easy. There's a line that gets crossed so often, after a while you don't even see it anymore. The last time your father got fired, he had to come to terms with the fact that he wasn't the only one with a good idea. That maybe your grandfather knew a thing or two about the business and that he should shut up and listen and learn. I'm not saying that you and your father can work together. I don't even know if that's what you want. But believe me when I tell you that, while your father might be unhappy with you right now as an employee, it doesn't change the way he feels about you as a daughter."

She poured some olive oil into a hot pan and fried up one of the steaks, then slid it into a plate and covered it in onions. "You're too skinny. Sit down and eat this or we're going to have to start calling you Cucumber instead of Tomato."

Sarah's car was parked in front of Grace's town house but there was no one in the car, which meant she was inside, waiting. It made perfect sense, since Sarah had her own key to Grace's place. Sarah wasn't waiting alone. She had reinforcements in the way of frozen margaritas. She'd even taken the time to rim their glasses with salt.

"Am I going to need that or are you?" Grace asked, taking the margarita Sarah offered.

"We both are."

"Sounds ominous."

"I listened to Speedway," Sarah said, lifting her margarita glass to her lips. The movement brought Grace's attention to the humongous diamond ring on Sarah's left hand. When had *this* happened? Grace tried not to stare. Was Sarah going to show it to her? Or should Grace mention it first?

What was the proper etiquette when your best friend ran off with your brother and didn't even have the decency to give you a heads-up?

"I think all of Daytona Beach listened to Speedway," Grace said.

"Grace, I'm so sorry about everything. Especially about losing your job." Sarah paused. "Your mother told Charlie, and he told me."

"I deserved it. Joe and I are through too." Grace tried for a bright smile, because this martyr gig really wasn't her thing. "It was inevitable. The St. Valentine's Day Curse, right? And you tried to warn me the boyfriend club was a bad idea. I just wish I'd listened."

"You don't really believe you're cursed, do you?"

"Why not? Someone has to be cursed." She downed some more of the margarita. Maybe she'd get drunk again tonight.

"Do you think Ellen has left her house yet?" Sarah asked, in an obvious attempt to lighten the conversation. "The last I heard, Speedway had upped the bounty on the panties picture to three hundred bucks."

"For three hundred bucks I'll take a picture of Ellen's panties myself. I need the money now that I'm out of a job."

They both laughed, but it felt fake.

*Have you told Sarah yet? Because she deserves to know the whole truth. The two of you will never be right until you do.*

Joe was right about one thing: She and Sarah weren't right. Only it wasn't because Grace hadn't opened up. This time, it was Sarah who was hiding something. Something big.

"Sarah, are you really in love with my brother? Because if this is some kind of rebound, then maybe it's not too late to—"

"Grace, I've never loved anyone *but* Charlie."

"Really? Because I thought you did a pretty good imitation with Craig."

"Craig was a mistake."

"No shit."

"Why are you mad at me? I thought you'd be thrilled! Wasn't it just last month you were trying to get me and Charlie together?"

"Yeah, get you together on a *date*. That's how it works. First you go on some dates, then you get serious. Then you get engaged, and then you get married. The whole process usually lasts longer than twelve hours." She knew she sounded like a bitch, but she couldn't help herself.

"You think I've taken advantage of Charlie."

"Does this have anything to do with what I told you the other night? About Craig cheating on you with Carla before the wedding? Is running off to marry Charlie some kind of revenge against Craig?"

"Grace, listen to me. I'm glad you told me about Craig and Carla! It made everything so much easier for me."

"*Easier?*" Grace began pacing the living room. "You'll have to explain that one, Sarah, because right now all I can think about is the sound of your voice six months ago when you called to tell me that you'd just caught your husband in bed with another woman. If you don't remember, maybe I can replay it for you, because *believe me*, that voice has pretty much haunted me every day since."

Sarah flinched. "I'm sorry. I should have told you the truth a long time ago."

"So tell me now."

Sarah downed the rest of her margarita like she was going to need it.

"The reason I was so hysterical on the phone that night wasn't because I was upset about finding Craig and Carla together. Although, I have to admit, it was a shocker. I was hysterical because I gave up Charlie for *nothing*. Grace, I've been in love with Charlie since . . . well, I could say that I've been in love with him since I was seventeen, only that wouldn't really be true. That was more of a schoolgirl crush. But I can honestly say that I've been in love with him, I mean *really* in love with him, for the past six years."

Grace stopped her pacing. *"What?"*

"Charlie's version of our getting together wasn't exactly honest," Sarah said. "He made up that whole story of me discovering my feelings Saturday night to protect me."

"You've totally lost me." Grace took a huge swig of her margarita. Sarah wasn't the only one who needed a little fortification.

"Do you remember the weekend that a bunch of us all went up to the Florida–FSU football game and we stayed at that bed-and-breakfast in Micanopy? I'd just gotten my interior design license and I was going out with Martin and you were dating that guy Pete."

"The one who kept doing the Seminole chop in my face every time Florida scored a touchdown? What an asshole!"

"Yeah." Sarah laughed a little. "And Charlie and some of his friends showed up, and he brought that girl with him, the one who laughed at everything he said like he was some kind of rock star and we kept making fun of her behind her back?"

"Trish the Dish. Blonde, long legs, big boobs."

"God, I think I still hate her."

Grace conjured up a fuzzy image of that weekend. She remembered Sarah acting strange. Oddly quiet one minute, giddy the next.

"From the minute that weekend started, I was a mess inside and I couldn't figure out why. And then it hit me: I was jealous of Trish. And I don't mean jealous in a little way either. I wanted to freakin' knock her out."

"*That's* when you realized you were in love with Charlie?" Grace asked.

"You remember how we tailgated after the game, and that by the time we got back to the inn it was really late? And everyone just crashed because they were so drunk and tired. But I wasn't drunk and I wasn't tired, so I took a walk to clear my head about . . . you know, all these *strange* feelings I was having. A cold front had come in and I hadn't brought my jacket with me, so I cut my walk short. And when I got back to the inn, Charlie was sitting on the porch in one of those big rocking chairs, smoking a cigar, which was weird because I'd never seen him smoke before. And he gave me his jacket and he showed me how to smoke the cigar the right way, but I just kept coughing and we started laughing. And I knew, I mean, I just *knew* that he'd seen me leave and that he'd been sitting there waiting for me to come back all that time."

Grace held her breath.

"We must have talked for at least four hours. And he told me . . . well, we kissed, and *oh my God*, Grace." The look on Sarah's face made Grace swallow hard. "It was beyond anything I'd ever felt, and I knew then that Charlie was the only one for me and I wanted to wake you up and tell you everything."

"Why didn't you?" None of this made sense. This was Sarah, her best friend, who told her everything. Only apparently not.

"I wish I had, because I wanted to tell someone. I wanted to tell *you*, but I was afraid you might . . . Remember how we used to make bets on how long Charlie's girlfriends would last? I think deep down I was afraid that you might try to talk me out of him."

"Talk you out of him? Why would I have talked you out of my own brother?"

But in that instant, Grace knew what Sarah said was true. On some level, just like Abuela and Mami, Grace had suspected there was something between Charlie and Sarah, only that level was buried so deep inside it hadn't found its way to the surface. Not until that night at Grace's apartment when she'd seen them bantering and caught the look of sheer longing on Charlie's face. But even then, Grace hadn't suspected the depth of those feelings. Or that Sarah felt them just as strongly. Grace hadn't wanted to.

Sarah took a deep breath and continued. "So I thought, okay, this is it. It all begins now and I won't have to tell Grace because she'll *see* it. Only the next day he was the old Charlie again, calling me squirt and acting like nothing had happened between us. Then, about a week later, we went out for coffee and he told me he was sorry, that it would be dumb of us to start something because if—and I could tell what he really meant was *when*—it went sour, it would be too awkward between you and me, since you were my best friend and I was already practically part of the family. So it was best to just leave things the way they were."

"Charlie got cold feet."

"I was so angry, Grace. I started yelling at him right in the middle of Starbucks."

"*You* yelled in public?"

"Oh, yeah. I showed out bad. I told him he was just a big coward and that he didn't deserve me and that one day he would be sorry."

How could all this have gone on and Grace not known about it?

Sarah, who was like a sister to her. Sarah, who Grace loved just as much as she loved Charlie, had gone through all this and had never said a word to her.

"Then I started dating Craig and we got serious and I thought, this is it again. I was at a crossroads, and surely Charlie would say something or do something, but he never did. It's not that I didn't love Craig in my own way. But I was settling and it was just stupid. Really, really stupid of me. And then before I knew it, Craig asked me to marry him and I said yes. And Mother planned this *huge* wedding, and everything cost a fortune, and a few days before the wedding Craig and I got in a big fight. He told me that he loved me but that if I wasn't really into it that we should call the whole thing off. And I freaked and told him that there was *no way* I was backing out.

"Then, the night before my wedding . . . the night *before* my wedding, Grace! Charlie knocked on my door at two in the morning. He'd been drinking. He asked me to call things off with Craig and give him another chance. If he thought he'd seen me angry before, he hadn't seen anything yet. What was I supposed to do? Call everything off because Charlie had finally come to his senses?" Sarah blinked, and Grace could see she was fighting back tears. "I told him he was too late and to get the hell out of there and to never talk to me again unless he had to."

*Sarah's stubborn and unforgiving.* Charlie hadn't been talking about Craig; he'd been talking about his own relationship with Sarah. The thought made Grace shiver.

"My brother is a total idiot."

"*I'm* the idiot. If I'd just swallowed my pride and had some guts, I'd have called off my wedding."

"But what he was asking . . . the night before your wedding! I don't know how he could have expected you to change your mind like that." Then something occurred to Grace. "If I'd told you about Craig and Carla, maybe you would have."

The realization that Grace's omission had done so much more harm that she'd even imagined was staggering.

"I don't know, Grace. I was angry at Charlie. And I wanted to hurt him the way he'd hurt me. Maybe this was how it was all supposed to happen. Maybe Charlie and I had to go through everything to get to where we are now."

"You think you were supposed to stay married to a lying scumbag for two years before you got your happily-ever-after?"

There was a long silence before Sarah spoke again. Her voice was low and Grace had to strain to hear her. "Craig didn't cheat on me until after *I'd* cheated on him. At least, not while we were married."

"But that's not possible!" Even as she said it, Grace realized that *anything* was possible. Everything she thought she knew about herself, about Sarah, even about her own brother had been challenged in the past few days.

"Last May, when Craig was out of town on business, I ran into Charlie at the gas station." Sarah shook her head. "Not the most romantic place in the world, but it was the first time since the night before my wedding that Charlie and I had been alone together, you know, without family or someone we knew around. We talked and I followed him back to his place and I think it took us about all of five minutes before we started tearing off each other's clothes. You have *no* idea what it's like to want something so badly for so long and then finally have it."

Grace wasn't sure she wanted to hear this. This was Sarah and Charlie, and it was just all so weird. Incestuous, almost. But not. She forced herself to listen.

"Charlie wanted me to leave Craig right away, to file for divorce. And that's what I wanted too, but even though I was deliriously happy, I couldn't get it out of my head that what I'd done was wrong. It was *adultery*, Grace." Sarah's voice started to shake. "I told Craig and he begged me to go to counseling, to see if we could give our marriage another try. And I felt like I owed him that at least. And Charlie was angry with me for giving in to Craig. And I was angry at myself and—"

"Wait! I'm confused. After you caught Craig with Carla and you decided to file for divorce, why didn't you and Charlie get together then?"

"Charlie and I left things so badly. He didn't understand how after we'd been together, I could . . . you know, try to make things work with Craig. But I swear I never slept with Craig again. I just couldn't. Not after being with Charlie."

"Male pride," Grace said, shaking her head in disgust.

"That night you told me Charlie was moving to Miami . . . I almost threw up in the car. I must have called him a dozen times and hung up before he could answer. Then, at the meeting Saturday night, when Phoebe accused Charlie of sexual harassment . . ." Sarah's face went red. "Well, you saw my reaction."

"You were awesome," Grace said. "I was so proud of you!"

"I realized then that Charlie and I had been playing some kind of stupid game to see which of us would be the first to cave in, and I didn't care anymore. So I drove to his house. I didn't even have to say anything. I rang his doorbell and . . . The look on his face when he saw me . . . He grabbed me and we started kissing and he threw some clothes in a bag and we jumped in his car and when I asked him where we were going he just kept laughing and telling me I'd find out. And we got to the airport and he paid this outrageous fortune for tickets to Vegas and I thought, okay, we're going on a romantic getaway. But then . . . right there at the counter, in front of everyone, he got down on one knee and he asked me to marry him.

"And I said yes. Well, I think I actually *screamed* yes, and everyone around us started clapping, like we were in some corny movie! And Grace, I'll be honest, even though it would have been nice to have you and my parents and your parents and Abuela there, I wouldn't have wanted it any other way."

Tears were running into Grace's margarita. She wiped her nose on the edge of her sleeve. "It's the most *perfect* thing I've ever heard."

Sarah nodded, her own tears running down her cheeks. "I'm going to hell, aren't I?"

"If you're going to hell, then so am I."

"No," Sarah said. "This isn't going to be fixed by saying three Hail Marys and two Our Fathers. I'm really going to hell. Or worse. There's probably a special place for people like me. Someplace like limbo where the dead babies who aren't baptized go, only it's for all the selfish Catholics who break commandments and don't care. I bet Sister Perpetua would know what it's called."

Grace began to laugh at the utter ridiculousness of it all, only Sarah was right. Not about the going to hell part, because Grace didn't believe God worked that way. At least, not the God Grace believed in. But they'd managed to make a big muck out of the sacrament of marriage, and Grace had to take some responsibility in it as well. The fact was, she should have told Sarah what she suspected about Craig before the wedding, no matter how uncomfortable the whole thing might have been.

"Sarah, remember that night outside Florida Charlie's when we were waiting in the car before the boyfriend club meeting and you asked me why I was trying to get you and Charlie together now? Why I hadn't tried, like, five years earlier?"

Sarah nodded.

"I think, deep down, I've always known you and Charlie had something going. And I think . . . I think I was jealous because I wanted to keep you all to myself. All my life, I've been envious of my brother. Charlie doesn't want to work at the store? Well, he doesn't have to. Charlie comes home late to dinner? Oops, we need to keep his plate warm! I could sense sometimes that he wanted to hang out with us. Not when we were kids, of course, but later . . . And I didn't want to give you up to him. I know that sounds stupid, but there it is."

"Oh, Grace, it's not stupid at all! I promise you, no matter what, we'll always be best friends."

"Charlie doesn't deserve you," Grace said, trying to laugh

away the tears. "*But I do*. St. Anthony couldn't have given me a better sister-in-law."

"What does St. Anthony have to do with it?"

"I'll tell you later." Grace grabbed Sarah's hand. "Right now, I want to hear all about this rock!"

They spent the rest of the night getting drunk on margaritas and laughing, and sometimes crying, and every once in a while Grace would marvel on how very dense she'd been about the whole Charlie/Sarah affair. But mostly she was just grateful to have the old Sarah back. The one who, *thank God*, had never been stubborn and unforgiving with Grace.

# 34

# Bless Me, Father, for I Have Sinned

"So Sarah confessed everything to me . . . And I mean *everything*," Grace said, unable to resist taking a poke at Charlie. It was Friday and Grace was eating lunch at Luigi's with her brother. It was something they'd rarely done before, she realized, because he was always too busy with work. Marriage to Sarah was softening him already.

Charlie looked resigned to the fact that his life was now forever linked to some kind of sister/wife/best friend ménage à trois.

Grace decided to take pity on him. "Don't worry, Sarah doesn't kiss and tell. Not every detail anyway." She ordered the spaghetti and meatballs and waited patiently as the server brought them their breadstick basket. "Ah, the delicious smell of Luigi's breadsticks."

The first couple of days after the fallout, she hadn't been able to eat. Now it was the exact opposite. She couldn't stop eating. It was binge eating, she knew, but she couldn't help herself. Food was the only thing making her feel better at the moment.

"So what do you think about Sarah and me?" Charlie said. "Honestly?"

"I think you're an ass hat and that you've behaved abominably. And that you and Sarah almost screwed up your lives. But you're my brother and she's my best friend and I love you both. And I don't know that, under similar circumstances, I might not have done the same thing. According to Abuela, I can be pretty stubborn too. And I have to admit, scooping Sarah off to Las Vegas was pretty romantic. I expect nothing but smooth sailing from now on. Oh, and a niece or nephew in the next couple of years would be nice too. Either one. I'm not picky."

"You'll be happy to know we're working on that."

Grace laid down her breadstick. "Charlie, I'm really sorry about Phoebe."

"You know the old saying, how every cloud has a silver lining? As awkward as the whole Phoebe thing has been around the office, it's her accusation against me that made Sarah admit she was still in love with me. So, in a way, I have Phoebe to thank for giving me Sarah."

"The partners at the law firm, they don't believe her, do they?"

"It's basically a case of he said, she said. I'm not worried about it and you shouldn't be either." The unspoken part being that Grace had enough to worry about. Like her own job. Charlie paused while the server brought them their orders. "I turned down the Miami promotion."

"Charlie, that's great! I mean . . . I'm sorry, I guess."

"Don't be. The only reason I was thinking of taking it in the first place was because of Sarah. It was hard, seeing her and . . . not being with her." Grace nodded. It still amazed her how clueless she'd been. "So how about you and Farrell? Any news you want to share on that front?" he asked.

"Charlie, did we both get the delusional gene?"

"What?" He put on a fake hurt expression that made Grace laugh.

"I've told you a dozen times, Brandon and I are good friends. End of story." She fiddled with her spaghetti and thought about what Joe had said to her about not opening up and not giving their relationship a fair chance. "The truth is, I've been seeing someone for a couple of months now. His name is Joe Rosenblum. But it's over."

"Name sounds familiar." Charlie frowned. "The dentist . . . Wickham?"

"I thought you overworked attorney types were too busy to listen to Speedway."

"Everyone in Daytona listens to Speedway."

"So I'm finding out."

"What are you going to do now? About a job?"

"I don't know," Grace admitted. "I haven't had time to think about it, what with best friends and brothers eloping and Speedway Gonzalez blaring my personal life for everyone to hear."

"It wasn't just your personal life. It was the personal lives of all the guys you reviewed in that club."

Charlie was right, of course. She just hated being reminded of it. "Brandon got me a pretty good lead on a job. A friend of his works at the Chamber of Commerce. Tourism PR, that kind of thing. I called him and he wants to interview me next week."

"Sounds perfect. If they offer, take it," Charlie said without blinking. "By the way, don't worry about that guy who was threatening to sue the store. I sent him a little nasty-gram the other day. He's already backed down."

"And this is why everyone should have a lawyer in the family," Grace muttered.

"Have you talked to Dad yet? He misses you."

"I've been avoiding him," Grace said. "I know, I know! Don't say it. I'm a coward. He's selling the store to Brandon, isn't he?"

Charlie stopped eating. "Go see him, Grace. Talk to him."

"I'm ashamed, Charlie. I've disappointed him and I've disappointed myself too."

"C'mon, Grace, stop being so fucking dramatic. You're his little Tomato, for God's sake. He can't stay mad at you." She must have looked surprised because he shrugged and said, "I know Pop loves me and he's proud of me, but it's not the same. I guess parents love their kids differently. They'd have to, because we're all different, right? You and Pop have always shared this special bond. It's like you get one another in a way he and I don't. When I was a kid, I used to be jealous." He chuckled. "And then I realized that he let me get away with shit he'd never let you get away with, so I figured it was a good tradeoff."

Grace felt her jaw go slack. "Charlie, this is too weird. You know I told Sarah that when we were kids I was jealous of *you?*"

"Of course you were. I was better looking, smarter, funnier—"
She threw her napkin at him and they both laughed.


Grace stopped on her way into the store to give the alligator a discerning look. He was now dressed in his St. Patrick's Day outfit. Not as sharp as his Santa costume or the new NASCAR look, but still, it gave him a certain flair. Penny spotted her. "Hey! What are you doing here? Not that you need a reason to come into the store, but . . ."

"I'm here to see Pop."

"That's good," Penny said. She studied Grace's face. "Sweetie, you have bags under your eyes. Are you not sleeping?"

"I stayed up all night finishing a book. Among other things."

Penny looked like she was going to laugh. "There wasn't a movie version?"

"Actually, there is; at least, I think there is. I stayed up reading *The Old Man and the Sea.* Joe loaned it to me a while back but I never got around to reading it."

"Isn't Hemingway a little morose under the circumstances? You should be doing things to cheer you up!"

Grace smiled. "Have you talked to Ellen? Has she gone back to work?"

"Oh my God. You haven't heard, have you? So you know how Ellen has been in hiding ever since Speedway put the bounty out on her panties picture. Each morning he's been upping the price, and this morning he offered five hundred bucks. And Ellen was so fed up with the whole thing that she took the picture herself. She walked right down to the station and demanded the money from Speedway."

"No!"

"Yep. He gave it to her too. She's going to take us all out to dinner next week. Her treat, she says. Plus, she finally took down the Yahoo! site."

"Thank God."

"I think over the past few days she's come to the realization that women's empowerment isn't all it's cracked up to be."

"Yeah, I have too." Grace glanced around the store. "So where's Pop? I saw his car parked in back."

"He's in the office." Penny gave her a thumbs-up. "Good luck!"

Grace knocked on the door. Pop yelled out a gruff "Come in." There were papers in stacks everywhere. On the desk, on the chairs, even on the floor.

Grace stared at the mess, bewildered. "Where did all these papers come from?"

"I pulled out all the invoices on the merchandise." He picked up a stack from the floor. "When did we start buying T-shirts from this place down in Miami?"

"Oh . . . that's a new vendor. But the quality and the price are first-rate. I swear. You won't find a better deal anywhere."

He laid the stack back on the floor. "I'll take your word on that."

Grace began eyeing some of the papers. "Pop, if you want, I can bring you up to speed on all this within a day or so. I know it seems confusing right now because you've been away from it for a while, but it's pretty cut-and-dry. You won't have any trouble figuring out the ordering system."

He showed her a pamphlet for a trade show to be held in Tampa next month. "What about this? You think you might want to go to this show? I've been thinking we need to start selling the back scratchers again. You know, the ones shaped like the manatee?"

"Those were terrible sellers. Don't you remember? We ended up having to put them on a two-for-one giveaway clearance rack, and even then it took forever to get rid of them."

"Oh, yeah."

"Pop," Grace said, taking a deep breath. "I know you went to see Brandon the other day. I don't think selling the store is a good idea."

"You don't, huh?"

"No. As a matter of fact, it's a *terrible* idea. The worst one you've ever had. I had lunch with Charlie yesterday. He told me . . . Well, never mind what he told me. I stayed up all night working on this." She pulled a sheet of paper out of her bag and handed it to him. "It's a business plan. Kind of like the one I wrote up about my idea to keep the store open on Sundays, but this one is more comprehensive."

He took the sheet and began to read.

"I read *The Old Man and the Sea*, Pop, and I *totally* get it. It's like you're the old fisherman, Santiago." She paused. "Not that I'm saying you're old or anything. And Florida Charlie's is the fish . . . or maybe the fish in this case is a symbol for success. I'm not sure, I'll have to ask Ellen. She'll know. The point is, you can't give up. You can't sell the store. Even if we end up going bust, we have to keep trying."

"Who says I'm selling the store? Farrell's bank is giving me a loan to get this place back in order. Charlie worked it out."

"He did? He didn't say anything to me about a loan!" *That sneak.*

"Your brother's a sharp negotiator. Got me a great interest rate. This place needs a new roof. And the bathrooms are a mess." He read a few more lines of her comprehensive business plan and locked eyes with her, surprised. "You really think we should resurrect the orange-head commercials?"

Grace cleared her throat. "I think it's worth a try. They were pretty successful, weren't they? We could do a whole retro ad campaign. I think people would really go for that."

"Did you know Stella wants four weeks off this summer to go visit her daughter up in Fort Walton Beach? I thought the longest we gave off was two weeks at a time."

"True, but you know, Pop, we have to make an exception for Stella. She's been here forever."

"Won't the other employees complain?"

"Let 'em. When they've been here fifty years, then they can take off four weeks too."

Pop grinned.

"About that trade show . . . I could go, but I'm not staying at the same hotel as last time. The rooms all smelled like smoke."

"Okay," Pop said. "Stay where you want. Within reason. Just don't forget the receipts."

Florida Charlie's wasn't getting bought out! And it wasn't getting leveled. And in that moment, Grace knew, she just *knew*, that no matter what happened to the store, there wasn't anywhere else Grace wanted to work but right here.

"You know, Tomato, I'm getting too old to run around the parking lot with the orange-head on. It's just not dignified. So maybe instead we could do a father/daughter orange-head commercial. We could do Big Orange Head and Little Orange Head. Do a kind of Burns and Allen routine. What do you think?"

Grace stilled. "I guess you're thinking . . . I would be Little Orange Head?"

Pop made an impatient sound. "You don't think *I'm* going to be Little Orange Head, do you?"

"On one condition: I get to say the punch line."

Pop sighed. "Okay."

*Your dad is weird and so are you*!

Richard Kasamati hadn't known it, but all those years ago on the third-grade playground he'd paid Grace the best compliment she could ever hope to get.

# 35

# Real Men Do Zumba

"You're late," Grace said to Brandon, ushering him into her town house. "What movie did you bring?" Monday nights had become their standard movie-and-popcorn night.

"*Pride and Prejudice*," Brandon said. "The Colin Firth version."

"You didn't! That's like a million hours long."

"Yeah, but I hear it's worth it."

"Good thing I have lots of popcorn."

"So how are things at Florida Charlie's?" Brandon asked as they settled into the movie.

"Technically I'm still on probation, but Pop and I are getting along. I'm officially the store manager and he's assumed the role of on-site owner and constant-meddler, which is fine with me because I need his advice. But he's letting me open the store one Sunday a month on a trial basis. I think it's really going to boost revenues."

It was the second week in March. Last Saturday, the first Saturday of the month, Grace had stayed late at the store, just in case. About fifty women (who apparently didn't read the ad Grace had put in the paper) had shown up for a boyfriend club meeting. They'd been disappointed when Grace had told them the club no longer existed.

"I'm training Marty to take over most of Penny's duties," she added.

Brandon got them a couple of beers from the fridge. "How are the wedding plans going?" He opened one of the beers and handed it to her.

"Good. Abuela is making all the dresses. Penny is going to look like a princess."

They were near the end of the first disc, the part where Colin Firth aka Mr. Darcy proposes to Elizabeth. "I can't believe your friends actually thought I resembled this guy. Does he really think any woman in her right mind is going to say yes to that messed-up proposal?"

Grace smiled. "You have to admit, there's an uncanny resemblance in our relationships. Except for the romance part," Grace said.

"Yeah, except for that."

"Ellen was one hundred percent positive you were Mr. Darcy. And she was convinced Joe was my Mr. Wickham."

"Yeah, I remember all that from the radio." Brandon turned pensive. "Do you still think of him, Grace? I know it's only been a few weeks, but you never mention him so—"

"Yeah, I still think of him." *Like all the time.*

"Maybe you should call him."

"Maybe he should call me."

"Is that you talking or that *Mal Genio* person inside of you?"

"I told you, *Mal Genio* means Bad-Tempered One, not Stubborn One."

"Whatever."

"I would feel weird calling him."

"I don't think he would mind."

Grace picked up the remote and hit the mute button. "How do you know?"

"I went out for a beer with him the other day. We talked. He asked about you."

"You and Joe had a beer together? I thought he didn't like you."

"We were friends in college. I did something he didn't like, but now we're okay again." Brandon stood and stretched. "I'll go stick another bag of popcorn in the microwave while you put the second disc in."

"So what did he say about me?" Grace yelled, since Brandon was in the kitchen.

"Call him. Or don't. That's your choice. But I'm not going to play messenger boy."

Grace bit back a retort. "So you're going to be my date for Penny's wedding, right? First Saturday in April. Dress is casual nice."

He plopped a fresh bowl of popcorn in her lap. "Is that you asking me or is that you assuming? Sorry, Grace, but no can do. I already have plans for that weekend."

"I thought . . . Oh, wow, I'm sorry! I've talked about the wedding so much and you're right, I just assumed you'd go with me. I didn't think I had to formally ask you. My bad."

"Ordinarily I'd love to escort you to this shindig, but it just so happens I have a date that weekend. I'm going to a regatta." Brandon kept munching on his popcorn and staring straight ahead at the screen.

"I didn't know you sailed."

"I don't."

When he didn't say anything else, Grace turned off the TV set. "So who is she? Do I know her?"

Brandon sighed heavily. "It's not a she."

For the longest time, they sat there not saying anything.

She covered her face with her hands and tried not to laugh. Not because there was anything funny really. It was just like it had been with Sarah. Staring at her straight in the face. "Am I the most self-centered person in the world? Or just dim-witted and clueless?"

"I really thought you suspected. Honestly, you didn't? Not even after our big kiss?"

"Well, now that you mention it, I thought— *Oh my God*. It's Joe's cousin, Phillip. *He's* your date!"

"He's actually my first . . . well, my first boyfriend. Joe introduced us in college and we hit it off right away. I'd suspected I was gay, but being with Phil confirmed it for me. He was ready to come out, but I was pretty freaked, so I broke it off with him."

"And pretended to like girls."

"I do like girls. I just like boys better."

"That's why Joe had such a problem with you."

"He knew I was nothing but a big fake. I never went out with the same girl more than twice. Everyone thought I was some kind of super stud." He laughed, then turned serious. "Honestly, Grace? I have you to thank for helping me get my shit together."

"*Me?*"

"That day at Chez Louis, when I told you walking out on me was the best thing anyone had ever done for me? I wasn't lying. That night I went home and started thinking about what an ass I was. Here you were, this really nice girl, and I was playing you so that my rep would stay intact. For a while I thought . . . maybe." He shrugged. "I thought maybe we *could* be together, but that kiss proved to me that it was impossible."

"Brandon, why didn't you just come out and tell me?"

"I hoped that you would say something first. It's not easy, Grace. Even now. Old habits are hard to break."

"I guess guys like Doug make it hard, huh?"

He munched on his popcorn and contemplated her question. "Guys like Doug like to give guys like me a hard time. But it's their own insecurities that make it a problem." A twinkle lit up his dark eyes. "Don't laugh, but I really think Zumba has improved my rugby game. All that extra coordination, you know? I told Doug he should look into signing up."

Grace held her breath. "What did he say?"

"He told me to go fuck myself. And then I beat his ass. On the rugby field, that is."

Grace smiled. "So, tell me about Phillip. Have you met his mom yet?"

"Not yet," he said, sounding a little nervous. "He makes her sound pretty fierce."

"Sarah calls her The Dragon. But don't worry, she's absolutely going to love you."

"We've only been dating for a couple of weeks, so don't make a bigger deal out of it than it is."

"Yeah, but you two have a history. No wonder you acted all weird at Chez Louis that night! Was that the first time you'd seen Phillip since college?"

Brandon nodded. "My heart was thumping so fast I had to leave. But seeing him again was the push I needed. So I mustered up my courage and called him a couple of days later. We went out to dinner and talked and, oh, get this. You're gonna love it. I told him that he makes me want to be a better man."

"You didn't!"

"He totally bought it. Hook, line, and sinker. Of course, I do mean it, you know," he said with a wink.

Grace started to laugh again, then caught herself. Something suddenly felt very strange. And oddly familiar. "Hey, Brandon," she said, opening her mouth wide. "Is there a piece of popcorn stuck in my bottom tooth?"

Brandon inspected her mouth. "No popcorn that I can—Uh oh, I think you chipped your tooth."

Grace ran to the bathroom with Brandon behind her. She smiled into the mirror above the sink. There it was. The same tooth she'd chipped four months ago was chipped again.

# 36

# Chipping Away at the Curse

Grace tried to ignore the infernal pounding in her chest. She picked up the phone and dialed.

"Sunshine Smiles, how can I help you?" said a serene, pleasant-sounding woman on the other end. Grace immediately recognized the voice.

"Is this Tanya?" Grace asked.

"Yes, it is."

"Tanya, it's Grace O'Bryan."

There was a slight pause. "Grace, how are you?"

"I'm fine. Well, actually, I chipped my tooth again, but it's not a big deal. Where's Melanie?"

"Melanie no longer works here. Joanna is the new receptionist, but she's got a cold today so I'm filling in for her."

Melanie no longer worked at Sunshine Smiles? *Good for you, Joe.*

"So I guess that means I talk to you. Kind of like old times, huh? I need to make an appointment, but it's not an emergency or anything." Now that she and Joe were no longer dating, there didn't seem to be a reason that he couldn't be her dentist.

There was a few seconds of thorny silence.

"How's Joe?" Grace asked.

"He's doing well." There was a crispness in Tanya's voice that could only mean one thing.

"Um, Tanya, did you hear about the boyfriend club?"

"Unfortunately, the whole office heard the Speedway show. It was very embarrassing for Joe. He had to let Melanie go after that, which"—Tanya lowered her voice—"was a big relief to everyone, so I guess some good did come out of it."

Grace could feel her palms go damp. She readjusted her grip on the phone. "Tanya, have . . . have any of Joe's patients said anything about the show?"

"I won't lie to you, Grace. We got so many calls asking about the boyfriend club and the Speedway show that we had to send out a letter downplaying the whole incident."

"Has . . . has Joe lost patients over this?"

"Well, some of Dr. Fred's patients left to go to other dentists when he retired. That was to be expected. But after Speedway's show we started getting a lot of cancellations, especially from our older patients who were a core part of the practice. I won't deny that things have been a little rough the past month. That's when we sent out the letter, giving Joe's side of the story."

Grace felt like she was going to be sick. "I don't remember getting a letter," she said.

"I think it would be very awkward for you to be a patient here after what's happened. I can recommend several very good dentists who I think you would like."

"Thank you, Tanya," Grace said, trying to keep her voice from wobbling. "I would appreciate that."


She opened the kitchen door to her parents' house to find Abuela hemming Grace's maid of honor dress.

"Perfect timing!" Abuela said. "Here." She handed Grace the gown. "Slip this on."

"Where's Mami and Pop?" Grace placed her bag on the kitchen table and pulled off the Florida Charlie's T-shirt over her head.

"They went out to dinner," Abuela said. "They wanted me to come along, but I had this dress to finish. And I knew you were coming, so I thought we would eat together. I made *tostones*."

"Yum."

Grace slipped the dress on. It was a simple cotton A-line halter sundress in lime green that hit just above the knee. For the actual ceremony, they would all go barefoot, since the wedding was taking place directly on the beach, but Grace had a pair of silver three-inch-heel sandals for the party afterward.

"You're going to look beautiful in this," Abuela said. "How are you wearing your hair?"

"Penny says she doesn't care, so I thought I'd put it up. Ten minutes on the beach and it'll be crazy looking if I don't."

"Good idea." She studied Grace a moment. "What's wrong?"

"Abuela, I . . . I need to apologize to someone, but I'm not sure how to do it."

"Just say you're sorry."

"I already told him I'm sorry. I need to do something more than just words."

"Didn't we have this same conversation a few months ago? You always make things too complicated! That's why you're the Tomato. It's all those seeds inside you."

Abuela laid her hand over Grace's cheek. It felt warm and firm and, for a second, Grace imagined she was a little girl again and she couldn't help herself. The tears began to flow. And flow. And flow. She'd cried a lot in the past few weeks, but this was like someone had stuck a stick of dynamite in the dam, and now all the water was rushing out and she couldn't stop it.

"Gracielita! What's wrong?"

"Abuela, I'm so miserable! Well . . . I'm not totally miserable, because I have my old job back and everything is okay with Pop.

And Charlie and Sarah are married, and now Penny and Butch are getting married, and Ellen doesn't have to hide out in her apartment anymore because Speedway already has the picture of her panites. So everything seems right, only it's not."

Abuela looked confused. "Let me get this right. You're miserable because you don't have someone special in your life?"

Leave it to Abuela to figure it all out.

"I *do* have someone special. At least, I did."

"Maybe a nice flan will do the trick."

"I already made him a flan."

Abuela smiled. "Gracielita, he's the man you're supposed to end up with."

"But you met Joe at the store and you told me he wasn't the one!"

"I did?"

"Abuela," Grace said, swiping the tears from her cheeks, "Did you even really have a dream?"

"Of course I had a dream! I dreamed you were happily in love and got married. And it all began with flowers," she insisted.

Grace narrowed her eyes. "When did you have this dream?"

"When you were a little girl."

"So, all those months ago when we were eating dinner and you made it sound like the dream was recent, it wasn't?"

Abuela shrugged. "I thought maybe if I told you about the dream it would give you a push. I certainly didn't think it would hurt."

"But . . . that day at the store. Why did you tell me Joe wasn't the one?"

"I knew there were two men," she said with a frown, "only I had no idea who the right one was. The one who sent you the roses, I thought he must be the one because, like I just told you, I saw flowers in my dream." She shook her head. "But I must have misinterpreted the meaning, because the man you made the flan for, he's the one you're supposed to end up with. I know that now."

"How can you be sure?"

"I saw the look in your eyes when you made the flan. That's all I needed to know."

Grace started to laugh. It seemed she'd been doing a lot of that lately. Crying one minute, laughing the next. "Abuela, I don't know what's wrong with me. I feel like I'm going crazy."

"That's what love does to you," Abuela sighed.

"Yeah, but I've had this happen before and I've always bounced back."

Abuela took off her sewing glasses. "Gracielita, how long have you and this man been broken up?"

"A month."

"Practically a lifetime!" She scowled. "A month is nothing. And if you've really gotten over your other big love affairs so quickly, then maybe that ought to tell you something."

"What do you mean?"

"The St. Valentine's Day Curse. Bah! What it is really, Gracielita? I'll tell you what it is. It's an excuse you've made up in that tomato head of yours filled with the seeds."

Abuela had been right about more than one thing. Grace had never had her heart broken before. Not like this. It had never occurred to her, but the truth was, *she* was the one who'd always done the breaking up. Or else, she'd pick some guy like Felix, who, deep down, she knew she could never really love. And if she could never really love him, then he couldn't really hurt her, could he? The stripper debacle had wounded Grace's pride more than anything else.

But to be truly in love meant to be vulnerable. To give up your power to someone else. Like Sarah had done with Charlie. It was scary, to be sure, but the payoff had been worth it for her.

"Abuela," Grace asked, staring at the *azabache* hanging around Abuela's neck, "do you even believe in curses?"

"Only the ones we put on ourselves, *mi amor*."

# 37

# What Goes Around, Comes Around

Grace picked up her phone. She dialed Sarah first, then Penny, and told them what she planned to do. They both tried to talk her out of it, but Grace was insistent. Ellen volunteered to come over for moral support and Grace decided to take her up on it.

"This is the bravest thing you've ever done," Ellen said.

"You did it."

"Yes, but at the time I had no idea. I mean, I knew he was powerful, but I wasn't expecting what I got," Ellen said.

"You make him sound like Darth Vader."

"He'll make you sound like an idiot. He does that to everyone."

"I know, but I have to do it, Ellen." Grace paused. "You met him, right? When you gave him the picture of your panties. What's he like?"

"Jerry's actually kind of cute. That's Speedway's real name by the way. Jerry Pike."

"Don't say he's cute. I like thinking of him as this big hairy tarantula sitting behind a desk with a mic."

Ellen giggled. "Think of him naked."

"Ew."

"That's what you're supposed to do when you're on stage and

you're nervous. You look out into the audience and you picture them naked and it gives you a boost of confidence."

"Okay, I guess I can try that." Grace picked up her phone and dialed. "What if he doesn't take my call?"

"Oh, he'll take your call. He gave you an open invitation, right?"

"Yeah, but that was more than a month ago. The boyfriend club thing has kind of died out."

Ellen made a pained face. "Not really, Grace. I get calls on it every day."

Ellen was right. Once the station personnel realized who was calling, it only took a few minutes to get to the man himself. Ellen turned up the volume on the radio.

"Hey, speedsters! This is Speedway Gonzalez, taking you round and round Day-to-na Beach. Guess who's decided to come out and play this morning? It's none other than the head honch-ess of the boyfriend club herself, Grace O'Bryan. So, Gracie, first things first. Are you fat?"

"Yes, I am. I tip the scales at four hundred pounds. Thanks for asking."

Speedway chuckled. "It's not going to be that easy, babe." He paused. "Gracie, we're having some technical difficulty. Do you have your radio on? And if you do, can you turn down the volume?"

"Oh, um, sure. Ellen, can you turn down the radio?" Grace asked. Ellen made a pouty face but she turned the volume dial down.

"That's better," Speedway said. "You weren't by chance talking to my new best friend, Ellen Ames, were you?"

"As a matter of fact, I was."

"Tell her I went to sleep last night looking at the picture of her in her panties. Tell her I think she's hot. Tell her that—"

"You can tell her yourself later. I didn't call to talk about that."

"So it's like that, huh? How long have you known you like to be on top, Gracie?"

"All my life, Speedway. That way I can crush my opponents. Don't forget, I weigh four hundred pounds."

"Now, Gracie, you know what happens to people who lie to Speedway. I've seen your picture. You're hot too. Don't deny it."

This was the part when people got stupid. Grace tried to focus on the goal. If she could just get in and say what she had to, then she'd take her chances with Speedway later. "Look, I didn't call to talk about myself, I called to talk about the boyfriend club."

"Okay, you got my attention. Tell us all about the club. But don't leave out any details. Because you know I'll find them out."

"It all started one Saturday night back in November when I ended up at the Wobbly Duck."

"You go there often, Gracie?"

"It was my first time, actually."

"That's what she said."

There was laughter in the studio background as Speedway's cronies laughed at his stupid joke.

*Patience, Grace.* "I went there to meet Brandon Farrell—"

"Mr. Darcy. Zumba guy, right?"

"Right. Some of his friends were drunk and they made fun of my family's store, Florida Charlie's, so I pitched a hissy fit and walked out on him. Oh, and I also knocked a pitcher of beer over and it spilled onto his crotch. But that was an accident."

"Remind me not to ever go out with you, Gracie."

"I don't think that will be an issue. Remember, I weigh four hundred pounds. Unless you're a chubby chaser. Are you a chubby chaser, Speedway?"

Speedway laughed. So far, so good.

"So, as I was saying, after my stint at the Wobbly Duck I went back to my book club meeting—"

"What kind of chicks meet on a Saturday night to discuss books? Fat ones, right? Oh, except you. We've already established that you're hot. You did say that, right?"

Grace could feel the sweat pooling in her armpits. It was a precarious road. She tried to think of all the different spins Speedway could put on her answers.

"I never said I was hot. And to answer your question, yes, all my friends are fat. Just like I am. So, I got back to my book club meeting, and I was angry and I wanted revenge, so I convinced my fat friends to change our book club to a boyfriend club so that we could diss on men. It was childish and petty of us— or rather, of me, because I was the main instigator. My friends Penny and Sarah didn't want to have anything to do with that, and Ellen, well, she just wants to develop her thesis into a book. But I was out for blood. The men you made fun of on your show were my victims."

"Gracie, am I hearing a big *mea culpa* from you on this?"

"Yes, Speedway, you are. I want to say I'm sorry. I'm sorry to all the men we discussed. Men aren't books that you can give a thumbs-up or thumbs-down to. They're like us. They have feelings and reputations, and all I can say is that it got out of hand and I'm sorry if anyone was hurt by this. Especially Joe Rosenblum, who by the way is a fantastic dentist and a terrific humanitarian—"

"Sounds like you've still got the hots for him."

"I . . . I do, Speedway. I think Joe is the love of my life."

"Is it the drill that turns you on, Gracie? You've already admitted you like to be on top."

Speedway wouldn't like that she wasn't going to answer directly, but Grace had just one more thing to get in. "Oh, and I also want to say that the boyfriend club is dissolved, so don't bother going to Florida Charlie's for a meeting. Although *please do* go to Florida Charlie's, because there's some pretty terrific stuff there, like the world's largest alligator tooth on display until the end of summer. And Felix, if you're listening, I'm sorry I told everyone about the Céline Dion thing, but I'm not sorry about anything else because you did cheat on me."

"No more boyfriend club, Gracie?"

"That's it, Speedway. No more boyfriend club."

*Whew.* She wasn't sure that she'd be able to get it all in, but she had. She'd even managed to get in a plug for the store. Grace smiled to herself.

"So Gracie, let's get back to you and that drill . . ."

She should hang up. Right this very instant. Any more time on the air would only end badly for her. But there was a certain seductive charm in Speedway's on-air routine. He lured you in and made it seem like you were secret friends. Like the two of you knew something that the rest of the radio audience didn't. She began to understand why all those people called in to the show. There was a chance—just a slim one, but a chance nevertheless—that you would be the lone caller who one-upped Speedway.

She tried to take Ellen's advice and picture him naked, and for a while it seemed to work because she was holding her own against him. But in the end, Speedway did to her what he did to everyone else who called in to his show.

# 38

# Reader, It All Worked Out the Way It Was Supposed To

"What do you think of this one?" Penny passed around a photo proof of her in her wedding dress. They were at Luigi's, only it wasn't Wednesday. It was the Friday night before the wedding. The official rehearsal dinner. And it wasn't just the four of them. Charlie and Sarah sat together on one side of the table, Butch and Penny on the other side, with Grace and Ellen sitting at the ends. Butch's family and Penny's aunt from Minnesota had left after dessert to go back to the hotel.

"Don't show it to Butch!" Penny said when the picture had made its rounds.

"Let me guess. It's white," Butch said.

"Wrong," Penny said. "I would never be that obvious."

Butch shrugged. "You know what I'm wearing. I don't know why I can't see the dress."

"It's bad luck for the groom to see the bride's dress before the wedding. I'll just tell you that it's not white, and it's beautiful."

Grace had to agree with Penny. And not just because Abuela had made the gown. It was lovely. A not quite taupe, not quite beige off-the-shoulder full-length mermaid wedding dress that brought out every curve in Penny's otherwise slender frame. Butch wouldn't be able to take his eyes off her.

Ellen reached into her bag and pulled out a pen and a yellow legal pad. "It's a new one," she said, before anyone could say anything. "Okay, so let's just make sure all the last-minute details are covered. Dress: check. Flowers—"

"Brandon has the flower situation under control," Grace said. "Even though he's not going to be here, he promised Benson's would deliver everything first thing in the morning." It had turned out that Brandon's investment group owned 50 percent of Benson's Flowers. Grace was beginning to wonder if there was anything in Daytona Beach that Brandon didn't own. Or at least a percentage of, anyway.

Ellen made a notation in the pad. "Flowers: check. Minister: check. Reception at Luigi's: check. Guest sign-in book." Ellen looked up from her pad. "Crap. We forgot the sign-in book."

"I figured I'd remember everyone who was at my wedding," Penny said. "It's not like I invited that many people."

Ellen ignored Penny. "Sarah, you're in charge of getting an appropriate guest sign-in book by tomorrow. The wedding is at dusk, but we'll need it by at least noon."

"Check," Sarah said.

Ellen continued reading off her list. "Music: I have a note that says Butch is in charge of that."

"Um, I have some bad news," Butch said.

All the women at the table turned to glare at Butch. Charlie just shook his head at Butch in sympathy.

"We still have the violinist who's coming to the ceremony," Butch said, causing Penny to let out a sigh of relief. "But the DJ who's supposed to do the reception canceled on me this afternoon. He's going to a bike show down in Fort Lauderdale."

"You got a biker friend to do the music at the reception?" Ellen asked incredulously. Before Butch could defend himself, she made a notation in her pad. "Never mind, I have it covered. It just so happens I have some very strong DJ connections."

"Oh, yeah? Who?" Butch asked. "I don't want any of that top-forty crap at our reception."

"Beggars can't be choosers, Butch," Ellen said.

"You're not talking about who I think you are." Grace gave Ellen a hard stare.

"Jerry and I have been out every night this week." Ellen's eyes glazed over in a familiar way. "He's absolutely wonderful, Grace. Wait till you meet him. I'm bringing him to the wedding as my date."

"Jerry who?" Sarah asked.

Grace didn't know whether to laugh or shake her head.

Everyone at the table looked confused. "His real name is Jerry Pike, and yes, his nom de guerre is Speedway Gonzalez," Ellen admitted.

Butch's face lit up. "You're dating Speedway? And he's coming to my wedding? Awesome!"

Charlie just laughed. Sarah and Penny began talking at once.

Ellen blushed. "I have a strong gut feeling that he's the one. He's . . . well, he's passionate and so well read. Do you know he has a master's degree in psychology? That whole Speedway thing is just an act. Jerry is actually very sensitive."

Sarah's jaw dropped. "Ellen! You've found your Heathcliff."

"Let's hope he doesn't go psycho on her," Penny muttered.

"Speaking of Speedway, I still think you were really brave, Grace, going on his show to talk about the boyfriend club," Sarah said. "I'm really proud of you."

"Have you heard from Joe?" Ellen asked.

Grace shook her head.

"Well, I'm happy to report one good thing came out of the boyfriend club," said Ellen. "Remember Karina and Matt Lakowski?"

"You mean Colonel Brandon?" Penny said.

"He read his review online and he was so flattered with how

highly Karina thought of him that they've gotten back together. She called me the other day to thank me."

The conversation at the table went back to Ellen and Speedway, so Grace took the opportunity to lean over and ask Charlie, "You and Sarah are spending the night at the house tonight, right?"

"Check," Charlie said, mimicking Ellen. Mami and Pop had gone on their thirty-fifth-anniversary trip to Europe and Grace and Charlie were taking turns staying at the house so that Abuela wouldn't be alone. "What are you going to do for the next couple of weeks? Lie around on the beach?" he asked.

Florida Charlie's was getting a much-needed overhaul. New roof, new bathrooms, new floors. Which meant the store would be temporarily closed. The new billboards announcing their grand reopening celebration next month had gone up on the highway, and Pop had hired a local PR firm to produce the new orange-head commercials. Grace had gone for a costume fitting yesterday. It was . . . interesting, to say the least.

"Hardly. I have a thousand things to do. I'll be at the store working while the renovations are in progress."

"Don't forget to wear a hard hat," Charlie joked.

"So what's going on with Phoebe?" Grace asked. "Any news on that front?"

"Phoebe's getting transferred to the Miami office. Not her idea," Charlie added. "And I've been made full partner."

Grace squealed. "Charlie! That's fantastic!" She stood up and hugged her brother. Everyone at the table wanted to know what was going on, and so Grace told them the good news and Sarah suggested they raise their drinks for a toast.

"Oh, and I have an announcement," Grace said. "Since I was the one who dismantled the book club, I thought it would only be fitting if I revived it again. Only we're changing the time and place. First meeting is at my town house, the last Sunday of the month at seven p.m."

"What book are we going to read?" Ellen asked Grace.

"I was thinking maybe we should stay away from Austen and the Brontës for a while. How about *A Farewell to Arms*? I happen to know where we can get an excellent price on a paperback version."

"Good idea!" Ellen flipped over the page on her legal pad and began scribbling. "What do you think about setting up a Yahoo! group? That way Penny can keep in the loop while she and Butch are on the road."

"Maybe we'd better stay away from Yahoo!," Penny said, catching Grace's eye. "You can just text me the info."

Ellen nodded. "Can I invite Janine and my other friends from the college?"

"Sure, but no flyers," Grace warned.

"None, I swear," Ellen said. "This is terrific. Hemingway is so *in* right now!" She paused. "Would you mind terribly if I invited Jerry? Honestly, he'll make a great addition to the book club."

"Why not?" Grace said. "But let me warn you, if he calls any of us fat, even once, he's out."

# 39

# Joe, Such a Little Name, for Such a Person

Grace said good-bye to Marty and told him she'd see him tomorrow at the wedding. After the rehearsal dinner at Luigi's she'd gone back to the store to take one last look. And to make sure the doors were properly locked, of course. Strange how she was picking up some of Pop's habits.

The sign on the glass double doors read "Closed for renovations. Will reopen in three weeks." She stood back a few feet and glanced at the store. On top of the roof, the big ten-foot pink flamingo next to the Florida Charlie's sign flashed brightly.

"Keep an eye on the place!" she shouted.

Not that she expected the flamingo to respond. That would be too much. But still, maybe if she gave the bird a name, it might loosen her up a bit.

She rearranged Gator Claus's bunny ears so that the right ear stuck up properly. "Sorry, I know how much you hate the Easter Bunny costume, but it's just for a couple more weeks. Then you can start your summer wardrobe."

Nothing.

Grace sighed. "Abuela is itching to sew you something new. I was thinking maybe a military look for Memorial Day. What do you think?"

Gator Claus stared straight ahead with the same benign look he'd had on his face for the past month and a half.

"How many times do I have to say I'm sorry? Pop has forgiven me. Why can't you?"

The right side of the alligator's upper snout curled up, ever so slightly. Or was it Grace's imagination? An idea occurred to her.

"Stay there. I'll be right back!"

She ran into the store, all the way to the back office, and picked up the orange-head costume the PR company had dropped off this afternoon and slipped on the giant head piece, adjusting the eye holes and the mouth section. She calmly walked back out to the front of the store and paraded herself in front of Gator Claus, making sure he got a good view of her from every angle. If this didn't thaw Gator Claus out, nothing would.

"I'm Little Orange Head, and I want *you*"—she paused dramatically and pointed her finger in Gator Claus's direction—"to stop by the one and only Florida Charlie's!"

Gator Claus grinned his appreciation.

"I thought you'd like that. Those are my closing lines for the big commercial," she said with a laugh.

Gator Claus was talking to her again!

Okay, not talking to her exactly. He'd never really talked to her, she knew that. But he was listening. She was sure of it.

"So, back to the new costume. What branch of the service would you like? Let's not do the Navy because white is a terrible color to keep clean. Plus, there's all those Village People jokes—"

"Grace?"

She froze.

Why hadn't she heard his car?

She had to maneuver her whole head around, because in the orange-head getup she couldn't see sideways, but there was Joe's black Range Rover parked in the far corner of the front lot. He must have driven up while she'd been in the office getting the costume.

She turned to face him. "Hi, Joe."

"I hope I'm not interrupting anything." There was a bouquet of flowers in his hands. But they weren't red roses. It looked like a mix of daisies and something else, something purple and pretty. Joe had never brought her flowers before . . .

Grace gulped. "Not at all. We were just deciding on a new look. Gator Claus and I." It sounded ridiculous. But he already knew she talked to the alligator, so what the heck. "How's business?" At the look of surprise on his face, she added, "Tanya told me what happened after the Speedway show. The one where, you know . . . all the boyfriend club stuff came out."

"I've picked up a few new patients this week. They heard you on the radio."

"That's great!" She brushed the edge of her toe over Gator Claus's right foot. Just for moral support. "So . . . you heard me?"

"Not live. But I've been listening to the best of Speedway."

Grace cringed. Speedway had replayed their interaction every morning this week. Apparently, Grace made for good radio.

"I heard you chipped your tooth again. Let me see." He came up to her, very closely, and gently tilted her orange-head piece back with the fingers on his free hand, the one that wasn't holding the flowers. Grace automatically opened her mouth. "What happened this time?" he asked.

"Popcorn kernel." Her heart was beating faster than Grace thought humanly possible. "I never told you how I chipped it the first time, did I?"

He shook his head.

"I was trying to open a shrink-wrapped tampon."

The expression on Joe's face was priceless. He laughed and shook his head as if to say *that could only happen to you*. "I could fix it. If you want."

"Actually, I think I'm going to leave it the way it is. You were right. I'm really the only one who notices it."

"It's kind of cute, actually."

"Joe—"

"I brought you something." But instead of handing her the flowers, he reached inside his pocket to produce a piece of paper. "I thought about mailing it, but then I figured I might need to explain a few things in person. I'm not as good with the bullet points as you are."

Her knees felt like rubber. She glanced down at the paper, but she was too afraid to look at it.

"Go on," he urged. "I promise, Grace, it's not going to hurt."

She unfolded the paper and began to read. "Number one: Punctuality." There was a ten written next to it. She looked up at him, confused.

"I don't ever remember you being late for a date." He shrugged. "Some girls are bad about that."

"What is this?"

"It's a girlfriend satisfaction survey. I figured I owed you one, in case you ever think about being a girlfriend again. Then you'll know what areas you excel at, and where you need to improve."

She cleared her throat. "Number two: Nag Factor. You gave me a *seven*," she said incredulously. "Please explain yourself."

"See . . . this is why I wanted to do this in person. If you look at the back of the page you'll see I went into some specific dated examples. Nag Factor is like when I'm driving and you tell me to slow down. Or when we're ready to go out and you tell me to go back inside and change because there's a hole in my sneaker and it looks bad. That kind of stuff."

"Okay . . . I suppose that's a fair score." She went back to reading. "Number three: Displays Affection. You gave me a 9."

"I would have scored you a 10 except for the time we were in the movies and I wanted to make out and you said we weren't sixteen. But other than that one time, I think you were very accommodating."

Her face went warm. "I agree." Her gaze skimmed through the remainder of the list, then rested on the last point, highlighted in yellow marker.

*Overall Score.* There was nothing next to it.

"That one's still in the air," he said quietly. He handed her the flowers. "But I'd like to see if we can hit that one out of the ballpark. You know how I feel about those tens."

"*Really?* Because . . . I have to warn you, Joe. I have this awful temper and I'm a little weird, and—"

"A little? Grace, you're wearing a giant piece of citrus on your head and talking to a plastic alligator. You think I don't already know that you're weird?"

"Joe," she said, her voice scratchy with unshed tears. "I've missed you so much. You were right. I was never *really* your friend. But I want to be, even though I don't deserve it. I think I was just scared to have everything all rolled up in one person. I want door number one, Joe. And I want door number two, and God, you have *no* idea how much I've missed door number three."

"I've missed you too, Grace. But I have *no* idea what you're talking about. What the hell are these doors?"

She laughed. "I'll tell you later, because right now I really just want to kiss you, Joe."

In the end, she had to get Joe's help to pull the orange-head piece off. (Had it been this tight earlier?) She walked into his arms, squeezed her eyes shut tight, and kissed him. Right there in front of Florida Charlie's with the alligator looking on. She'd get Gator Claus's opinion on that later, she was sure.

Joe wasn't a Wickham. And he wasn't her Mr. Knightley, or her Laurie (thank God), or even her Heathcliff. He wasn't anybody someone else had made up in their head.

He was just Joe. And that was more than good enough for Grace.

# Flan De Queso

*(This is the flan my mother makes. Simply delicious!)*

1 (8-ounce) package cream cheese

1 teaspoon vanilla

1 (12 ounce) can evaporated milk

1 (14 ounce) can sweetened condensed milk

½ cup sugar

5 eggs

Pinch of salt

2 cups sugar (for the syrup)

Combine all the ingredients (except the 2 cups of sugar) in a blender and set aside.

In a large skillet, melt 2 cups of sugar over medium-high heat until the sugar completely melts into a syrup. Pour the syrup into a baking pan with a circle in the center (like a Bundt pan), making sure to cover as much of the pan's surface with the syrup as possible. Let it set for a few minutes. Carefully pour the liquid egg mixture into the pan over the set syrup. Place the pan inside a larger pan filled with an inch of hot water (a *baño de Maria*) and place the whole thing in a 350 degree oven. Cook for 35 to 45 minutes until set. Let cool to room temperature and chill well. Before serving, let the chilled flan sit out on the counter for about 20 minutes (so the syrup warms up a bit), then flip it onto a plate, letting all the syrup drip over the custard.

# the
# boyfriend of the
# month club

## READERS GUIDE

# DISCUSSION QUESTIONS

1. Discuss some of the incidents that Grace's spiritual alter-ego, *mal genio*, gets her into. Why do you think she blames them on the spirit instead of herself? Do you think Grace is indeed inhabited by *Mal Genio* at times, or is it an easy excuse for when she gets herself into trouble?

2. Do you think *Mal Genio* has anything to do with the curse Grace believes has been cast on her love life?

3. Discuss the O'Bryan family dynamic and how it changes over the course of the book, especially with Pop as Grace's boss.

4. Why do you think Penny said no to Butch's proposal initially? Discuss how and why things changed by the end of the book.

5. Why does Grace fight her attraction to Joe so much, especially in the context of the story?

6. Why do you think Grace isn't swayed by Brandon's apologies of roses and Dom Perignon? Is it a point of pride for her or more?

7. Grace feels guilty about knowing about Craig's infidelity before his marriage to Sarah. How does that guilt manifest itself in their friendship?

8. Do you think the description of the Boyfriend of the Month Club as a "woman's empowerment group" is apt?

9. Do you believe in Grace's quote of "never say never" when it comes to men and dating? Was it smart of her to give Brandon a second chance, and do you think he redeemed himself in her eyes?

10. Do you agree with most of Ellen's assessments of the men discussed in the club, especially Joe? Have you ever dated someone who fits a literary archetype?

11. Who is your favorite literary leading man or woman and why?

12. Do you think fate was at play to connect Grace and Joe? Did her relationship with Brandon confuse that or did it act as a contrast to what she truly was looking for?

13. Why isn't Grace ready to introduce Joe to her family as her boyfriend? Do you think it has to do with his description of being dubbed a Wickham by the Club or is there another reason behind her hesitation?

14. Do you think most women want a hero in their lives, and might this be why the women deviate to literary heroes and villains in the Club?

15. Do you agree with Mami's quote: "I don't think you should put a timetable on happiness"? Was the Vegas elopement the right move for Sarah and Charlie? Why or why not?

16. Do you think the second chipped tooth was the sign Grace needed to realize she and Joe belonged together? Were there other signs she ignored?

17. Discuss how fate has worked for the characters' love lives in the novel.

18. Why do you think Grace has always been afraid of true love in the past? Do you think she is finally willing to let the idea of the curse go? Will *Mal Genio* disappear as well?